INHERIT THE EARTH

INHERIT
THE EARTH

Audrey Willsher

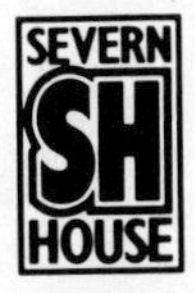

This first world edition published in Great Britain 1995 by
SEVERN HOUSE PUBLISHERS LTD of
9–15 High Street, Sutton, Surrey SM1 1DF.
First published in the USA 1995 by
SEVERN HOUSE PUBLISHERS INC of
595 Madison Avenue, New York, NY 10022.

British Library Cataloguing in Publication Data
Willsher, Audrey
  Inherit the Earth
  I. Title
  823.914 [F]

  ISBN 0-7278-4815-1

Typeset by Hewer Text Composition Services, Edinburgh.
Printed and bound in Great Britain by
Hartnolls Ltd, Bodmin, Cornwall.

To Joan, Gean, Norah and Christine
With love and friendship

Chapter One

Leicestershire – 1814

It would take no more than a moment to do what he'd come to do and the lanthorn illuminated his face only briefly. But in that passing second Rachel saw that he was young and that the muscles in his jaw were knotted with anger. Alert to his every move, she watched him take a length of straw and hold it to the candle, then with a slightly unsteady hand, bend and push it into the corn stack. He didn't wait to see the consequence of this action but instead, extinguished the light then turned and fled swiftly across the dark midland fields. And as the girl caught his shadowed outline, she could almost taste his fear and felt the sympathetic hammering of her own heart.

At first the straw smouldered and Rachel thought it had gone out. But the sheaves were tinder-dry and a night breeze soon fanned the fire into life. Gradually it took hold. Flames began to lick round the base, the rick crackled and spat then erupted into a pyrotechnic display of shooting stars that quickly burnt themselves out in the night sky. The air shimmered in the intense heat, making it impossible for Rachel to follow the movements of the young man and soon he was no more than a ghostly blur. But as she stood there by the window, she found herself willing him to reach the safety of Rooks Spinney before the farmhouse candles were lit. For she knew if he was caught it could mean a hanging.

1

Her attic room was at the north end of the house over-looking the stackyard and the flames were now so high she realized that a spark blowing in the wrong direction could set fire to the thatch. She didn't move from the window, but stood there enjoying the acrid smell of burning in her nostrils and the spectacle of her master's harvest going up in flames.

The barking dogs finally alerted the sleeping household. There was shouting, doors slammed, then old Man Pedley, still in his nightshirt, came rushing into the yard, bellowing like his prize bull and waving his fists at the heavens. "I'll get them for this, whoever it is and they'll hang by the neck for it!" he threatened above the roar of the flames and began pumping water into a bucket.

Mrs Pedley, the ribbons on her lace nightcap flowing out behind her, followed closely on her husband's tail. When she saw the arsonist's work she began wringing her plump hands in despair and crying, "Oh Joseph what shall we do?"

"We'll put it out of course you stupid woman," yelled her husband brutally. "Here, take this." He handed her the overflowing bucket and began filling another.

Esther Pedley staggered to the burning rick but the red-hot heat forced her back and she stood there helplessly, tears running down her face.

Sam, the young hired hand, had emerged from his sleeping quarters in the hayloft. Half awake and hardly able to credit what was happening, the lad stood scratching himself and gawping at the chaos around him. Shouted obscenities from farmer Pedley finally brought him to his senses and he made a fruitless charge at the stack, now a great golden cave into which one sheaf would collapse then another.

So far the children, George and Matilda, had remained undisturbed by the commotion. Then Rachel heard George's voice. Moving closer to the window, she peered down and saw that they were standing well back from the burning rick and surveying the scene in their normal indolent manner, apparently unperturbed that the barn and thatch were in imminent danger.

"Don't stand there gawping, form a chain with your mother and Sam, you great larkin," Joseph Pedley yelled at his son and heir.

"You're wasting your time, Father," answered George, but he did condescend to take a bucket from Sam and aim it in the direction of the flames.

"And you too Tilda, come on."

But Matilda's only concern was what the fierce heat might do to her complexion. Staring accusingly at the small room under the eaves, she called back to her father, "Where's Rachel? Why can't she help?"

Joseph Pedley stopped pumping and followed his daughter's gaze. "Yes, where is she? Go and get that lazy wench immediately Tilda and bring her down here."

"Yes Papa." As Matilda moved towards the house with a self-satisfied expression, Rachel slipped back into the shadows. But there was a defiance in her stance and she waited until she heard the latch being lifted before leaping back into bed and pulling the blanket over her head.

Placing the chamberstick on a chair, Matilda went over to the bed and began shaking Rachel roughly. "Wake up, you idle girl!" she ordered.

Rachel feigned sleep, but when Matilda began spitefully nipping her flesh, she was forced to roll over and sit up. "Whatsa matter?" she mumbled, rubbing her eyes. The leaping flames lit up the small room and through her half-closed lids she could see that Matilda's hair was screwed tightly in rags. This was to achieve the curls she so favoured and which she always insisted were natural.

"A corn stack's on fire, that's what's the matter." Matilda pointed to the window. "Are you so stupid you can't see it? And how you could sleep through the noise, I don't know. Now get dressed and go down and help."

3

As she gave her orders, Matilda stood looking down at Rachel, at the thick black hair falling loose around her shoulders, with envy and dislike. The fire threw up shadows that seemed to emphasize Rachel's high cheekbones and finely arched eyebrows, and there was a quality about the face that no serving girl rescued from the workhouse was entitled to have.

A movement diverted Matilda's attention and she turned to see her brother in the doorway. He was wearing a brocaded dressing gown and although his curls were boyishly ruffled, he appeared unsullied by either smoke or flame. "What do you want, George?" she asked crossly.

"Rachel's to hurry, there's nothing more we can do about the fire but Papa wants ale and cheese." His eyes were on Rachel as he spoke and he stared so hard at the outline of her breasts under her shift, that she instinctively drew the blanket up round her neck.

"I can't get up while you're standing there, now can I, Mr George?"

"Yes, go," ordered Matilda. She was well aware that her brother lusted after Rachel. But it would be more than his life was worth to touch her. For if he did his father would beat him within a inch of his life. Not out of any concern for the girl's virtue, but because he'd invested hundreds of pounds on having them taught the manners of gentry. A good marriage was what he was after for them both and no son of his would go dallying with serving girls.

At his sister's insistence, George departed. But he went reluctantly because the sight of Rachel in bed, her dark hair loose, and with only a nightgown covering her nakedness, had aroused him so much he'd wanted to leap on the bed and ravish her there and then. Before he went away to London to finish his education she'd been nothing more than a little kitchen maid, someone to taunt when he was bored. Then he'd come back to find her grown into a rare

4

beauty and now he couldn't get her out of his mind and he had dreams about her when he was asleep and erotic fantasies when he was awake. Always they were lying in the hayloft together, he was caressing her firm naked breasts while she lay there, abandoned in her desire for him, head thrown back and moaning with pleasure. But the reality was that so far she'd shown not the slightest interest in him, in fact she seemed to dislike him and frustration was making him impatient. He was determined to have her, though, and before some undeserving, country bumpkin got his calloused hands on her. In fact he felt her maidenhead was something he was entitled to, like the *droit de seigneur* of medieval France.

But how this seduction would be accomplished was a matter that occupied the twenty-year-old George most of his waking hours. For practical purposes it would have to be somewhere away from the house, which rather limited his opportunities. And his father must never find out or he would be cut off without a penny.

George was at the bottom of the attic stairs when saw the light of his sister's candle behind him, heard her berating Rachel to get a move on. As the petulant tones moved nearer, he stepped into the shadows, waiting until she passed. Rachel was a only a second behind but without any light to guide her she had to feel her way down the dark staircase. As she reached the bottom step, George stepped out blocking her path and she gasped with fright.

"It's all right, it's only me."

But she didn't seem reassured. "What do you want Mr George?" Her voice had an edge of uncertainty to it and this excited him even more. By now his self-control had gone completely and he was about to reach out and grab her when his father's voice came bellowing from below. "Rachel, where the devil are you? Get down here immediately or you'll feel my belt round your backside."

5

"Just coming Master," Rachel answered, ducked under his arm and was gone.

"Hell's teeth," George muttered and in an agony of frustration kicked the wall. But he only succeeded in stubbing his toe, which brought forth more oaths as he limped after her to the kitchen.

The intense heat had finally forced Joseph Pedley to abandon his attempt to douse the fire and he stood at the end of the long oak table, glowering at his wife and daughter. His face was blackened with smoke and Rachel could see that rivulets of sweat had drawn an uneven pattern down his face. And his beard was singed, his nightshirt scorched. She could also see that not one villager sat at his table which meant that none had come to his assistance. This didn't surprise her since he was the most hated man in Halby. And tonight someone had dared to express that hatred openly.

Smoke was now seeping through windows and doors and curling amongst the cured hams, plum puddings and copper saucepans hanging on hooks from the ceiling. It also made the candles burn less brightly and by keeping to the outer reaches of the kitchen, Rachel hoped to slip past to the pantry without being seen. The whole family had to walk on tiptoe round Joseph's irascible temperament, but Rachel knew that if he lashed out physically it would be at her. She eased her way past him and had almost reached the pantry door when he smashed his fist down so hard on the table the beer tankards leapt in the air, his family jumped with fright and Rachel herself stood frozen in *bas-relief* against the whitewashed wall.

"It's insurrection," he roared, "and Squire Bennett will have to be told, the Yeomanry sent for." He swung round to Rachel. "You girl, you're on that side of the house, did you see anything?"

Rachel swallowed hard. "No . . . no . . . Master," she lied, certain guilt was written all over her face. Then to avoid further cross-examination she hurried into the pantry. She took her time filling a pitcher with home brewed ale, hugging the secret to her, savouring the power it gave her and wondering who the young man was. She'd only caught a glimpse of his face but she knew every family in the village and he wasn't a local. So perhaps he'd come from Nottingham or Leicester. Maybe he was one of General Ludd's men. At the idea, Rachel shivered so much with fear and excitement she slopped beer over the stone-flagged floor.

When she went back into the kitchen Joseph was still blasting away, Mrs Pedley looked cowed, while his children's expressions had glazed into indifference. "I'm not waiting until the morning, I want this incident reported to the Squire now."

"At this time of the night, dear?" enquired Esther Pedley anxiously. Although the family were freeholders and Joseph proudly declared that he bent his knee to no one, she knew it was unwise to upset Squire Bennett, who had a temperament almost as dyspeptic as her husband's.

Mr Pedley gave her a bad-tempered glare. "Why should I care what time it is. A capital offence has been committed, he's the Magistrate, and I want those responsible found and brought to justice. The girl can walk up and tell him."

"Me?" Rachel had long ago learnt never to speak unless she was addressed directly but she'd been surprised into comment.

"Yes you."

"But everyone will be abed."

Joseph Pedley lifted his hand. "Less of your insolence. Go! Now!" he roared and Rachel turned and fled, forgetting in her haste to take her shawl.

Sam, who was staring into the the dying embers of the fire, looked up in astonishment as she tore past. "Where you going?"

But Rachel knew better than to stop. "I've to take a

message to the Squire, about the fire," she called over her shoulder. Not until she reached Blackthorn Lane, which lead down to the village, did she feel secure enough to slow down and enjoy her solitude, away from the turbulent and hostile atmosphere of Thatcher's Mount.

Rachel, as an orphan, had no personal experience of home life. However she could see that there was a disunity about the Pedleys and as a family they found little happiness in each other. And she herself had to cope with Joseph's brutish manner and George and Matilda's spitefulness. Mrs Pedley showed her small kindnesses in a furtive way, which was brave of her because most of the time she seemed totally crushed by her husband. Her one consolation was a firmly held Christian faith and from this she drew the small reserves of strength that enabled her to withstand her husband's bullying ways.

All her daughter had to console her was the prospect of marriage. But Matilda had been educated above her station, which made her an unsuitable wife for a yeoman farmer. And though her father was prosperous, he was still trade so it was unlikely that even sons of minor gentry would look on her favourably as a match. At two and twenty and hemmed in by village life, Matilda's mouth was pinching into querulous lines of discontent as hopes of an acceptable union slipped away.

If, in a way, Rachel could find it in her heart to pity Matilda, she wasted no such emotion on her brother, from whom, in an instinct of self-preservation, she always fled. Even as a bewildered girl of five, straight from the workhouse, George had shown her no pity, but had taunted her, pulled her hair, once even submerged her face in a pail of milk until she'd nearly drowned. Now he frightened her in a different way, for her watched her all the time, and it was a look that shamed her and stripped her of dignity. At every opportunity he would touch her, press himself against her so that she had to be constantly on her guard. Fortunately she didn't have to endure his attentions too often because he worked in his father's hosiery warehouse in Leicester, had lodgings there and was only home for the occasional weekend.

Although the farm was about half a mile from Halby, Rachel didn't feel threatened by the darkness. She relished her solitude, the balmy night air, nocturnal rustlings in the hedgerows, the polite cough of a cow. The village lay in a valley, and as she paused to get her breath, she could discern the outline of the church steeple, see the lights of the Weavers' Arms, while higher up on the other side of the village, a windmill stood, its great white sails for the moment stilled. Reassuringly Halby remained as it had always done. It was the surrounding landscape which had changed. The old medieval open field system had disappeared and in the past three years common and waste had been enclosed with quickset hedges or fencing, and ditches dug.

Rachel didn't understand exactly how it had happened but she remembered strangers arriving in the village, "from the government," it was whispered. Then they left and suddenly many of the villagers who farmed in a small way had lost their land and the cottagers their ancient grazing rights.

Pigs no longer snuffled for acorns in the oak woods, nor, were they even entitled to gather furze for fuel. Not unnaturally, the outrage of the villagers at the loss of these privileges, and the destruction of a way of life had manifested itself in various acts of vandalism. Under cover of darkness, fences were thrown down, hedges pulled up and as happened tonight, cornstacks fired. There was also a deep bitterness amongst the village folk that was directed towards three people who had done very well out of enclosure; Squire Bennett, The Reverend Cornelius Dobbs and Joseph Pedley.

The church clock striking eleven reminded Rachel that she ought to be deciding what to say to Squire Bennett, even supposing he was sober, which was unlikely. Trent

Hall had been built by the Squire's grandfather and was set apart from the village to establish his superiority. Charnwood granite had been used in its building and although it wasn't large it had a handsome porticoed entrance and had once stood proud. Unfortunately Francis Bennett, a widower of fifty and a notorious drunk, had allowed the house to fall into disrepair. Now slates were falling off the roof, windows rotting and there was an air of dereliction about the place.

The driveway was long, Rachel stumbled in potholes and overgrown bushes seemed to reach out at her like witches' fingers. A fox barking made her jump, then she thought she heard footsteps, remembered the arsonist and felt a prickle of unease. Supposing he'd seen her at the window, knew that she could identify him. He was a desperate man already at odds with the law, a bit of blood on his hands would mean little to him. She paused, alert to any sound.

Then someone so near she could hear his jagged breathing called out, "Rachel, you're to wait, do you hear me, I've got something to tell you." That she recognized the voice offered her no comfort. In fact the prospect of being alone in a dark driveway with George terrified her even more than being waylaid by a murderous Luddite.

Ignoring his pleas, she started to run, but her legs felt leaden, brambles tore at her skirts and branches whipped against her face. She had seen bulls mount heifers and knew what George's intentions were. She also knew she wouldn't stand a chance against him here in these dark woods where her screams would go unheard. From somewhere she found an extra surge of strength and as the driveway curved and the house came into view, a dim light drew her forward. Her breath rasping in her throat she reached the kitchen door. Hammering at it with both fists she managed to cry out, "Let me in Mrs Sawyer, let me in!"

"What the devil . . .?"

"Let me in, sir . . . please." Rachel's breasts were heaving, her unbraided hair was in disarray and her skirts torn but Harry Bennett hadn't seen such a delectable sight in a long time. Responding to her pleas, he held the door open and as the girl stumbled into the kitchen, he caught her to prevent her falling.

The kitchen was cavernous, walls and ceiling blackened with the soot of smoking rushlights. Because she knew that in a moment Cook would emerge from the gloom to take care of things, Rachel allowed herself to be led to a chair where an officer's blue army jacket edged with gold lace hung.

"Now whatever is the matter? You came through that door as if the hounds of hell were at your heels." Standing over her, Harry tried hard to adopt a tone in keeping with a master addressing a servant, but found himself mesmerized by the rise and fall of the girl's breasts. By God, he thought, who would have expected to find such a rare gem in Halby, and appearing like a gift from nowhere.

Still trying to shake off the horror of George's pursuit, Rachel found it difficult to collect her thoughts and for a few minutes the reason for her visit eluded her. But she knew the young officer was waiting for an answer and she managed to stutter out, "I . . . I . . . was looking for Mrs Sawyer sir. I have a message from my master for the Squire . . ."

"Is that so? Well you seemed to be in a mighty hurry." But Harry, not a perceptive young man, seemed prepared to accept this answer. Besides, at that moment one thing interested him, the maidservant's astounding physical attributes.

"Oh I was. It be most urgent sir."

"Well I'm afraid Cook has retired for the night, so has my uncle. Your master's message will have to wait until morning."

"But it can't wait." Rachel half stood, then minding her manners, sat down again. "The Squire is the Magistrate, he must be told otherwise my master . . ." Her voice trailed off.

11

"Your master will what?" asked Harry gently.

"Nothing." He was likely to give her a beating, something she was too ashamed to confess.

"Give me the message and I promise I'll pass it on first thing in the morning."

Rachel knew she had no choice but to do what the young man said. "Well my master . . . Master Pedley that is, wants the Yeomanry sent for. One of his corn stacks was set fire to tonight, it could have been one of General Ludd's men."

"Mmm . . . that's interesting. But why should anyone want to damage your master's property?"

"I don't know, sir." There were of course many reasons, but Rachel wasn't prepared to risk being accused of nursing Jacobin ideas.

"Did anyone see him?"

Rachel gazed at him steadfastly. "No."

"Well, never mind." But Harry began to feel excited. He relished the idea of pursuing Luddites. It would make a change from killing Froggies. "I will write a letter to your master, explain to him that my uncle could not be disturbed but that he will see him after church tomorrow. Does that satisfy you?" Harry smiled at her, thinking to himself that it was a pity that in the poor light she couldn't see his eyes, which were a clear blue, ringed with long dark lashes and recognized as being his best feature.

Harry, who was a captain in the Dragoons, had come through the recent wars in the Peninsula unscathed and now had only three ambitions in life. One was never to fight another battle, the other to accrue some wealth and the third was to seduce every pretty girl he met. As the younger son, he also had little in the way of private income and with the war over, he was now in the unfortunate position of having to live on reduced pay while his debts continued to spiral. So when, by coincidence, he found his regiment stationed near Halby, Harry decided it might be to his financial advantage to pay his childless uncle a visit. He'd arrived the previous day but since his uncle seemed to be perpetually in his cups, it was difficult to know whether he was making the right impression or not.

And Halby was dull, with nothing in the way of society, unless one counted the two monstrously ugly daughters of the vicar, and until the hunting season started, no sport. He'd even begun to question whether it was worth cultivating his uncle if it meant dying of boredom. But now he'd met this delicious creature and there was still nearly two weeks of his furlough left. Plenty of time to enjoy a dalliance with her. Harry never stopped to wonder if he might be unsuccessful in his pursuit of women. That was a negative thought and Harry was a young man with too much conceit in him ever to consider failure.

He went to find some ink and a pen and when he returned to the kitchen bearing a sealed letter, Rachel was gazing into the dying fire. He stood for a moment watching her, admiring the soft contours of her cheeks, the graceful curve of her neck and wondered what her history was. Perhaps she was the bastard child of a camp follower, perhaps sired by some foreign mercenary. Certainly she hadn't sprung from these cold northern shores for her skin reminded him of apricots ripening in the sun and she had the same warm-blooded look as the flamenco dancers he'd enjoyed in Spain. He felt a sudden compulsion to reach out and stroke the long black hair, to recapture those hot nights of throbbing guitars and the bold glances of the girls, as they sent out coded messages of love with their urgently tapping feet.

Harry lifted his hand, hesitated and let it fall. No he mustn't risk frightening her away. Beneath his easy charm he was a heartless young man who didn't give a fig for anyone. But he did differ from George in his approach to women for he loved paying court to them; loved the amorous glances, the secret *billet-doux*, the declarations of love. And the less interested a woman was the more he enjoyed it. He often likened wooing to fox hunting, the chase being almost better than the kill. Congratulating himself on his own self-restraint, Harry handed her the letter. "Here you are, take this to your master." As Rachel took it from him she looked up with a smile that was totally without guile and Harry realized with something of a jolt that she was still unaware of the power – and the curse – of beauty.

Rachel stood up, bracing herself for the journey back down the driveway where George lay in wait for her. And this time, she knew, she was unlikely to get away. She shivered and glanced at the Captain. He was nice, and seemed kindly disposed towards her. Perhaps he would walk with her some of the way. But in spite of her fear of George she was held firmly in check by a rigid social code. Maidservants didn't make such bold requests. Besides which, he'd just lit a small cigar and was inhaling it with obvious pleasure. But fear sucked away her strength and she felt her legs tremble as she walked to the door.

"Just a moment." As the Captain spoke, Rachel turned with a flicker of hope. "Before you go you might as well help me with my boots." He sat down and languidly extended a long leg towards her.

Ordinarily Rachel might have been somewhat taken aback by the request, but she was so pleased to do anything that would delay her departure, she moved back into the circle of the fire. He was now wiggling his foot at her in a peremptory manner but there was something so intimate about the task that she hestitated, hardly daring to touch him.

"Go on pull," he ordered.

As Rachel took hold of the heel and toe of the boot the masculine, faintly erotic smell of leather assailed her nostrils. This so distracted her that when the boot suddenly slipped from his foot, she staggered back across the room.

"Hey, steady on." The Captain laughed and held up his

14

other foot. When Rachel had freed him from the restricting footwear, he flexed his toes and admired his well-shaped calves. "Thank you . . . eh . . ." His voice held an enquiry.

"Rachel sir. Rachel Arden." She repeated, to make sure he remembered.

"Rachel . . . mmm . . ." He rolled the name round on his tongue. "A nice name, I like it."

"Good-night sir." Still she hesitated by the door.

"Good-night." He'd picked up a glass of brandy and was stretching towards the fire.

Rachel read the signals, she was being told to go. Mercifully, it had started to rain. She felt the soft touch of it on her face with gratitude. If anything could dampen George's ardour it was rain. He wouldn't have waited around, not if it meant getting wet and spoiling his clothes. Nevertheless, she still had to make her way down the driveway. And the wind had become stronger and as she ran she felt menaced by thrashing trees and the scuttering leaves.

To be back in Blackthorn Lane was like reaching a safe harbour. She didn't stop running until she'd reached the farm. Here the rain had doused the fire and the house was in darkness. Relieved to be spared the ordeal of facing Joseph Pedley again that night, Rachel put the letter on the table, slid the bolt across the kitchen door and went upstairs. She was so tired that if she hadn't been soaked to the skin she might not have bothered to undress. So when she fell into bed she expected sleep to come immediately. But too much had happened that evening and her brain raced with disturbing images and impressions.

For a long time she lay tossing and turning, knowing that dawn would come soon and she'd have to get up and go about her daily business blank-eyed with fatigue. When sleep did come it was fitful and disturbed, and although no one heard her, once in the night she cried out. For in her dream she was being pursued by a blue-coated Dragoon. She could see his features clearly, unsmiling and wrathful as they bore down on her. It wasn't the Captain, or George, she was fleeing from, but the young arsonist who that night had set fire to Joseph Pedley's corn stack.

Chapter Two

As she did every morning of the week, Susan Levitt walked up from the village to Thatcher's Mount with her daughter, a large ungainly girl of thirteen, trailing some way behind. Because it was Sunday she didn't have to start until half past seven. Even so she moved with urgency, so that when she heard the cry of, "Wait Mam," she gave a vexatious sigh. Stopping, Susan Levitt turned to wait for her daughter, watching with a mixture of guilt, love and exasperation as Polly lumbered up the hill, panting noisily in her effort to catch up. Sometimes the kids in the village would taunt her with names like daffy or loony but the wasn't daft, just not quite all there. She'd been such a little runt when she was born, it hardly seemed possible she would survive. And Susan remembered with a further rush of guilt how she'd prayed that she wouldn't. And because her feelings towards her daughter were so confused she tried to curb her irritation.

"You'll have to try a keep up wi' me, Polly. The Pedleys won't thank me if their breakfast is late. And you know how the old man goes on. You don't want your mam shouted at do you?" As she spoke, Susan, in a gesture of tenderness, took the corner of her apron and wiped beads of perspiration from the soft down of the girl's upper lip.

"No Mam, I don't," answered Polly, her placid features briefly animated as she gazed adoringly at her pretty, fair-haired mother.

"Take my hand then love and keep up."

The girl did as she was told, dragging on her mother's arm and hindering her progress so much Susan had to grit her teeth to hide her impatience.

Susan hardly gave the charred circle where the corn stack had once stood a glance, but hurried on into the kitchen. Here Rachel was down on her haunches trying to coax life into the new fangled range she had yet to get to grips with. When Polly saw her she gave an excited squeal, rushed over and hugged her so enthusiastically they both toppled to the floor where they lay giggling. Susan watched them fondly, as always, touched by Rachel's easy acceptance of Polly's handicap. If only . . . well if only a lot of things. With a resigned sigh she said to her daughter, "Go and set the table, there's a good girl, while Rachel and me gets on wi' breakfast."

Susan curbed her impatience until the door snapped shut. She even curbed it long enough to unhook a flitch of bacon and begin slicing it. "I see you had a bit of a fire up here last night." The tone of her voice was casual.

Rachel, who was now pumping away with bellows, looked round. "Oh you saw it, did you?"

"Oh no. I'd have been fast asleep when it happened."

"Well the whole village must have been fast asleep, 'cos not one person turned up to help."

"Are you surprised?"

"No, not really," answered Rachel.

"Lucky for him it was only a corn stack and not the barn."

Rachel gave a quick glance towards the door then lowering her voice asked, "Who do you think it was, Susan?"

"I shouldn't think it was anybody. Probably just a stray spark from a chimney."

"Oh no, some person did it."

Susan gave the girl a sharp look. "You sound very certain. You saw someone, did you?"

18

Rachel shook her head. "No, it's just what Old Man Pedley said. He wants the Squire to call the Militia in."

Susan laughed. "Over one corn stack?"

"Yes and he made me go all the way up to Trent Hall last night. I was supposed to tell the Squire but he was was dead drunk. His nephew was there though, so I told him instead. He's in the Dragoons." Then without thinking added, "he's really handsome too," and blushed scarlet.

Even as she spoke she could see a reproof forming on Susan's lips. But fortunately Esther Pedley came bustling into the kitchen and Rachel was spared the acid comment.

"You must have heard about the fire by now Susan." Mrs Pedley said, looking even more anxious than normal.

"Yes ma'am."

"Terrible business, Susan, terrible. But why should anyone want to do such a thing to us?"

"I'm sure it weren't deliberate, ma'am."

"Well Mr Pedley thinks differently, and he's determined to catch the culprits. Anyway it was all too much for Mr George so he won't be getting up for breakfast. Which I suppose means he won't be coming to church." Esther Pedley sighed, for she wasn't quite reconciled to the fact that her beloved son was past redemption anyway.

While the breakfast and dinner menus were being discussed Rachel went to fetch milk from Percy Weddeburn, the cowman. He was a taciturn, awkward man who'd never married, lived in a cottage that was little more than a hovel and even Joseph Pedley was disinclined to cross swords with him. Clean was not a word that sprung to anyone's lips when describing Percy, and his bushy whiskers were stained brown by the clay pipe jammed perpetually in the corner of his mouth.

"So there was somethin' of a fire then, last night," said Percy transferring the pipe from one side of his mouth to the other.

19

"How did you know Perc?"

"I saw'd it didn't I? It would a' bin bloody hard not to. Lit up the sky. Everyone wa' standing at their gates cheering."

"Why did no one come and give a hand then?"

"Help Old Man Pedley, that wud be a joke. You know everyone hates his guts." To reinforce this point, he removed the pipe from his mouth and aimed a stream of nicotined spittle in the direction of the floor. Then muttering to himself, Percy went back to his cows, whose company he maintained, was preferable any day to that of humans.

Before returning to the house, Rachel skimmed off the specks of shag tobacco that were floating across the milk like boats on a lake, and thought about what Percy had told her. For his interpretation of the events of the night before certainly differed from Susan's. But then that was her own business, just as certain matters were hers.

Susan was already married with a two-year-old infant when Rachel arrived at Thatcher's Mount from the workhouse. A frightened little girl, it was Susan who took Rachel under her wing and protected her from George and never thought twice about sending him packing if she caught him out in any spitefulness.

It was Susan too who had taught her letters and numbers. Every Sunday afternoon as a child, Rachel would trot down to the small cottage Susan shared with her husband Robert, and under her stern eye laboriously scratch out multiplication tables on a slate and struggle to make sense of words and sentences in a dog-eared primer. At the time Rachel hadn't felt any particular enthusiasm for learning. Sunday afternoon was her only free time and she would sit chewing on her slate pencil and gaze longingly out of the window at the children playing on the green.

But Susan would brush aside her complaints. "You'll thank me for it when you're older. An unlettered person is at a great disadvantage in this world." Which of course was true, although it wasn't until she grew to know the pleasure of reading that Rachel ceased to regret those lost hours of play. "You're not to tell them up at the house I'm giving you lessons either." Susan would warn. "They think that learning, for the likes of us, is as dangerous as putting a keg of gunpowder in our hands. So, remember, if you ever have to sign anything, just put your mark."

Not understanding what Susan was on about, she would nod her head. Obedience, Rachel had learnt, meant reward, usually in the form of a slice of seed cake and a small glass of cowslip wine. Anyway, she wouldn't have missed going to Susan and Robert's for anything. She loved the homely atmosphere of the cottage, with its shining brass candlesticks and pewter mugs lined up on the oak dresser. Winter afternoons were spent round the hearth making toast, and in summer the clove scented smell of gillyflowers wafted in through the diamond framed open window. But what fascinated her most as a child was the stocking-frame Robert worked and which like everyone else in the village, he hired from Joseph Pedley. The work was noisy and arduous but to see the yarn turn into finished hose had always seemed to Rachel a miracle.

Susan was standing flushed-faced over the range cooking Joseph Pedley's mutton chops when Rachel got back to the kitchen. She looked up briefly from her task, "You've been long enough."

"I was talking to Percy. He saw the fire from his house. Said the whole village was cheering."

"I think there's enough been said about that fire. Now go and get yourself changed before this food spoils and there's the devil to pay."

Rachel, who knew better than to argue with Susan, hurried off to change into a clean white apron and mob cap. Because, although she had to be at church with the family by ten, she first of all had to serve breakfast.

*   *   *

"Polly. Come up here, I've got something for you." George called softly from the trap door of the hay loft.

Polly looked up at him and grinned. "Is it cake, Master Georgie?" she asked with a hopeful expression, for she had an insatiably sweet tooth.

"Something even better, sugared plums. And Dusty's had kittens, six altogether and they're up here. Do you want to come up and stroke them?" George coaxed.

The girl nodded. "I can have the sugared plums as well, can't I Master Georgie?" Polly always liked to negotiate favourable terms.

"Of course you can," answered George, trying to keep the impatience from his voice. "Come on." He held out his hand and the girl climbed the ladder.

"Where are the pussies?"

"Over here." Beckoning to her, George walked to the far end of the loft and had a quick squint through a cobweb covered window which looked out on to the yard and gave him a good view of the kitchen. He had chosen his time carefully for apart from Susan, who would be busy preparing the Sunday dinner and Percy, who was working in the top field, everyone else was at morning service. Even so he knew there wasn't time to waste and satisfying himself there was no one around he knelt and called to the girl, "Look, here they are." As she reached him, he pulled her down beside him in the hay. "Now you're my little kitten, aren't you? And Master Georgie's going to give his little kitten a sugared plum just as long as she does what he says. You will, won't you?"

"Yes, Master Georgie," answered Polly with a giggle and ran her fingers through George's blond curls.

George knew he was lucky with Polly. She might be simple but she was also accommodating and didn't cost him a penny. A whore in Leicester could charge as much as half a guinea and was likely to give you the pox into the bargain. But he had to be careful. Apart from his father there was only one other person who put the fear of God into him and that was Susan Levitt. If she found out what he did regularly to her daughter she was likely do him a serious injury. But there were times when his frustrated need for Rachel became so intense he took the risk.

George unwrapped a sugared plum and held it in front of the girl. She tried to snatch the sweetmeat but he pulled it away and wagging his finger at her said, "Now you're to promise not to tell your mam what we get up to because if you do, she'll say you're a bad girl a slap your backside. And Georgie would never give you anything ever again. And you wouldn't like that would you Polly?"

Polly shook her head and smiled and her eyes, brown, bovine and trusting gave George a momentary twinge of guilt. But the need within in him was too urgent, too powerful and as he allowed her to make a successful grab for the sweetmeat he pushed her into the hay and threw back her skirt and petticoat. Her legs were long and straight, the thighs white and firm, the mount of venus just beginning to sprout baby fine hair. He leaned back on his haunches and with some urgency began to undo his trousers.

"Open your legs Polly," he ordered and as she complied he only had to imagine it was Rachel lying naked before him with her legs carelessly spreadeagled, and he was erect in a second. Moaning "Rachel, Rachel," he flung himself down on the girl and came almost as soon as he entered her.

Chapter Three

The lane leading from the farm down to the village was little more than a track and in wet weather mud made it impassable to all but the sturdiest waggon and strongest horse. In summer the surface was hardly better because by then the ruts had been baked hard by the sun, and were capable of snapping the axle on a carriage in two. This morning the trap in which the Pedleys were travelling to church lurched and bumped over the ridges like a ship in a storm, throwing the occupants from side to side and creating so much dust Matilda announced she could stand it no longer. "Put me down, this minute, Mama."

"As you wish, my dear," said her mother. "But don't be late or you'll miss the parson's sermon."

"Oh fiddle sticks!" Matilda mouthed to the backs of her departing parents. Who cares about a boring old service, who cares about anything in this God forsaken place, she thought, gazing around her with a discontented expression. The only thing that gave purpose to her day was her new bonnet. It was made of plaited straw and green velvet ribbons, which were tied under her chin in a large bow. Time and energy had been squandered that morning in arranging her curls so that they tumbled in pretty disarray on her forehead and cheeks. But the finishing touch was her parasol, which cast a flattering shadow, and gave mysterious depths to her rather pale blue eyes.

Matilda felt she looked exceedingly becoming and it peeved

her that there was not one man in the village worthy of such effort. What she would have to settle for was being gawped at by the village yokels and ogled by the Squire. Still there were Jane and Grace. The parson's daughters rarely had anything new and the ill-concealed envy on their faces when they saw her bonnet, would make up for a lot.

Matilda was now just a few yards from the entrance to the Manor and the sound of hooves on gravel gave notice of the imminent appearance of the Squire. If he saw her, he would stop and offer her a lift and she had to balance the prestige this gave her in the eyes of the community against the fact that he was so gross she could hardly bear to be near him. In that split second she had in which to make a decision, Matilda darted behind a bush facing the gates, snapped shut the parasol, drew in her skirts and held herself very still.

As he reached the end of the drive, the Squire slowed the horse to a walking pace before turning left into the lane. And in that brief pause Matilda saw Harry. He was in uniform and looked so dashing beside the dropsical Squire, her mouth fell open in astonishment. She'd never seen anyone so handsome in her life. But who was he? By now she was in such a fever of curiosity she could hardly bring herself to wait. In her haste the hem of her dress caught on a bramble, and as she tugged at it impatiently there was the sound of rending muslin. "Dash it!" she exclaimed, then without stopping to examine the damage, Miss Matilda Pedley set off towards St Philip's church with an expectant gleam in her eyes and all the bounce of a high stepping filly.

Rachel and Sam, who were sent to church each Sunday more for the good of their souls than because they wanted to go, were some yards behind when this episode took place. Both of them watched the girl then Sam said in a puzzled voice, "What's got into her? She's in a mighty hurry all of a sudden."

But the significance of this small tableau hadn't been lost

on Rachel. "I'll tell you if you can't guess. She's just seen the Squire's nephew right? And she's two and twenty and still not wed, right?"

Sam nodded.

"Well it's orange blossoms and wedding bells that have got into her, that's what."

"What a daft idea," answered the twelve-year-old Sam dismissively.

But Rachel acknowledged Matilda's right to nurse such hopes even though it was an idea she found depressing. Because for the Captain's benefit she herself had washed and dressed with special care that morning. Her white cap and kerchief were freshly starched, her hair neatly plaited. In the garden, she'd picked some sprigs of lavender, released the scent by rubbing them between the palms of her hands, then tucked the small posy down the front of her bodice.

The day was warm, the sky the same washed-out blue as Rachel's calico dress, the clouds mere brush strokes. The previous night's rain had been the first for several weeks and the grass verge was a biscuit colour, the sloes and blackberries almost ready for picking. Sam was gorging himself on ripe blackberries and on any other occasion Rachel would have joined him but she didn't want to risk staining her dress, just in case the Captain looked in her direction. The church bells were now summoning the last few stragglers, and calling out to Sam, "Are you coming?" Rachel hurried with the same eagerness as Matilda had done towards St Philip's church.

It might have been God's house but here in church, just as in the ouside world, every villager knew his or her place in the scheme of things. The Squire and the Parson's family had their own pews, then behind them in order of social standing sat the Pedleys, the innkeeper, blacksmith, miller and carpenter with their families. After this came the Squire's servants, while right at the back sat Rachel, Sam and the field labourers, the humblest members of the community.

It was a small, plain church with only one stained glass window, donated by the Squire's father shortly before his death in the hope that it would atone for some of his more outrageous sins. It was no hardship for Rachel to sit at the rear of the church, particularly when it was warm like this morning and the verger had left the door open. From the back too she could observe Matilda and at the same time admire the Captain's broad shoulders.

Although Jane, the vicar's elder daughter, played the harmonium rather badly, Rachel knew most of the hymns by heart and sang them with gusto. The Parson's sermon, as usual, seemed interminable, his voice sonorous. Through the open door she could hear the soporific buzz of bees and once or twice she had to smother a yawn. She tried to look attentive as the Reverend Cornelius Dobbs went on about the sin of envy and the virtues of being satisfied with that station in life which providence had seen fit to call one, blinked hard when she felt her eyes closing. But she couldn't fight off the drowsiness and her head finally dropped on to her chest. A nudge in the ribs and Sam hissing "Hey, wake up," startled Rachel so much she leapt to her feet and sent a hymn book banging to the floor.

The whole congregation turned and stared. All of them, looked disapproving. Mortified she slunk down low into the pew. However her clumsiness did at least bring the parson's sermon to an end, for which everyone was secretly thankful. The last hymn had been sung and people were gathering up shawls and bibles when the Parson held up his hand.

"Before you leave I have two points to raise, one pleasant the other unpleasant so I will deal with that first. As you probably all know by now, there was a fire at Thatcher's Mount last night, and a corn stack was destroyed. This wasn't the first incident of this kind and there have been other insurrectionary acts, such as fences being pulled up around newly enclosed land. If anyone here has any information about the incident, for which there is an award of three guineas, and they are keeping quiet about it I want them to remember that this is God's house and they will have their consciences to answer to."

As Parson Dobbs cast a stern eye over his erring flock, Rachel sat absolutely still, certain someone was about to leap up, point an accusing finger, and denounce her in front of the whole congregation with the words, "She knows who it is!" But although there was some clearing of throats, every bottom remained affixed to the pews, and, having done his duty by Farmer Pedley, the Parson moved on to the next point.

"Well, if no one has anything to say, I shall proceed to more pleasant matters. It has been decided by the Parish Council that we should celebrate our deliverance from Bonaparte and the glorious victory of our matchless hero, Field Marshall the Duke of Wellington, with a public rejoicing here in Halby a week on Wednesday. Generous contributions have been made by various members of the village . . ." Here the vicar paused and smiled benignly at the first four rows of pews, ". . . and the day will be declared a holiday so that the whole village can participate in the festivities."

At this news a murmur of excitement ran through the church and Rachel turned to Sam. "Do you think we'll be able to go?"

"He said everyone didn't 'e. Well that means us then."

"What about the master?" Rachel was doubtful whether Joseph Pedley's charity, even on an historic occasion like this, would extend to her and Sam.

"If it's a holiday for everyone he can't leave us out, now can he?" Sam reasoned.

Although Rachel hoped Sam was right she decided not to take any chances. Kneeling, she closed her eyes, pressed her hands together, and prayed. Very hard. "Please dear Lord, let me go the the party. And Sam as well of course," she added as an afterthought.

Satisfied she could do no more, Rachel opened her eyes to find the Squire and his nephew leaving the church. She jumped to her feet and as they passed, gave a deferential bob. She tried to keep her gaze modestly cast down but the Captain caught her eye and winked, which caused her cheeks to turn pink with pleasure and embarrassment.

With a clatter of hobnailed boots, and in order of precedence, the rest of the congregation took their leave, with Sam and Rachel bringing up the rear. Outside, they stood blinking in the sunshine then Sam, seeing boys of his own age, said briefly, "I'll see you later," and shot off to enjoy a brief spell of freedom and the rough and tumble of childhood games.

The warm weather had seduced people into lingering and gossiping in the churchyard. Some were discussing the coming celebration, others, Rachel guessed, from the lowered voices and slightly furtive glances in the direction of the Pedley family, the fire. Stretching her neck and standing on tiptoe, she tried to see over their heads. She'd just caught a glimpse of the Captain and his uncle by the lych gate and was pushing her way through the crowd towards them when Peter Fellowes, the miller called out, "Come here girl," beckoning her with a peremptory wave of his hand.

"What do you want?" she asked warily. She knew full well of course, he wanted to poke his nose in, quiz her about the fire. She also knew from Susan that the miller was an untrustworthy man who cheated folks out of their full measure of flour. He probably thought he could winkle a few things out of her then go toadying to Joseph Pedley. But Rachel cherished her secret knowledge. No one would find out anything from her.

"I just want a word with you." Peter Fellowes answered, breaking away from his friends. But Rachel was too quick for him and as he came towards her she turned and went zigzagging between the gravestones.

She'd almost reached the lych gate when she saw the

Captain get his first glimpse Matilda and turn her faint hopes to cinder. The girl was walking towards him between the dark yews that lined the path, and all his attention was focused on her. Although Rachel was familiar with Matilda's little tricks it was easy today to see why. She looked very engaging in her new bonnet, the petulant droop of her mouth had gone and her expression was animated. Even her mother managed to say something to amuse her and her laughter rang out, clear as spring water.

But it wasn't just Harry who was admiring her performance so was the Squire. "Morning Pedley, Mrs Pedley, Miss Matilda," he called out to the family, lifting his hat and feasting his eyes on the girl.

"Good morning to you Squire," answered Joseph Pedley in a cordial tone. Rachel knew he found being civil to anyone hard but to a man like the Squire, whom he despised, he must have found it an almost impossible task. But she knew he was aware of Francis Bennett's growing interest in his daughter and was enough of a businessman to want to see a return on the investment he made in piano, painting and elocution lessons. Matilda as Lady of the Manor would be a fulfilment of one of his most cherished dreams.

"Let me introduce my nephew, Captain Bennett of the Dragoon of Guards." Rachel heard the Squire say.

"At your service," said Harry and bringing his heels together he gave a deep bow.

Matilda smiled, dimpled, went pink and twirled her parasol with a becoming confusion and Rachel's heart sank.

But the girl's interest in his nephew wasn't helping the Squire's temper, which was unfortunate for Joseph Pedley, who wanted to discuss the loss of his corn stack.

"A word with you about last night, Squire," he said but without that deference Squire Bennett felt was his due. Feeling it was about time Pedley needed reminding he was his his social inferior he turned and glared at him splenetically. "What about last night?" he barked.

"The fire. I had a note from your nephew assuring me you would discuss the matter this morning."

"Well go ahead, say what you've got to say."

"Not in public with all the busybodies listening," answered Joseph Pedley equally forcefully. He had worked his knuckles bare to get where he was and now he had a bit of freehold land, a hosiery business in Leicester and his credit was good. He'd be buggered if he was going to defer to the Squire. He'd been slighted by the County set once too often and was deeply resentful of them. But it was his opinion that they would be worth nothing soon. Many, like the Squire, were deeply in debt, didn't know how run their estates, were terrified of having their names tarnished by being associated with trade and consequently were rapidly going to the dogs. But what he really couldn't stand was the way they looked down their aristocratic noses at his Tilda, considering her an unsuitable match for their sons. And yet you only had to look at her to see she was as much a lady as any of them. God almighty, she should be, he spent enough money on making her one.

The Squire was glaring at Joseph Pedley balefully but since they were men with the same implacable natures, the hosier just glared back. "All right, we'll talk over here, come on," Francis Bennett said with a jerk of his head.

No one was more relieved than Mrs Pedley when the two men walked away. She'd half expected a full blown row to develop in front of the whole village and was now in a state of high nervous tension. And when she was nervous Esther Pedley was inclined to chatter inconsequentially. "And what did you think of the Parson's sermon this morning, Captain Bennett?" she asked, with an agitated rubbing of her hands.

"Excellent ma'am," replied Harry, who had slumbered through most of it.

31

"Oh good." Esther Pedley beamed, thinking to herself what a nice young man and obviously devout too. "I'm sure the Parson will be delighted to know. Ah . . . there he is, I'll just go and have a word . . ." and without finishing her sentence, darted away after her spiritual guide and mentor.

At last Harry and Matilda were alone together. Unfortunately Matilda felt so overwhelmed by the Captain's handsome features, his proud military bearing, that instead of engaging with him in the witty conversation she'd rehearsed in her head during the long sermon, she found herself tongue-tied.

However, silence in women never bothered Harry. The less they said the better. And over the years he had devised various strategies which had proved to be very successful in the game of seduction and he liked to keep his hand in. One which always proved effective was to gaze deep into the eyes of the young woman without speaking, as if drinking in her beauty. Few women could resist this and while he waited for Matilda's trembling hand to flutter to her mouth, he appraised her in a detached manner. Skin good, teeth too small. Figure not bad and nice breasts. Not a stunner like the serving wench but not bad for a place like Halby. She was dying for it too he could see that, he just hoped she wasn't going to be too damned easy, that took the fun out of it. Still there would be an added piquancy in bedding the maidservant and her mistress at the same time.

Matilda knew that by allowing a man to stare at her so boldly, her own behaviour might be construed as immodest. But not for the life of her could she have averted her gaze. His eyes, which were an intense blue and spoke of danger, ignited strange sensations in her body and she felt a most pleasurable throbbing between her thighs. She had to grip the parasol hard to prevent her hands trembling and felt so lightheaded she wondered if she might actually swoon into the Captain's arms. Finally Matilda broke away from his hypnotic gaze and embarrassed by her own behaviour, said the first thing that came into her head. "Er . . . ah . . . are you staying with your uncle for long, Captain Bennett?"

"Two weeks."

Matilda did a quick calculation. "So you'll be coming to the victory celebrations then?"

"I most certainly will." He treated Matilda to another of his intense glances.

Matilda's spirits soared like a skylark's. Hardly half an hour before, the thought of sharing a table with an unwashed cottager or field labourer had filled her with distaste and she had determined not to go. Now she was already planning her outfit for the day. "There's to be dancing I believe." she said, almost unable to contain her excitement.

"Well I certainly hope, Miss Pedley, that you will save the first dance for me."

"Oh I will Captain Bennett," she breathed almost beside herself with joy.

Esther Pedley, who had decided the young couple had spent more time alone together than was perhaps seemly, now rejoined them and Matilda tensed herself for one of her mother's foolish remarks that could always make her cringe with embarrassment. Instead she surprised and, for once in her life, pleased her daughter by smiling at the Captain and saying, "I've invited the two Miss Dobbs up to take tea with us this evening. Perhaps you and your uncle, Captain Bennett, would like to join us as well?"

Chapter Four

Rachel was halfway back to the farm when Sam finally caught up with her. He'd expected a wigging so to find himself ignored was slightly disconcerting. To make his presence felt, he began to engage in swordplay, cutting and jabbing at an imaginery foe with a stick. But even this failed to make any impression. At twelve, Sam had yet to be beguiled by a neat ankle and dimpled smile, had yet to be tormented by the bittersweet ache of love, so her behaviour puzzled him. What bewildered him even more was when she stopped, and tearing the spiky heads of lavender from the bodice of her dress, stamped them angrily into the dust.

"Eh oop Rachel, what's that all about then?" Sam asked in astonishment.

"None of your business!" she snapped.

Sam shrugged, thinking to himself, it wa' true what old Perc said; woomen wa' a funny lot, moody one minute, laughing the next. And Rachel wasn't half the fun she used to be be. In the last year or so she'd changed, didn't want to play games, sometimes even tried to act the lady. But Sam was a lad who approached life with an unabashed optimism and deciding what Rachel needed was a bit of cheering up, he pulled a broad blade of grass from the verge, stretched it taut between his thumbs, placed his lips against it and blew hard. The discordant sound, split the midday calm and carried so far it set all the dogs in the neighbourhood barking. Well pleased with his effort he grinned widely and waited for Rachel to have a go.

Instead she gave him a cold, grown-up look. "Do that again and you'll get a clout."

"Oh yeah," he jeered, blew a penetrating chord close to her ear, then tore off up the road but glancing over his shoulder to see if she was following him.

But Rachel was in no mood to go chasing after anyone. She was too preoccupied with the meeting she'd witnessed between the Captain and Matilda. She was daft to think that he could have the slightest interest in a serving girl. But he had seemed to like her. And he was so different from George with his crude advances, or the callow youths in the village, either leering and incoherent or measuring her worth as a prospective bride by the number of cows she could milk in an hour. Rachel had never given it a thought before, but she decided that nothing on earth would induce her to marry an uncouth village swain. She'd rather go to her grave a spinster.

Rachel wasn't a girl to be downhearted for long and such a positive decision made her feel much more cheerful. When she saw Sam appear in the dusty lane, she waved cheerfully. But he didn't wave back. Instead he cupped his hands against his mouth and called, "Susan says your to stop day-dreaming and get a move on. There's table to set and vegetables still to be done."

Joseph Pedley paused in the task of carving a large sirloin joint and glared balefully at his wife and daughter. "Will you two women stop wittering on about that soldier boy. I had to put up with it all the way home, but if I hear the name Captain Bennett mentioned again at this dinner table I'll send a note telling him not to come tonight, I swear to God I will. Do you understand?" he thundered, then made several vicious stabs at the air with the carving knife to reinforce his point.

"Yes, dear." Esther Pedley's tone was dutiful, submissive, but her thoughts were less so. Why does he have to shout? She wondered, regarding her better half with dislike. She would have loved to step out of character and ask him but she didn't quite have the courage. Besides there was Matilda and her happiness to consider. His threats were all too real and a word out of place could put the evening her daughter was so looking forward to in jeopardy.

Matilda herself didn't even bother to answer her father. Only when she was sure he wasn't looking, did she dare to extend a small pink tongue at him.

While he harangued his nearest and dearest, Rachel handed round the plates and served vegetables. And although she listened intently to every word that passed between the family, her expression remained impassive. It even remained impassive when George tried to get his hand up her skirt under cover of the damask tablecloth. It was unfortunate, though, that he commenced his groping as Rachel was serving him gravy. Even more unfortunate that it was scalding hot and she held the gravy boat awkwardly. Because as she tried to move out of his reach it tilted, and a stream of steaming brown liquid shot straight into his lap. George let out a yelp of pain, leapt up and clutching his crotch, danced around the room, yelling obscenities of a kind the women in the room had never heard in their lives before. Still clasping the gravy boat, Rachel stood immobile, gazing in horror at the spreading brown stain on George's best nankin trousers.

Everyone was on their feet now and the drama seemed to unfold in slow motion as George took a step towards Rachel and delivered her a stinging blow. Her head reeled under the impact and as the ring he wore dug deep into her cheekbone, she let out a cry of pain. To protect herself from further violence she shrank back against the wall, pressing her hand to her face and wincing as she felt the scored flesh and blood, warm and viscous, on her cheek.

"You did that deliberately, you stupid bitch," George accused. "Damn you to heaven girl, you'll pay for this."

"George, stop it!" He went to make another lunge at the girl but his mother grabbed his arm.

Knowing it would be useless to protest her innocence, Rachel blinked back her tears. But she stared at George with an expression of such naked hatred in her dark eyes even his tongue was stilled.

In the attack the gravy boat had slipped from her fingers and the dregs were now spattered all over an expensive Chinese carpet. Rachel also found herself unable to staunch the flow of blood and the sight of it fusing with brown gravy stains almost made Joseph Pedley apoplectic. "Christ almighty get that girl out of here, she's bleeding like a stuck pig!" he bellowed.

Esther Pedley studied her husband for a moment, and wondered as she did several times a day, how she'd ever come to marry such an uncouth, disagreeable person. The truth, of course, was that she'd been so plain she been humbly grateful for any man's attention, even though she realized early on in their courtship it was her father's hosiery business Joseph had his eye on rather than her. And no matter how much she tried to ignore it, George seemed to be a vessel fashioned in the same clay. Burdened with these unpleasant thoughts about her own flesh and blood she put a protective arm around Rachel's shoulder. The girl was trembling like a small bird that has just been rescued from a cat and briefly she found herself disliking her son almost as much as her spouse. "Come along, my child, let's get you cleaned up," she said gently and led the maidservant from the room.

Susan was taking a plum pie from the oven and Percy, Sam and Polly were sitting at the table waiting for the remains of the joint to come through from the dining room. So three

37

pairs of hungry eyes turned with hopeful expressions, as footsteps approached the kitchen. Rachel was holding the white apron to her cheek and at the sight of the spreading stain of blood there was a simultaneous, shocked indrawing of breath. Then in the silence, Susan who had almost dropped the pie, rushed round the table exclaiming, "Good Lord, what's happened?"

"Just a slight accident, Susan that's all." answered Mrs Pedley. Acting with a calm authority that was never evident when her family was around, she handed Sam a bowl. "Get me water from the pump, and gather the tops of some nettles," she ordered, then dispatched Polly to get clean sheeting from the linen press and oil of lavender from her room. When Sam returned, he was set to pounding the nettle leaves with a mortar and pestle while she diluted the lavender oil.

Rachel, still dazed from the blow, stood in docile silence while Mrs Pedley bathed her cheek. But the oil stung the raw wound and brought tears, that were already dangerously near the surface, to her eyes.

Mrs Pedley paused and gazed at her solicitously. "Are you all right my dear?"

Quickly Rachel rubbed the tears away with her index finger. "It was the lavendar oil, it stung," she lied.

"It might hurt but it will prevent a scar. You're young and healthy so it won't take long to heal." Esther Pedley kept her tone optimistic, but deep inside, her soul trembled for her son.

Although she had great faith in her mistress's remedies, all written out in copperplate in a large leather-bound book, as the cold compress of crushed nettles was applied to the wound, Rachel did begin to have doubts. What would the folks in the village say if she showed her face today?

"Don't fiddle, there's a good girl," Esther Pedley ordered as Rachel fingered the compress. "The nettles are to stop the bleeding." Standing back, she surveyed her with a critical

38

eye, then said, "But you look a bit of a mess, I must say." Turning to Susan she went on, "I'm afraid you'll have to finish serving the meal, Susan. Rachel's not in a fit state to go back in there."

Esther Pedley had one last look at the girl's gashed cheek then satisfied she had done all she could, she returned to the dining room. But she approached it with a sinking heart. Voices were raised. Although she longed for tranquility, Mrs Pedley had long ago accepted that with a family like hers, it was something she was unlikely to achieve in this life.

"As if I haven't got enough to do without serving that lot," Susan grumbled. But she might as well have been talking to a brick wall. All the other three were interested in was Rachel's injury and they clustered around her, eager and curious, all of them talking at once.

"What happened Rachel? . . . Yeah, go on tell us . . . did the old man give you one . . .?" But the jumble of voices was just too much for the girl and she had to press her hands against her ears to shut out the noise.

Instantly Susan was at her side. Putting a protective arm round Rachel's shoulder, she spoke sharply to the others. "Leave her alone, can't you see she's upset. If she wants to tell you it'll be in her own good time."

"I'm all right. Anyway I want everyone to know. It was that pig George, he hit me."

"Whatever for?" asked Susan.

She told them of the accident then, haltingly at first but as she went on to describe George's anguished dance round the room she started to giggle. "It didn't half make him jump, that hot gravy. And the language! Well . . ." A wild laugh ripped through her, releasing the tension and soon the others were joining in, their dislike of George voiced in a great explosion of laughter which had them rocking backwards and forwards, while tears ran down their cheeks. Their outburst deadened the sound of the footsteps in the passage, and George, on his way to change his trousers, heard the shrieks of laughter, guessed it was at his expense and walked on with murder in his heart.

Rachel huffed on the base of the copper saucepan, gave it a final polish with the sleeve of her dress, then holding it up like a mirror, she tried to peer at herself in its burnished surface. However, her features remained obstinately blurred. Slamming the saucepan back down on the table she gave a restless sigh and went over to the window. What was she doing here? After all this was her afternoon off and by now she'd be down at Woodbine cottage, if everyone hadn't undermined her confidence by telling her what a mess she looked, and how by the morrow the yellow stain on her cheek would be the colour of ripe damsons. But her decision not to go was beginning to lose its appeal and her few precious hours of freedom stretched emptily ahead. Matilda would be titivating herself for the Captain's visit too and if she thought Rachel had time on her hands there would be work found for her to do. Perhaps hair brushed and curled or ribbons sewn on to a dress. Anyway Rachel thought defiantly, I've done nothing wrong, why should I hide myself away like a leper? Let anyone who likes ask, I'll tell them who hit me.

With a sudden resolution she sat down, applied a generous application of powder to the remaining saucepans and began polishing them vigorously.

She executed this task at record speed, hung the saucepans up on their hooks over the fireplace, then stood back and briefly enjoyed the bright glow of polished copper in the firelight. Her job done, she went outside and bathed her face clean of the cold compress under the pump. Her cheekbone still throbbed but after gingerly checking that it had stopped bleeding, Rachel set off towards the village at a brisk pace and with her chin held obstinately high.

It had clouded over since the morning but it was still warm, with a hint of thunder in the air. At some risk to her fingers, Rachel paused every now and then to pick sprays of rosehips from the hedgerow, all that she could ever offer Susan in the way of a gift. She had her food and clothes from the Pedleys but nothing else. As a child she'd accepted this unquestioningly but as she grew older she realized that not to earn a wage reduced her to the status of a slave. Although it could land her in prison, she had thought of running away, perhaps at the time of the next hiring fair. She'd even wondered about moving north and getting work in a cotton mill. But without money in her pocket she knew she was unlikely to get far and parishes were suspicious of anyone likely to become a burden on the Poor Rate.

Before enclosure, although most of the cottagers might have lived at a subsistence level, the common rights they'd enjoyed gave them a certain independence. Deprived of these rights many of them had sunk to a state of abject poverty. But Sunday was the one day in the week when every man made sure his wife and children had full bellies, even if it involved a bit of poaching on the Squire's estate. And a heavy meal needed to be slept off, so apart from a few children playing on the Green, Halby had a somnambulant air. Woodbine Cottage too seemed to stand silent and the windows had a blank uninviting air. Even the door that usually stood open, was closed although it swung to at Rachel's touch.

She stepped into the small room with a certain feeling of unease, not sure what to expect. At first it seemed empty but a movement made her start and glance towards the chimney corner. Someone stood up and as he moved towards her across the stone-flagged floor, Rachel bit hard on her lip to try and control her involuntary gasp of fear. For standing in front of her was someone whose features she'd seen only briefly in the glow of a lanthorn but which were etched, like a line drawing, on her memory.

41

Chapter Five

When she thought about it later, Rachel never knew why she didn't turn tail and run. But since nothing could have prepared her for the shock of coming face to face with the young arsonist in Susan's parlour, her brain didn't have time to make that connection between his presence and her own personal safety. So her immediate feeling was one of outrage, and indignation gave her voice the weight of authority. "Who are you? What are you doing tresspassing here, in this house?"

"I could ask the same of you." The young man's manner was equally abrasive, his grey eyes so cold, Rachel felt she was being impaled on splinters of ice. He advanced towards her as he spoke, and although she despised herself for doing it, she took a step back.

She knew he was trying to intimidate her when he stepped forward again. And although he was tall and strongly built, this time she stood her ground holding the spray of barbed orange berries against her breast in an unconsciously defensive action. "I've got a right to be here, you haven't."

"Oh who says so? And why should I believe you anyway." He enquired, staring at her in a most hostile manner.

"Uh . . . uhmm . . . because Susan and Robert are friends of mine, that's why." As she floundered to explain herself, Rachel realized he was cleverly trying to manipulate the situation to his own advantage. Determined this shouldn't happen, she stood tall trying to match his height as she fought to regain control. "Anyway I'm not answerable to you. You're the intruder not me. Just tell me who you are and what your business is."

"His name is Jed Fairfax." At the sound of Susan's voice, Rachel swung round. Her friend had been standing by the door leading to the room where the stocking frame was kept but now she moved into the parlour and stood by Jed, linking her arm in his as if to protect him from further questioning. "He and me is kin, cousins if you want to know. He's just brought news from Leicester that my aunt's been took ill."

Rachel fought hard to hide her astonishment, her glance moving from Jed to Susan. But although Jed's hair was several shades darker than Susan's, their common ancestry was evident in the similarity of features, the same grey eyes and good looks. As Rachel reluctantly absorbed this knowledge she felt a growing sense of unease as she tried to come to terms with the idea that Susan must have known of her cousin's criminal act. Her immediate instinct was to warn, urge her to get Jed out of the house, because if she was caught harbouring him, she would be seen to be as guilty as he was and they could go to the gallows together.

But Rachel also sensed that a careless remark on her part, the slightest hint that she'd been witness to Jed Fairfax's lawless deed could make her a marked woman too. For there was a steely ruthlessness in his eyes which told her that he wouldn't hesitate to silence anyone who had the misfortune to stand in his path.

These thoughts came tumbling one upon another and buzzed around in her head like a captive fly. Keep calm, she told herself firmly. Even so the minutes seemed to stretch to an hour as she ran her tongue over her dry lips and searched for something to say that wouldn't incriminate her.

"I'm sorry to hear about your aunt, Susan," she managed

to say at last. Then hoping her voice sounded suitably concerned, she turned to Jed. "Is she ailing badly?"

"Badly enough. She has the fever."

"Yes and don't forget you're taking one of my herbal remedies when you go. In fact I'd better give it to you now, then you can be on your way." Susan began to draw Jed towards the back kitchen.

At the door he turned and after appraising Rachel coolly for a moment, said, "it's been nice making your acquaintance."

But his tone mocked her and she felt her hackles rise. "I wish I could say the same," she replied tartly, hoping to discompose him. But he just laughed, as if at a child, then followed his cousin out of the room.

There was a pewter jug standing on the table and Rachel felt a strong desire to pick it up and heave it after him. She wasn't a judgemental girl, neither was she quick to anger, but at the moment her dislike of Jed Fairfax was intense. For years she'd had to endure the jibes and insults of the Pedley family, bite on her tongue and say nothing. But what gave him the right, a common criminal, to talk down to her, she thought angrily and was only comforted by a sudden awareness that she knew a good deal more about him than he did her.

Not sure whether to stay or go, Rachel stood listening to the low murmur of voices on the other side of the door. Finally, overcome with curiosity, she tiptoed closer and strained her ears to hear what they were saying.

"Rachel! We weren't expecting to see you today."

At the sound of Robert's voice behind her, Rachel jumped. "Oh . . . he . . . hello Robert." She turned slowly, hoping the guilty flush had left her cheek, and was saved from further embarrassment by Polly rushing over and flinging her arms around her waist.

"Susan knows I'm here," she said lamely. "She's just seeing her cousin off."

"So you've met our Jed have you? A rare and handsome lad, isn't he? Just like my Susan," he added proudly.

Rachel pretended to think about it for a moment. "Yes, I suppose he's good looking enough," she answered. And indeed he was, although a moleskin waistcoat could in no ways be compared with the blue and gold uniform of a Dragoon.

"How old are you now?"

"I'm seventeen or thereabouts."

"You'll be looking to be wed soon then and you could do a lot worse than our Jed."

Silenced by this astonishing suggestion, Rachel wondered if Robert was unaware of Jed's activities. He was a large man, ungainly in appearance and with a thick thatch of black hair that would never lie flat. In all her life Rachel had never known him do anything dishonest, and though he refused point blank to enter St Philip's, claiming that religion was just another way of controlling the poor, he was a man of high moral principle and good in a way that many so-called Christians could never be. But Susan and he were too close not to share every secret. Best to go along with the deceit, Rachel decided, gave a small, protesting laugh and answered, "But I've not spoken two words to him in my life." She restrained herself from adding that any woman unwise enough to take on a man with Jed's wild ways would find herself no sooner wed than widowed.

"Well we'll soon see to that, won't we Susan," Robert called over to his wife, who had just come back in the room.

"What's that Robert?" Susan looked distracted and Rachel could see she was paying little attention to what her husband said.

"I think we ought to give Rachel and our Jed a chance to get to know each other. He needs a wife, it'll settle him down."

45

Susan didn't reply, but Rachel saw a silent signal pass between husband and wife and Robert suddenly found he had work to finish on the stocking frame.

"I think you'd better go too, Rachel," Susan advised. "George will be here soon to collect the hose and to settle up for the week. Go the back way home, across two acre field, then double back on yourself, that way you ought to miss him."

"Mam, can I walk some of the way wi' Rachel?" asked Polly.

"Course you can, love. But no further than the stile."

Outside, at Polly's insistence, Rachel had to stop by the sty to scratch the neck of Bessie the pig, then admire Robert's vegetable patch. Nothing that was growing in the garden would be wasted. Later herbs such as sage, rosemary and hyssop would be hung up to dry in the kitchen, beans salted, onions pickled and the large purple plums hanging from a twisted, lichen covered tree, turned into preserves by Susan to see them through the hard winter months.

Robert was one of the many villagers with a bit of land who'd fared badly during the recent enclosure. It was land he insisted which his forbears had tilled since Saxon times. But he'd had no deeds to prove it so the arable strips which had supported his family for generations, had been grassed over for the Squire and Joseph Pedley's sheep. And now Robert, who'd never been beholden to anyone before, found himself solely dependent on what he could earn as a common farm labourer or on the stocking frame which he was also forced to hire from Joseph Pedley.

Polly, affectionate and physical, grabbed Rachel's hand as they crossed the field, swinging it backwards and forwards and chattering all the while. But since Polly's conversation never amounted to much and she was too preoccupied with thinking about Jed Fairfax, Rachel hardly listened to her childish prattle until George's name caught her attention.

Stopping, she took Polly's other hand and pulled her around to face her. "What was that you said about Mr George?"

Polly, dimly remembering George's warning and seeing a possible curtailment of her supply of sweetmeats, suddenly looked sly. "Nothing," she answered. Then with a giggle and pulling her hands from Rachel's clasp, she turned and ran back towards the cottage.

"Hey, what's the hurry!" Rachel called after her. But the girl just kept running and Rachel rebuked herself for not listening more carefully. Troubled by something she didn't know, Rachel absentmindedly climbed a stile. But instead of taking the path that she'd intended, she made her way across a field of stubble towards the river. The Squire's pheasants panicked at her approach, weaving a nervous, zigzag path in front of her as if incapable of flight. The day and its dramas had left her neck and shoulders stiff and as she tried to massage away the tension, her skin felt clammy. Heavy grey clouds, distended with rain, were massed in the sky, but she would welcome a downpour, just to rid the air of the humidity.

Reaching the river she followed a path along its bank, eased by the sound of water on stone. Dragonflies hovered on transparent wings, and she caught the brief, brilliant blue and orange flash of a kingfisher. In no particular hurry Rachel stopped when she came to a spot where overhanging willows dipped their long fingers into the water. Kneeling, she scooped some water up in her hands and patted it over her face and neck. Invigorated by its coolness, Rachel sat down, rolled off her stockings and dangled her feet in the river, splashing great arcs of water high in the air. Then, throwing caution to the winds, she looked quickly around, pulled her dress over her head and slid down the bank into the river. Almost immediately swarms of midges gathered for the attack. But it was such a liberating experience, the cold, dappled water lapping around her naked flesh, that

Rachel felt it was worth enduring the odd bite. Someone, a long time ago, must have dammed the river at this spot for the purpose of swimming in it and although with the trees it was gloomy and the earth smelt dank, the floor of the river was stony and the water clear.

Healed by the spirit of the place, Rachel relaxed into the water. Lying on her back, her hair, loosened from its plait, floating out behind her like delicate tendrils of weed, she closed her eyes and allowed her thoughts to drift. The cracking of a twig made her open her eyes and directly above her, through the silvery green leaves of the willow she saw Jed Fairfax, sprawled full length along one of its branches and giving her his undivided attention.

Her body stiffened with shock and embarrassment and as she tried to get a foothold she went under, swallowing great mouthfuls of water. She surfaced coughing and gasping, "Go away you Peeping Tom!"

Ignoring her, Jed climbed swiftly down the tree and stood watching her from the bank. "Actually although I can't claim any territorial right to the place, I was here first."

"So what? If you were a gentleman, you'd go now."

"Well I can say with my hand on my heart, that's something I've never pretended to be. Not like George Pedley. By the way, is it true he gave you that shiner?"

"I'll thank you to mind your own business," Rachel answered tartly and briefly touched her bruised face. "And if you don't want to be tarred with the same brush as George, you'd better go." She'd begun to shiver, whether from nerves or cold, she wasn't sure, but she was desperate to get out of the water.

"Why should I? Are you the only person entitled to enjoy the river?" As he spoke he pulled his shirt over his head. "In fact I think I'll join you."

"Don't you dare!"

"No one tells Jed Fairfax what to do," he replied

48

unbuttoning his breeches. He stood for a moment, proudly naked and as Rachel flushed and turned away he slid down the bank and into the river beside her.

"Go away you horrible man!" she shouted, trying to use her wet hair as a cloak and crossing her arms protectively across her breasts. "If your mother's so ill, why aren't you getting the medicine back to her?"

But he was relieved of the necessity of answering that question by a great clap of thunder. It was so unexpected, Rachel cried out in fright then ducked as a jagged flash of lightning was followed by hammering rain which quickly penetrated the canopy of leaves. Then without pause there came another explosion, rolling around the heavens like the wrath of God.

"I'm going," Rachel announced. "If we stay here we'll be struck down." Past caring about her modesty, she waded to the bank and scrambled up its muddy slope. She snatched up her clothes and ran, head down against the elemental forces and with the sound of laughter following her across the field. She made for a rickety lean-to where sheep were sheltering. They scattered at her approach and then stood baaing at her reproachfully from a distance. Their thick, oily coats were designed to throw off water but even so they had a bedraggled air about them and had soon decided to return and share her flimsy cover.

Rain was spouting through a hole in the roof and Rachel stood dejectedly among the sheep droppings and puddles, her teeth rattling with the cold, her long wet hair clinging to her body like a glossy pelt of fur. She pulled some strands out of her mouth and peered out at the sodden, dripping landscape. If she had to endure another moment of Jed Fairfax's arrogance she would scream. But to her relief there was nothing to be seen of him and she could only hope it stayed that way.

Out of a need to do something positive Rachel tried to

49

dry herself on her sopping clothes and as she bent to rub her legs she saw that her bare feet and ankles were cut and bleeding from the sharp quills of stubble. If weeping would have solved anything she might have burst into tears just then. But that wasn't her way. Besides she knew this wasn't the time to start feeling sorry for herself. First and foremost she had to decide how she was going to get back to the farm. She was solely in charge of the arrangements for the party that evening, and before she even started the preparations she had to clean herself up and dry her hair.

Although it was still raining, the interval between each flash of lightning and roll of thunder was lengthening. Deciding it was impossible to feel any more wet and uncomfortable than she already was, she wrung out her stockings and dress and put them back on, wincing at their dank coldness. The dress clung to her, rather indecently outlining the curves of her body, but there was nothing she could do about that except pray she didn't meet George.

When the rain finally let up enough for her to venture out, she found a gap in the hedge and squeezed through into Blackthorn lane. It had been turned into a quagmire by the storm and as the mud sucked at her shoes it occurred to Rachel that the Squire, even with the tempting prospect of an evening with Matilda, might be disinclined to try and get his horse and trap up to the farm. And she knew that if the guests failed to appear, the household would have to endure one of Matilda's tantrums, which usually began with stamping feet, progressed to tears and ended with the vapours and smelling salts. Rachel had to admit too, that her own disappointment would hardly be less acute if the weather denied her the pleasure of seeing the handsome captain that evening.

The small drawing room, as the Pedleys grandly called it, looked its best, Rachel thought, by candlelight. The wallpaper had a delicate pattern of roses and ivy leaves and instead of the usual dark, crude oak furniture of the country, Mrs Medley had brought with her on her marriage, fine pieces in walnut veneer crafted by skilled cabinet-makers. Placed around the room were porcelain figurines from the Chelsea and Bow factories and oriental rugs were scattered over a wooden floor that shone with elbow grease and bees wax. All this, as well as a small table set out for cards, and the pianoforte standing open with music upon its stand, was illuminated in a large gilt mirror that hung over the fireplace.

Matilda, who was sitting on an upright chair, wore a low necked silk gown of blue and silver stripes, and a tense expression. George looked as if he'd have preferred not to be there. Mrs Pedley prattled nervously, Mr Pedley as usual, ignored her. Then through the window they all saw the lights of the gig, heard voices and laughter. Mrs Pedley's sigh of relief was plainly audible, Matilda nervously fingered a gold locket at her neck, while Rachel went to the door, teasing curls from beneath her cap and smoothing her apron.

"Dearest," cried Grace and Jane Dobbs in unison, and rushed to embrace Matilda as if it were months rather than a few hours since they'd last met.

The Squire lumbered in behind them, but Harry paused and after handing her his cloak, gently stroked her bruised cheek and said in a low voice, "What has my beautiful Senorita done here?" before following the rest of the party into the drawing room.

Rachel stood with a sort of dazed pleasure, nursing his cloak in her arms, rubbing her face across its rough surface and inhaling the masculine smell of cigars and horses. She saw him bow low over the hand Matilda extended, heard him say, "Miss Pedley, may I congratulate you on your appearance," but all she could think was; he said I was beautiful!

She was about to steal a glance at herself in a small mirror

51

when Mrs Pedley came out into the hall. "Now put the wraps away Rachel and come and hand round the Madeira."

As she waited for Joseph Pedley to fill the glasses, Rachel kept glancing shyly in the direction of Harry. But he appeared to be listening intently to Matilda's prattle and didn't look up.

Farmer Pedley's task was taking him longer than usual because he kept pausing to discuss the stack-yard fire with the Squire.

"But what evidence have you got that it was deliberate, Pedley?" asked Mr Bennett, eyeing the bottle of Madeira thirstily.

"None," the farmer admitted. "But that doesn't mean . . ." Here, Joseph Pedley, who preferred to be on the offensive rather than the defensive, decided to change tack. "Look, there's a mob out there who respect no one's property, machine-breakers, bread rioters, murderers even. If we don't put down insurrection immediately, England will find itself in the same position as France and with a bloody revolution on its hands, you mark my words."

The Squire, who didn't want to be lectured by his host, hurrumphed loudly, grabbed a glass of Madeira and downed it in one go. In its early stage, alcohol could make him quite civil and he answered affably enough, "Well Pedley, I'll pass your remarks on to the Chief Constable, and see what he says." Then he turned his attention to Matilda, gazing at her greedily with bloodshot eyes, but acknowledging to himself that the only chance of having her would be in the marriage bed.

Balancing her tray carefully, Rachel moved on to George and Jane. She pitied Jane, a kind girl who rather resembled a sagging mattress. She also nursed an unrequited passion for George, which she rather innocently imagined no one knew anything about. Her thick arms and large breasts were totally unsuited to the slim fitting, high waisted classical line and although she had a natural affinity with horses, she was ill at ease in company. It didn't help either that hot coals and nervous excitment had turned her neck and cheeks a scarlet that clashed rather unfavourably with the plum-coloured gown she had chosen to wear. "Duchess, you know . . . my mare, well she foaled this morning, a beautiful long-legged stallion," the girl squeaked, desperate to engage George in conversation. A discussion on cock fighting might have aroused his attention but now he just smothered a yawn and adjusted his neckerchief in the mirror, and poor demoralized Jane reached out and took a glass from Rachel like a sailor grabbing for a lifeline.

"Jane, come and play for us, the Captain wants to hear you sing," Matilda called to her.

"Does he really?" Relief and gratitude shone on the girl's face and flattered by her friend's attention, Jane excused herself and went and sat down at the piano, a willing victim to her friend's little scheme.

Mrs Pedley and Grace, were playing a quiet game of cards, but not for money since it was the Sabbath, and after she'd served them, Rachel carried the tray over to Harry and Matilda. Matilda was sitting, Harry standing with his hand resting on the back of her chair. Rachel knew he was trying to catch her eye but she refused to look at him. Instead she watched Matilda who, whenever Harry spoke to her, would lift her face like a flower receiving beneficence from the sun. There was no doubt that Matilda looked radiant this evening but Rachel could never look at her without thinking of a vixen, for she had small, sharp teeth, that she felt sure would give a savage bite.

She'd served everyone and was on her way back to the kitchen when Jane started to sing, slightly off key and accompanying herself on the piano. Rachel paused for a moment to listen, knowing Matilda well enough to guess what her scheme was. As a musician she was hardly more accomplished than her friend, and her voice was thin. But a kettle could sing better than Jane, so the Captain could only find the comparison favourable. And Rachel wondered, as she had done since childhood, when poor old lumpy Jane was going to wake up to the fact that she was outrageously exploited by Matilda.

At nine o'clock Rachel took in tea and small cakes and placed them on a table in front of her mistress. Matilda was well into her repertoire of songs, had just finished 'The Ash Grove,' and was now trilling 'Sweet Polly Oliver.' Harry was turning the pages of the music for her and the Squire, now well in his cups, glowered jealously at the young pair from the other side of the room.

"I'm gonna shing now," he announced drunkenly, stood up, swayed then fell back into the chair, accidently knocking his glass to the floor.

At the sound of breaking glass the room went silent and Rachel saw dismay writ large on Mrs Pedley's face. She dearly loved a *soirée* as she called it, loved presiding over the tea table, and delighted in knowing an evening was going well. She hated it when in spite of her best endeavours events spun out of control. Quickly she poured a cup of tea and pushed it at Rachel. "Here, take it to the Squire," she instructed.

But Matilda rose from the piano and brushing Rachel aside, took the cup from her mother. "I'll see to it, Mama," she said, and seating herself beside Squire Bennett, handed him the cup. "Now what are you going to sing for us, Mr Bennett?" she asked sweetly.

"A song, for you." He heaved himself up again and went to the piano and began to play "Greensleeves" surprisingly well to everyone's astonishment, the large fingers stroking the keys with some delicacy. His singing didn't quite reach the same standard, but this didn't deter him and as he sang, he gazed blearily up at Matilda, whose smile was so fixed her jaw ached. But she was carefully trying not to antagonize him, because with his unpredictable temper, he could quite easily

54

turn nasty and send Harry packing. And she knew she would just die if she couldn't see him again. For love had hit her, hard, like a sharp blow between the shoulder blades, leaving her breathless with wonder.

With an indulgent mother prepared to cater for every whim, Matilda had never known what it was like to want something desperately and not have it. But since reaching womanhood she'd had two specific ambitions in life which Mrs Pedley had been unable to satisfy. One was to improve her social standing, the other was to marry. And even in love she was clear-eyed enough to see that with Harry she could fulfil both aims perfectly. It didn't matter that he was penniless, Papa would take care of that, only that he was well connected.

Unfortunately Harry didn't strike her as a young man looking to settle down, so she realized that the route to becoming Mrs Harry Bennett might be strewn with obstacles. However what Matilda did have, was her father's ruthless single-mindedness, and it was a formidable weapon as anyone who'd come up against it could testify.

The Squire seemed to have a vast repertoire of romantic songs and with each one he grew more maudlin and damp eyed. In the end Matilda was so terrified he would actually start sobbing, she agreed to sing a duet with him, bringing the evening to a close with a song from John Gay's rather saucy *Beggar's Opera*.

Harry was disgusted to find the evening finishing so early, and all because George had to leave at dawn to return to Leicester. But Harry, who'd spent whole nights carousing, then faced a horde of Frenchmen the next day, found this a very feeble excuse. Still, he thought, as he levered his uncle up, it hadn't been a bad evening's work. He now had both girls practically eating out of his hand and it was still over a week until the celebrations . . . by God they'd be begging for it then. And with luck and careful management he might manage to have both girls on the same night.

Matilda stood at the door as the party left and Harry turned to her with a smile and a final salute. "Good-night, Miss Pedley."

"Good-night Captain Bennett," she answered demurely. It was as well he couldn't read her thoughts, and couldn't guess at her plans and schemes. Because if he had, that vain young man might have decided to proceed in his wooing of her with perhaps a little more caution.

Chapter Six

A cock crowing followed by the grandfather clock in the hall chiming four woke Rachel. She rose at once, dressed then while the rest of the house slept on, crept downstairs to the kitchen. She stumbled around in the dark searching for a light, quickly found the lantern, lit it, then slipping her feet into pattens, unlocked the door and stepped out into the muddy yard, shivering in the chill, pre-dawn air.

By the pump, Rachel stopped and sluiced water over her face. The water came from a spring deep in the earth and was so cold it made her gasp. But it was also invigorating and washed away the last vestiges of sleep. Hurriedly drying her face on her apron, she walked towards the barn and climbed the ladder to the hayloft. Sam never slept in the same place twice and it took several minutes of searching before she found him curled up under a blanket, the only part of him visible his hair, which was as bushy and red as a fox's brush.

Although she was as much alone in the world as Sam and like him worked hard and had few pleasure in life, Rachel still felt strongly protective of the boy and if the choice had been hers she would have let him sleep on undisturbed. So to lessen the shock of waking she crouched down beside him and shaking him gently, called in his ear, "Sam come on, time to get up, it's market day."

Sam groaned, pulled the blanket over his head and snuggled down into the hay.

"It's no good doing that, there's Daisy to be harnessed yet and I shall want help loading the cart. And if you don't get a move on there'll be no time for breakfast and I don't want to listen to you moaning you're hungry all the way to Leicester."

"Arright, arright, don't keep on Rachel, I hear you." Resigned to the inevitable, Sam sat up and reached out for a brown smock frock and pulled it over the shirt and breeches he wore even in bed. Then he stood up, stamped into a pair of ankle boots, combed his fingers through his hair and was ready for anything the day had to offer.

Back in the kitchen there was only time to gulp down some milk and parcel up bread and cheese for them to eat on the way. Then while Sam harnessed the mare, Rachel went over to the dairy. This was Mrs Pedley's domain, and it was here that butter was churned and the cheeses that went to market each month ripened. For as long as she could remember it had been her job to stir the great tub of milk and rennet until the curds were separated from the whey and then pressed in cloth-lined moulds. It was a solitary occupation but soothing and Rachel enjoyed her hours in the cool, high-ceilinged room with its blue Dutch tiles. Today, as well, there were eggs, honey and a couple of dressed fowls to be loaded on to the cart and the five o'clock start-of-work bell was peeling by the time they drove through the village.

"If you like I'll take the reins first, you have something to eat," said Rachel, handing Sam the parcel. "And see you leave some for me," she added, when she saw the speed at which the food was disappearing into his mouth.

There was no hurrying Daisy, her pace was measured, and by nature she was obstinate. But as long as they got to Leicester by six, Rachel knew they would get a pitch. And the early morning was a time she particularly loved, a leisurely period when the world itself seemed to be stretching and yawning before the tempo accelerated into a normal working day.

They rattled along, brushing sticky invisible cobwebs from their faces and shouting cheerful, "good-mornings" to villagers on their way to the fields. As the sun rose, setting the sky on fire, crows on their lofty perches commenced their harsh cawing. For some way the road ran parallel with the river and the boy and girl watched as a heron rose with a great flapping of wings from the mist, spindly legs dangling awkwardly, with its breakfast clamped firmly in its beak. "He don't get done for poaching off Squire, do 'e?" Sam remarked ruefully, and although they both laughed there was no real mirth in it.

They reached the busy turnpike road, joining a stream of carriers' carts and waggons, and had just changed seats so that Sam could take over the reins, when from some way in front of them there came the imperious blast of a post-horn. "It's the mail coach Sam, quick, into the side of the road," Rachel urged and the boy eased Daisy on to the verge just as the coach came round the corner, travelling at a perilous speed and covering everything and everyone in a film of dust. A flock of sheep being driven to market scattered in panic, and the angry farmer raised his fist and shouted, "you stupid sod!" at the driver. But the man, arrogant and self-important and with the full weight of the Post Office behind him, just laughed, waved his whip, and proceeded on his on his way, secure in the knowledge that nothing would impede his progress; traffic would always give way and at a blast from the guard's horn, turnpike gates would fly open all the way from London to Derby.

By the time Sam and Rachel reached the Belgrave Road the thoroughfare was clogged. Here cattle, hogs, sheep, carts and packhorses converged and brought the traffic almost to a standstill. Tempers became frayed, angry words were exchanged, and the din was indescribable. "At this rate we're never gonna get there, Rachel," Sam complained, impatiently flicking at the reins.

"Yes we will, don't worry," Rachel reassured him. And sure enough shortly after they'd paid their penny at the Belgrave Gate tollbar they were trundling towards Coal Hill and Gallowtree Gate.

"Tether Daisy," Rachel ordered Sam when they reached the market place, then immediately she began unloading the waggon while eyeing the other stalls at the same time. But Rachel had an artistic eye and first of all she draped sacking over her stall, spread this with good clean straw then placed on top of it large firm cabbage leaves on which to display the cheese. Butter was placed on beds of parsley, the fowls garnished with sage and rosemary, the eggs displayed in nests of hay, then finally the whole stall was decorated with ivy leaves.

The woman on the next stall came to have a look, standing well back and with her head cocked critically to one side. She had several baskets of hard looking plums and small green apples, and since Rachel wasn't in direct competition, she could afford to be generous in her praise. "My, you've made a nice job of that, me duck," she said admiringly.

"I'll do your stall if you like," Rachel offered generously.

"Would you?" said the woman and watched in admiration as Rachel carefully formed the plums and apples into several concentric circles, which greatly enhanced the appearance of the fruit and its chances of being sold. "Here, take this," said the grateful woman when she'd finished, and pressed a penny into Rachel's hand.

"Look what I've got," said an astonished Rachel to Sam.

"Coo a penny," said Sam, goggle eyed.

"Now what shall I buy with it?" Rachel mused, thinking first of the bright baubles on the trinket stall, then the ribbon stall with its brilliant display of silks and satin and embroidered Coventry ribbon. For a penny she might be able to buy an end piece, long enough to tie in her hair. Maybe even catch the Captain's eye, if she was permitted to go to the party.

But a street vendor was walking by, a tray balanced on his head, ringing a bell and crying: "Hot pork pies, hot pork pies, one penny for two and the best you'll taste in Leicester!"

As he passed, Sam sniffed the air, savouring the rich aromatic smell. He gave Rachel a sideways glance, assessing his chances of getting her to part with her new-found wealth on something sensible rather than on a bit of useless female frippery. Adopting a beseeching expression he gazed up at her. "Go on, get two of those, please . . . Rachel, I'm starvin'."

"You're always starving," replied Rachel, remembering how he'd devoured most of the breakfast. But the smell tempted her too and reminded her of her own hunger. She saw Sam's eyes fixed on her, dithered briefly as she thought of the scarlet ribbon, then reminded herself that her chances of going to any celebration were pretty slim anyway. Deciding to settle for the here and now she said finally, "Oh all right, but see you keep an eye on things here. And no mistakes with the money or we'll both get a box round the ears when we get home."

But market day was a social as well as a business event and Sam knew from experience how easy it was for Rachel to be diverted by the bonnet stall or a meeting with a friend. "Well mind you don't keep stoppin' on the way. 'Cos you knows I be bad wi' giving the change," he answered craftily.

"I'll be no more than five minutes," Rachel promised and went in search of the pie-man.

Every available inch in the market square was crammed with booths and stalls, and anything could be bought, from chipped crockery to rusting farm equipment and second-hand clothes. Also on market day, matters of health could be dealt with, and tucked away discreetly in one corner of the square

61

was the tooth-drawer, his instruments of torture laid out on a white cloth. There was a great crush of people and Rachel was pushed and jostled so much by bargain-seeking housewives she'd soon lost sight of the pie-man.

To get her breath back she paused for a moment to listen to a ballad singer. The man, who was wearing a ragged army jacket, was supported by a crutch and one of his trouser legs flapped emptily. He was trying, against enormous odds, to make himself heard above the raucous exhortations of the stall-holders and his hungry expression and empty hat so reproached Rachel she nearly threw him the penny coin. Then she remembered Sam, imagined his disappointment if she returned empty-handed and slunk away.

In spite of her promise to Sam she found herself drawn to the ribbon stall. She was fingering a length of scarlet silk and thinking wistfully of Harry when she heard the woman say, "Go on give yerself a treat, me dook. You'd look real pretty wi' a bit of that tied in your lovely dark hair. Turn a young man's head you would."

"Do you think so?" Rachel asked eagerly.

Sensing a sale coming off the woman warmed to her theme. "Not just one, several shouldn't wonder."

"How much is it?" Rachel found herself asking.

The woman lifted up a short length of ribbon. "This bit's the end of the roll. Say you gives me an 'alfpenny for it."

Rachel hesitated, then thought; the devil with Sam. It was her money so surely she was entitled to treat herself. "All right." she said, the deal was struck and she walked away, refusing to be burdened by guilt. After all, she still had money enough for one hot pie.

"A bob a yard on the hod," the butchers in their blood-stained aprons yelled, making the chant sound almost lyrical. But Caggy Row, with its stinking fly-blown carcasses, was the one part of the market where Rachel held her nose and hurried past. The rest she found endlessly fascinating. Even after she'd caught up with the street vendor and made her purchase, she was still diverted and distracted by everything around her. The second-hand book stall in particular, with its rows of fusty books which nobody seemed to be minding, caught her eye and she stopped to study the titles. Although she could never have afforded a book herself, Matilda belonged to a circulating library, and Rachel, by secretly reading a page at a time while she was cleaning her room, had managed to get through several highly charged gothic tales and was now addicted to this type of novel. Some of the books on the stall were so ancient, their spines so battered, the titles had almost been obliterated. But amongst them she did make out one called, *The Confessional of Valombre*, by Louisa Sidney Stanhope, a much favoured authoress. Rachel blew off the dust, then with a quick glance around, eased it from out from under the disorderly heap. She was just about to dip into it when she saw Jed Fairfax approaching with a pile of books balanced under his chin. This so confounded her, her fingers went stiff and the novel slid from her grasp.

"Ah, the little water nymph," he said, as he dropped the books on to the stall and brushed himself down.

To be reminded of her humiliating retreat across the field was so ungentlemanly, Rachel felt, that she would have walked away from him in disgust if his next remark hadn't offended her even more.

"And one who can apparently read too. My word what talents the young lady has."

Incensed by his condescending tone and the assumption that she would be unlettered, Rachel's ears went pink with annoyance. "Of course I can read," she answered haughtily. "If you want to know, your cousin learnt me."

"It'll do you no good, you realize that. People who learn to read can get dangerous ideas about democracy and that would never do. And I'd better warn you, some of these books are considered very inflammatory stuff by our masters." He lifted one from the heap, "Take this one for instance: *The Rights of Man*. Booksellers have been thrown in prison just for having it on their shelves."

"Why are you selling it then?"

"Because like Tom Paine who wrote it, I believe in democracy and political freedom."

He was talking way above her head but when he pushed another book at her and said, "Here's one that should interest you, *Vindication of the Rights of Women*, why don't you take it and read it?" she backed away.

"I've no money to go buying books."

"I'll make you a gift of it."

"Why should you want to do that? Do you want to see me in the Bridewell?" Rachel asked suspiciously.

This remark seemed to amuse him and his grey eyes, which previously she'd thought so hard and cold, crinkled into a good humoured smile. "Hardly. Just put it down to my essential good nature."

She might possibly have accepted a novel from him but not a book on politics, about which she knew nothing other than what she overheard in the Pedley's dining room, usually at breakfast time, when Joseph Pedley read out pieces from the *Leicester Journal* to his wife. Also common sense told Rachel it would be unwise to be beholden to anyone as dangerous as Jed Fairfax or to get mixed up in his dubious political activities. "Thank you anyway, but I'd have nowhere to keep it at home and supposing my master found it."

"Yeah, he certainly doesn't believe in the rights of men, or women, does he?"

Was that why you fired the corn stack, she almost blurted out. But although the astonishment on his face would have recompensed for his cheap jibes, she knew the risks were too great.

"You haven't answered my question."

"It's not something I wish to discuss. Now if you'll excuse

me . . ." Rachel was walking away in what she hoped was a dignified manner when Jed called out to her,

"Hey, you've forgotten something."

She looked round, He was dangling the greasy package containing the pie between his thumb and forefinger and looked highly amused.

She turned and snatched it from him, and by the time she got back to Sam she felt in a thoroughly bad temper.

"You said you'd be gone five minutes, more like five hours you mean. And I'm so hungry me guts ache."

Sam's complaints did little to improve Rachel's mood. "Shut up and eat this," she answered, breaking the pie in two and handing him a piece. "And before you say anything, I bought some ribbon with the other halfpenny."

"What you wanna do that for?" Sam asked grumpily. Girls were the giddy limit, he thought, always wanting to pretty themselves up with frills and furbelows.

"Because it's my money that's why and I can do what I like with it."

Surprised by the sharpness of her tone, Sam gave Rachel a quick glance. What's upset her now, he wondered.

"Anyway, have you sold anything yet?"

"'Fraid not, Rachel," he answered through a mouthful of food.

Rachel gave an exasperated sigh. "Just as I thought. You're hopeless do you know that?"

Sam shrugged, swallowed and wiped his hand across his mouth. "Well at least you can't blame me for giving them the wrong change. Can I go an' have a look round now?"

"Yes, go on clear off, but for half an hour only mind. I want you back here by nine of the clock and not a minute later."

If business hadn't been brisk with Sam it certainly picked up with Rachel. And she watched the butter disappear with a sense of relief, because if the day became warm then the butter would turn oily and rancid and no one would buy it.

65

It got so that she could have done with an extra pair of hands. But the clock struck nine then the quarter hour and Sam still hadn't appeared. Just wait till I get my hands on him, she thought grimly as she sliced cheese into neat quarter and half pound wedges and weighed it with the hand scales. She waited until there was a lull, then upturning a box, she stood on it, balancing precariously and craning her neck. But to find a boy of Sam's small stature in that crowd was like looking for a needle in a haystack. Who she did see though, was Jed Fairfax and he seemed to be pushing his way towards her. Quickly she climbed down off the box, straightened her cap and apron and and became very busy swatting flies with a cheesecloth.

"I'll have a half a pound of the strongest cheese you've got."

When he spoke, Rachel turned and gave him her most gracious smile. "Certainly sir."

"And I might as well have half a dozen eggs while I'm at it. Are you here every week?" he asked as Rachel handed him his goods and he counted the money into her hands.

"Once a month," she answered distantly, for she still hadn't forgiven him for his remarks.

"Well perhaps by the next time you come I'll have my own bookshop, I'm looking for premises to rent. If I have, you must come and visit me."

"Oh I don't have time to pay social calls, we're always far too busy," answered Rachel.

Jed shrugged. "As you like. Well I'll wish you good day then."

"Good day." Already regretting her offhand manner, she watched him, tall and broad shouldered, as he became part of the crowd and disappeared. Her feelings towards him, she accepted, were ambivalent and although she found it difficult to reconcile herself to the two sides of his character, the destructive man and the bookish man, he did intrigue her. Yes, she would definitely like to know more about him.

Chapter Seven

Rachel's hands were still when they should have been busy, her eyes more interested in a squirrel in the garden than the pots in the sink, so Mrs Pedley's footsteps on the flagstones made her jump guiltily. But her mistress seemed unaware of her idleness. Instead, coming over to her, she said, "Stand up straight, dear, I want to see if this fits you," and held a dress up for Rachel's inspection.

Drying her arms, Rachel stared open mouthed at the short-sleeved, high-waisted, sprigged muslin frock. "Fit me?" she asked in a bewildered voice.

"Yes, I thought you could wear it tomorrow. Hold still now while I measure it against you."

But as Mrs Pedley held the dress up to her shoulders, Rachel's face still wore an uncertain expression. Although Sam had speculated endlessly on whether they would be allowed to participate, after the unfortunate accident with George, she had given up any idea of going. "Am I to go to the party then? Me and Sam . . . both of us?"

"Why of course, the whole village is to go."

"And you say I can wear this?"

"Yes child. I ordered it for Matilda, but it's a little on the large size," she answered, hoping God wouldn't punish her for her small fib. The truth of it was, her daughter had in fact turned up her nose at the dress, considering it far too plain for such an auspicious occasion.

Rachel was so bemused by this sudden turn in her fortunes

that she couldn't even find her voice to say thank you. Instead, in an excess of emotion, she threw her arms round Mrs Pedley and kissed her on both cheeks.

"There, there, my dear," said Mrs Pedley, patting her serving maid on the back in a slightly embarrassed fashion. "I'm sure you're going to look very pretty, almost a match for my Matilda." And as she hurried away she had to admit to herself that the girl might prove more than a match for her daughter, because although she might not have the manners of a lady, she certainly had the looks.

The remaining pots were washed and dried in record time that night, then Rachel tore up to her room to try the dress on. It was white with a small design of pink roses and Rachel had never worn anything so lovely in her life. She felt a little doubtful about the low neck, which displayed rather more of her breasts than she felt was seemly but otherwise it fitted perfectly. But then she noticed how the dress emphasized certain imperfections, her red, coarse hands, the shoes that were broken down and old. Then there was her hair, what should she do about that? She fingered it with a sense of dissatisfaction then remembering how Matilda acquired her curls, she shot downstairs to the linen press and quickly grabbed a scrap of linen. Back in her room she tore it into strips and tied her hair up in corkscrew curls, torturing her scalp. But Rachel felt it was worth any amount of pain if her ringlets did justice to the dress. Just before getting into bed, she knelt, and pressing her hands piously together, prayed that Wednesday would be fine.

And the good Lord obliged. Rachel knew it, as soon as she opened the door the next morning and stepped out into the yard. The faint mist lying over the fields and meadows told her it was going to be a perfect September day. With a feeling of intense joy she closed her eyes and stretched as if to touch the heavens. But her solitude was interrupted by footsteps behind her and recognizing them, she dropped her arms and immediately went tense.

George didn't say a word as he passed her to go to the stables, just glared hard and thrashed his riding crop against his leather boots. One of the positive things to come out of the accident was that he'd given up pestering her, for the time being at least. The negative side was the hate she could sense emanating from him and the knowledge that he would most certainly be at the party had the power to cast a cloud over what she'd hoped would be a perfect day.

She didn't stay to watch him mount his horse, instead she went back into the kitchen and began blackleading the grate, bringing it to a shiny perfection in her effort to work off the fear he always induced in her. But the cross fertilization of Anglo-Saxon with Latin blood had produced a fusion that made Rachel both spirited and determined. And nothing, and no one would spoil her day. Youthful, romantic longings beckoned and George could go to the devil.

Washing wasn't something Sam really cared for, but today in a clean smock frock, his thick hair flattened into submission by a good dousing of water, face scrubbed and shining, he looked fairly presentable. And proud too to be seen with Rachel. He'd been waiting for her in the kitchen and growing impatient at the time she was taking when she came downstairs in her new gown, and with her ringlets tied up in scarlet ribbon. For a moment he didn't recognize her. "Gosh," he'd said as the vision glided towards him, followed by "cripes," when he realized it was her.

"Do I look all right, Sam?" she asked, self-consciously fingering her ringlets and smoothing down the dress.

"You look real pretty," Sam answered, acknowledging to himself something he'd suspected for a while, that Rachel had grown up. "Happen you'll put Miss Matilda's nose out of joint," he went on, his brown eyes warm with admiration.

69

"Don't say that Sam," Rachel exclaimed in alarm, for she'd had trouble enough with Matilda that morning, enough, in fact, to last her the day.

Earlier after carefully tucking her locks up under her cap, she'd gone to Matilda's room to help her dress and found her curled up in a chair, a thumb stuck in her mouth and twiddling her hair like a bad tempered child. As Rachel stood studying the girl's sulky profile and awaiting instructions she pondered on the relationship, or rather the lack of a relationship that existed between them. Although they were separated in age by no more than five years and she knew every habit and detail of her life, Matilda had never encouraged any sort of girlish intimacy and Rachel was required always to mind her Ps and Qs. She sensed now that Matilda was ignoring her out of a sort of immature wilfulness and Rachel felt her patience being stretched to its limits. What young madam needs is a good spanking. Her fingers itched to reach out and administer a slap, hard enough to leave marks on her plump cheeks, and at the same time tell her what a spoilt, silly creature she was.

Instead she bit on her tongue and took refuge in silent scorn, moving her weight from one foot to the other and clearing her throat as audibly as she dare. Then when the girl continued to ignore her she finally said, "The missus sent me to see if you wanted help with dressing."

Matilda straightened and clasping the arms of the chair, glared at her. "How can I get dressed? I've got nothing to wear." Her tone inferred that somehow this was Rachel's fault.

Rachel said nothing but looked around her at the confusion of dresses, underwear, silk stockings and shoes tumbling out of drawers or scattered over the floor. Wondering if Matilda really believed what she was saying, she scooped up a beautiful dress in pale primrose she'd have given almost anything to own. "What about this, Miss Matilda?" she

70

asked, prepared to humour and cajole, otherwise she could see herself there all morning.

"It's horrible, throw it away!" Matilda's small white teeth snapped together like a man-trap.

Rachel groaned in silent frustration and picked up another, this time the colour of musk rose and with a fashionably vandyked hem. "This is lovely and the colour will really suit your complexion," she said persuasively.

Miss Matilda Pedley, who was a young woman very susceptible to flattery, at last began to show an interest. "Do you think so? Tighten my stays for me then and I'll try it on." Standing up, she threw off her wrap, grabbed hold of the bedpost and held her breath as Rachel pulled on the lacing.

"Is that enough?" Rachel asked at last, sure that if Matilda's waist was constricted any more she would faint.

"No tighter, tigher," the girl ordered, pushing up her breasts. They were smaller than she would have liked and it was necessary to emphasize their shape. All her hopes were pinned on today and she was prepared to endure any amount of agony to captivate Harry. Only when she was sure her waist was small enough for the Captain to encircle it with both hands did she allow the dress to be dropped over her head and buttoned. After this her curls were arranged so as to appear prettily dishevelled then Rachel knelt and eased her feet into grey stamped kid slippers.

Rachel still held her breath as Matilda walked to the cheval-glass, for when she was in an ill-humour, she could wreak havoc on the whole household. But as she preened and twirled, Rachel could see she was entirely pleased with what she saw.

"My waist is the smallest in the county, do you know that?" Matilda informed Rachel, her hands resting on her hips.

"I'm sure it is, Miss Matilda," answered Rachel dutifully as she edged towards the door.

"And my hair, do you like my hair?" She shot round just as Rachel placed her hand on the door nob. "I've heard it's now quite the ton in big cities for girls to have their hair cut short as a boy's. Should I have mine done?"

"I think not, Miss Matilda, it's pretty as it is," said Rachel, already imagining the hysterics that would ensue if the cut wasn't to her liking.

"Well perhaps not," Matilda responded, but thought nevertheless she would get Harry's opinion on the matter.

"Can I go now, Miss Matilda?" Rachel asked at last, not quite brave enough to open the door.

"Yes, of course, of course." With an indifferent wave of the hand Matilda finally dismissed her. And since choice of dress wasn't a problem Rachel had to deal with, she was soon ready to be escorted down Blackthorn Lane by a rather proud Sam who insisted Rachel should hold his arm, although he barely reached her shoulder.

But they were too full of high spirits to maintain a sedate manner for long. The noise and laughter carrying up from the village made them quicken their footsteps then break into a run.

But outside the Squire's drive Rachel grabbed Sam's arm, checking his pace. "Let's slow down a bit," she said. There was a chance they might bump into Harry and she wanted to be seen comporting herself with dignity, not all disheve..ed and behaving like some hoyden.

But Sam, impatient to be part of the celebrations tugged his arm away. "You can do what you like but I'm going on," he answered and sped off.

"Beast!" she yelled, momentarily forgetting herself. Then straightening her shoulders, Rachel walked into the village unaccompanied but with all the poise of a lady.

But even her newly acquired poise fell away when she saw the transformation that had taken place. "Wow!" she exclaimed, and gazed around in astonishment.

Union Jacks, attached to broomsticks, fluttered from the upstairs windows of every cottage and crumbling walls were blanketed with dark green laurel and flowers. In the woods, oak boughs had been sawn down and were now being dragged across the Green by sturdy youths to enclose the two long rows of tables. Nearby a whole ox was being turned on a spit over a huge fire, and men were already helping themselves to ale out of large wooden barrels. Their wives, finding more to do, hurried back and forth with freshly baked bread and whole cheeses, at the same time doling out sharp slaps to any offspring who made the mistake of getting under their feet.

Sam, she saw, was helping turn the spit. Looking around it seemed that everyone had a set task. Amidst all the bustle, Rachel felt self-conscious and a little lost. This was something she was unused to, time on her hands. So it was with a sense of relief that she saw Robert hurrying towards Woodbine Cottage, looking preoccupied like everyone else. Calling his name she ran after him, following him into the cottage.

Immediately the door closed behind her Rachel was enveloped in steam. It billowed round the rafters, misted the windows and ran like tears down the whitewashed walls. And by the spicy mouth-watering aroma, the cauldron hooked over the fire and Susan's rather cross expression Rachel knew she was boiling plum puddings for the party.

Susan, who already looked hot and weary, didn't even bother to look up when Rachel entered but went on spooning the dark mixture into floured linen cloths. But Rachel had been ignored long enough. "Can I have a taste?" she asked, then without bothering to wait for a reply, hooked her forefinger into the bowl.

This at least produced a reaction in Susan. "Leave it alone!" she snapped and rapped Rachel sharply across the knuckles. "If you want to make yourself useful tie these puddings up."

73

"But my hair!" she wailed, "If I stay in here the steam will make the curl fall out and I might spoil my dress too."

For the first time Susan seemed to notice her. But some moments passed before she spoke. "Well I'll be blessed!" she exclaimed finally. Then over her shoulder, "Polly, Robert, come here!"

The whole family was now standing staring at her and in a self-consciously embarrased gesture, Rachel fanned out her dress and asked shyly, "Do you like it? Mrs Pedley gave it me."

Robert shook his head in wonderment. "Well I allas knew you were a good-looking lass, but I'd no idea . . ." He turned to his wife, "did you, Susan?"

"Now don't go giving the girl a swollen head, Robert," Susan admonished. "You'll unsettle her, talking like that. Encourage her to give herself airs, which will do her no good in the end. Now we've done admiring her, can we get on? Robert, you go down to the miller's, he's got pigeon pies in his oven and they'll have to be on the table by two. Rachel you go and see if the band has arrived. If they're here give them a tankard of ale each. They've come all the way from Sheepshead so they'll be thirsty and looking to wet their whistles. And be generous because we'll want them to give us a good rendering of the 'Sir Roger D' Coverely' later on."

In the end, after a great deal of indecision and rearranging of places, either to sit with bosom friends or avoid sworn enemies, it was gone two before the gathering finally sat down. Several eager hands immediately shot out to grab food and were reprimanded with a stern glance from the Reverend Dobbs. "We will now say Grace," he said severely, folding his hands together and bending his head.

"For what we are about to receive . . ." his flock chanted after him obediently, but speeding it up a bit, because their stomachs were rumbling and the tables already beginning to sink under the weight of pigeon pie, rabbit pie and huge home cured hams.

Although Rachel sat with Robert, Susan and Polly she was well placed to keep an eye on Harry and Matilda. Earlier Harry had caught her on her own and she remembered with a quiver of excitement what he'd said. He come up behind her when she was helping to set the tables. Catching her by the waist, he'd whispered into her ear, "You look absolutely delicious and I swear I'll get a kiss from you before the day is over." Then he'd gone before she'd had the chance to turn around. Now, though he was gazing at Matilda as if she was the only girl in the world, Rachel tried not to care. Instead she closed her eyes and with her lips slightly parted, imagined herself held fast in Harry's arms. She'd never been kissed by a man and wasn't sure how it was done.

"Come on, Rachel, stop day-dreaming and have this."

Startled out of her reverie, Rachel opened her eyes to find Susan pushing a plate of rabbit pie towards her. "There are three hundred folk here, all of them hungry so if you want your share you'd better eat up quickly."

But even love couldn't dull her appetite and she tucked in with the same vigour as everyone else. Looking down the table as she ate, Rachel could see that just for today, social distinctions had been forgotten and cottager and Squire sat down together. And since some of the men had already had more than their fair share of John Barleycorn and were in high good humour, there was none of the restraints usually felt when in the presence of the local nobs. Tongues were loosened and the conversation flowed. In place of honour at the head of the table sat Thomas Pick, who at ninety, was Halby's oldest inhabitant. Hardly larger than a child, with a body twisted and deformed by rheumatism, he had a skin that was as brown and wrinkled as a newt's. But he was alert as a young man, and Rachel could hear him telling

Harry how he'd been impressed into the Navy as a lad and fought in the War of Jenkin's Ear.

By four o'clock every platter of meat had been consumed, the ham bones picked clean and any left-over gravy soaked up with bread. Everyone was leaning back and declaring they couldn't eat another mouthful when Susan and several young women hurried off to their houses. They came back minutes later, bearing aloft the rich, dark plum puddings, and for their efforts were treated to a well-earned round of applause. Somehow room was found in distended stomachs and the puddings were rapidly demolished. By five, the men were belching exhuberently, the ladies more delicately. With sighs of contentment belts were loosened on breeches while those women, like Matilda, who were wearing stays, would have given anything to ease their tight lacing.

The Reverend Dobbs once again stood up. But this time the noise and hilarity had reached such a level, he had to bang the table several times before he could make himself heard. "Right, before we finish I'm going to call on Thomas here to give the loyal toast, after which the dancing will commence."

Tankards were refilled and Thomas asked them to be upstanding. First he toasted poor mad King George, then his dissolute son the Prince Regent, then as he got in his stride, the Duke of Wellington, the Dragoons, the first Regiment of Foot and finally, the Yeomanry Cavalry of the County.

Hepzibiah Fellowes, the Miller's wife, who was standing next to Rachel, was obviously less accustomed to strong ale than her husband. For suddenly she found her legs weren't supporting too well and with a surprised, "Oh my God!" then a giggle, sat down heavily on the bench and put her head in her hands. But the rest of the village was in such high good humour that when Thomas finished, he was lifted up by four young men and chaired through the village, with skipping children, barking dogs and those that could still walk, forming a procession behind and singing, "For he's a Jolly Good Fellow."

When it got dark there were to be fireworks but in the meantime the fiddler and the man who played the serpent, were tuning up their instruments so that the dancing could start.

This was something Rachel had been looking forward to all day but to her intense disappointment the band struck up a German waltz, a new and fashionable dance she couldn't do. Determined to master the steps, she watched Matilda being swung round with an easy grace by Harry, saw how her face glowed with a rare happiness and envied her. George was partnering Jane who stomped round the floor with all the grace of a Shire horse. It didn't help that the girl apologized humbly every time she trod on George's highly polished hessian boots and he wore an expression of such pained irritation, Rachel was forced to cover her mouth with her hand to hide her amusement.

When the music stopped Jane was unceremoniously dumped. Almost immediately another waltz tune was struck up and this time George strolled over to Rachel and held out his hand.

Disconcerted she stuttered, "But . . . I . . . I can't do a waltz Mr George."

"Nonsense. Anyway, you couldn't be any worse than that great galumping creature it's just been my misfortune to push around the floor." His tone was sneering and he made no attempt to lower his voice. Ignoring further protests, he dragged her on to the dancing area. Here he clamped an arm round her waist and pushed his hand so firmly into the small of her back, she could feel her breasts being crushed against the buttons on his jacket. She tried to wriggle free but his grip on her became pincer-like and just to make sure she realized what a privilege it was to dance with him, he squeezed her fingers painfully. "Now

77

follow me," he instructed. "One, two, three, one, two, three."

To begin with, Rachel felt tense and self-conscious and she stumbled against his feet more than once. But in spite of the feeling of revulsion George induced in her, he was a good dancer and she soon found herself caught up in the rhythm of the music. She'd just begun to relax when she noticed that George's hand had moved lower down her back and his fingers were now splayed out across her buttocks. Then she felt something hard through her flimsy dress.

"Let me go you disgusting pig," she muttered between clenched teeth.

But he just held on to her and didn't answer. His eyes had gone glazed and he was rubbing himself insistently against her belly. After a moment he gave a convulsive shudder, let go of her and hurried away, leaving her feeling defiled and ashamed. Rachel glanced around her to see if any villager had witnessed her degradation. But it was obvious that even if they had they were past the stage of moralizing or even caring. Curls and plaits had shaken loose under caps, clothing was dishevelled and their broad country faces were flushed with exertion and drink. There'd never been a day like it, nor was there likely to be another in the foreseeable future, and they were damned well going to make the most of it.

But for Rachel the joy had gone out of the day. Although she'd done nothing wrong she felt unclean and pushing her way through the roistering crowd she fled to the other side of the Green where there was a large chestnut tree, whose branches were so wide and heavy, they touched the ground. This tree, planted, it was said, by one of Cromwell's men, had witnessed many an illicit assignation. Children plundered its branches for conkers in autumn and once an old man had actually been found propped against its thick trunk quite dead. Now protected by the cool mantle of leaves and well away from prying eyes, Rachel flung herself down, and overwhelmed with shame, pressed her face into her knees and shed copious, bitter tears.

And this was where Harry found her. He'd witnessed her flight, noticed her distress but had had some difficulty extricating himself from Matilda who, although he'd grown a little weary of her company, had clung to him all day like a leech. The call of nature had finally been his excuse for parting from her and by making a careful detour round the edge of the green he finally came upon Rachel as if by accident. Parting the branches, he gazed down at her.

She looked a forlorn sight. Her dress was crumpled, her face tear stained, the ringlets beginning to lose their curl. And at that moment Harry was startled by a feeling quite foreign to him of tenderness. It took some effort but he managed to curb this unfamiliar emotion sufficiently to enquire, "What is it my pretty little thing? You seem upset."

Rachel was no longer weeping but her eyes were dull and expressionless as she looked up at him. And no man in the world could have consoled her at the moment. She hated all men and their needs, which always seemed to be at the expense of women. "Go away please, I want to be on my own."

Rejection wasn't a thing Harry took kindly to and bending on his haunches so that their eyes were level, he said, "Am I not to get that kiss, then?"

This was Harry's one blunder in an otherwise very successful amorous career and when Rachel suddenly stood up, brushed the grass from her dress and said fiercely, "Leave me alone, can't you," he couldn't take her seriously.

"Come now, you don't really mean that." He smiled, put out a hand and lightly stroked her arm. But Rachel shook him off, and turning from his attentions, she hurried back across the Green.

He watched her with a slightly perplexed expression. She'd done the unimaginable and rejected him, for the time being

79

at least. And he must be on his guard, for he was in danger of becoming enamoured of the girl, which would never do. Emotions had to be curbed at all costs, his mind kept on conquest. And meanwhile there was Matilda, who he felt sure would be much more accommodating than the serving girl, although he would have to wait until dark before he knew for certain.

A sea of expectant faces were lifted to the dark canopy of the sky. The fireworks exploded, then fell like showers of stars to satisfied exclamations of, "ooh" and "aah". And while the crowd was thus diverted, Harry slipped his arm round Matilda's waist. "Shall we go for a little walk," he whispered in her ear.

"But what about Mama and Papa?"

"They'll not even miss us with all this going on," he cajoled.

"Well . . . all right," Matilda tried to sound uncertain, reluctant, but she was tingling with excitement from her head to her toes.

The quietest place, Harry had worked out, would be the churchyard. No doubt there would be other couples there, spread out on the gravestone or under the trees, but he reckoned it was dark enough and big enough to accommodate a few more lovers.

Taking a firm grip of Matilda's hand, he led her up between the path of yews. "Oh it's ever so dark and creepy," she said with a shiver, as doubts began to surface. "Hadn't we better turn back?"

Harry stopped. "Do you really want to?" His voice was soft, persuasive.

"Aaah . . . well," answered Matilda indecisively, knowing full well that if she did turn back it would be the last she would see of him.

They were now at the rear of the church and Harry could

see that if he didn't play his cards right the day could end badly for him. "Shall we sit down here on the grass?" he asked, guiding her in the direction of a large family vault surrounded by wrought iron fencing.

"Oh no," said Matilda, backing away with a shudder then a nervous giggle.

"All right," he said, fighting to keep the exasperation from his voice. But he'd been patient long enough and pushing her against the rough stone of the church wall, he silenced any further protest with a kiss.

Matilda felt his hand on the back of her neck and his mouth on hers with a sense of surprise. She wasn't sure at first how to respond and her mouth remained firmly shut. But as she felt the pressure of his tongue on her teeth, her lips softened and opened like a flower as it is plundered by a bee. Then he was kissing her throat, pulling down the sleeves of her low cut dress and lightly nibbling her shoulders. A hand was plunged down the front of her dress and he began caressing her breasts in a way that had her clinging to him in feverish ecstasy.

But just then she heard the crunch of feet on gravel and went tense. To be seen in this sort of situation, dishevelled, and up against the wall like some common slut would ruin her reputation for all time. Pushing Harry away, she shrank against the wall and tried to readjust her clothing. But the couple moved off into the grass and in a very short while there were giggles, then a mild protest from the girl, followed by the loud, orgiastic grunts of two people engaged in and enjoying sexual congress.

This was just too much for Harry and he began pulling urgently at Matilda's dress until the hem was somewhere around her waist. Here however he was thwarted by her tightly laced stays. Stays he knew from long experience, rendered any woman as impregnable as a fortress. Cursing silently, he let the soft material slip from his hands. Then

81

he thought: control yourself Harry old boy, don't be too impatient. He would have bet his last guinea on her being a virgin still, and her deflowering shouldn't take place against a church wall. The place and time had to be carefully chosen and he was sufficiently sure of his hold over Matilda to know she would find every opportunity she could for them to meet.

He'd been right too about her being the willing sort. In fact she seemed a bit too damned eager, whereas that little serving maid . . . reticent and mouth-wateringly beautiful, didn't appear at all ready to fall into his arms. Realizing he might not, after all, achieve the double seduction he'd so set his mind on, Harry gave a deep, very audible sigh of regret.

Misinterpreting his sigh as an ungovernable longing and passion for her, Matilda pressed herself hard against him and asked softly, "What's the matter, Harry?"

His response disappointed her deeply. Instead of a declaration of undying love, Harry answered casually, "Nothing, but we best be getting back," adding as he gave her a pat on the backside, "and next time, my darling girl, you could you do me a favour and leave off those wretched stays."

Matilda and Harry were unaware that Rachel had watched them disappear in the direction of the church. She also noted their return, and when she saw the girl's dishevelled appearance and the way she clung possessively to the Captain's arm she felt a final hardening of her heart against him and all men. For her money there wasn't one of them who was worth a groat.

And her antipathy towards the opposite sex wasn't helped by the feeling that had persisted that somehow she was unclean like a leper. Even when, at Robert's insistence, she'd joined in the set dances, she hadn't felt part of the celebrations and her sense of self-disgust was almost as powerful as the loathing she felt for George. She had hoped he would quickly tire of the company of country folk and take himself off back to Leicester. But he'd continued to hang around, drinking large quantities of ale, fondling any girl he could lay his hands on and becoming more objectionable as the day passed. Then she noticed him talking rather urgently to Polly, and she was so disturbed by the way the girl giggled and leaned against him she found herself calling out, "Polly, you come here now your mam's looking for you!"

If looks could kill, thought Rachel as George glowered at her. But he did push Polly away from him, saying as he did, "Go on, she wants you, clear off."

"What was Master George saying to you Polly my love?" Rachel asked, as the girl skipped over to her.

Polly's simple features took on a guarded look. "Nuthin'," she answered.

"Are you sure?"

Polly nodded her head up and down emphatically.

"Where are your mam and dad then?"

"Gone 'ome. Mam says she's had enough and all she wants to do is put her feet up."

"Shall we go and see them then?" asked Rachel, taking the girl's hand. "With a bit of luck your mam might have the kettle on for a cup of tea."

If the red and white check curtains hadn't been drawn across the parlour window, Rachel would have seen Jed Fairfax. And since their last meeting had been less than friendly, this might have caused her to change her mind about going in. But she was already well over the threshold before she realized that it was his long legs sprawled out towards the fire. It would have been difficult to retreat but his presence made her feel awkward and it wasn't until Robert beckoned and said, "Shut the door, Rachel," that she felt confident enough to move towards the fire.

"Here have this," said Jed, jumping up and offering her his chair.

Rachel shook her head. "No thank you, I'm not staying."

"Of course you're staying, I'm just about to mash some tea," answered Susan in a matter of fact tone. "Sit yerself down."

Since there was never any point in arguing with the strong-minded Susan, Rachel did as she was bid, while Jed squatted cross-legged on the floor and continued with the discussion they'd been having when she walked in.

"Yes those people are out there enjoying themselves tonight, but there are hard times coming," Jed prophesied. "Demand for hose is going to fall and with all the soldiers home from the war and wanting work, the hosiery trade is going to be overcrowded. Wages are bound to fall. And mark my words, your Mr Pedley and his obnoxious son will be the first to beggar people."

Although she listened intently as they aired their grievances, she felt far too ignorant to offer an opinion of her own so it was some moments before Rachel realized he had addressed his last remark to her. "Don't blame me for what they do, I hate them both as much as anyone." she replied sharply. That she reserved a particularly deep hatred for George she kept to herself.

"Aye," Robert went on, "and now that he's stolen land that was ours by right, he and the Squire and that black fly Parson Dobbs, how are we to live, where are we supposed to graze our beasts, gather our fuel?"

"There's trouble coming Robert, you can see it a mile off," Jed answered. "It's been a good harvest this year so they'll be spared the sort of bread riots we've had in the past. But it'll not always be so. And when people are starving and reduced to living off the poor rates, there'll be unrest, revolution even."

"Stop talking like that Jed," Susan scolded as she poured tea and handed it round. "We don't want revolution here. Look what happened in France. All that killing, people

84

guillotined who I'm sure didn't deserve it." She shook her head. "No I draw the line at that."

Denied a topic of conversation dear to their hearts, the two men lapsed into silence, leaving Rachel and Susan with the chance to indulge in a little gossip; the unfortunate cut and colour of Miss Jane Dobbs new dress, how the normally prim Mrs Fellowes had been seen staggering tipsily around the village, cursing like a sailor. But Jed soon made it clear he had no interest in such trifling matters.

"I'll be off then." As he walked to the door the grandfather clock chimed ten.

"Gosh, is that the time? I must go as well." Rachel leapt to her feet.

"In that case I'll walk up the hill with you."

"Thank you, but I'll be quite all right on my own," she answered coolly, still not having forgiven him for the personal remarks he'd made last market day.

"Let him see you back to the farm Rachel," Susan interceded. "It's dark up that lane."

Susan was right, of course, and she had to think where George might be lurking. And because Rachel knew that every rustling in the hedge would set her nerves on edge, she allowed Jed to follow her out of the door.

She knew the rabble had taken over the party when she saw a youth leaning over the wall vomiting into the garden, while a gang of village louts shouted encouragement. Without checking to see if Jed was behind her, Rachel hurried away in disgust. She was picking her way between bodies out cold on the Green when a leering drunk swayed towards her. Terrified, she backed away and found herself enfolded in the security of Jed's arms, heard him say quietly. "It's all right, I'm here." He held her long enough for her to feel the regular beating of his heart, then he let her go. "Come on, let's get you away from this lot." And taking her arm, he led her from the coarse, suggestive songs and the roistering that was likely to go on all night.

They were in the lane before he spoke again. "I bet there'll be some sore heads and regrets in the morning."

"And serve them right too," Rachel answered unsympathetically. The air struck chill on her bare arms and she walked close to Jed, glad to feel the warmth emanating from him and grateful now of his presence. They walked in silence after this, but the words of the bawdy songs followed them up the hill and made Rachel blush in the darkness. Finally to cover her embarrassment she blurted out, "I didn't see you at the party."

"That was because I didn't go," he answered, making it clear by his tone that he considered such mindless frivolity way beneath his dignity.

She cleared her throat and tried another topic. "Your mam, is she better now?"

He seemed a little put out by this question. "Oh . . . err . . . yes. Fully recovered thank you. In fact she plans to remarry, unfortunately to a gentleman I have little liking for, and move to London with him."

"Your father, how long is it since he passed away?"

"Just over two years." His voice immediately took on a hard quality. "He died in the debtors prison of a broken heart when his hosiery business failed. It was the Pedleys' fault. They set out deliberately to put him out of business by lowering their prices and by making shoddy cut-ups instead of fully-fashioned hose. Then when they'd done their worst they bought his frames at a knock-down price. That's how old man Pedley's made all his money, by fraud. It's the same with the folks who rent frames off him, they all work for a pittance. His father was a drunken turnkey at the prison in Leicester you know, and where he learnt every dishonest trick in the trade. But he keeps it legal, just. He'd sell his daughter to the highest bidder and he lives in perpetual hope he'll be able to buy himself a place in society and turn that obnoxious son of his into a gentlemen."

So that was it, thought Rachel, the key to Jed's hatred of the Pedleys. The reason why he'd fired their corn stack. And yet here he was, walking up the lane as cool as cucumber. Rachel sensed something in Jed's nature that was halfway between recklessness and stubborness, and she was in no doubt that his walking her home was a defiant gesture; a sort of fingers to the nose at the Pedleys. But by now they were less than fifty yards from the house, far enough Rachel felt, for even Jed to feel that honour had been satisfied. Pausing she turned and was about to assure him she'd be all right now, when a figure moved out of the shadow of the hedge and stood swaying in front of them, blocking their path.

"Wha' are you doin' snooping around here, Fairfax?" George asked, his voice slurred with an excess of ale.

"My intention was to see this young lady home. Now if you'll just get out of my way . . ." Jed took Rachel's hand and made as if to brush past, but was prevented by George extending both arms.

"Lady, huh. That's a good one that is. The serving wench you mean."

Jed moved very close to George and waved a clenched fist under his nose. "Watch it Pedley or you'll feel this."

"It's you who ought to watch it. Your voice carries you know. I heard all those slanderous remarks and the aspersions you were casting on the good name of our family."

"There wasn't a word I said that I wouldn't be willing to repeat in court. And as for your family name, well it stinks of corruption."

If George had been sober he might have had more regard for the size of Jed's fist and been a little more circumspect in his next choice of words. But drink had driven out what little wit he had, besides which he seemed unaware of the real depth of Jed's loathing. So rather incautiously he went on, "The reason your old man lost his business was because he was incompet . . ."

But the sentence remained unfinished as Jed's fist shot out and caught George fair and square on the nose. He gave an astonished "ouch!" and then, because of his inebriated state, lost his balance and sat down heavily on the ground.

"Come on, get up and fight like a man, you empty headed coxcomb," ordered Jed, bouncing up and down like a prize fighter.

But George was holding a handkerchief to his nose and had no intention of rising to face his opponent. "Look what you've done. Made my nose bleed, and ruined my best trousers," he wailed.

Rachel didn't even try to suppress the laughter that rose in her throat. George had humiliated her too many times and to see him felled by one blow from Jed's fist and blood dripping on to his starched neckcloth was one of the most joyful moments of her life.

"Shut up you bitch!" George shouted angrily.

"Watch your tongue, Pedley," Jed warned, stabbing him in the behind with the toe of his boot. None of this helped Rachel, whose laughter was now so out of control she was in danger of choking.

Amid all the confusion and shouting, none of them heard the horse's hooves, and the buggy was almost upon them before they heard Joseph Pedley's voice booming out of the darkness. "What the devil..!" The buggy lamp now illuminated the scene sufficiently for him to see his son on his backside in the middle of the lane, bleeding into a handkerchief, while the wretched maidservant and a stranger stood over him apparently relishing his distress. To discover what was going on, he jumped down from the buggy, closely followed by Matilda and her mother.

"What are you doing down there, for heavens sake, George?"

"Yes, my poor child, what ever has happened to you?" cried Esther Pedley, swooping to embrace her son.

George, who for the benefit of his mother and father, had been moaning in a most exaggerated fashion, removed the handkerchief briefly from his nose and pointed an accusing finger at Jed. "Fairfax gave me one."

"Fairfax?" Joseph Pedley's voice held a note of enquiry. "What on earth's he doing here?" He turned to face Jed, peering up at him in the darkness.

Deciding it was time she said something, Rachel stepped forward. "Mr Fairfax were seeing me home."

"What did I tell you Mama," Matilda interceded, "give her one of my dresses and she immediately starts giving herself airs and graces."

"Shut up, Tilda. Now I'm going to get to the bottom of this. You say Fairfax was seeing you home?" asked Mr Pedley. Rachel nodded. "So why has he bloodied my son's nose? You weren't fighting over this wench, were you?" He glared suspiciously at his son who was being assisted to his feet by his mother. "I've warned you not to go tampering with serving girls."

"Her? Why I wouldn't touch her with a pair of tongs," answered George, in a tone of high moral outrage.

At Matilda's snigger of disbelief Rachel felt a powerful urge to expose him for the liar he was. But knowing it would do her little good, she held her tongue.

"Anyway," George went on, "if you want to know I was defending our family name, which Fairfax here seems intent on defaming."

"I've heard enough," shouted Mr Pedley. He turned to Rachel. "Right you wench, go to your room. I'll deal with you later. And you Fairfax, clear off and don't show your face in these parts again. There's been some dirty work round here lately and I wouldn't put anything past you."

"I'll go in my own good time. Anyway, you're in no

position to talk about dirty work. A past master at it you are."

"The insolence . . .!" For a moment the older man seemed lost for words, but then he pointed a finger in the direction of the village. "Go," he roared, "before I have my hounds on to you."

"I'll go when I'm ready. But before I do you can take that." Again Jed's arm shot out, there was a crack of knuckle against jaw, then taking Joseph Pedley's advice, he turned and vanished into the night.

Rachel, forgetting in the general mayhem that she shouldn't be there anyway, had watched Jed's foolhardy behaviour with a sort of dazed admiration, almost wanting to cheer him on. But now as her master staggered back with a yell of fury and pain, she decided it might be wise if she too put some distance between herself and the fracas. Edging away, she then moved swiftly round to the back of the house and let herself in.

Lying in bed she heard the hubbub outside gradually die down to a low buzz of complaint. Then the family moved inside and doors were locked. But Rachel knew that for her this wasn't the end of the incident. Joseph Pedley would want to vent his spleen on someone. But even knowing it would be her who would have to face the consequences of Jed's reckless behaviour, Rachel felt it was worth it. She'd never known vengeance could taste so sweet and she savoured the image of George grovelling in the dirt. It was a memory she would cherish all her life.

The last door clicked shut and beds creaked in protest as they received their night's burden. Through her open window she could hear a breeze lightly stirring the leaves in the tall elm trees. Tranquilized by the sound Rachel had almost drifted off to sleep when she heard footsteps on the stairs, heavy with retribution. Then her door was thrown open and she lay rigid, her eyes squeezed tightly shut, steeling herself for the bruising lashes of her master's belt. When nothing happened she opened one eye a fraction. Joseph Pedley's bulky frame almost filled the small room and he held the chamberstick high and was looking about him. "Right, where's that dress?" he barked and snatched it up from the chair. "I'll see you don't go titivating yourself up in this again so that you can lure unsuitable men up here, you whore." And with a sleeve in each great fist, Joseph Pedley took the the beautiful dress and ripped it savagely in two.

After he'd gone Rachel lay in the bed cradling the ruined dress in her arms. And as she stared dry-eyed into the darkness, she began to wonder how much longer she could safely go on living at Thatcher's Mount.

Chapter Eight

After discovering how cold winds could ravage the skin, Matilda had decided she didn't much care for riding. Nevertheless as she rested her riding crop on her shoulder and struck a pose in front of her mirror, she had to admit, that in the green velvet habit and small black beaver hat, she looked rather pleasing to the eye.

A ride over to Charnwood Forest had been Jane's bright idea, but it was Francis Bennett who had come up with the suggestion that they should picnic there. For what reason, Matilda couldn't imagine. Certainly to her way of thinking, as a day out it had little to commend it. But since Harry had seemed just as keen as the other two, she'd had no option but to fall in with their plans. Because by tomorrow he would be on his way back to his regiment and she now had to contemplate weeks, maybe months even, of separation.

When it suited her, Matilda could be sweetness itself, although she found it an exhausting business, being constantly pleasant, particularly when there was little to show for it, not even a declaration of love. But whatever Harry felt about her, she was in no doubt about her own feelings. With a guilty pleasure, Matilda closed her eyes and as it always did when she remembered their tryst in the churchyard, her body grew warm and languorous. The sweetness of his kisses, the pressure of his hands on her breasts were recalled with a delight that sent convulsive shudders through her body and made her light-headed with desire.

But then as it frequently did, a little nagging doubt began to surface. Should she have yielded quite so willingly? It was a well attested fact that men didn't approve of fast girls and although they might take them as mistresses they rarely made them their wives. Remembering her own, over eager responses, she suddenly felt hot with shame and had to press her face against the cold glass of the mirror to cool her burning cheeks. But it was no good, to be parted from him would be like dying of thirst. Matilda was rarely aware of anyone's feelings but her own, but she now felt a slight wave of sympathy for her brother, because she finally had some inkling of the urges that drove him to continually pester the serving girl.

Matilda's daily routine was normally so dull it was no more than half a life, and often as she sat stitching some tedious moralistic proverb on to a sampler and listening to the clock ticking her youth away, she would fret and fume at the emptiness of her existence. More than once she'd caught Harry watching Rachel. And it was a look that made her feel uneasy. What if the unthinkable happened and she lost him to a maidservant, what would she do then? Confronted with such a possibility, Matilda felt a tremor of fear. It wouldn't happen though: there was no way she was going to let him slip from her grasp. In fact she was prepared to do anything to retain his interest. Harry spelt danger, but with him she knew she was alive and that was worth almost any sacrifice.

To be standing on the edge of a cliff face might be exhilarating but it was also dangerous, for one false move . . . but she wouldn't think of that. Because anything, surely, had to be better than the monotonous certainty of her normal everyday existence.

Her mother calling up the stairs, "Matilda, darling, your friends are here," jolted her out of her introspection and with an eager lift of her head she hurried to join them. On her way down, for the sheer pleasure of it, she paused at the landing window and looked down at Harry astride his horse. Noticing the ease with which he controlled the animal, the muscular bulge of his thighs, she felt again such a hot rush of desire for him, it almost crushed the breath out of her and she cursed silently at having to share him for the whole day with Jane and the Squire.

Matilda, who had been hoping to savour the sweet pleasure of eloquent glances, felt disappointed by Harry's casual, "Good morning, Miss Matilda," and wondered if the intimate hour they'd spent in the churchyard had meant anything to him at all. And she'd hardly mounted when he moved off down the lane with Jane, while she found herself bringing up the rear, with the Squire, thick and solid as his horse, riding beside her. Matilda would never have dreamt that she'd ever have an occasion to be jealous of Jane. Until today. Because Jane was a superb horsewoman and mounted on a frisky filly she'd bred herself, she was transformed from a gauche non-entity into a self-assured young woman. Matilda, in spite of the superior quality of her habit felt at a definite disadvantage. She could see Harry was impressed too, where before he had hardly given Jane the time of day. Just wait, she thought glaring at her friend's broad back, I'll have something to say to you Miss Jane Dobbs.

"You look very becoming, my dear," commented Francis Bennett, hardly able to credit his good fortune at having Matilda to himself.

Matilda, who was by now in a foul mood, gazed indifferently in front of her and didn't even bother to answer. And since the Squire, who had never been at ease with women anyway, had exhausted his stock of flattering phrases and could think of nothing that might engage her attention, they rode on in silence. He'd mourned the death of his wife, God rest her soul, but her passing had relieved him of the necessity of making small talk. She had also been barren and he desperately needed an heir. Oh he knew the young mountebank in front had hopes of getting his hands on what was left of his estate, but not if he knew anything about it. He might not be in the first flush of youth but he knew he had it in him to sire a healthy brood of sons, with the right woman, he thought with a sideways glance at Matilda, wondering at the same time what sort of marriage portion she might bring with her and if it would be enough to mend the roof. She was pouting very prettily and he understood why, and he also knew there wasn't a chance in hell of Harry marrying a girl of her social standing. That young man had his sights set on something far grander and richer. But he himself would be quite happy to settle for Matilda. Otherwise it might have to be one of the parson's daughters, and it would require a great effort of the imagination to be aroused by either of them. Poor girls, they were both so plain and he did have a penchant for pretty women.

They had now reached the drove-road which crossed the Squire's land and would bring them out eventually on to the turnpike. Here at last there was room for Matilda to catch up with Jane and Harry. But no sooner had she done so than Jane said, "Come on, I'll race you Harry," and the two of them cantered off, closely followed by Francis Bennett.

"Wait for me," called Matilda in a querulous voice, but nobody heard her and she was left fuming at the perfidy of her friend and trailing some way behind. The day had turned warm too and the green velvet habit which previously she'd thought so becoming now stuck to her skin, making her feel hot and cross. Furtively she dabbed at her forehead and upper lip with a small lace handkerchief, knowing it would never do for Harry to see her doing anything so vulgar as perspire.

Charnwood was a forest in name only, most of the trees having been having been felled long ago for timber or charcoal. Now it was a landscape of rocky outcrops, rough pastures of bracken and gorse, with small copses of oak here and there. But if Matilda had cared to look around her she would have seen that with its views of Bradgate Park and Old John, it was pretty enough. But she was in no mood t0 admire the scenery. All she wanted to do was find somewhere cool where she could sit down and maybe when she regained some of her energy, strangle Jane.

Because the bridle paths were narrow they now rode in single file, the Squire in front and Harry at the rear. "Not much further now," Francis Bennett called and after about a quarter of a mile they finally reached the small wooded area where they were to picnic.

"Now isn't this a delightful spot, Matilda?" asked Jane as she dismounted and tied up her horse. Then without waiting for her friend's reply went on, "And how clever of you, Mr Bennett, to find it."

"Yes, it is a pleasant spot, isn't it," answered the Squire, pleased to be complimented. "Although it is many years since I was last here."

Why does she have to be so effusive about a wretched picnic, thought Matilda bad temperedly. She was about to dismount when she realized her skirt had become tangled in a pommel. She was tugging at it impatiently when Harry came towards her, hand extended and seemingly unaware of his heartless neglect of her. "Allow me Miss Matilda."

Well before she'd reached womanhood Matilda was aware that society was structured entirely to men's advantage and they could behave as they liked. She on the other hand, as a woman, must beguile, charm, please, for they were the only weapons she had. Controlling her murderous thoughts, she gave Harry her sunniest smile. "Thank you." At her most gracious, and taking his hand, she released her skirt and slid to the ground. As her feet came in contact with the earth, Harry held her a fraction longer than was necessary and she felt something being pressed into her hand. He returned her startled expression with a warning look then turned and walked away, while Matilda quickly stuffed the note he'd given her into the pocket of her habit. But as she fingered it, the sharp edge of her misery evaporated and Harry was forgiven.

The worst part of it now was the suspense, not being able to read the letter, having to guess at its contents. Could it be a declaration of love? Or . . . Matilda caught her breath and looked across at Harry, hardly daring to hope . . . a proposal even. But whatever was in it, she knew she'd have to wait until she got home before it offered up its secrets. To be caught reading it here could compromise them both. But the day had already taken on a happier aspect, a feeling of goodwill flowed through her and she now felt well-disposed towards everyone, even Jane.

A servant of the Squire's had driven on ahead and he now presided over a cold collation spread out on the ground. It was a pretty meagre table. Some cold chicken drumsticks, a sad looking pork pie, pickled onions, a lump of sweating cheese and a few jam tarts on which several wasps were drunkenly gorging themselves.

"Right, sit yourselves down and tuck in," said the Squire rubbing his hands heartily, proud to be playing host to the small party.

"It all looks delicious, Mr Bennett," said Jane, not quite truthfully and helped herself to a slice of pork pie.

Matilda squeezed herself down between Harry and Jane and surveyed the repast without much interest. And it was only because the Squire insisted, that she ate a stringy chicken leg. But if the quality of the food was poor, the same couldn't be said of the drink. Even Matilda recognized that the claret was excellent and there seemed to be a plentiful supply. Because no sooner was one bottle emptied than Hodge, the manservant uncorked another.

"Your health, Miss Jane and Miss Matilda," said Harry lifting his glass.

"I know you're joining your regiment tomorrow, but will

we being seeing you when the hunting season starts?" asked Jane, helping herself to another slice of pie and holding up her glass to be refilled.

Matilda went on chewing her chicken bone with a studied indifference but she waited for his reply with a nervously fluttering heart.

"It rather depends on Uncle."

The Squire was now well into his second bottle of claret and feeling expansive. "Come when you like, Harry m'boy there's always a bed for you at Trent Hall. I like young people around me, it livens up the place. We might even manage a dinner party next time you come."

"Thank you uncle," answered Harry giving no indication by his tone whether he intended taking up the offer or not.

Matilda tried to imagine who the Squire might invite to this dinner party. The house was crumbling round his ears, the furnishing and tapestries were home to an army of moths and woodworm, while his cook, Mrs Sawyer even when she was sober, couldn't be relied on to cook a leg of lamb without burning it.

Matilda could see that there was going to be little in the way of sparkling conversation at this picnic. Jane never had a lot to say for herself and Harry looked as if he was regretting the whole exercise. In fact Francis Bennett seemed to be the only one really enjoying himself and he was giving his full attention to the food and drink. "I think I'll just have one of these," he said and reaching over, helped himself to a tart.

"There's a wasp on it Mr Bennett," Jane warned.

"Why so there is," he said, gazing at the tart with a slightly befuddled expression. Then brushing the wasp from the crater of burnt jam, he stuffed it into his mouth. As he ate, crumbs joined the particles of food adhering to his shirt from meals past and when he'd finished he hooked his finger round his gums, then sucked his teeth noisily and with obvious relish.

Matilda gazed at him with an almost open contempt. With

his grimy fingernails and greasy neckcloth he was hardly cleaner than some of the squatters who took up residence in the village from time to time and she turned from him with a shudder of disgust. But not before she noticed that the level of the bottle of brandy Hodge had now opened was falling rapidly and she wondered how long it would be before Francis Bennett toppled over.

Within the hour he was flat out on his back, arms spreadeagled and snoring loudly. "Give me a hand here, Hodge," said Harry, and levering his uncle to sitting position the two men lifted the Squire and dumped him in the buggy. "Take him home, Hodge, I'll bring his horse." Then leaving the servant to clear up, the three of them moved off with one riderless horse.

Matilda forced herself to wait before opening Harry's letter. She got Rachel to help her off with her clothes, demanded that her hair be brushed and only after these tasks had been seen to and she was alone did she slit open the envelope with slightly trembling fingers. But there was no declaration of love, no proposal of marriage just a request. "Dearest heart," it said, "meet me tonight in Rooks Spinney. It will be our last chance to spend time together so I shall wait from eleven until midnight. Devotedly, Harry."

Matilda crushed the letter against her breast in a state of some agitation. She couldn't go, it was impossible. How was she to get out of the house without being seen or without alerting the dogs? And the stairs creaked, bolts would have to be undone, great keys turned in locks. Why her parents would be awake in a minute. It was cruel of Harry to expect her to compromise herself so. She read the letter again, tapping a fingernail thoughtfully against her teeth. Of course she could leave a downstairs window open . . . perhaps in the drawing room. It was immediately under her bedroom and well away from the kennels. There was no moon tonight either, and if she wore dark clothes and kept close into the hedge no one would see her. The risk was tremendous, but if she didn't go, would Harry bother about her again, or would he turn his attention to Rachel? The very idea made the palms of her hands damp with anxiety. In a fever of indecision she stared at herself in the looking glass. "Well my girl, what are you going to do?" she enquired of her reflection. "Take a chance, go," the other, braver girl seemed to say and immediately Matilda felt sick. But she must go. For wasn't this what she craved for? To taste danger, to reach out and touch the stars.

Matilda thought her mother would never go to bed. Her father always retired early and usually Esther Pedley followed shortly after. But tonight for some reason, even after she'd had her nightcap, it seemed to her impatient daughter that she hung around needlessly, driving her mad with her inconsequential chatter.

When the clock struck ten, Matilda closed her book, yawned and stood up. "Well . . . time for bed. Aren't you coming, Mama?"

"In a little while dearest," her mother answered as she did battle with a length of wool and a square of canvas that one day might cover a footstool.

Matilda ground her teeth in exasperation then, as an unwelcome thought entered her mind, she focused on her mother with a growing suspicion. Had she guessed what she was up to? Matilda crossed to where Esther Pedley was sitting and as she bent to kiss her on the forehead, she studied the placid features intently. No, it was a silly idea, her mother couldn't possibly know. It was just her own over-active imagination playing tricks.

At the door she hesitated. "Good-night Mama."

"Good-night darling," her mother answered serenely and went on with her sewing.

As she climbed the stairs, Matilda reflected on her mother's behaviour. For a simple woman she could be excessively awkward at times. Although in most matters she was inclined to defer to her husband, Matilda often suspected that she was far more astute and aware of what was going on around her than her family gave her credit for. Which made it essential, if her escapade was to succeed, to proceed with caution.

Leaving the bedroom door ajar, she undressed, fumbling with buttons, trying to unlace stays with fingers that felt all thumbs, then quickly covered her nakedness with a wrapping gown. As she sat down and the full implication of what she was about to do hit her, she began to perspire under her armpits and her legs turned to jelly.

Downstairs she heard Rachel go into the drawing room to clear the tea things away. Matilda could never understand why her mother showed such an interest in the girl and for a moment her nervousness was displaced by resentment as she listened to the low conversational murmur of voices.

After what seemed like an eternity Rachel returned to the kitchen then shortly afterwards climbed the attic stairs to her room. But still her mother didn't stir. "Come on, come on," Matilda muttered impatiently gnawing at her fingernails and watching the hands of the small carriage clock on the chimney-piece move to half past ten.

Matilda, as the evening advanced, had alternated between a state of high excitement and doubt. Previously, as far as any romantic attachment was concerned, she'd been just paddling in the shallows. Now she was about to embark on a momentous adventure where the waters were turbulent, the risks high. For the first time in her life she'd been awakened to the possibility of pain and her emotions were raw. She was risking everything by meeting Harry, she knew that. But then who said she had to go? She could climb into bed, Harry would wait for an hour then return home and no one would be any the wiser.

"Not in bed yet, dear." Matilda in the end hadn't heard her mother come up the stairs and she jumped guiltily when her head came round the door.

"Oh . . . no," she flustered, then regaining her composure, added, "Actually I decided to finish my book."

"Well don't strain your eyes, and don't sit up too long."

"I won't Mama," answered Matilda, so meek and obedient, it really should have aroused Esther Pedley's suspicions.

At last her mother went, there was a few minutes silence, then as she'd expected, her father's grumbles as his wife joined him in bed. Even so she still waited until she heard their snores emerging, in counterpoint, from under the door. Then in a state which alternated between agitation and a bemused wonder at what she was actually doing, Matilda donned a dark dress and black woollen cloak, concealed at the back of the wardrobe.

Feeling like a heroine in one of the gothic novels she read so voraciously, she tiptoed out onto the landing. Her heart was beating so violently she could hardly breathe. At every furtive step she took the stairs creaked. Then the grandfather clock wheezed out eleven ponderous strokes, echoing through the silent house with such an intensity of sound, Matilda was convinced she was done for. She stood rigid, mouth dry with terror, waiting for her father to come charging out of his bedroom demanding to know what she was up to. But apart from the mice, nothing stirred. Relaxing slightly she moved to the drawing room. Here it was hardly better. The window was stiff and as the struggled to open it, Matilda wondered if Harry had any real understanding of the risks she was taking on his behalf or even of the consequences, heaven forbid, if she was caught. She finally managed to raise the window, and squeeze through but she banged her knee on the sill and had to a smother a yelp of pain. When her feet came into contact with solid earth, Matilda felt jubilant. She'd done it! Surely no other obstacles stood between her and Harry now. Drawing the hood of the cloak over her head, she moved swiftly through the garden and climbed over a stile to a footpath leading directly to the woods.

The trees in the spinney were tall and when they swayed and the wind rustled their leaves, it sounded to Matilda's fevered imagination like the whisper of ghosts. And she remembered how as a small girl when George wanted to frighten her he would say the spinney was haunted and that the rooks were the souls of dead witches. By now her nerves were in tatters and if she hadn't seen the signal from the lantern she might have turned tail and run.

"Over here, Matilda," Harry called in a loud whisper and she hurried towards him, in her haste stumbling over extruding roots and nearly falling.

"Oh Harry," she cried when she reached the sanctuary of his arms. "I was so frightened . . . I thought there were ghosts."

"Silly goose," he said affectionately, reassuring her with his kisses. "There's nothing to be afraid of now my darling, you're here with me and quite safe."

She looked up at him, his features, handsome, mysterious in the glow of the lantern. "But Mama and Papa . . . supposing they should find out?"

"Why should they?"

"I don't know . . . it's just that I feel sort of . . . guilty."

Dear God, thought Harry, don't say she's going to be difficult, just when he thought he'd bagged one. "Look I've brought a blanket, let's sit down. And some brandy," he added, unscrewing a small silver flask and handing it to her. "Have a swig, it'll warm you up and make you feel better."

Matilda took the flask and held it to her lips. The brandy scorched her tongue and throat but she enjoyed the sensation of it warm in her stomach and the feeling of wellbeing it induced as it coursed through her veins. She handed the flask back to Harry, waited impatiently for him to drink from it, snatched it from him again, this time quaffing liberally. Then she lay back on the blanket and began to giggle.

"Hush," said Harry, leaning over her and silencing her with a kiss, forcing her mouth open with his tongue and at the same time trying to unbutton the top of her dress.

But Matilda wasn't sure she liked his tongue in her mouth and tried to push him away. "Don't do that Harry."

"Don't do what, sweetheart," Harry murmured, undoing a couple more buttons.

"Don't do anything, I'd better go home." Matilda tried to rise, found to her surprise that her head was swimming and sank back on the blanket again.

The last of the buttons were undone down to the waist then Harry began to lightly kiss her neck, caressing the small breasts until the nipples went hard like nuts. When he felt her relax under the gentle manipulation, one hand moved down her body, fumbling for the hem of her dress. Sliding his hand under the garment, Harry felt her warm naked flesh and smiled in the darkness. Protest as much as you like, young lady, you know what you're here for just as much as I do.

Matilda felt his mouth on her nipples and his hands between her legs with a sense of shock. "No Harry," she cried in alarm, knowing there was no going back, and not sure now if this was what she wanted.

But he pressed her back on to the ground with a kiss and as his fingers began their skilful exploration; to ever so gently stroke and probe, she felt her body relax and respond and her feeble protests ceased. She had one more moment of doubt and that was when he heaved himself on top of her and grasped her bottom firmly. Then something very hard was being pushed into her, a tearing sensation made her cry out and she knew she didn't like what was happening at all. "Get off Harry, you're hurting me," she ordered tearfully, trying

104

to push him from her. But Harry didn't seem to hear. Instead he was moving up and down on top of her with deep, urgent thrusts, his exertions making him pant noisily. She was about to indulge in silent tears of self-pity when she realized that what Harry was doing to her wasn't so unpleasant after all.

The pain had diminished and moistly responsive she found herself moving to his rhythm, head back, eyes closed, body arching. She wanted it to go on too, so much so that she cried out, "Don't stop, don't stop." Then she seemed to reach some sort of peak, followed by a falling away that was like a long deep shudder, exquisite and fulfilling in its intensity and starting somewhere in her head and finishing at the tips of her toes.

She lay, her head swirling from drink and lovemaking, staring up through the trees at the starry heavens, with Harry inert and heavy on top of her. So that was it, she thought, the great mystery, revealed to her at last. She quite enjoyed it too. Very much in fact after the initial discomfort. She tried to cling on to Harry because she liked the weight of him on her, his physical closeness. But after a few minutes, he rolled away from her and sat up. Then without any expression of love or affection, he pulled down the skirt of her dress and began tidying himself up.

"What's the matter, Harry?" Matilda asked, reaching up to stroke his neck. After all, in yielding to him she'd just made the ultimate sacrifice. Bestowed without thought of the consequences, the most precious gift a woman could give to a man and it deserved a few words of love. "Do you love me Harry?" She hated asking but she wanted to be assured that her surrender hadn't been in vain.

He turned and kissed her on the nose and then stood up. "Course I do," he answered holding out his hand. "But we'd better be getting back, it's nearly twelve o'clock."

"But when shall I see you again?" Her shoulders sagged under the pain of his indifference. Her lips trembled but she swallowed hard, sensing that tears might be wasted on Harry. Oh why had she been so foolish as to come, why had she let him use her so.

"In about two weeks' time." A woman penetrated was already a woman who bored him and Harry was dying to get his hands on the little maid, although that might not be as easy as he'd initially thought. So it would be unwise to burn his boats with Matilda at this early stage. After all he could hardly continue to visit his uncle and ignore her. He put his arms round her waist, pulling her close. "Are you going to let me meet you here again?" he breathed huskily in her ear.

"Oh yes, Harry," Matilda whispered, reaching up to kiss him. Unquestioning and adoring and totally happy. Harry wanted her and that was all that mattered.

Chapter Nine

It was February with a sleety rain that might soon change to snow. Rachel edged her way along Loseby Lane careful where she placed her feet, for the wet cobblestones – known locally as petrified kidneys – made walking hazardous and she had no wish to end up on her backside in the slush. It was always a bit risky, leaving Sam in charge but business in the market had been so bad recently it had hardly seemed worth setting up a stall that morning and what custom there was had dwindled to nothing by ten o'clock. However she was still anxious to be rid of the letter Susan had asked her to deliver and get back to the market before any real damage was done.

Although the weather was miserable Rachel knew this wasn't the real reason for the fall off in trade. It was the war ending that had done it. The balls, the bells ringing and parties that had celebrated Boney's defeat and imprisonment on Elba had soon given way to desperation. It seemed all Jed's predictions were coming true. The demand for hose, webbing and worsted pieces that war inevitably brought had tailed off, along with the town's prosperity, and the wages of stockingers had fallen to near starvation level. And then there were the returning servicemen swelling the ranks of an already overcrowded trade. Rachel was used to beggars, they were part of the fabric of every day life, but now there seemed to be more than ever. And children in particular, some hardly more than six-years-old, with emaciated features and haunted eyes. Without hope or even the energy to speak, they just reached out and grabbed her garments as she passed. "Sorry, but I've got nothing," she said, feeling crushed by her own inability to do anything to relieve the distress in those small pinched faces. And although her cowardice shamed her, she hurried from their despair, guiltily relieved to reach the High Street and to be clear of their tiny clutching fingers.

Here she turned left and weaving her way between the traffic, crossed the road, thinking as she did that in spite of George she should count her blessings. She might be chilled to the marrow but unlike those poor mites, she knew she had somewhere to rest her head that night. Her destination was High Cross Street and when she reached it, Rachel paused and peered through the sleet. Surely it couldn't be much further, then saw by the numbers that the shop she was looking for must be quite a way along. She trudged on, past the Free Grammar School and County Gaol, noticing that while the right-hand side still retained many of its rat infested, dilapidated, medieval half timbered buildings, in contrast, the shops opposite were modern, with large bow windows in which merchants could display their goods. Eyeing them from across the street, Rachel wondered who could afford such luxuries as jewellery, rosewood pianos or even fine linen, in hard times like these. She'd almost reached the end of the street before she saw what she'd been searching for. A sign hanging over a door and proudly inscribed in gold lettering the words: 'Jedidiah Fairfax, Bookseller'. She also read, before she pushed open the door, that from here she could purchase ledgers, bibles and grammars and join a circulating library.

A bell announced her entrance. The interior was dim, the wooden floor dusty and uneven. The pervasive, fusty smell of old books made her nose tickle and although she held her fingers under her nose, Rachel sneezed violently several times.

"Good heavens!" exclaimed a voice from the bookshelves above her head. Then, "just a minute I'm coming down."

Rachel watched Jed descending the ladder with some interest. This was the first time she'd seen him since his altercation with the Pedleys and the change in his appearance was noticeable. Where before he'd worn the clothes of a working man, now he had on a well-cut frock coat and brocaded waistcoat and looked every inch the man about town. He'd been in London for a few months (and she could only imagine what he'd been up to, down there amongst all those radicals) and although he'd never been been uncouth in his manner, the great city had obviously smoothed away some awkward provincial ways.

The first hint Rachel had that Jed was no longer a resident of Leicester was when she found that his usual pitch in the market had been taken by someone else. She'd made enquiries amongst the other stall-holders, who told her he hadn't been seen for a couple of weeks. Puzzled, she mentioned this to Susan, who'd answered her with a brief, "He's gone to London to visit his mam."

She no longer wanted to think the worst of Jed but there'd been an outbreak of machine breaking, which had coincided with his sudden disappearance. But the man who stood before her didn't have the look of a criminal and she pushed to the back of her mind the idea that had grown in the intervening months, that Jed might be General Ludd himself, the brains behind the campaign. Because surely even he wouldn't be so foolhardy as to come back and open a bookshop if that was the case.

"It's nice to see you Rachel," he said, banishing her last doubt with a smile. Then he saw that she was shivering. "Why you're soaked to the skin, no wonder you're sneezing. Get that bonnet and cape off before you catch your death."

"Oh I haven't got a cold, it's the dust," Rachel answered, truthfully but tactlessly and sneezed again.

Jed laughed. "I take your point," he said, glancing around him. "It could do with a bit of a sweep in here, but I haven't had much time to spare for domestic matters since I moved in."

"Oh I didn't mean it was dirty," said Rachel rushing to make amends.

"Don't worry about it. Anyway are you going to part with those wet clothes?"

"I can't I've got to get back. I've just come with this." She drew a damp piece of paper on which the ink had run from under her cape and handed it to Jed. "It's from Susan," she explained.

Looking thoughtful, he turned the letter over in his hand went to break the seal, then changed his mind and stuffed it into his pocket. Rachel was trying to imagine its contents when he looked up at her with a smile. "You've got time for a cup of tea at least."

Tempted by something warm, Rachel hesitated. "Well . . . perhaps." Untying the short cape, she shook the rain from it then handed it to Jed. "But I can't stay long, I've left Sam in charge of things and . . . well, he not always reliable."

"Come into the back at least, I've got a fire there," he said, and he led her into a small room. It was obviously his living quarters, for there was a narrow bed against one wall covered with a tartan rug, an oak gatelegged table against another and a few windsor chairs. But most available space was taken up with books and political pamphlets, and he had to remove some from a chair and dust the seat with a handkerchief before she could sit down. But the fire was well stoked and a kettle was singing on the hearth. Cocooned in that small warm room, the blood returning to her fingers and with Jed engaged in the domestic task of making tea, it was impossible to think ill of him. As Rachel stretched luxuriously towards the fire she even forgot she had duties elsewhere. Until she happened to look out of the window. It had started to snow, quite heavily. "I must go," she said and leapt up from her chair. "I can't leave Sam any longer."

Jed handed her a cup of tea. "A few minutes won't make any difference, you can drink this first."

The tea scolded her throat but she gulped it down gratefully. Then Jed helped her on with her cloak and showed her to the door. "Come and see me again," he called as she sped down the street. "Come any time you like, I'm always here."

Rachel felt uneasy as she approached the market. But she relaxed slightly when she saw there was nothing amiss. Sam had packed everything back into the cart so that they could be on their way immediately and was now crouched by a glowing brazier belonging to one of the more prosperous stall-holders, chatting amiably. His first words to her were like a punch between the eyeballs. "Mr George has been here. Wanted to know where you were."

Rachel's heart began to thud erratically. "You didn't tell him, did you?"

"Course I did. You were only delivering a letter. No harm in that is there?"

"Oh Sam . . ." she wailed, "why couldn't you have made something up. You know how he hates Jed."

"To tell the truth Rachel I couldn't think of anything else to say. He sort of caught me unawares."

"Well, what did he want me for?"

"He didn't say."

"Well how did he look then?"

"As he always does, bloody bad tempered."

Rachel gave a resigned sigh. "Well we'd better be on our way. Whatever it was he wanted me for, I'll find out tonight won't I?"

Rachel had hoped that rather than make the journey home in worsening conditions, George would decide to spend Saturday night at his lodgings in Leicester. But hope faded when, late in the afternoon, she heard his voice and a short while after he came into the kitchen.

"Can I have tea please, Susan?" Rachel noticed how he was careful to be pleasant to Susan even though he ignored her. Not that there was anything unusual in his attitude and she had schooled herself not to allow his tortuous little games to affect her too much. His sole intention in going to the market place had been to spy on her and sooner or later, her minor transgression would be reported to his papa.

Percy, who was as good a judge of weather conditions as anyone Rachel knew, had grabbed Sam as soon as they got back from Leicester. "Come on lad, you and me's gonna bring those ewes down to the barn. It's near lambing time and I'm not gonna risk losing any." Then as soon as they'd done he and Susan left early for the village and Rachel realized with a queasy sensation in the pit of her stomach, that the house, with George in it, could be snowed up for several days.

Since Sam only had the clothes he stood up in, Rachel made sure he dried himself off before he returned to his sleeping quarters in the hay loft. She was glad to have his company too and they sat, watching the fire burn low while the wind wailed like a banshee round the chimney pots and blew, with Siberian ferocity, across open fields, forcing the snow into undulating drifts, piling it up against hedges, and pushing it through cracks in windows and under doors.

All evening she expected Joseph Pedley to come stamping into the kitchen snorting like an enraged bull. Nothing stirred, though, except the embers of the fire. At nine o'clock, she pushed a protesting Sam out into the blizzard. "Normal folk wouldn't put a dog out on a night like this," the boy grumbled as his feet sank into several inches of snow.

"I'm sorry Sam," Rachel replied, "but I'll be skinned alive if the beds haven't been warmed before that lot get into them." If it had been up to her she would have let him sleep on the floor and trying hard not to let the burden of someone else's guilt bear down on her, she watched the small figure, shoulders hunched, disappear into a swirling void of wind and snow. She couldn't bring herself to shut the door until she felt certain he'd reached his sleeping quarters and as she stood shivering on the step, the wind seemed like a living, malevolent force. It blasted through the kitchen extinguishing candles, rattling the saucepans like church bells and frightening the house cat from its slumbers, so that it stood up, spitting and arching its back at something unseen and which only he understood. Rachel had to hold her shoulder against the door to force it shut and although she knew it was fanciful of her she felt she was closing it on something truly diabolical. And as she shovelled hot coals from the fire into a warming pan and struggled with it upstairs, for the second time that day, she thanked God for a roof over her head.

She heated the beds, swishing the warming pan backwards and forwards across the cold linen sheets. After this she did the fires in each bedroom, banking the coal up so that it would burn slowly and maintain an even temperature throughout the night. When the blankets had been turned down, the night attire laid out, Rachel went back downstairs and prepared a hot chocolate drink for the family.

She was carrying it through to the drawing room when she was intercepted by George, who was hovering in the hall. She stopped short when she saw him, the hairs rising on the back of her neck, the chocolate drink slopping on to the tray. This was what she'd been waiting for all evening, to be confronted with her small transgression, after which would come the denunciation to his father.

Instead, to her utter astonishment, he tried to prise the tray from her hands. "I'll carry that in for you if you like."

"It's all right I can manage."

"I insist," he answered, tugging at the the tray and spilling even more of the drink. Such thoughtfulness was hardly in character but Rachel had been up since four o'clock that morning and was too tired to question his motives. So she relinquished the tray without further argument and went back to the kitchen. But there could still be other tasks and she had to sit there and wait until every last member of the family had gone to bed. To stop herself falling asleep, she sat upright on the hardest chair and with elbows resting on the kitchen table, wearily massaged her temples.

In spite of her best endeavours she did doze off and woke with pins and needles in both arms but to a blessed silence. Flexing and rubbing her arms to renew the circulation, Rachel went to the kitchen door. Reassured that neither sound nor light was coming from the drawing room, she lit her own candle, wrapped a hot brick in an old crocheted blanket and dizzy with exhaustion, dragged herself up the long flight of stairs.

Very little heat ever managed filter through to the top part of the house and moving from the warm kitchen made Rachel's room under the eaves seem doubly glacial. Even with the hot brick clutched to her breast, the shock set her teeth chattering. But she could only focus her thoughts on one thing, sleep, she must have sleep. Unable to fight her need any longer and still fully clothed she collapsed on to the bed, pulled the blankets over her shoulders, and in a instant was dead to the world.

In the dream she was suffocating. She struggled and tried to cry out but no sound came. Then as she fought through the stupor of sleep to consciousness, Rachel felt an enormous weight on her chest and heard George's snarling in her ear. "Make a sound and I'll kill you. So help me God I will. You do it for Jed Fairfax so tonight you'll do it for me."

Her brain was still fogged with sleep, so it was several moments before the full and horrifying implication of what was happening hit her and then Rachel's heart began to

114

thud with terror. George was sitting astride her, he had her wrists pinned above her head and his other hand was clamped over her mouth. Fighting the almost paralysing fear she knew would be the end of her, Rachel gave a convulsive heave and tried to dislodge him. But she was no match for someone of George's weight and size and as the hopelessness of her situation became clear, Rachel stopped struggling and concentrated instead on trying to think coherently and keep panic at bay. She also knew she needed to conserve her energy. It was his clear intention to rape her and if she resisted he would do it brutally, and even if she managed to scream out there was no certainty anyone would hear. Better to give in then, let him have his way and be done with it. But whatever the cost, Rachel knew she couldn't, she detested him too much. And this loathing of him fortified her; much better to die, she thought, than submit to someone she had such a deep hatred for.

Her stillness caught George off guard and mistaking it for compliance, he tried to lever open her knees. It was a fateful mistake because as he did, he relaxed his hold on her mouth. And in that one second of inattention Rachel managed to clamp her teeth over his thumb. Unable to articulate her hatred, all her pent up fury went into that bite and she held on like a bull terrier until she felt the crunch of bone and the taste of blood in her mouth.

Suppressing a yell of pain, George let out a stream of profanities and retaliated by grabbing her round the neck. Pressing two fingers against her windpipe, he proceeded to bang her head up and down on the mattress, at the same time chanting compulsively, "You bitch, you whore! You did it for him and you'll do it for me or you'll never lie with another man again."

As Rachel felt the life being squeezed from her, her nerveless fingers groped frantically around in the bed. The world was growing dim when she found it but in one last desperate move she managed to grasp hold of the brick and with all the strength she could muster, smash it against George's skull. There was sickening crack, a surprised grunt then he slumped on top of her, pinning her to the bed. Her moment of dazed relief at being able to breathe again was quickly followed by the terrible certainty that she had killed him. But as he lay there, intimate as a lover, Rachel felt the faint beating of his heart. But knowing he was alive was like being presented with a double-edged sword, for it meant her own life was still in jeopardy.

The wonder of it was that not one member of the family had been roused by the noise and a suspicion began to grow in Rachel's mind. She ought have known that a kindly gesture was beyond George and it was her guess that the family's hot chocolate had been liberally dosed with Mrs Pedley's sleeping draught. He was too weak to defy his father, feared his towering rages and she couldn't see how he would have dared to come to her room otherwise.

Rachel, with what little strength she had left, finally wriggled out from under George. She studied the dim outline of him on the bed with a clear-headed dislike, but then as she felt the grittiness of drying blood on her fingers, she began to shake violently and retch, the sour bile filling her mouth, the room spinning like a top. She fell back on the bed taking great gulps of air, pulling a blanket round her shoulders and trying to think about what she should do. She could no longer stay here. They'd both have a different story to tell, and her version of the events would count for nothing against George's loathsome untruths. If she was glad he wasn't dead, she thought as she pushed her feet unto her boots, it was only because he wasn't worth hanging for.

But where should she go? Susan and Robert's house was where they'd look first so that was out of the question. She was buttoning up her cape when she remembered Jed's small room and his last words to her, "Come any time you like,

I'm always here." Except that she had to get to Leicester first. Rachel went to the window, scraping away at the ice on the pane with her fingernails. The snow still fluttered down like thousands of dissolving white butterflies but she noticed that the wind had dropped fractionally and she was grateful for that.

Well it's now or never. She gave the inert body on the bed a brief glance, hoped it would never be her misfortune to set eyes on him again and stole downstairs. After hurriedly parcelling up some bread and cheese she let herself out, and as she pulled the door closed she promised herself that no matter what happened or how difficult she found it to survive in the world, she would never return to Thatcher's Mount.

The snow had eased up slightly. With luck, she thought, it would have stopped by morning. The dogs growled in warning as she ran across the yard, but she called out to them softly by name and they settled down again to sleep. In the barn she stumbled over sheep who baaed fretfully at being disturbed. It was pitch dark in the loft and she had to crawl around on her hands and knees searching for Sam in the hay. She found him finally, curled up like a dormouse. He muttered something and stirred as she crept under the blanket beside him. But he didn't wake and snuggling up to him, Rachel found solace in his small, warm body.

It was peaceful in the hay loft. The sweet smell of hay, the faint chomping of sheep, their emanating warmth. But George's assault on her remained a fixed image in her mind. What right had he? What made him feel entitled to take her by force. Was it because he was bigger and stronger? Or because she was only the maidservant or merely a woman, born to service a man as a mare does a stallion. Of course if he came searching for her, her footprints would lead him straight here. Unless fate felt more kindly disposed to her than of late and George remained unconscious until they were obliterated by the snow. But just in case, she knew

117

she mustn't let herself fall asleep. Rachel fought to keep her eyes open . . . I must stay awake she told herself . . . keep my eyes on the window so that I can be away at first light . . .

But someone was shaking her . . . George! She shrieked in mortal terror and leapt up, arms and legs jerking as if being manipulated by a puppet master.

"Rachel? Whatsa matter. What you doin' here?"

"Oh Sam I thought it was . . ."

"You thought it was who?"

"Never mind." Rachel shook her head to clear it and looked towards the small window. It might just be the snow but it seemed to her it was getting light. But whatever the weather conditions, she must leave this place, before it was too late. She scrambled to her feet, brushing straw from her clothes and hair. "It's too long a story. And its probably better for you if you don't know. I'll tell you another time. But I'm leaving Thatcher's Mount this minute and for good. I've had as much as I can stand from George Pedley. If anyone asks, you haven't seen me. Is that clear, Sam?"

Sam was confused. "Won't I ever see you again?" He considered himself too much of a man to cry, but his bottom lip trembled. Rachel had bossed him, mothered him, fought with him, been his companion and friend, and it was unthinkable that she was deserting him.

"Course you will. I'm only going to Leicester. Jed Fairfax will probably put me up until I find a job."

"But you'll never get through in this weather."

"Yes I will, it's stopped snowing. And I'm off this minute." She stooped to pick up the cloth she'd wrapped the bread and cheese in the night before, saw with dismay that it was punctured with teeth marks and knew without looking that its contents had been devoured by mice. Already too she was hungry. "Bye Sam. Not a word to anyone now. For your own sake as much as mine."

Sam was glad it was dark otherwise Rachel would have seen that tears were running down his cheeks in a most unmanly fashion. As he lay stretched out on the floor watching her descend the ladder, he called out, "You shouldn't go, you'll freeze to death."

But his warning went unheeded. "Go back to bed," she answered, then there was a blast of cold air as the barn door opened and closed. He scrambled to his feet and ran to the window, banging against it with his knuckles until it hurt, willing her to turn round. But she just walked on and as he let his bruised hand fall to his side, he watched with great gulping sobs, the small, toiling figure, somehow insignificant against the vast winter whiteness, disappear round the corner of the house.

It was a mile to the main road and the longest one Rachel would ever walk. In some parts the snow was piled high as a mountain, while in others it looked as if someone had taken a broom and swept it clean away. Even with her head bent submissively to the killing wind it still felt as if it was stripping the skin from her face and she heard her own breath like a rasping sob. Dragged down by the soaking wet weight of her dress and exhausted with the effort of struggling through deep drifts, Rachel had to fight the urge to surrender. What kept her going was an incident she recalled from the previous winter. Like most news, no matter how tragic, it was something she'd read about and almost immediately forgotten. But the circumstances were so similar to her own, the event came back to her now with a chilling clarity. A young woman had gone with her small child, to see her soldier husband off to his regiment in the same sort of weather conditions. They'd said their goodbyes and that was the last time the man saw his small family alive. For on the way home they were caught in a blizzard and not found until a week later when workmen dug their frozen bodies out of the snow. Although she had to keep telling herself that the weather last winter had been much more severe than this, the possibility of freezing to death filled her with such horror it kept Rachel struggling on. And remember why you're here too, she muttered, lifting one weary foot, then another. Surely she hadn't escaped from George's clutches just to die on a bleak country road.

Her resolve and step did falter slightly at the turnpike. Here she'd expected conditions to be better and had taken it for granted there'd be traffic, a waggon or carrier's cart from whom she could cadge a lift. But the road unfolded in either direction like a bolt of bleached linen, and was devoid of vehicles or any form of life. It's like being the only person in the world, Rachel thought and shivered. But still she tried not to let it depress her. Something would come along in a moment, and she'd be all right just as long as she kept moving.

She plodded on, glancing over her shoulder every now and then, certain it was only a question of time before transport of some description materialized. After all work didn't stop just because the weather was bad. But the road remained empty. Church bells resonating across the white wasteland finally told her why. It was the Sabbath and no sensible person would move his feet from his hearth today. Rachel gave up then. Never had she felt so desolate, so abandoned. Salty tears scoured the chapped skin of her cheeks and defeated by exhaustion, cold and hunger she began to stagger drunkenly.

She never knew, and neither did he, how she reached Jed's shop, what instinct for survival guided her there. Because by the time he opened the door to her, took one look at the state she was in and swept her up in his arms, Rachel was beyond caring about anything.

Chapter Ten

The possibility that Rachel might die did occur to Jed so he gave no thought to her modesty as he rapidly removed the sodden clothes and spread them out in front of the fire. His manhood had reacted in the way nature intended that first time he caught her unawares and naked by the river. But now he had only one purpose in mind and that was to see that there was no further deterioration in her condition. Unburdened by desire, he gently massaged her half-frozen body, his hands strong, life-giving. Only when he felt her soft skin begin to thaw under the easy manipulation of his fingers did he move to a drawer and pull out a nightshirt.

Then clasping her firmly he brought her up to sitting position, tugging the garment over her head and guiding her arms into the sleeves as if she were a child. From time to time he would call her name but there was no response. So laying her on the bed he gathered up all the blankets he could find and piled them on top of her. Sleep and warmth is what she needs, Jed thought, looking down at the pale features, that way the healing process would take its natural course.

Initially his only concern was to keep her alive so he hadn't wasted time wondering what had brought Rachel to his door. But as he sat by her bed he had time in which to deliberate on her seemingly foolhardly action. Only someone driven by desperation would have ventured out in such appalling weather conditions, he knew that. Someone in flight. But from whom? George? His father? Perhaps both. Jed only had to think of the Pedleys and his ire rose. By God how he hated them. They were destroyers, the pair of them, and they made him want to destroy too, to crush the very life out of them.

Rachel slept restlessly, tossing and turning and mumbling incoherently all the while. Once she sat up and with her eyes wide open, screamed, "No!" then fell back on the bed again. Although her pulse remained strong and her forehead cool, Jed grew anxious, wondering if he should call in the apothecary. After a time, though, the crisis passed, her breathing became less laboured, the bad dreams no longer troubled her and she settled into a deep sleep.

It was five o'clock when Rachel woke. Her body ached, her mouth was dry, her mind confused. She ran her tongue over her cracked lips, moved gingerly then opened her eyes. The room, which was lit only by firelight, was full of shadows and when she saw the dark figure of a man move towards her, terror filled her mind and she sat up with a jerk, pulling the blankets protectively around her.

"So you're awake?"

"Jed?" Her voice held a question but he heard the relief in it too.

"Why, who did expect it to be?" He sat down beside her and put a cup to her lips. "Here, drink this."

She took a sip of the hot tea before answering. "For a minute . . . I . . . I thought it was George."

"Was that who you were running from?"

Rachel nodded.

"I guessed it. What's that lump of primeval slime been up to now?"

"He . . . he came to my room last night . . . and tried to . . . tried to . . ." Shame made her stumble, ". . . to force himself on me," she managed to finish, then hung her head to hide the embarrassed flush that stained her skin.

Jed's lips narrowed into a thin line of disgust. "I'll

122

kill that bugger one of these days, so help me God I will."

Rachel's head shot up. "Oh you won't have to. I took care of him myself." She made the confession with pride.

"Are you telling me you killed him?" Jed didn't try to hide his astonishment.

"No, not quite, I just knocked him senseless with a brick," she said matter of factly.

"A brick?" Jed looked so totally bemused Rachel giggled and proceeded to fill him in on the details; George's savage attack, her own retaliatory measures and escape, omitting only the crude allegations he'd made about them both.

When she finished Jed threw back his head and laughed. "Good for you. It was a brave thing to do, though."

"I had no choice. It was self-defence. Me or him. Anyway he had it coming to him for all the beastly things he's done to me over the years. Mind you I did think I had killed him at first." She examined her fingernails, which were encrusted with blood then looked at Jed. "You don't think there's a chance I could have, do you?"

"With that thick skull? Not on your life. No he'll be around to plague us for a while yet, I shouldn't wonder."

But something else now begun to trouble Rachel. "You didn't mind me coming here, did you Jed? Only there was nowhere else I could go."

"Of course not," Jed answered gallantly, proud that Rachel trusted him enough to see his small room as a safe haven. Not that her problems were over. Just because she'd put a distance between herself and George, didn't mean that was the end of it. The Pedleys weren't people to let a matter rest. And they could call in the law, which would make matters awkward for him. Looking at it practically too, he had very little room and it was hardly proper for a young woman and young man to be seen residing under the same roof and in such close proximity. But what was the alternative? He couldn't throw her out on

123

the streets. No, for the time being at least, he had a penniless waif on his hands, and one who was probably very hungry. He stood up. "Now what about something to eat. Could you manage some bacon and potatoes?"

"Yes please."

"How many rashers?"

"Four."

Jed raised an eyebrow. "My you must be on the mend."

Not used to being waited on, Rachel felt she ought to offer to help. Except that her legs had very little strength and Jed appeared entirely capable anyway. So she watched him from the bed as he set the table, fried bacon and cut bread with the efficiency of a man well used to looking after himself. With her empty stomach the smell of frying bacon was almost unbearable and when Jed set the food down in front of her she had to restrain herself from falling on it and gobbling it down like turkey being fattened for Christmas.

It was Jed's opinion that problems solved themselves more easily on a full stomach than on an empty one, so he waited until they were drinking tea in front of the fire, before broaching the subject of Rachel's future. "Have you given any thought to what you're going to do now that you've left the Pedleys?"

"No. But I won't have trouble getting work, then I can rent a room." Rachel said confidently. "And I can work a frame, Robert learnt me."

"There are more stockingers than there are jobs at the moment. And women aren't always made welcome in frameshops, they're seen to be taking work away from men."

"Well there are plenty of farms needing hands or maid-servants, aren't there?" Rachel answered, knowing that if she didn't take a positive attitude her courage might fail her. "There's not much I can't turn my hand to. Then when I've got a bit of money behind me I might

124

move north to the cotton mills. I've heard the pay's good there."

"Oh you don't want to go all that way," Jed hastily interjected. He didn't like the sound of that at all. Rachel far away in another county where he might never see her again. "There are plenty of rich hosiers up in the Newarke with wives and daughters trying to adopt the manners and ways of gentry. I'm sure you'll get work in one of their houses."

"It might take me a day or two that's the trouble. So could I stay here, until I'm fixed up? I'm sure it wouldn't be for more than a couple of nights, and I'll sleep on the floor."

Against all his instincts and better judgement, Jed heard himself say, "Stay as long as you like," then wondered about sleeping arrangements.

It was a well attested fact that a man travelled more swiftly, and further, unfettered by domestic matters, so Jed had always fought shy of emotional involvement. He often congratulated himself on his ability to live a detached, monk-like existence, and now Rachel had come along to disturb these certainties. He was damned if he was going to be another George, but sleeping in and sharing a room with her was going to put a severe strain on his self-control.

Later, as he made up a bed on the floor, which he gallantly insisted he would sleep in, Rachel noticed again that his economy of movement spoke of a high degree of self-sufficiency. Did he have a sweetheart, she wondered and tried to imagine what she would be like. Well he would be able to take his pick amongst girls, so she'd be pretty, and educated, probably from a family of some standing in the town.

He looked up suddenly from tucking the blankets in, caught her watching him and smiled, a smile that made her hope that the paragon of a girl she'd imagined for him didn't actually exist.

For modesty's sake Jed undressed in the small scullery. When he came back, he extinguished the candle, wished her a chaste good-night, climbed between the blankets, and in spite of the hard floor, appeared to fall asleep immediately.

In the dark, listening to his regular breathing and with no one to reassure her, the bright confidence she'd maintained for Jed's sake deserted Rachel. Worries crowded in and she wondered what an earth we going to become of her. Supposing the Pedleys found her and dragged her back forcibly to Thatcher's Mount. Prosecuted her even, had her sent to prison for assaulting George. There was no doubt that the serpent would have already honed his own version of events into a fiction acceptable to the ears of his parents. She really needed to get away from the area, but she couldn't do that without money. Once she'd got that, she could make a fresh start. After all she was hardly likely to be missed. Sam would be upset and perhaps for a little while so would Susan and Robert. But she'd fade from their memory in time. Occasionally in the midst of some task that reminded them of her they might pause and say to each other, "I wonder whatever became of Rachel." But really if she lived or died was of no importance to anyone. Often she tried to imagine what it must be like to have parents, two people who'd invested time and love, who really cared. But it was beyond her comprehension that, to be loved unreservedly. Overwhelmed by a great yawning loneliness, tears of self-pity began to trickle down her cheeks. As she sniffed and wiped them away with the rough blanket, she was startled to hear Jed's voice.

"Why are you crying Rachel?"

"I'm not crying," she answered and started to sob loudly.

"Come on there's no need for that." Hard-headed, unemotional was how he saw himself but a woman's tears were his Achilles' heel and in the face of them Jed had often made avowals he'd afterwards regretted. Wrapping a blanket round himself, he lit a candle, padded to the bed and as he sat down, Rachel flung her head on his lap, letting the misery pour out of her. Tears were cathartic, he knew that, so he let her cry, stroking her hair and rashly making promises. "I know you're worried about your your future," he heard himself say, "but you mustn't be, I'll look after you."

Rachel gazed up at him. "Always?"

Tears shimmering on lashes, dark eyes full of gratitude were just too much for Jed and in the face of them his last vestige of self-preservation crumbled. "Yes, always," he answered rashly. "But now you must sleep."

"All right." Calmed by his reassurances, Rachel lay back and closed her eyes. She felt safe, protected. The Pedleys couldn't touch her now.

Jed covered her up, blew out the candle and he went back to his own hard bed. But it was now his turn to lie awake worrying and fretting. Dear God, he muttered to the ceiling in dismay, just what had he let himself in for.

She was being shaken. Stretching and yawning, Rachel slowly opened her eyes and in those brief, dislocated seconds between sleeping and waking, she saw Jed Fairfax standing over her and shot up in bed. "Jed? What are you doing here?"

Jed laughed. "It's where I live, remember?"

Oh yes, she remembered all right, with a sudden clarity that made her cringe. The tears and with them the promises exacted. She of all people, who despised that sort of conduct in women, had carried on just like Matilda.

"Here, drink this," said Jed, handing her a cup of tea. "The letter carrier will be here shortly so I've got to open the shop. But there's no need for you to hurry. Just take your time, get up when you want to."

Rachel took a quick sip of the hot strong liquid, then looking him straight in the eye, said firmly, "Jed, I'm sorry

127

I made a fuss last night, it was unfair of me. What I'm going to do today is look for a job then when I've got one, find myself a room to rent and trouble you no more."

"I keep telling you, jobs aren't easy to come by. And Robert and Susan, they'd want me to look after you, wouldn't they? Just imagine what they'd think, if I left you to roam the streets."

"You've done enough for me," Rachel answered stubbornly.

Jed shook his shoulders to express irritation, both at himself because he now appeared to be fighting to keep her under his roof and at Rachel for making him behave so irrationally. But he had made a promise and he liked to think of himself as a man of his word.

Deciding to ignore Jed's gloomy predictions about the job market, Rachel finished her tea and swung her legs out of bed, eager now to get on with the day. Optimism, that was what you needed, she thought. After all she was young and healthy. Suddenly the opportunities appeared limitless. Although of course there was the weather. That could hinder her search for gainful employment. However, for some time she'd been aware of a persistent sound of dripping. Now she listened more carefully. Yes, there it was, the gurgle of water in gutters. "It's thawing, isn't it?" she said to Jed. "Thank heavens for that. Now there's nothing to stop me."

"Nothing except great piles of slush and huge puddles. I hope your boots are up to it."

Rachel followed Jed's glance to where her boots were, propped on the fender. The cheap leather had dried hard and was cracking, while the soles and uppers had well and truly parted company. It was obvious to both of them that they were past mending or patching up. "Well they're all I've got, so they'll have to do. But as soon as I've had my first week's wages I'll go out and buy a new pair."

Jed was a fairly opinionated young man but even he knew

it would serve no purpose to destroy Rachel's buoyant mood with a further lecture on unemployment and its causes. So best let the matter rest, he thought. She'd find out for herself soon enough anyway. Though in many ways she'd been harshly treated by the Pedleys, she'd never had to fight for the essentials of life. A bed, food and a roof over her head had been something she'd taken for granted. She'd never had to elbow someone else out of the way to get the one and only job, probably never gone to bed with an empty belly. But there again she was so darned pretty who would dare deny her work and she could be lucky, find something immediately. With these hopes for her future, Jed left her then so that she could get washed and dressed. And when he looked round the door about half an hour later he wasn't surprised to see she had already gone.

The sun shone, the world sparkled and a breeze gently wrinkled the surface of puddles that mirrored a world turned upside down. In comparison with the arctic conditions of the weekend, the air felt almost balmy to Rachel. But snow did have an antiseptic, cleansing effect and hid the filth of the streets; the debris thrown from shops and houses, the night soil that still hadn't been cleared away. The country had its own strong smells but to Rachel the stench of towns was stomach-turning, and it so overpowered her this morning she had to press her hand against her nose or she would have retched.

Leicester lay low in the Soar valley and with the rapid thaw there was danger of basements and lower floors of houses flooding. So some householders and shopkeepers had already inserted sliding boards in their doorways as protection against such an eventuality. But Rachel herself found it difficult to avoid the water that dripped from the over-hanging eaves or the occasional lump of half melted snow that dislodged itself from a deeply sloping roof and slid with a thump on to the footways below. In the end, for safety's sake, she took to the middle of the street. But this was almost as hazardous, because as well as dodging between waggons and carts she also had to run the gauntlet of the bad tempered comments of the drivers for daring to get in their way. Here too her ill-clad feet squelched in horse droppings that had stained the snow the colour of tobacco, and before she'd even reached the end of the street her woollen stockings were not only wet through but had also acquired a rather pungent odour.

Prior to leaving Jed's, Rachel had quickly scanned the advertisements in the *Leicester Journal* and noted several addresses. One of them, a millinery and dressmaking business in the High Street, sounded quite hopeful, since several apprentices were required, and immediately too. She considered herself a fairly accomplished needlewoman and as the shop was nearby, Rachel decided to make it her first call. But she had never applied for a job, had no idea how she should conduct herself so by the time she had reached the shop her nerve had quite failed her.

She hovered uncertainly in front of its bow fronted window, read that the proprietress's name was Mrs Dumelow, stared at the solitary, but elaborately decorated bonnet displayed there. When there seemed to be no movement inside the shop, Rachel became a little more bold, and shading her eyes, peered in. But her hands fell quickly to her sides as a well-dressed woman brushed passed her and entered the shop. Immediately there appeared from behind a curtain a woman well past her first youth but of rather startling appearance. She had an abundance of auburn curls, rouged and patched cheeks and was bedecked in a pink satin gown that wouldn't have been out of place at an Assembly Rooms' ball. The conversation between Mrs Dumelow and her customer quickly became animated. Mrs Dumelow gesticulated wildly, her curls bounced, and her plump cheeks wobbled in an excess of emotion. Although Rachel couldn't hear a word of the conversation she guessed that the exchange was less than friendly. This was shortly confirmed when the customer turned and flounced out of the shop, banging the door violently.

The proprietress quickly followed her, calling down the street in shrill tones, "You'll pay me by the end of the month or else . . ." Leaving the threat unfinished, she turned to go back into her establishment, saw Rachel and blinked at her suspiciously. "Was there something?" she asked, staring at the girl's shabby clothes and tattered boots with an expression of haughty distaste.

"I've come about the . . . the job ma'am," Rachel managed to blurt out.

"Of all the impertinence!" Mrs Dumelow shrieked. "You? In my shop. I'm looking for respectable young women, not tramps. Now clear off before any of my customers see you. Go on, shoo! shoo!" Beady-eyed and malevolent, she advanced on Rachel, flapping her hands irritably, as if shifting a worrisome bee, so that the girl was forced to make a backwards, shamefaced retreat down the street, while several passers-by looked on in amusement.

Although Rachel knew she looked shabby, Mrs Dumelow's rudeness had made a great dent in her pride. She tried to comfort herself with the thought that she wouldn't have liked working for such a painted and powdered creature anyway. However she still approached the employment registry office near the Corn Exchange with a diminished self-confidence. And with every good reason. The skinny self-important youth behind the desk took one look at her and told her with a sneer in his voice that the position she'd been after as an under servant had already been filled.

It was no better at the Crown Inn. In fact the innkeeper laughed at her. "My advertisement was for a steady, middle-aged woman and you're just a spring chicken. And there's the whole of the cooking to do. Would you be up to it?"

"Course I would," Rachel answered stoutly.

She was a pretty little thing, thought the innkeeper, rubbing the stubble on his chin and eyeing her lasciviously. He could try her, see what she was like, then imagined his wife's reaction and had second thoughts. "I'm sorry me duck, I'd like to but . . ." He gave Rachel an apologetic shrug.

If Rachel had been a person to give up, she might have done so then, but she was determined not to go back to Jed's without employment of some kind. From what he'd said, she'd gathered there was little chance of her getting work as a framework knitter. But frameshops still needed winders and hose had to be seamed, she reasoned, as she plodded off down yet another grim back street. But even though she knocked on umpteen doors and enquired at even more warehouses, she couldn't persuade one hosier to take her on.

The soles of her boots were so thin that by late afternoon the cobblestones had chafed her feet raw and walking had become an agony. And her limbs still felt weak from her long trudge through the snow. So with the light going, tired and defeated, she hobbled back to the book shop.

Realistically Rachel knew she couldn't stay with Jed for long. Apart from the small scullery, there was no privacy for either of them, besides which tongues would soon start to wag. And anyway she wanted her independence, a place of her own, some money in her pocket. However, these small ambitions seemed a mile away as she let herself in through the back door. She'd flung off her shoes and was massaging her aching feet when she heard Jed wish the last customer good-night, pull down the blind and lock up.

"Well, how'd it go?" he asked, when he came through from the shop. But only out of politeness, because he already knew by the defeated slump of her shoulders that it had been a wasted day.

Rachel didn't even look up. "Nothing."

"Never mind, I've just sold a couple of books and they were rare so I got a good price. Tomorrow we'll celebrate by going out and buying you some shoes. Not a new pair," he went on when he saw her startled expression, "I couldn't run to that, but there's a woman who has a shop in Shambles Lane who sells good second-hand clothes so we could see what she's got."

Rachel shook her head. "It wouldn't be right. Anyway, you've done enough for me already."

"There are lots of things aren't right in this life young lady, but I don't consider buying you something you're desperately in need of to be one of them. If it makes you feel better you can pay me back when you're earning. And just look at it this way, with decently shod feet you might find that job a bit more quickly."

On any other occasion Rachel might have gone on disputing the rights and wrongs of a man buying her shoes, but she was defeated by fatigue. "All right but just as soon as I've got a job I'm paying you back."

"Done," he answered, although he knew from her tone, she resented his generosity.

At seven o'clock he got ready to go out. Although Rachel didn't ask, he told her he was going to a meeting and would be back about ten.

Rachel hadn't wanted Jed to see the real state of her feet, so she waited until he'd gone, then went and bolted the front and back doors. With time to herself, she sat down, pulled off her filthy stockings and examined the soles of her feet. As she'd suspected they were badly blistered and she touched the engorged sacs gingerly and with a sharp indrawing of breath. If she didn't do something about them right away, it was unlikely she'd be able to walk the following day let alone look for a job. Casting her eyes around the room she saw a cast iron pot high on a shelf. Hobbling over, she reached up for it, turned it upside down to remove the corpses of several spiders, then filled it with water and hooked it over the fire. She waited until it was steaming, then poured it into an enamel bowl and stripped off. Enjoying the luxury of hot water, she washed her hair first, then worked slowly and methodically down her body until she reached her dirty, blistered feet.

All water for household use had to be fetched from a pump further along the street near the Cross, and was too precious to waste. So Rachel found her stockings and submerged them in the murky water, kneading at them with her knuckles. A thick scum now floated over the surface and it was barely lukewarm. But she still wasn't done. Every part of her must be clean, she'd decided, and not until the mud splattered hems of her dress and worsted petticoat were also immersed in the water, scrubbed and wrung out, did she finally feel she reached her own required standard of cleanliness.

She was in Jed's rough calico nightshirt and kneeling in front of the fire, head down, the dark mane of hair draped forward over her face, when she heard the knocking on the back door and the handle being tried. Thinking it was Jed returned early, Rachel tossed her hair back and stood up, She was about to move through to the scullery, when she heard a voice that for evermore, whenever she heard it, would chill her blood. "Fairfax, come on open up. I want a word with you."

For a moment Rachel stood rigid, then her eyes swept wildly round the room searching for escape. A further pounding of fist on wood brought her to her senses and she found the presence of mind to extinguish the candle and scramble to the end of the bed. But crouched there, fingers in ears, eyes squeezed shut, she could still hear the banging and exhortions, to 'open up'. Dear God in heaven, Rachel thought, was she to be pursued by George for the rest of her life? After a short while, tired of the lack of response, she heard him move away. Thinking he'd given up, she dared to move from her cramped position, straightening her legs and moving her head to ease the tension in her neck and shoulders. But it soon started up again, the curses, the handle rattled so violently she thought the glass would break, but this time at the front of the shop.

But the gruff voice of a nightwatchman interceded between George and his violent tussle with the door. There was a sharp exchange of opinions then the sound of footsteps moving reluctantly away. But even when the arguing voices came back as a mere echo, Rachel was still too terrified to move. Because she was certain now George would return and like a dog on heat, vault the six foot high wall into the back yard.

And it did come again, as she'd known it would. Huddled in the corner, rocking backwards and forwards, teeth pressed hard against her knees to muffle her sobbing, she heard the rapping and a loud male voice demanding to be let in. "Rachel, it's me, Jed."

She lifted her head and listened. Jed? Relief flowed through her. "Jed!" She sobbed, "Thank God," tried to stand up but her limbs were still fettered by terror and she slumped back on the floor. At her next attempt she managed to haul herself up and drag herself to the door, making no effort to check her tears which came in great hiccuping sobs.

"Rachel, what on earth's the matter with you?" Jed asked as she opened the door and fell into his arms.

Her tears redoubled. "It's George . . . he's been here."

"Has he by Christ!"

"I thought he was going to break down the door," she sobbed into his shoulder.

With his arm round her waist, Jed supported her back into the small room and sat her down on the bed, and while he lit the candles, cursed at his stupidity in leaving her alone. He'd expected trouble, of course he had, but not quite so soon. H'ed imagined the flooding would have prevented George from getting through from Halby for at least a day. As he stirred together some hot water and brandy that he hoped might calm Rachel, he watched her. The tears had subsided to long, deep gulping shudders, but she was now raking her fingers through her long hair, and he saw in those compulsive repetitive movements something very disturbing. Here was a girl, he realized, nearly at her wit's end. Moved by a savage hatred of George, he made a silent avowal. One of these days I'll kill that evil specimen, so help me God I will.

Gently untangling the strands of hair from her fingers, he crouched in front of Rachel and placed the tankard of hot toddy in her hand. "Drink it," he ordered, "it'll make you feel better."

The brandy fumes were strong in her nostrils and as Rachel took a tentative sip she made a face. But to please Jed she persevered and managed to finish it. Any calming effect the alcohol might have had however, was offset by the throbbing over her left eye. Massaging her swollen lids she said listlessly, "I need a handkerchief."

"Here, let me." Pulling one from his pocket, Jed gently dabbed her eyes, noticing as he did that they were filling with tears again. "Please don't cry any more Rachel," he pleaded.

"I can't help it."

Her hopelessness called on all his reserves of pity and letting the handkerchief fall, he explored with his fingers the contours of her face. Aware of her stillness he allowed his hands to follow the graceful curve of her neck, until he could feel the small jutting bone at the top of her spine and her hair damp on his fingers. Overwhelmed by her soft womanliness he slowly drew her towards him, His heart was thumping wildly but he was impelled by something more powerful than reason and when she didn't resist, he leaned forward and kissed her on the mouth.

"Oh!" she exclaimed tremulously.

Emboldened he took her in his arms, but she started to

struggle, pushing her hands against his chest and shouting, "Let me go, let me go!"

Sick with shame, Jed's arms fell away and he stood up. He could feel himself shaking, and he pressed his hands together in an effort to control the tremors. He couldn't look at her and even in his own ears his voice was harsh and accusing when he spoke. "I'm sorry Rachel, but it's impossible, you can't stay here, you'll have to go, first thing tomorrow."

Chapter Eleven

The news that Bonaparte had escaped from Elba and landed in France with an armed force to reclaim the crown, earned itself barely half a paragraph in the *Leicester Journal* in mid-March. By the twenty-fourth, however, the editor, perhaps realizing the seriousness of his intentions, allowed the ex-Emperor over half a column, giving in some detail his exploits; the fact that he'd taken Grenoble and been welcomed with open arms in Lyons.

Since she wasn't a girl to concern herself with world affairs, these momentous event went unnoticed by Matilda. Much more real to her that day was the blemish on her chin. It appeared regular as clockwork when she had her ladies' trouble and she always fretted about it so much even her mother was inclined to lose patience with her.

"For goodness sake Matilda, it's a spot no bigger than a pin head. I can hardly see it."

"Well your sight must be failing then, mother, that's all I can say," Matilda answered coldly, picking up a small silver backed looking glass and poking at the the spot fretfully. She sighed, with a mixture of boredom and unhappiness, put down the mirror and took up her needlepoint. She hadn't seen Harry for over three weeks and was in almost total despair. She stabbed at the canvas viciously, almost hating him for daring to neglect her. Searching around for someone on which to vent her bad temper, she said, "Anyway, what's happened about that girl Rachel? Has she been found yet?"

"A description of her went in the paper but we've had no response, fortunately."

Matilda's needle was now poised in mid air. "Why do you say that? The ungrateful girl ran away, didn't she, whilst under Papa's guardianship. It would serve her right if she was caught and sent to prison."

"Come Matilda, no one in their right mind would run off in that weather, without a penny to their name, not unless they were desperate. And you know as well as I do, that George was forever pestering her. I'm reluctant to say this about my own son, but he was never able to provide a satisfactory explanation for that gash on his forehead, and from what information I could prise out of Sam, I've good reason to believe George went to Rachel's room that night. If we pursued the circumstances of her disappearance, there could be a scandal, so I've persuaded your father to let the matter rest."

"You always made far too much fuss of that girl."

"And I make no apology for it. I always tried to remember that she was a human being, something, unfortunately, the rest of my family refused to recognize."

Matilda shifted her bottom uneasily on her chair, surprised by her mother's sharp tone. "Well are we to get another girl? I need someone to help me with my toilet."

"Your father has a lot on his mind at the moment, Matilda. But no doubt when he can find the time he'll make a call on the overseer at the poorhouse and choose another girl. And like any new servant, she'll need training, so in the meantime if you really can't manage on your own, Polly can give you a hand."

"Oh God, not that imbecile."

"Matilda!"

Slightly ashamed, Matilda threw down her canvas. "I've had enough, I'm going out for a walk."

Yes do, it might improve your temper, Esther Pedley

wanted to say, but she bit on her tongue and instead asked serenely, "Where dear?"

"I don't know, do I?" Matilda answered irritably. "Perhaps I'll go and see Jane. She can bore me with her talk about horses, it'll make a change from being bored here."

Understanding the reason for her daughter's misery, Esther Pedley listened to the door slam with a heavy heart. If only she could introduce her to some more young men, it might possibly take her mind off Harry. In desperation she'd even suggested to George that he bring some friends home for the weekend, but he'd just laughed at the idea and said that two days of Halby would have any friend of his dead with boredom. She had two children who'd been denied nothing, clothes, money, education and yet who were dissatisfied and unhappy. So where had it all gone wrong? She wished she knew. With a sigh, she put down her needlework and smoothed her hair. She would go and talk to Susan in the kitchen. Susan's common sense could always restore her to some sort of serenity. And at the same time she could find out from her if there was any news of Rachel.

As she walked into the stable yard, Matilda guessed from the affectionate tone of her voice that Jane must be talking to her hunter, Hercules. He was a large beast who rather terrified Matilda, but now as he stood in his box being lovingly groomed by his mistress, he looked as docile as a lamb.

"Do you always talk to yourself, Jane?" asked Matilda, creeping up on her friend.

Jane started and turned round. "I wasn't talking to myself," she answered defensively, "I was talking to Hercules."

"Well that's the same thing, isn't it? After all he's hardly likely to answer you back," Matilda pursued, intent on needling as many people as possible that day.

"Oh shut up, Matilda!" Jane returned to brushing Hercules'

140

glossy chestnut coat. Then aiming to get her own back said slyly, "Are you coming out with the hunt tomorrow?"

"You know I'm not. I hate hunting."

"Pity, Harry's coming."

"How do you know?"

"The Squire told me. But he's not stopping. Apparently he's off to a very grand ball in Nottingham that same evening."

Because of Harry's often callous disregard for her, Matilda's emotions had become as sensitive as an exposed nerve in a tooth during the past few months. But today after an inward struggle with her pain at this latest act of perfidy she managed to say, "Perhaps I'll come out with you after all then."

"You had a bad fall last time, do you remember."

"I just won't take any fences that's all."

"Will George come?" Jane asked casually.

"I expect so, if he's home. You know George, he enjoys watching any animal being torn to pieces. Cocks, rats, dogs, it doesn't bother him what it is."

"That's rather an unkind thing to say about your brother, Matilda."

"Oh yes, I'd forgotten, you're rather sweet on him, aren't you?"

Jane hid her blushes in Hercules' shoulder. "Don't be so beastly, Matilda, just because, you haven't seen Harry for a couple of weeks."

"Three actually. Look, there's something I want to show you. Turn round," she ordered as her friend ignored her and went on grooming the gelding.

Reluctantly Jane ceased her labours and turned to face Matilda.

"There's a spot on my chin, can you see it?"

Jane studied her friend's unblemished skin. "Ooh . . . yes," she said cruelly and stepped back as if she might be similarly contaminated.

141

"Can you really?" Matilda wailed.

"I said I could, didn't I? And by to tomorrow I reckon it'll be full of pus."

"I hate you Jane Dobbs," Matilda retorted and stomped off.

Jane retaliated with, "Bitch!" but not loud enough for Matilda to hear because she was, after all, the parson's daughter. She watched her friend's departure with relief. Matilda's moods were hard to cope with at times, and she could only think or talk about Harry. Besides she didn't share her friend's blinkered infatuation for that young man and had grown weary of hearing his virtues endlessly discussed. Much better to give your love to a horse. He would never be untrue, utter harsh words, cause you pain. "Would you, my love?" she asked the uncomprehending Hercules, then wrapping her arms around his neck, Jane kissed him with great tenderness.

The Hunt was already there. Men, women, children, panting excited hounds, were all gathered in front of the Weavers' Arms, when Matilda rode into the village with her father and George the following morning. It wasn't a smart hunt like the Quorn or Belvoir, for the most part it was just a raggle taggle of prosperous yeoman farmers hunting over their own land, with people like the vicar, the Squire and Harry, who was of the few men wearing scarlet, adding a touch of class. A large group of villagers, who had a noticeably sullen air about them, stood around observing the pack and as the stirrup cup was handed round an anonymous voice shouted provocatively, "God bless the Squire and his relations, and keep us in our proper stations."

"Who said that?" barked the Squire, swinging round on his saddle and staring into the blank features of people whose faces had acquired a leaner, hungrier look over the past few months.

142

"Yes remember, 'tis our land you'll be riding over this morning, land you stole," someone else called out, a woman this time.

"The downright insolence . . ." Looking as if he was about to have a seizure, Francis Bennett swung round again, and lifted his whip threateningly. Daring him to use it, the crowd took a step forward, closing in on the riders. Apart from the scraping of the horses' hooves, and the occasional rattle of a bit, a silence had descended, but it was an ugly, threatening silence of landowner lined up against the dispossessed.

Matilda had just noticed, with a tremor of fear, that some of the men were carrying staves and pitchforks, when Harry moved over to his uncle's side. He didn't say a word, just put his hand in his pocket, extracted, copper, silver and gold and threw it to the crowd, and in the undignified scuffle that followed the hunt was able to move off.

Unnerved by the incident, Matilda made sure she kept well to the front, jostling to ride beside Harry. "You showed great presence of mind there, Harry," she said, gazing up at him admiringly.

"Yes, could have been nasty," he agreed. "Still I might be dealing with nastier things soon."

"What do you mean?"

"Haven't you heard, Boney's on the loose and with an army too."

"Are you talking about war?" asked Matilda, and felt a sickening lurch in her stomach.

"Could be." Harry lowered his voice. "Listen, meet me next Friday night in the usual place, it might be our last chance."

"I'll try Harry but it's not always easy," answered Matilda, although she knew as long as she had two legs to carry her, she would get there somehow.

"Good girl." He smiled, then as the pack picked up the scent of a fox he was off, leaving Matilda to trail well to the

143

the rear with some of the younger children. She rembered her own initiation into the hunt. How excited she'd been, a miniature adult in her new outfit and confidently perched on her dappled pony, Rufus. Until the kill. Although she had no idea what he was going to do, she'd still recoiled from her father when he'd come up to her, holding the beautiful golden brush dripping with blood. Then horror of horrors, he'd lifted it to her face and smeared the still warm blood down both her cold cheeks. "You've been blooded now Matilda," her father had informed her proudly. But she hadn't been listening. Instead the still, frosty air was filled with her hysterical screams, which had only stopped when her indignant, humiliated father slapped her soundly. Weeks of nightmares had followed and although at her father's insistence, she continued to follow the hounds, since that day she'd always been on the side of the fox and contrived never to be in at the kill.

Although she could hear an occasional blast from the horn in the distance, Harry and the rest of the field had gone. But Matilda was happy enough. She'd achieved what she'd set out to do, spoken to Harry, made a tryst with him. And she saw no point in risking her neck by taking a fence. So long before the hunt had drawn blank at several coverts, she'd turned her horse round and trotted briskly home.

Matilda read the *Leicester Journal* with rather more interest the following Friday than she had on the previous one. In fact she snatched it from her father's hand as soon as he came through the door. "Let me have a look," she said, then as her father expostulated at her lack of manners and demanded to have it back, Matilda gave him a quick kiss. "I won't be a moment, Papa."

Slightly mollified by the kiss, her father said gruffly, "All right, but don't be long. I can't imagine what all the interest is though, you never usually look at a newspaper."

144

But Matilda already had it spread out on the table and was reading with a troubled expression that Bonaparte had entered Paris. She read on with a heavy heart and strong sense of foreboding that he'd been denounced by the allies as an enemy of civil and social order, that vast military preparations were going on and the Duke of Wellington was expected in Brussels. The black typeface jumped in front of her eyes as the full significance of those words were brought home to her. Military preparations. That could only mean Harry. He was bound to have to go. She looked towards her father, who was stuffing his pipe with tobacco. "Might there be a war, Papa?" she asked, gripping the table and preparing herself for the answer she so feared.

Her father bent foward to light a taper from the fire. "Let's hope so, business might pick up then."

"How can you say such a thing?" Matilda burst out, stamping her foot angrily, and already visualizing Harry, his tunic soaked with blood, lying dead in some foreign field.

Her father stopped puffing on his pipe and stared at her with a hard expression. "If you read the papers a bit more you would have seen for yourself that the stockingers have been petitioning us for higher wages." Joseph Pedley snorted. "I don't know where they think it's coming from. And you're always wanting new gowns and bonnets, aren't you? Aren't you?" he repeated more loudly, when Matilda didn't reply. He waited for her silent nod, then went on, "Well you canna pluck feathers from a toad. Money's got to be earned my girl, sommat you might find out for yourself sooner than you think, if the hosiery trade don't improve."

"Are we . . . you're not going bankrupt, are you Papa?" Oh the humiliation, the shame of it if he were. Their names in the paper, Papa in prison, their home and belongings auctioned, while she and her mother were left to survive as best they could in one mean room in Leicester.

Her father turned in his chair, giving her his full attention.

145

"Let's just say this, missy, find yourself a husband, just in case."

"I'm trying to, aren't I?" Matilda wailed.

"And you'd do well to look to Squire Bennett, not that penniless nephew of his, he'd never be able to keep you."

"I loathe and detest Francis Bennett," Matilda screamed, then rushed from the room and upstairs where she flung herself on the bed, sobbing into her pillow, "Harry, Harry, please . . . please, don't leave me."

Being in love with Harry, Matilda had come to see over the months, was like being adrift in a stormy sea without a compass. She just didn't know where she was with him and although when she asked – and only then – he said he loved her, she knew what her father said was true, and the possibility of marriage seemed as remote now as when they'd first met. Sometimes she even regretted what she saw as her Great Sacrifice, feeling that if she'd held out, she might have maintained a stronger hold over him. But Matilda knew it was far too late for any such regrets, besides which she herself was well and truly ensnared by her own needs.

Sex had come as a surprise and delight to her and during the winter months, when it had been too cold for them to meet in Rooks Spinney, Matilda had become adept at finding places of assignation. In fact she came to find it altogether a most enjoyable sport. The plotting and scheming, and the risks, had only heightened the pleasure of their lovemaking. On one occasion she'd slipped round to the back door at Trent Hall when the Squire was having his afternoon nap and cook was out, and Harry had taken her there and then, abruptly, up against the kitchen wall, so that as he pushed into her she could feel her bottom being grazed against the cold, rough stone. Another time it had been on the floor in the church, cramped between the pews. Walking home afterwards, enjoying the sensation of Harry's fluid running

146

down between her legs, she remembered their noisy excesses and had to smother a giggle as she imagined the vicar's expression of astonishment, then disgust if he'd walked in and found them there, clothing in disarray, arms and legs entwined. And now the excitment was to come to an end, her life was in ruins, and all because of that loathsome Corsican *parvenu*. Harry was being taken from her, perhaps for months, perhaps, although she hardly dared consider the possibility, forever.

Towards the end of April troops received orders to hold themselves in readiness and as Matilda slipped across the fields to meet Harry for the last time, she kept telling herself she mustn't cry, must try not to think that tonight might be the last time she'd spend in Harry's arms. He hated tears, a fuss as he called it, and was inclined to turn away coldly if she ever showed any sign of creating a scene.

"Hold me tight, Harry," she whispered as she collapsed against him in the dark. Feeling his warmth, she wanted to melt into him, to capture the essence of him to console her in the empty months ahead.

"I want us to make love unhampered by clothes tonight. I want to feel you completely naked against me," Harry murmured and began unbuttoning her dress.

"But supposing someone should come?" Matilda said uncertainly, not out of any sense of modesty but because a poacher could always chance upon them and it would be easier to flee with clothes on rather than completely naked.

Harry laughed. "The only people who'll come will be you and me, my love, several times, if I know anything about it," he said a trifle coarsely.

Matilda giggled and protested no further. They took their time discarding their garments, each removing an article of clothing from the other, until they stood nude as Adam and Eve before the fall, their pale, anglo-saxon skins luminous

147

in the darkness. When he laid her down on the blanket, Matilda wasn't aware of the chill April air, the hard ground, but only of Harry's slow and leisurely exploration of her body. He'd never shown her such tenderness before and she sensed that he too was savouring these last quiet hours together, perhaps to remember amidst the putrifying smell of carnage on some blood soaked battlefield. And she knew she would never forget, not until her last breath, his naked muscular soldier's body against hers, the smell of dank earth, the stars through the trees. His thrust was slow at first but then their rhythmic moving together became more frenzied, increasing to an explosion of tension as they climaxed, then lay panting together in happy, fulfilled exhaustion.

"Come here, my love," said Harry and drew Matilda into his arms. Her frantic adoration irritated him at times but he had to admit his tumbles with her had been some of the best ever. Watching the changing emotions on her face as they made love then her long, wild cry at the end, made him feel powerful, omnipotent. "I'm going to miss you, Tilda, do you know that." He offered this information with a sincerity that surprised him.

She didn't say anything but he could feel her warm, silent tears on his chest. He was so certain of her feelings, he'd often deliberately neglected her in the past and, regretting now the way he'd trifled with her emotions, Harry was tempted to throw caution – and fortune – to the winds and ask her to marry him. But he quickly curbed such weak, perilous feelings. His financial situation was desperate and he could only be available to the highest bidder.

But the next day in a sentimental gesture, Harry had gone into Leicester, before joining his regiment, to consult a lawyer. Although he hadn't greeted the news of Bonaparte's escape with quite the same enthusiasm as his fellow officers, Harry was consoled by reports that Brussels was an even gayer town than London. All society had apparently taken itself off there; both the *demi-monde* and *beau-monde*, and by all accounts it was impossible not to have a good time.

However, Harry had a premonition that in any future engagement with the French, his luck would run out. He had no wish to die but viewed it with the fatalistic detachment of a professional soldier and made sure his affairs were in order. He had very little to leave anyone, just his gold repeater watch which somehow or other had always managed to avoid being pledged or sold, plus a small private income. So he'd given instructions in his newly drawn up will that his batman should have his watch and personal effects, Matilda what money there was. For there was no one else he wished to have it. His mother had been dead so long she was no more to him than the faint smell of lavender in a sick room, and since his father was a cold, unloving man who, when his wife died, had packed him off to boarding school, where he'd been flogged for the slightest misdemeanour, he had no wish for him to benefit from his death. That left his brother Gerald, ten years older than he was, pious and dessicated, but who'd determinedly, and to the detriment of his wife's health, sired eight children, just to make sure Harry wouldn't get his hands on the estate.

Having concluded his business to his satisfaction, Harry was standing on the step of the lawyer's office in Friar Lane, his mind wandering this way and that, thinking, would it rain; should he have stuffed carp, beefsteak and oyster pie or boiled mutton and capers for dinner; how was he to fill his time until the the Post Coach left at midnight, when he saw Rachel. At least he thought it was her, because the girl had already turned the corner into Hotel Street.

Calling, "Rachel, Rachel," he raced after her. Although he'd picked up pieces of information here and there, Harry had never dared to show too much interest in her disappearance. He had his suspicions, of course, guessed George was implicated in some way but although he'd tried to nudge

149

Matilda into a disclosure, she'd remained surprisingly tight-lipped about the whole incident. Usually, once a woman was out of his sight, he could hardly remember her name so he'd been disconcerted to find Rachel frequently in his thoughts over the past few weeks.

Harry was now certain the girl was Rachel by the way she proceeded in a zigzag fashion, down Cank Street and into Cheapside as if trying to throw him off. Exasperated by her elusiveness, he called out "Rachel," again and this time she hesitated then stopped and turned around but with a reluctance that irked him.

"It is you then," Harry said, then paused to draw breath. "I thought I might be accused at any moment of accosting a stranger."

Her skin flushed pink but she answered politely, "Good day to you Captain Bennett."

"Why didn't you stop when I called the first time?"

"I was in a hurry. I've got to get back to my place of work."

"Where is that?"

Rachel waved her hand vaguely. "A few streets from here."

While they talked, Harry studied her features intently. Although she looked shabbier, her beauty was undimmed and he was jolted again by a strange and troublesome feeling almost akin to tenderness. It was like a persistent itch, which no matter how much you scratched, continued to irritate. To his relief though these uncomfortable emotions were quickly superseded by more basic desires. He'd often wondered if George had beaten him to it but her face still had an unawakened, virginal quality and Harry reacted to it instantly. Because what was denied him he must possess.

"I'm going to the Continent to fight, Rachel, this is my last night in Leicester, can you see me?"

Rachel stepped back from him and her face had taken on a cornered look. "No, I'm sorry. And I must go."

But as she turned to walk away Harry gripped her wrist, forcing her to turn and look at him. "Well at least talk to me for a few minutes. Just think, Rachel, I could be killed. You'd never see me again then. Perhaps that wouldn't bother you though. But I did hope you liked me, just a little bit." His blue eyes sought her dark ones and as he'd hoped, Rachel responded to the tragic expression in them.

"Oh I do," Rachel innocently assured him.

"Well you could prove it by coming and having a tankard of ale with me at least."

Rachel hesitated. He still had hold of her wrist and to break away from him in the middle of a crowded thoroughfare would have involved an unseemly tussle. "Yes, all right, but only for a short while, the wife of the man I work for is very sick and I don't like leaving her."

He hid a look of triumph behind his dark lashes. She was about the most desirable creature he'd ever met in his whole life . . . if he could just get her up to his room, half an hour would be long enough. "We'll go to the Bell Inn, that's where I'm staying until the coach leaves."

Aware of her own shabby appearance, Rachel kept several paces behind as she followed Harry into the tavern. It was too dark and noisy inside for anybody to pay them much attention. Nevertheless, she was relieved to find herself being led by Harry to the far corner of the tap-room, away from curious eyes, and where a few old men played dominoes. Even so, the hefty serving wench who came to take their order, looked at Rachel, then the handsome officer and made her own assessment of the situation and Rachel felt herself shrivel under the implication that in the girl's eyes, she was nothing more than a common harlot.

Rachel was becoming increasingly tired of the way she was perceived by the world, and by the way she was used and abused by the people in it and she wanted to reach out and strike the girl, hard, across her podgy cheeks. Except that Harry was beguiling her with one of his most dazzling smiles and ordering food for them both. "Two tankards of ale," he said to the girl, "and a couple of plates of cold beef, cut from the sirloin."

"Thank you Captain," the serving wench simpered, then giving Rachel a final hostile stare, she hurried off.

"You shouldn't have ordered food for me, I won't have time to eat it. I told you, I should be getting back. I only came out to get some physic for my mistress."

"So who is your mistress now?" asked Harry, turning to Rachel and giving her his full attention.

"I'm employed by a hosier here in town."

"And what do you do?"

"It would take less time to tell you what I don't do. I look after his wife, who is confined to bed and expecting her fifth baby soon. Then there are the four other childer to attend to, and when there's a free moment I'm expected to go down to the frame-shop and wind yarn or seam hose. I get very tired."

"I can see you do," Harry said, rubbing the dark smudges under her eyes with the ball of his thumb.

Rachel jerked her head away from him. "Don't do that."

Oh dear, thought Harry, setbacks. "I'm sorry. Look here's some food, tuck in," he said, as the serving girl banged two large plates in front of them. Although she ate more with the manners of a lady then a serving maid, he could see she was hungry. It must be some damned awful place she's working at, he thought. She's probably even more exploited than she was at the Pedleys. "And the wages at this place, are they good?"

"Mr Brewin, my master, promised me four shillings a month and my keep, but I've haven't seen a penny of it yet."

Harry indolent, self-centred could rarely be roused to anger but now he felt a great surge of fury and it was directed at the unknown Mr Brewin. "You must have wages. I'm coming back to that place with you and demand he pays you."

Rachel stopped eating and put her hand on his arm. "Oh no, you can't do that. You see they don't know who I really am. I goes by the name of Abigail Smith there. And they need me, particularly Mrs Brewin and the little un's, I couldn't leave, not just yet. And it's a roof over my head. It's that or the poorhouse."

Seeing here an opportunity to slip in the question that troubled him for so long, Harry said quietly, "Why did you run away from the Pedleys, Rachel?"

Rachel threw him a quick frightened glance. "You won't tell them you saw me, will you?"

"Of course I won't," Harry reassured her, although he knew that if they were really desperate to find her they could do so without much difficulty.

"It was George, h . . . he pestered me."

"In what way?"

But her expression had become blank, withdrawn and Harry knew he was being told not to pry any further. Left to draw his own conclusions, he had to admit rather guiltily his own intentions were hardly more creditable than George's, although he would never sink to anything as despicable as rape. But seduction . . . well that was an entirely different matter, he thought, absent-mindedly stroking Rachel's hand.

Why can't men leave me alone, thought Rachel pulling her hand away. I never flirt with them or throw them bold glances like some girls do. Even Jed, she thought bitterly, who she thought she could trust, had proved to be no different from the others. And yet surely she had a basic right to go unmolested by the opposite sex. She remembered that last night, how frigidly polite to each other she and Jed had been

153

as they moved around the cramped room trying not to touch. Jed had apologized later of course, said he'd spoken in haste when he asked her to leave, said she could stay until she found a situation. But her own confused feelings had made that impossible and so she'd left.

Fortune, she supposed, had been on her side when she'd come upon Jack Brewin later that morning, leaning against the door of his house with four small girls clinging to his trouser leg.

With a quick glance she'd ascertained there was a frame-shop at the back of the house, then without much hope had asked, "Do you need any hands mister?"

"What can you do?" the man she presumed to be the father of the children asked.

"Anything. Cook, clean, work a frame. And I'm very good wi' childer," she wisely added, as she saw four pairs of eyes weighing her up.

"And what about an ailing wife? To add to my problems I've got one of those upstairs too. And just about ready to drop another kid, God help me. Could you manage her d'you think? If you can, the job's yours."

And that had been the easiest part of it, being taken on, because she'd worked like a galley slave ever since.

Rachel glanced at Harry. It was all right for him, she thought resentfully, and felt a sudden wave of anger at the injustice of life. "Your kind don't know what it's like to have nothing, to wonder where your next meal's coming from. Will you have a roof over your head that night? Can you afford to have your shoes mended? That's something you've never had to cope with, is it Captain Bennett?"

Taken aback by her outburst, but with no ready answer to her questions, Harry, carelessly and unthinkingly, felt in his pocket and drew out five gold coins, which he placed in a pile on the table. "Look, here's five guineas, enough to tide you over. Leave that place."

Mortified, Rachel stood and with an indignant sweep of the hand, scattered the coins, which rolled away over the sawdust floor to be quickly snatched up. "How dare you!" Her face was scarlet with indignation. Everyone in the tavern would assume she was a whore now. "I'm going, let me past please."

But Harry was hanging on to her skirt like a child. "I'm sorry, Rachel, it was thoughtless of me I know, but there was no ulterior motive I can assure you."

The look Rachel gave him was withering. "Oh no? Shall I tell you something? There are times when I hate all men." Although she had heard plenty of bad language in her time it wasn't part of her normal repertoire. But an incandescent anger freed her of any inhibitions and the obscenities tripped easily off her tongue. "You're bloody selfish bastards, every one of you!" she hurled at the astonished Harry, then tugging her skirt from his grip, she strode off. A silence had descended in the tap-room. Even seasoned drinkers ceased their quaffing to enjoy what they imagined was a lovers' tiff and watch Rachel's straight-backed, enraged departure, followed by Harry looking uncommonly discomposed.

There was something grandly operatic about the way people made a path for her to the door and as Rachel swept out, she found herself bestowing upon the customers a queenly nod. Immediately she'd passed, the crowd closed in on her again, impeding Harry's progress, and she could still hear him calling, "Rachel, wait for me," as the door swung shut behind her.

But she refused to lessen her pace and hurrying from him, Rachel found it difficult to understand why, when just a few months ago, she was devising all sorts of schemes to catch his eye. How absurd she must have seemed to him, how obvious, how childish. It made her blush to think of it. But circumstances had matured and toughened her and now she was more conscious of the weakness of his chin than the blueness of his eyes.

However, Rachel wouldn't have been human if she hadn't been flattered by the attentions of a Captain in the Dragoons. So although she could see through his charm, when he caught up with her and offered an abject apology for his crass behaviour, she graciously allowed him to walk with her a little way.

When they reached Church Gate, Rachel held out her hand. "Goodbye Captain Bennett," she said in her formal way.

"Harry, you must call me Harry," he murmured and taking the small, work-scarred hand in his, clasped it to his breast in a theatrical gesture. "Listen to how my heart beats for you Rachel. Surely you wouldn't be so cold and heartless as to deny a soldier, perhaps about to die for his country, just one small kiss."

Rachel shivered. "Please, don't talk about dying."

"Would it grieve you, never to see me again?" Harry asked, gazing at her steadily and depending on his blue eyes to weave their sexual spell.

Forcing herself to look away, Rachel stared at the cobblestones. "Of course it would," she mumbled.

Harry drew her closer and put his forefinger under her chin. "You said you liked me. Perhaps you even care for me a little too?"

His voice was low, persuasive, thrilling, his lips hardly an inch away.

Rachel forgot her suspicions as she gazed into the compelling blue eyes. Her heart was acting queerly and she felt frightened, yet excited. "I like you . . . a lot," she admitted.

"Prove it by letting me kiss you then."

"All right, but only there," Rachel said primly and pointed to her cheek.

"One chaste kiss, I promise," said Harry, and pressed

his lips against her flushed cheek. Then, with some clever manoeuvering, he found her mouth, soft, sweet and not altogether surprised. Her response was shy, uncertain but she didn't draw away and Harry was just about to gather her up in his arms, when there were footsteps and voices. She immediately sprung away from him and Harry silently cursed the two men at that moment walking towards them.

"Good-afternoon, Rachel, Captain Bennett," said Jed, lifting his hat as he passed.

Rachel kept her gaze fixed on the wall and didn't reply. She waited until Jed and the man he was with had turned the corner, then in spite of Harry's attempt to prolong their farewell and a plea for just one more kiss, she bade him a brief goodbye and fled.

Chapter Twelve

Her immediate reaction at being caught in Harry's arms by Jed had been shame and embarrassment in equal measure, although after a few minutes Rachel was asking herself why. After all what was her crime? A kiss, no more than that, and hardly any business of Jed's.

Besides what about his own companion? A rough-looking, swaggering young man if ever she'd seen one. In the awkwardness of the moment she hadn't paid much attention to him, but even a fleeting glance told her he was someone who spelt trouble. There was also something vaguely familiar about the face and it exasperated Rachel that she couldn't immediately put a name to it. When she did it brought her up short with an agitated indrawing of breath. That was it! James Towle.

Good Lord, she thought, was there no limit to Jed's reckless behaviour. Certainly James Towle was not a person, if you valued your good name, to be seen in company with. A man of extremely dubious character, he'd been well known for years as a trouble maker. But his notoriety – and bravura swagger – rested on the fact that he'd recently been acquitted at the Assizes after a Luddite raid and it was the opinion of many that he was fortunate not to have been hanged.

Rachel's long-held suspicion that Jed had allowed himself to be drawn into that dangerous and murky world of secret oaths and blackened faces, now stiffened into certainty and made her fear for his future.

It had been about four years earlier, after three failed

harvests, falling wages and with a quarter loaf of wheaten bread reaching one shilling and eight pence, that she had first seen a handbill posted up in the village cautioning against framebreaking and spelling out the consequences of such action, which was punishable by death. A reward of fifty pounds for information that would lead to the conviction of a Luddite was also offered. When she'd put her puzzled question to Robert as to who, or what, a Luddite was, he'd been surprisingly uncommunicative. "I don't know nowt about them lass and it would be better if you didn't neither, for it could get you into a deal of trouble."

Since then Rachel had learnt plenty about them because their exploits had become part of the folklore of many counties, stretching from the Midlands to Yorkshire.

Petitions by desperate stockingers to Parliament and master hosiers to stop payment by 'truck', the system of paying wages with goods rather than money, adopted by the more unscrupulous employers, had fallen on deaf ears. So had their pleas to have frame rents and the taking on of unapprenticed labour regulated. It was a crass, short-sighted attitude: this failure to recognize their distressed conditions. Hunger and bitterness together are highly combustible forces. With nothing to lose, the stockingers' anger erupted into violence. Ill-considered it might have been, but soon well-organized gangs, anonymous and terrifying, and often in different villages on the same night, were forcing their way into workshops, removing jack-wires and smashing to pulp frames of unpopular hosiers. The Midlands was in turmoil and the authorities, with the guillotine still echoing in their ears, called in the Dragoons.

Unlike Sheepshead, where twenty frames had been destroyed in one night, Halby had escaped the destructive blows of the great hammers called Enochs. Rachel never understood why, since Joseph Pedley owned most of the

159

frames and there could be few men more unpopular than he was.

Because the majority of people were connected in some way with framework knitting, there was a general sympathy with their cause. But as well as hammers, many Luddites carried pistols and muskets. It also became an umbrella under which other crimes were committed, an excuse to settle old scores; rob and murder, even. For it, men had been transported and hanged and it had become an altogether bloody affair. It was known too that the government had a network of informers and spies prepared to fan rumour for financial gain. Incautious behaviour could soon land a person in gaol.

And Jed appeared to lack that streak of self-preservation necessary to operate outside the law, which made Rachel feel his days of freedom might be numbered. Now she wanted to rush after him with a warning to trust no one otherwise she might soon be praying for his soul.

But she was already in Church Gate and without a ready excuse for her long absence, she knew she daren't turn back. And Jed was hardly the sort of person who would welcome interference in his affairs. Besides, she thought, if he was involved in illegal activities he obviously felt strongly enough about them to consider it worth taking the risk, and nothing she said was likely to change his mind.

As Rachel turned into Butt Close Lane, she heard St Margaret's clock strike three and realized, with a sinking heart, that she'd been gone on a simple errand for well over an hour. An explanation would be demanded from Mrs Brewin. But she had none to give. And lies still didn't come easily to her even though she'd had plenty of practice lately, what with having to invent a new background for herself and changing her name.

The Brewin house was three storeyed and had bulging walls of lathe and plaster. The elongated upper windows showed that the top floor must have once been home to several knitting frames. On this top floor was also the small room in which Rachel slept. From her window she could see directly into the Great Meeting burial ground with its grassy mounds and the grey slate headstones. Sometimes when she felt she couldn't cope any longer with four quarrelsome children, she would take herself off there and stretching out under a tree, savour its tranquility.

Now as she reached the house, the walls seemed to vibrate with the screams of children locked in deadly combat. It was a situation that had become exhaustingly familiar to Rachel over the past weeks and she'd hardly got the door open before two small figures threw themselves upon her, each protesting vehemently about the other.

"Whatever is the matter?" she exclaimed as she tried to extricate herself from their clutching fingers and at the same time dump the shopping down on the kitchen table.

"She bit me!" four-year-old Lily sobbed, holding out her small plump arm for Rachel to inspect.

And indeed the skin had been punctured so deeply by sharp teeth, blood had been drawn and the arm was beginning to swell. "Did you really do that, Rose?" Rachel asked angrily, pulling Lily protectively towards her.

"Well she kicked me, look." Rose, hardly a year older, extended a leg for her inspection. This was bruised and swelling too.

Her sympathy for both children evaporated. "I'm tired of your perpetual quarrels. Now run along, I've got see how your mama is."

The bedroom when she entered it was stuffy, and the heavy dark oak furniture, low ceiling and small window, gave the room an oppressive air. As a reluctant concession to his sick wife, Jack Brewin allowed a fire in the room, the only one outside the kitchen. But it was a sullen thing which

161

no matter how often Rachel attacked it with the bellows, she could never persuade to burn with any real warmth. Mrs Brewin, who lay in the large half tester bed clutching a small dog in her arms, appeared to be asleep. This was a relief to Rachel who otherwise might have been called upon to explain her prolonged absence. Unfortunately, as she tiptoed towards the bed, the dog, a smelly creature of indeterminate breed, growled and bared its teeth and Mrs Brewin opened her eyes.

"Now, now, sweetheart, don't be grumpy, it's only Abigail come to see your mummy. She's been an awfully long time too hasn't she, my love."

Rachel, who occasionally had trouble with the name she'd adopted for herself, glanced over her shoulder, looking for this stranger called Abigail. Then remembering it was herself, she blustered, "Mr Randall had run out of your physic so I had to go all the way up to Belvoir Street and the chemist there kept me waiting ages."

"I don't believe Abigail's telling me the truth, do you pumpkin?"

The dog, who went by the name of Caesar, disdained to answer.

In an attempt to change the subject Rachel asked quickly, "Would you like me to make you up a dish of caudle before I give the children their lessons?"

Mrs Brewin, who found making any decision an exhausting business, sighed. "What do you think Caesar? Shall we have some caudle?"

Rachel ground her teeth in exasperation. It irritated her beyond measure the way Mrs Brewin rarely addressed a remark directly to her. But the woman was ill, it was evident in the waxy texture of her skin and her bloodless lips. The physic she swallowed daily was supposedly for her blood, but she looked as anaemic now as the day Rachel had followed Jack Brewin up the narrow stairs to be introduced to her.

"Catherine, I've at last found someone to help us out. She'll see to the children, look after you, cook and help me out in the frameshop."

His wife had given Rachel a perfunctory once over then said to her husband. "What's her name?"

"Abigail Smith, Ma'am," Rachel answered with a polite bob.

"What's her name?" Mrs Brewin repeated as if Rachel hadn't spoken.

"She's just told you, Abigail Smith," Jack Brewin's tone was short. "Anyway, I've got to get back to the shop. Leave those men too long and there's no telling what they might get up to."

He departed and a silence had descended on the room. Rachel stood waiting for instructions but when none seemed to be forthcoming she ventured to ask, "Is there anything else I can tell you about myself, Ma'am?" She'd invented a colourful past life and was keen to test its credibility.

Still Catherine Brewin didn't answer, but stroking Caesar's mangy coat had said, "I hope this young miss doesn't think, just because I'm lying helpless up here, she can go setting her cap at my Jack."

Rachel took an astonished step backwards. Jack Brewin was hardly likely to set many women's hearts afire with passion. He had small acquisitive eyes almost hidden by eyebrows which straddled his bulging forehead like two hairy caterpillars. An added misfortune was that the good Lord had seen fit to deny him an equally luxuriant growth on his head and no matter how carefully he arranged the few sparse hairs, he couldn't hide his bald pate. He was also short, bow-legged, minus most of his teeth, and had a skin pitted with smallpox scars.

"If that's what you think of me," Rachel expostulated, "I'll go, right now." Aware that she was about to make herself homeless and jobless again, she stomped to the door.

163

"A proud miss isn't she? Can't even take a joke Caesar." Mrs Brewin addressed the dog, but it was also an obliquely offered apology and Rachel had no choice but to swallow her pride. But the relationship between her and Mrs Brewin, even after several weeks, remained uneasy and she felt that some of the resentment was due to her efficient running of the household and her competent handling of four difficult children.

It quickly became obvious to Rachel that neither Brewin was much interested in the four daughters they'd brought into the world. Catherine Brewin reserved all her affection for the odious little dog and her husband made no secret of the fact that he considered them nothing more than a financial burden and what he wanted was a son. But several miscarriages had ruined Catherine Brewin's health and while she awaited the birth of this latest child, she'd been forbidden by the doctor to leave her bed.

The house was tall and narrow, the staircase winding, the shallow steps too hazardous for a quick descent. But ear splitting squawks reached Rachel when she was still only half way down, so disregarding life and limb, she lifted her skirt and took them two at a time. Wondering which child was in the process of being garrotted, knifed, suffocated or otherwise dispatched this time, she flung open the kitchen door. "Right, I've had enough, to your beds both of you."

"It wasn't me it was her," each of them said in their childish piping voices. Then there followed the usual monotonous litany of complaints, one against the other, rounding it off with, "please don't send us upstairs Abigail, it's cold."

"I'm giving you one last chance. Get your slates and write out the alphabet. If it's neat and correct I might change my mind. Now I've got to prepare some caudle for your mama to make her better, so one word out of either of you . . ." Rachel left the threat unfinished but both girls knew they'd gone far enough and her patience was exhausted. Settling

164

down at the kitchen table, their small pink tongues extended in the effort of concentration, the blessed silence was broken only by the squeak of pencil on slate.

But even as Rachel stirred hot gruel on to egg, sherry and sugar, she still had to keep one eye on the clock. Because soon the two eldest girls would arrive home from school, hungry, demanding and equally as quarrelsome as their sisters.

Rachel spooned the unappetizing slop into the caudle cup, had a quick taste, gave a grimace of disgust, then in an attempt to improve the flavour, grated it liberally with nutmeg. To be ill was bad enough, she felt, but to have to eat such stuff was a double misfortune. After a final, "Now remember what I said," to the girls, she speedily negotiated the stairs. Lukewarm food was never well-received by the invalid.

Today Catherine Brewin hardly touched it though. Instead she emptied half the contents into the saucer, blew on it, then held it out for Caesar to devour.

Although Rachel watched the food disappearing down the dog's throat with more than a passing irritation, she wisely held her counsel, even when the rest was tipped into the saucer and slurped up by Caesar.

"The girls exhaust me, tell them I can't see them today," Mrs Brewin said in a tired voice as she handed the empty cup back to Rachel.

"They'll be so disappointed. Can't they come up for just five minutes?" Rachel pleaded, knowing if the girls were deprived of a visit their behaviour would deteriorate even more.

With a weary sigh Mrs Brewin let a transparent white hand fall on to the counterpane. "Well just for a couple of minutes then and I expect you to keep them under control."

In the kitchen, Primrose, ten, and Marigold, eleven, finished for the day at their Dame school, were engaged in their favourite pastime of taunting their younger sisters. But although they could be a plaguesome quartet, Rachel had

165

grown attached to the girls in the couple of months she'd been with them. She'd quickly recognized that even though they had parents, the children were starved of love and this struck an immediate cord with her.

Unfortunately for them, the sisters all bore a remarkable resemblance to their father and in spite of their flowery names, were plain as pipe-stems. With their lank hair, pale, doughy faces and small eyes, she feared Mr Brewin in later years, unless he could provide an extremely generous dowry, might have trouble getting them off his hands. Obviously this thought had crossed his mind too and probably served to fuel the exasperation he felt at having fathered four girls.

Jack Brewin complained about idle workmen, the drop in the sale of hose, the cost of an ailing wife, constantly. If Rachel approached him about her wages, he would wave her away with an irritable, "later, later." She was required to feed seven of them on a pittance and every farthing had to be accounted for. Fortunately she'd learnt skills such as breadmaking from Susan and with very careful budgeting, could just make the money go round.

Today, as always, the children were clambering for food. In defiance of Jack Brewin's instructions that she was to feed them only on stale bread, she took a crusty loaf she'd baked only that morning from the shelf and cut it into thick slices.

She'd hardly finished spreading the bread with dripping when eager hands shot out to grab it. Rachel restrained them with a sharp tap on the knuckles.

"Your manners are deplorable. Do you want to go out in the world as ladies or hoydens?"

"Hoydens," they shouted cheerfully, which although she knew she shouldn't, made Rachel laugh.

She gave them milk, then when they'd finished, brushed the crumbs from the fronts of their dresses, attempted to bring some order to the wispy, dun coloured locks,

166

then marched them in single file up to their mother's room.

Outside the door she put her finger to her lips. "Quietly now, remember, your mama isn't well."

They tiptoed across the creaking, uneven floor, then Lily, the baby of the family, spoilt it all by hurling herself upon her mother and disturbing Caesar, who snarled nastily.

"Now look what you've done, Lily, upset poor Caesar," complained Mrs Brewin. Then testily to Rachel, "I thought I told you to keep them under control."

"Sit down girls. No not on the bed," Rachel said hastily, as they all went to perch on it.

"Well, where then?" asked Marigold, "there's only one chair."

"Just stand," said her mother, "you won't be staying long."

The conversation that followed was awkward and desultory. "Will you be better soon Mama?" Rose asked, feeling they'd been left to shift for themselves long enough.

"I don't know, do I?" answered her mother fretfully.

"Are you very ill?" Marigold asked.

"Do you think I'd be here if I wasn't? I've had enough of these silly questions, go."

The girls' faces fell. "Kiss your mama," said Rachel. Each of them went in turn to the bed and bestowed a hesitant kiss upon Catherine Brewin's parchment cheeks, then with heads bowed, hands clasped in front of them and unnaturally subdued, they filed out of the room, their brief visit to their mother over for yet another day.

But Marigold, who was a bit more persistent than her sisters, was tired of being fobbed off, and as soon as they'd settled themselves in the kitchen, she began quizzing Rachel.

"Papa says he'd rather have six boys than one girl. Is that why Mama is ill? Is it because she's going to have a baby?"

"I'm sure I don't know," answered Rachel, who'd been given strict instructions not to discuss with them the reason for Catherine Brewin's delicate state of health.

"Well I know how you get babies anyway. Freda Jones told me at school." Marigold sat back, arms folded, a look of extreme satisfaction lighting her plain features and enjoying the astonishment of her sisters.

"How?" Primrose, a year younger, indicated by her tone that it would have to be good for her to be impressed.

"You have to go and look for them in the garden under a rhubarb leaf."

Unable to bring herself to accept this, Primrose turned to Rachel for confirmation of this biological detail.

"Is that true, Abigail?"

"Yes, dear of course it is," Rachel lied calmly and for once was relieved when Jack Brewin appeared with a pile of hose.

Throwing them down on the kitchen table, he said, "Come on you cackling females, make yourselves useful and get on with seaming this lot. There's plenty more where they came from too, enough to see you through the rest of the evening."

Lily and Rose were too young and their small fingers lacked the dexterity to sew neat seams. But although the two older girls made faces at their father's retreating back and grumbled loudly at this imposition on the free time, they knew they had no choice but to do as their father said.

Jack Brewin wasn't a man to concern himself with initiating apprentices into the "craft mystery" of framework knitting. Neither did he waste time making fully fashioned hose, that is stockings shaped on the frame. For this process required the stockinger to continually adjust his machine, a skill which was time consuming and therefore more expensive. His stockings were the crudely made and despised cut-ups, strips of knitted fabric made on wide frames by unskilled hands then roughly shaped with scissors. Cheap to make and buy but quickly splitting, unravelling or losing their shape in the wash.

Rachel sewed neat seams, making sure there were no uncomfortable bulges in the feet. Primrose and Marigold weren't half as bothered but there was no point in reprimanding them, for their father certainly wouldn't have thanked her if she'd made them unpick the seams. His only concern was a quick financial return, which reminded Rachel she must approach him for her wages again.

By seven, Lily and Rose, whose job it was to turn the finished hose outside in and tie them in neat bundles, had their heads on the table and were fast asleep.

Gently shaking them awake, Rachel sent them up to their beds. When Primrose and Marigold joined them at eight the pile of hose still to be stitched seemed to have hardly lessened. Rachel knew it would be well past midnight before she finished and her eyes and fingers already ached.

She was further delayed when Jack Brewin came in shortly afterwards demanding his supper. The best food was reserved for him and he demanded meat twice a day. He was a taciturn man but as he noisily ate his chops and supped his ale, Rachel decided that the only way she was ever going to get what was owed to her was to threaten withdrawal of her labour.

"Mr Brewin . . . about my wages . . ." she began.

"I know, I know, you haven't been paid, but I shall settle up with you at the end of this month."

"You're always promising me that and I still haven't seen a penny."

"You're always harping on, yet you've got a roof over your head and you get your vittles. And it don't grow on trees you know, money."

Some vittles, thought Rachel, bread and scrape more like. "Perhaps not, but I work hard for you and I deserve a wage. I need clothes. Look at my dress it's nearly in rags. She fanned the skirt out for his inspection.

He lifted his eyes briefly from his plate. "There's years of wear in it. But if you're that bothered ask Catherine, she'll let you have one of her dresses."

Rachel very deliberately folded the stocking she'd been seaming, smoothed it with the palms of her hand and placed it on the table. "Mr Brewin, either you pay me tonight, or I leave this house." Although she had nowhere to go, she was able to press her demands in the certain assurance that Jack Brewin could ill afford to lose her.

"Oh all right," he answered irritably. "Why it's my misfortune to live in a house full of women. Nag, nag, nag, that's all they're good for. Can't leave a man alone. No wonder I've got indigestion." He picked up the chop bone and began gnawing at it wolfishly.

Try eating a bit more slowly, instead of stuffing your face like a pig at a trough, Rachel wanted to say as she watched rivulets of grease dribbling down his chin.

He finished, flung the bone on to the fire, ran his hand along his mouth and belched loudly.

"Are you going to give it to me then?" she held out her hand.

"Good God girl, at least let me get my supper down."

"I'm doing nothing more, no seaming, no cleaning until you hand over what's mine by rights."

Suddenly Jack Brewin's features took on a sly expression. "What I'd like to know is, where you was afore you came 'ere."

Rachel quickly turned away from him and made herself busy poking the fire. "I've already told you, when me mam died, I was thrown out of our cottage in Loughborough and I had to go looking for work."

Jack Brewin swung back on the legs of his chair and inserted both thumbs into the leather belt at his waist. "You wouldn't 'ave run away by any chance?"

"Course not." With a great show of industry, Rachel swept ash into a dustpan.

"Funny then that there were this notice put in the paper recently about a servant who'd run away, and the description would just about fit you."

Rachel had collected her wits sufficiently to realize what he was up to; a little bit of blackmail to browbeat her into silence on the question of wages. Best thing to do, she decided was brazen it out, play him at his own game. Taking her time, she finished sweeping the hearth then turned to face her employer with an expression of calm assurance. "It weren't me. I've already told you where I came from."

"Well just let's hope your tellin' me the truth. I wouldn't want to be harbouring a criminal. You know a servant can get seven days hard labour for running away don't you?"

"If you thought it were me, why didn't you get in touch with these people before?" she asked with bold contempt.

But Jack Brewin was saved from answering this awkward question by a low moan which made them both turn.

In the doorway stood Catherine Brewin, clutching her small dog in one arm and supporting herself against the door frame with the other. In the candlelight her skin had a greenish pallor and her nose and mouth were pinched with pain.

Responding to the mute appeal in her eyes, her husband righted the chair and stood up. "Catherine, what ails thee?"

"The baby . . . it's coming." She clutched her belly as another spasm gripped her.

Jack Brewin turned to Rachel. "Hurry, go and fetch Mrs Spence the midwife, she's three doors down."

The panic Rachel heard in his voice carried her swiftly from the house, all thoughts of unpaid wages forgotten. The midwife's house was in darkness, but she banged and called loudly until a head was thrust out of an upstairs window and an irritated voice demanded to know what she wanted.

171

"It's Mrs Brewin, the baby's on its way. You're to come immediately."

"Why do they always choose to arrive at night?" Mrs Spence asked no one in particular. Then, "Go and boil up plenty of water, girl, I'll be with you within two shakes of a lamb's tail."

Rachel was building the fire up and filling cast iron pots with water when Mrs Spence came bustling in, her white apron creaking with starch. "Get your sleeves rolled up and an apron on, I'll want some help."

"Me?" said Rachel faintly. "But I don't know nothing about delivering babbies."

"Well you will by the time the night's out. Because if it's anything like the others, it's going to be a long one." Mrs Spence glanced quickly around the kitchen then lowered her voice to a confidential level. "It's a crying shame the way he keeps putting that wife of his in the family way, and all 'cos he wants a boy. He'll kill her if he goes on like he does." She paused and gave a hurrumph of disgust. "Mucky sod. He needs to tie a knot in it. Anyway what's your name girl?"

"Abigail."

"Well Abigail, first of all you can make me a pot of tea."

"Ooh, I'm not allowed to touch the tea. Mr Brewin keeps it locked up."

"Go and get the key from him then. I've been woken from my sleep and I'm doing nowt until I've had something hot to revive me. And tell him," she called after Rachel as she hurried up the stairs, "he can thank his lucky stars it's not gin I'm after supping."

When Rachel tiptoed into the room Catherine Brewin was lying back on the pillows. Her eyes were closed and already she looked too exhausted to cope with the ordeal that lay ahead of her. Her husband, more solitious than Rachel had ever seen him, was leaning over her wiping her damp forehead with a cloth. As she gave a low groan and

172

gripped his arm, he turned sharply to Rachel. "Where the devil's Mrs Spence?"

"Downstairs. But she says she's doing nowt until she's had a cup of tea?"

"That bloody woman, and the price tea is," he muttered, reluctantly drawing the keys to the dresser and tea caddy from his pocket. "And you can tell her from me it'll be deducted from her bill, and that'll be exorbitant I'll wager."

Rachel had no intention of doing any such thing. They could fight that out between them later, after the baby was safely delivered. Mrs Spence was clean. She was also a Methody so didn't drink and since these were virtues not easy to come by in a midwife, it would be risky upsetting her at this late stage. Her proud boast that she rarely lost a baby – or mother – was something Jack Brewin ought to have regard to as well, Rachel felt.

"Make it good and flavoursome," said Mrs Spence. And to make sure her instructions were carried out, as Rachel spooned the dark leaves from the tea-caddy into the pot, she slyly nudged her elbow into profligacy. Then in a firm voice as the girl went to lock the tea away again. "Just leave it there on the table, love. You'll be making me a few more pots afore the night's out."

Even after Mrs Spence had had two cups there was still enough in the pot for Rachel, although she gulped the liquid down in furtive haste, fearful that her employer might suddenly appear and accuse her of theft.

"Right, I'm ready for anything now," said Mrs Spence and picked up her bag. "I'll call you when I need you. Keep your ears open, don't fall asleep and bring some water with you when you come. I'll need clean linen too and some swaddling to wrap the infant in when it's born," were her final orders before she disappeared up the stairs.

Unceremoniously ejected from his wife's bedside, Jack Brewin appeared in the kitchen shortly afterwards, one minute sitting with his head in his hands in an attitude of despair, the next restlessly pacing the length of the kitchen, back and forth, back and forth.

In spite of her earlier threat, Rachel took up some hose and began seaming. But although the work occupied her hands, her mind was free to fret and worry, and wonder what was going on upstairs and how long it would be before she was wanted and how she would cope. At Thatcher's Mount she'd often been called out to help Percy at lambing time, so she was familiar with the mechanics of birth, and the pain of ewes so stoically borne. But a confinement like this, which was obviously going to be difficult, was another matter.

Jack Brewin's restless pacing had now begun to get on her nerves so when he suddenly made for the door and announced, "I'm going out for a drink." she was glad to see the back of him.

He must have been out of earshot or he'd have heard it, the scream of torment that ripped through the house and caused Rachel to leap to her feet, her heart thumping and scattering hose, wool and needles all over the kitchen floor. Her hands, clammy with anxiety, stuck to the banister as she climbed the stairs. She was waiting too for childish voices but when she eased open the girls' bedroom door she could tell from their regular breathing that their mother's agony had failed to pierce their youthful slumbers.

Although she felt ashamed of her own cowardice, Rachel held back for several moments before entering the room where Catherine Brewin lay. That frightful scream had come from someone way beyond human assistance and she might indeed have already passed on. A weak cry finally gave Rachel the courage to enter, but as her eyes moved fearfully to the moaning, sweating figure on the bed, she found herself making a silent avowal that if this was what having children was like, then she would have none of it.

Although there was little evidence of Mrs Spence's earlier

breezy manner, she was professional enough to keep her anxieties to herself as she delivered her instructions. "We've got something amiss here. I shall need help. Tell your master to fetch the doctor and he's to run as fast as his legs will carry him."

"Mr Brewin's gone out."

"Gone out?" Mrs Spence exclaimed in astonishment. "At a time like this. Typical of a man. Do you know where he is?"

"At the Bunch of Grapes, I think."

"Go and haul him out. Say if Doctor Lewis isn't here within the half hour I can't be responsible."

"Yes Mrs Spence," answered Rachel, already backing out of the door. Then after a last terrified glance towards the suffering woman, she turned and fled from the horrors of the childbed.

But Jack Brewin showed a marked reluctance to leave the warmth and *bonhomie* of the tavern, and it was only the determined pressure of Rachel's hand upon his arm that finally drew him out into the street. "Mrs Spence says you've to fetch Doctor Lewis," she said when they were outside in the Lane. "The mistress has been taken real ill, screaming out in agony she is."

"Good God, the woman must be off her head, I can't afford that man's fees. Everyone round here seems to think I'm made of money. Has she put a knife under the bed? I've heard that cuts the pain in two."

"No she hasn't." Rachel snapped, restraining an urge to take him by the shoulders and shake him until what few teeth he had in his head, rattled. "It's a doctor, not witchcraft the mistress needs. Do you think more of your pocket than her life? Are you going to go back to the house and sit and listen to her screams? And when she is dead what will you tell your motherless girls? Will you tell them their mother died because you were too mean to fetch a doctor? Because if you don't, I

175

will, Mr Brewin. In fact I'll tell everyone in this town, damn me if I won't."

Whether it was the contempt in her voice, the threat to expose his penny-pinching ways or another shattering scream carrying down the lane that sped Jack Brewin on his way, Rachel wasn't sure, but one moment he was standing there cracking his knuckles, the next he was no more than a darting shadow. Even so, as he was briefly illuminated by the flaring torch of a linkboy guiding a couple home, Rachel found herself calling after him. "And for God's sake don't start haggling with the doctor over fees. Wait until the babby's safely delivered first."

She continued to stand in the lane long after the linkboy had delivered his customers to their door. Even back in the house she found herself doing small jobs, anything to avoid going up to the sick room, although she was forced up the stairs finally by Mrs Spence calling down demanding hot water. But she still needed to stand for a moment on the landing and take several deep breaths before she was able to edge open the door.

A troubled conscience must have put wings on Jack Brewin's feet because he arrived back with the physician in less than a half hour. Doctor Lewis's wig was askew and his nightshirt poked out from under his coat tails, but his presence had a reassuring affect on everyone, even the patient.

"Right, first of all we'll have that dog out of here." With a peremptory snap of his fingers, the doctor ordered a truculent, cowering Caesar from the room.

Rachel looked on curiously as vials were plucked from various pockets in his voluminous coat, shuddered when torturous looking instruments were removed from a box and laid out on the table, pulled a face as he poured one of his evil looking concoctions into a glass.

Indicating that she should give it to the patient, he handed

176

the draught to Rachel. Supporting her thin shoulders, Rachel eased Catherine Brewin to a sitting position and persuaded for her to swallow the potion. Her nightgown was soaked with sweat and her skin seemed to burn through the thin material. Even the effort of raising her head exhausted her and as she sank back on to the pillows, she said weakly, "I'm going to die, aren't I?"

Moved by a terrible pity, Rachel grasped her hand. "Of course you're not. We've got Doctor Lewis and Mrs Spence here, they'll see you're all right."

Mercifully, the draught seemed to do its job, she became drowsy and her eyes closed. Doctor Lewis pushed up his sleeves in a workmanlike manner then after ordering Mrs Spence to bring the candle nearer, adjusted his spectacles and peered at the lower regions of Catherine Brewin's pain racked body. "We have a breech presentation here, Mrs Spence, I'm afraid." he said and selected a particularly sharp looking instrument.

As he bent towards his patient, Rachel felt sure she was going to vomit. Then the room began to sway and the candles grow dim. From a long way off she heard herself being sharply reprimanded by the midwife. "Pull yourself together girl, we've got enough to do without you passing out on us." And only by gripping hold of the bedpost and inhaling deeply was she able to avoid making an exhibition of herself.

Rachel lost all sense of time that night but the candles burnt low and had to be renewed several times before she heard Dr Lewis, and Mrs Spence exclaim together, "It's coming!" and a tiny slippery form was lifted on to the mother's stomach.

"What is it?" Catherine Brewin asked, lifting a weary head from her pillow.

Rachel saw the doctor and midwife exchange glances. "A boy, Mrs Brewin."

"Thank God for that."

177

But the small blue creature smeared with blood and mucus looked lifeless to Rachel and when Mrs Spence lifted him by his heels and slapped his buttocks, no sound came. She tried again but still nothing.

"What's wrong, why isn't my baby crying?"

No one spoke.

"He's dead, isn't he?"

"Yes, poor wee crittur. But spared this vale of tears, God rest his soul," answered Mrs Spence with a sob in her voice. She wrapped the dead infant in linen and offered him to Catherine Brewin. "Would you like to hold him for a moment, my dear? It sometimes helps."

After all her mistress had been through and then to be delivered of a stillborn child, was enough, Rachel was sure, to send any woman mad with grief. But there was no sign of emotion on her face, not even a tear. Turning away from the midwife, she rejected her dead son with a shake of the head. "No. I want to see Caesar. Will someone go and get him please."

"What about your husband, Mrs Brewin? Surely you want him here with you at this unhappy time?" The doctor, who thought he'd become inured to most human foibles, couldn't keep the surprise from his voice.

"Just send in my little dog."

"It would be better if he stayed outside for the time being," the doctor answered firmly, as he wiped his instruments free of blood, inspected them then returned them to their box. He completed his task with neat efficiency then turned to Rachel. "Go and fetch Mr Brewin, he must be told."

"I don't want him, I want Caesar!"

"Later Mrs Brewin, later!" There was now a noticeable edge of exasperation to Doctor Lewis's voice.

But it was evident that Caesar had been keeping a night-long vigil outside the bedroom, because Rachel had hardly opened the door when he squeezed through, almost sending her flying

178

in his haste to be reunited with his beloved mistress. Then with his stump of a tail wagging furiously, he hurled himself on the bed and began licking Catherine Brewin's face with such frantic delight, no one had the heart to remove him.

Downstairs in the kitchen Rachel opened the shutters to a gold-streaked dawn. But the night had left her drained both emotionally and physically and she was in no state to appreciate the beauty of the morning. All she saw was a fire that had gone out and Jack Brewin fast asleep in the chair, mouth hanging slack and snoring loudly. Her own eyes were grainy with fatigue, her body chilled and as she stood looking at him, she shivered and rubbed her arms apprehensively. What was she going to say to him? Although she'd never found much to like about her employer, as she shook him gently awake, her heart was scoured by a deep pain at his loss.

"Doctor Lewis wants to speak to you," she said quietly as he blinked, then jumped up.

"Has the babby come? What is it, a boy?"

Rachel knew she was abdicating her responsibility but she just couldn't answer. Instead she parried his question by repeating tonelessly, "Doctor Lewis wants to talk to you."

But he'd obviously caught something in the inflection of her voice for he glanced at her sharply. Then with an, "Out of my way woman," he pushed past her and sprinted up the stairs as fast as his short bandy legs could carry him.

Rachel, coming into the bedroom behind him, realized it wasn't his exhausted wife he was concerned about, for he hardly gave her a glance. His whole attention was concentrated on the small still form laid out at the end of the bed. With a great shuddering sob he gathered up the tiny lifeless bundle and clutching it against his chest, he fell to his knees, wailing in anguish, "My son! my son!"

Rachel could only turn away from such raw, uncontained grief but the weary doctor becoming impatient, exhorted

179

Jack Brewin to pull himself together. "Your wife is still alive and that is the main thing. But I must speak plainly and tell you there are to be no more children. She survived this night, by my skill and the grace of God. You'll have to put aside all thoughts of a son, Mr Brewin. Just be thankful your daughters still have a mother." Then having delivered this homily he pocketed his two guinea fee and leaving the midwife to deal with the afterbirth, he departed.

Chapter Thirteen

Hearing the heavy footsteps of workmen shuffling into the yard, Rachel hurried with a guilty sense of relief from the stifling misery of the room.

The men were waiting, eight of them, sullen and uncommunicative, and as she unlocked the frameshop they filed past her without a word of greeting.

"Your master's not himself this morning so he probably won't be down. Mrs Brewin was delivered of a babby last night but he was . . . was dead." A small sob escaped her lips, but there was no murmur of regret from the men, a sure indication of their feelings towards Jack Brewin.

Like any eighteen-year-old Rachel was certain she would live forever and had never pondered on such weighty matters as life and death. But that night she had been brought face to face with human pain and suffering, and been made aware of her own mortality. And as she groped her way up to her room and fell on to the straw mattress, the idea of death began to haunt her. She tossed restlessly from side to side, trying to cast out these morbid thoughts and longing for sleep. From outside came the ponderous clop of horses' hooves, and from downstairs, the girls' voices, chirpy and quarrelsome as the sparrows under the eaves. Life goes on, she thought, for some at least. But not for that tiny dead baby. He hadn't been given the opportunity to taste life, its bitterness and sweetness, not even for a few hours. Mourning the unlived life, a few tears squeezed out from under her closed lids and on to the rough ticking of the mattress. In spite of her troubled thoughts, noises gradually grew fainter and she was just sinking into a drowsy languour when she felt herself being shaken violently.

"Abigail, Abigail, wake up!"

"What do you mean, wake up," Rachel complained, "I haven't been to sleep yet Mrs Spence."

"And nor you're likely to my girl this day. Mrs Brewin's bleeding something terrible, so downstairs wi' you." She pulled on Rachel's arm, almost dragging her from the bed. "You'll have to fetch Doctor Lewis this time. Jack Brewin's drinking himself under the table and is of use to neither man nor beast."

Rachel was so dizzy with fatigue that when she stood up the room swam before her eyes and she slumped down on the bed again. But a sharp, "Come on girl, buck your ideas up," from the midwife quickly had her on her feet and struggling into a dress.

In the kitchen the girls were sitting looking unusually subdued, while Jack Brewin stared morosely into a tankard of ale. When the children saw her they rushed towards her, clamouring for her attention, their small faces pinched with anxiety as they bombarded her with questions. Finally Rachel put up a hand to silence them. "One at a time please."

"Is Mama ill?" Primrose asked, delegating herself spokesman.

Rachel glanced at Jack Brewin. "What has your papa told you?"

"Nothing," answered Primrose, biting her lip as she gamely fought back her tears.

Deciding it would serve no purpose to hide the facts from the girls, she said quietly but she hoped reassuringly, "Yes your mama is rather poorly, but I'm on my way now to fetch Doctor Lewis and I'm sure he'll soon make her better. But while I'm gone I want you, Primrose and Marigold to get

182

yourselves off to school, and you, Lily and Rose to keep still as mice so as not to disturb your mama and get on with your school work. Will you do that?"

Four small heads nodded vigorously and Rachel hurried off. She ran all the way up the High Street and arrived panting outside Doctor Lewis's establishment. Here she met an invincible force in the shape of Mrs Lewis, who was adamant her husband could not be disturbed.

"But ma'am, Mrs Brewin is bleeding real bad and Mrs Spence can't do nothing about it."

"Find another physician, my husband must sleep, he's been called out three nights running."

Rachel weary and defeated, began to cry. "There's no time. She 'll die if nothing's done."

Irritated rather than moved by her distress, Mrs Lewis was about to slam shut the door when Rachel heard the Doctor's voice further along the hall calling, "Who is it, my dear?"

From behind the door his wife hissed, "The Brewins' serving girl. They want you again but I told her you'd given strict instructions not to be disturbed."

"What is wrong?"

Mrs Lewis, who found a perverse pleasure in turning patients from the door answered tetchily, "According to the girl, Mrs Brewin is bleeding, badly she says, but that's probably an exaggeration."

"I doubt it my dear. Mrs Spence wouldn't send for me unless it was serious and it was an extremely difficult delivery." Rachel heard his footsteps moving along the hall and a moment later he was standing on the step in his nightcap and dressing gown. With a kindly expression, he said, "It's all right young lady, you can go and tell Mrs Spence I'm coming right away." And as Rachel turned to go she was pleased to hear the doctor upbraiding his wife for her lack of humanity.

Dr Lewis arrived at the house only a few minutes after

Rachel, and was immediately drawn into a corner of the room by the midwife. She spoke in a low, troubled voice and Rachel who had been put to work tearing up sheeting, had to strain her ears and move nearer to catch what was being said.

"It's the afterbirth, it hasn't come away."

From the doctor's grim expression Rachel knew this was serious. "Then I'm afraid I have no alternative but to extract it by hand, Mrs Spence," he replied and as he moved to the bed her was already discarding his coat and rolling up his shirt sleeves. And Catherine Brewin, weak from the long labour and loss of blood, now had to endure the torment of the good doctor's intrusive investigation of her womb as he searched for the placenta.

It seemed impossible she would be able to cope with this further ordeal and when her cries of pain brought two frantic small children banging at the bedroom door, Rachel guiltily crept back downstairs with them.

She was still comforting the girls when she heard a door open and voices on the landing. A moment later the physician came into the kitchen.

Pushing the girls from her lap, Rachel stood up.

"Where is your master?" he asked. "In the frameshop?"

"I think not, sir."

"In the Bunch of Grapes then, I'll be bound."

Rachel nodded her head.

"The man's a self-pitying fool. Just don't let him say he can't find the money for my fee, that's all. Anyway, your mistress is sleeping now, but tell him I'll be back tomorrow."

Following him to the front door to let him out, Rachel ventured to ask, "Is the missus going to be all right now, Doctor Lewis?"

His shoulders slumped and he suddenly looked tired and grey. "I hope so my child, I hope so."

And it seemed his hopes might be fulfilled when she rallied

184

sufficiently the next day for the children and Caesar to visit her. However a day or two later a rash appeared on her back, her temperature soared and the room had the smell of putrefaction. Even though blankets were piled on top of her she developed violent shivering fits. After this her condition deteriorated so rapidly that when the children were brought in to say their last farewells she didn't appear to recognize them, although she did call faintly for Caesar to be brought to her.

Less than four days after she had been delivered of a stillborn child, Catherine Brewin died. She was laid out by Mrs Spence and on the widower's instructions, measured by the local carpenter for the plainest and cheapest of deal coffins. Rachel insisted though on festooning the cart that carried her to her last resting place in St Margaret's graveyard, with black ribbon, rosemary and yew.

In all this time Jack Brewin had rarely been sober and it had been left to Rachel to run the household and frameshop as best she could. With four grieving children to console she managed to remain dry-eyed during the committal. But after the funeral, her eyes blurred with exhaustion, she went into Catherine Brewin's bedroom to uncover the draped pier glass and re-wind the clock Mrs Spence had stopped at the moment of death. Here she found Caesar curled up on the bed and fast asleep. But today he didn't leap up with a warning snarl. And Rachel somehow knew, even before she reached out and touched him, that the one creature Catherine Brewin had loved was dead, of a broken heart, she hadn't a doubt. And although she'd never cared for the animal, it was the final straw and sinking into a chair she put her head in her hands and wept.

Chapter Fourteen

When the small blemish failed to appear on her chin at its appointed time of the month, Matilda felt more than a faint stirring of unease. By the following month she was retching miserably in the mornings and panic had set in.

The awakening loveliness of the countryside; Rooks Spinney where she'd lain with Harry, misty with bluebells, yellow primroses tucked under hedgerows left her completely unmoved.

In the first frantic weeks, her mind could contain but one thought. It was with her when she woke and before she slept; the terrible and unforeseen predicament she found herself in and the humiliation that awaited her. Oh how they would enjoy it, the village folk, to see Joseph Pedley's daughter, humbled and brought down like any serving girl. Already she could hear their crude jokes and smothered laughter. And worse, she had no idea what she should do to stave off this disgrace. Neither did she have anyone she could turn to. All she could do was rage silently against Harry and in the privacy of her room weep copious, bitter tears.

Until the practical side of her saw that this was a self-indulgence which would get her nowhere. First of all, Matilda realized, she had to accept that her situation was desperate, decide what options were open to her and proceed from there. Not in a state of blind panic but with a clear eyed, logical calm. She had to get in touch with Harry, that was her priority, tell him of her condition. Except that she had no address to write to.

What about getting rid of it then, this unwanted child? After all there were women in the back streets of Leicester, who for a price would do what was necessary. But how to get there? To even explain her absence from home? There might be someone in the village of course. Dare she ask Susan? Canvass her help? No, it would be a deal too risky, since Susan might feel obliged to tell her mother.

Her emotions were fragile as eggshells and her secret, weighing heavily, made her even more short-tempered than usual. She longed to unburden herself, confide in Jane but knew it was out of the question. When her last hope, a search through her mother's book of herbal remedies, failed to come up with an antidote to her condition, Matilda took to wandering apathetically around the village. She'd always found other people's distress easier to bear than her own, so on these aimless meanderings she didn't notice the increasing poverty of the villagers, and wasn't perceptive enough to sense a simmering discontent that could easily erupt into violence.

Totally self-absorbed, just two scenes were played out in her head. The first was optimistic. Marriage to Harry and respectability. Because when she was in a hopeful frame of mind she was certain that if only she could get a message to him, he would marry her. After all, his reputation as an officer and a gentleman demanded that he do the honourable thing. And she was sure Papa would make a settlement generous enough to keep Harry from regretting marrying slightly beneath him.

On her pessimistic days, she saw herself disowned by her parents and banished to the other end of the country, there to give birth to a child that would immediately be taken from her and fostered by some hag, where no questions would be asked if it happened to contract some fatal disease.

To add to her general depression, nobody did anything but talk of war. The pages of *The Times* were full of it and it seemed to be the sole topic of conversation at any social gathering. And a great terror grew in Matilda's mind that Harry would be killed before he could even acknowledge that he was the father of her child.

At school she'd found geography so tedious she hardly knew where Belgium was. But she quickly corrected this gap in her knowledge by getting hold of an atlas and studying it in detail. She also poured over *The Times*, memorizing the names of villages like Quatre Bras, Ligny and Waterloo, followed the movement of British and French troops with such diligence that when she opened the paper one Sunday morning and read: 'Hostilities began yesterday 15 June,' she wasn't entirely surprised.

Although Matilda knew Harry might already be dead, she didn't swoon on reading these words and there was only the slightest suggestion of a tremor in her fingers as she folded the newspaper. But that phrase had put a seal upon her future. Totally repugnant as it was to her, she knew she had no choice but to put into action an idea that been fomenting in her mind for some days. So after refusing a lift from her parents, she donned her most becoming dress and bonnet and with a purposeful gleam in her eye, set off down the lane to church.

But not straight there, because outside the gates of Trent Hall there was a wide strip of uncultivated ground. Here Matilda paused and plunging in amongst the tall grasses, she began gathering up great armfuls of wild flowers. Ankle deep amongst the blooms, buttercups spilt their pollen on to her dress, turning it into a cloth of gold. She allowed her bonnet to slip to her shoulders so that the breeze could nudge her glossy curls into a becoming disarray. Aware that she was a sight to nourish even the most rheumy eye, Matilda could only regret that there wasn't an artist on hand to immortalize this moment of rural charm on canvas.

Her arms, now overladen with poppies, scabious, cornflowers and lacy fronds of cow parsley, were beginning to tire when she heard the sound she been listening for. But she still gave every appearance of being absorbed in her task and managed to feign surprise when the Squire pulled up beside her and called, "Good morning to you, Miss Matilda."

"Oh, Mr Bennett, you quite startled me," Matilda exclaimed, treating him to a smile equal in brilliance to the flowers she clutched to her breast. Then holding them out for his inspection, added with an air of grave spirituality, "They looked so lovely, I thought I might decorate the church with them."

But it was the flesh not the spirit that moved the Squire at that precise moment. Matilda's naked flesh, to be precise. And as lascivious images flashed through his mind, he felt his member stiffen. Glancing furtively down, he saw the embarrassing bulge in his trousers, shifted uncomfortably, then instead of offering Matilda a lift, he hurriedly flicked the reins and ordered the mare to "walk on."

Astounded at his abrupt departure, Matilda stood in the middle of the lane, glowering after the squat, overweight figure and grinding her teeth in rage. "Fat old toad," she muttered, slung the flowers over the hedge, dusted her hands, and undefeated by this minor setback, stalked determinedly after her unsuspecting quarry.

And outside the church after the service, Matilda did manoeuvre him into offering her a lift home, while still appearing to hesitate. "Well . . . it is such a lovely morning I feel I ought to walk." she said, when the Squire extended his offer. Then more hurriedly as he went to move off, "However, with such bad news coming from the Continent, to have a companion such as yourself, Mr Bennett, would, I am sure, cheer me up." And linking her arm familiarly through the Squire's, she walked with him down the path, favouring several members of the congregation with a gracious smile, and behaving as if she were already Lady of the Manor.

To feel her small hand on his arm, to inhale the faint scent of roses, set the Squire's heart pounding like any lovesick young swain. Perhaps now was the time to press his suit, while that good-for-nothing nephew was out of the way.

"This war is a terrible thing, is it not, Mr Bennett?" Matilda asked as he helped her into the buggy.

With much huffing and puffing, for his gout was playing him up, the Squire climbed in beside her. "It is indeed," he replied, when he managed to get his breath back.

"Have there been many casualties do you know?"

So that was it, Francis Bennett thought: Harry. He might have guessed. And there he was thinking his luck had changed and she was feeling more kindly disposed towards him. Well she would suffer a bit for that. "There's been no casualty list published yet, but rumour has it thousands of men have already been killed. And of course there will be worse to come. It'll be a blood bath I shouldn't wonder," Francis Bennett said cruelly, gave Matilda a sideways glance and saw her turn pale. Of course it would be convenient if one of Boney's men did oblige. Just one shot from a musket, a sword scything the air or the deadly thrust of a bayonet, then the problem of Harry would be solved, permanently. After all, wasn't that every cavalry officer's wish? To die a hero's death on the battlefield, covered in blood and glory. Not that his nephew would consider marrying Matilda. Nevertheless he was an irritant, a fly in the ointment as long as he hung around. And if he could be disposed of . . . well so much the better.

Lapsing into a sentimental day dream, Francis Bennett saw himself comforting Matilda in her grief, while quietly hinting that the old enemy time wasn't on her side and she ought to be married. Although he expected no opposition he'd need to speak to her father first. There might not be any love lost between himself and Joseph Pedley, but they understood each other perfectly and for social advancement, Matilda's father would happily sell his soul.

In spite of the Squire's chilling words, Matilda had managed to maintain a cheerful countenance all the way home. She had smiled winningly, even managed to say, as they reached Thatcher's Mount, "Would you care to come up for a game of whist tonight, Mr Bennett?" But although her lips curved into a smile her eyes remained blank and the words screamed in her head, I can't marry him, I can't! Her whole being shrunk from the idea of physical contact. For that was what marriage would mean, doing with him what she'd done with Harry. And the idea was so totally repellent to her, by the time she reached her room she was retching into her handkerchief.

Staring at her pale features in the gilt-framed looking glass, she thought, no it's impossible for me to go through with it. He's a pig! Disgusting! Awful! But if Harry is dead, what choice have I? Matilda's head sank on to her hands. Why had she been so foolish . . . so careless? Because she was like a weather vane to his breeze, that was why, and quite simply, because she loved him.

Matilda's interest in the war now became obsessive. When she read that, 'All our troops performed prodigious acts of valour, but we have lost a great many men,' she prayed Harry wasn't among those mortally wounded. At night she stood at her window knowing that the moon, shining with such brilliance on the peaceful Midlands landscape, was also casting its light, filtered through a pall of gunsmoke, upon flattened cornfields and scenes of total carnage: abandoned weapons, mangled corpses, strewn limbs, carrion crows, pecking at the bloated carcasses of horses.

However, Matilda still continued to alternate between hope and despair and although without her mother's piety, she took to going to church daily. She had just returned hot

191

and tired from St Philip's one morning and was listlessly sipping ginger beer when George suddenly appeared, waving a newspaper jubilantly above his head.

Matilda glared at him. "What are you doing home?" she asked in a peevish voice.

Ignoring her question, George continued to wave the paper like a flag. "It's over! We've won! Official from Downing Street. Bonaparte's defeated."

"Let me see." Distrusting her brother's word, Matilda leapt up and snatched the paper from him. Her eyes quickly scanned the dispatch from the Duke of Wellington, confirming that Bonaparte had indeed been routed. Limp with relief, she slumped back down in the chair. So it was over, after only a few days. And she'd thought it might go on for months, years even. That meant if Harry was alive he could be home soon. She'd be able to tell Francis Bennett where to go then. There'd be no more having to endure his fumbling overtures, the damp kisses he'd taken to planting on her lips with increasing frequency. No more having to count the days wondering how much longer she'd manage to disguise her shape. If Harry was alive. But George had taken the paper and was now reading it.

"Is there a casualty list, George?"

"Worried about your soldier boy, are you? Well you'll have to worry on, they're not printing any names until next week."

A whole week to wait? Why she'd go mad with the uncertainty. She didn't mind if he came home blind, with an arm or even a leg missing, just as long he came home.

At the same moment as the church bells began their victorious chiming, Mrs Pedley came rushing in and embraced each child in turn. "Isn't it marvellous, my darlings? We're at peace again. The slaughter is done with. What a great man the Duke is to finally defeat that horrible little corporal."

George stood up. "Well I don't know about anyone else,

192

but I intend to mark the event with a pot or two of ale down at the Weavers' Arms."

"Wait for me, I'm coming with you," said Matilda, whose mood fluctuated so rapidly between hope and despair she was glad of any distraction.

"Why don't we all go?" suggested Mrs Pedley. "Susan, Polly and Sam too."

"You're suggesting we give the servants the day off?" George expostulated.

"Yes I am. It's a great victory. Surely they're as entitled to celebrate as we are."

"But what will Papa say?" asked Matilda.

Mrs Pedley looked her daughter straight in the eye. "Your father is in Nottingham and won't be back until tomorrow. So there's no reason why he should ever find out. Unless someone decides to tell him."

Matilda bridled instantly. "Don't look at me like that, Mama, I'm not a sneak, although I can't answer for George. But I'm not walking down to the village with the servants. I wouldn't be seen dead with that dolt, Polly. And as for Sam . . . well our scarecrows are better dressed than he is."

"Now come on, show a little Christian charity, my love."

Although George might be a lost cause, Mrs Pedley could generally shame Matilda with a mild rebuke. She was concerned about her, though. Over the past few weeks her face had lost its plump freshness, she'd become pale and listless and spent long hours alone in her room. Listening through the closed door, Mrs Pedley often heard tears and although she would have never dared intrude on her daughter's misery, she guessed they were being shed for Harry. And such tears. Enough to fill a lake. He was handsome, no one could deny that, but not worth such unhappiness. A bit of a gay blade too, a man quite happy to trifle with a girl's affections, a philanderer even. And that could be it, she thought, with a sudden cold feeling. Her eyes slid to her daughter's waistline.

193

Was it thickening or was her imagination getting the better of her. No . . . it was unthinkable, impossible. Dear God, not that. Esther Pedley closed her eyes, sank down in a chair and clasped her erratically beating heart.

"Mama, whatever is the matter?" cried Matilda in alarm, and rushing to her mother's side, began massaging her hand.

"It's nothing dear, I just felt a little faint, it's the excitement, I expect."

"George, quickly, go and get the smelling salts."

"There's really no need to fuss," protested Mrs Pedley, then thought, if Matilda is pregnant, how am I going to deal with it? But she couldn't be. It's just me getting fanciful in my old age. She might be wilful at times but she wouldn't be so foolish as to allow herself to get in such a condition, surely. Of course there was one way of finding out and that was by asking. Or checking when she had her 'menses'. One way or another, now that her suspicions had been roused, she would keep a watchful eye on her daughter's figure, look for the telltale signs, early morning sickness, strange fads. Because if she was in that unfortunate condition and Harry was dead, drastic measures would have to be taken. Here her mind turned to the Squire. Should she mention her fears to Joseph? No, she must be sure first, otherwise she could risk giving him a seizure.

George returned with the smelling salts and kneeling beside her mother, Matilda held the small bottle to her nose. But Mrs Pedley pushed her hand aside and stood up. "I'm all right, darling, really, let's go and celebrate."

Matilda, looked doubtful, "Well if you're sure."

"Yes I am. You wait here, I'll go and tell Susan they have the rest of the day to themselves then we'll be off."

They reached the village to find a huge bonfire had already been built on the Green and straddling it was an effigy of Napoleon, awaiting a fiery end. The Squire, more to impress

194

her, Matilda felt, than in any genuine spirit of goodwill, was ordering free barrels of ale to be set up outside the Weavers' Arms.

She'd have to go over in a minute, coyly flatter him, remark on his generosity and try and find out if there'd been any news of Harry. As always when Matilda thought about her predicament, tears welled up in her eyes. But she knew the last thing she could afford was for her distress to be made public. Hurrying from her mother she found a log some distance from the main festivities. Here she sat down, pulled a small lace handkerchief from her reticule and blew her nose and wiped her eyes. Then when she'd recovered her composure, Miss Matilda Pedley straightened her back and gazed around with an air of disdain that came naturally to her.

The village, she could see, was working itself up into a fine drunken roustabout. Youths, already well lubricated, were chasing screaming pink faced girls. She saw Jane emerge from the vicarage, then stop and look about her, possibly with the intention of waylaying George. But George was talking to Polly, something so unusual, it made Matilda sit up and take notice. Whatever it was he kept it brief. But before he walked away, he nodded in the direction of the church, and a moment later, Polly, with her heavy, shambling gait, made her way towards St Philip's.

Her curiosity aroused, Matilda looked around for George and saw that he was heading in the same direction but by a more circuitous route. He looked shifty too, kept glancing over his shoulder, and Matilda felt a frisson of unease. What's he up to? She'd known for a long time he couldn't keep his hands off anything in a skirt, but dear God in heaven, not poor simple Polly, surely?

Matilda jumped down from the log. Well if that is his little game, she thought grimly, he'd better be stopped, before Robert finds out and slaughters him.

Tight lipped, Matilda set off in pursuit and found them in the long grass amongst the gravestones. The girl was lying on her back with George already on top of her and when she saw Matilda, she giggled and gave a warning tug at George's curls.

Preoccupied as he was, George sensed there was something amiss, saw the hem of a woman's dress and thinking it was Susan, leapt to his feet in sweating terror. However, when he saw it was Matilda interrupting his pleasuring of Polly, his expression turned to one of venom. "What are young doing here?" he asked, as he pushed his shirt back into his trousers.

"I hardly need to ask you the same question, you despicable little worm. Good God, is no woman safe from you? First Rachel, now this simpleton."

"It's the pot calling the kettle black, isn't it?"

"What are you talking about?"

"Well let's just say that some of your nocturnal wanderings haven't gone unnoticed. I bet you wouldn't want father to know about those. But I'm a reasonable sort of chap, so let's make a bargain. You keep your mouth shut about this little business, and I'll keep mum about you."

"I had no intention of saying anything. If I did, Robert would probably kill you. I don't know how long you've been exploiting this girl, but I suggest you keep away from her in future. If you're that desperate find a whore, not someone with the mental age of a child."

Turning to the girl, Matilda held out her hand. "Straighten your clothes, Polly," she ordered, "I'm taking you back to your mam."

Matilda had just about reconciled herself to an interminable, nail biting wait for the casualty list, when about three days after the peace celebrations, her mother called up the stairs

196

to her that the Squire was in the drawing room and wanted to speak to her.

"What about?" she called back indifferently.

"He didn't say, but I think he's got a letter."

Matilda didn't swoon, her mind didn't go blank, she just thought 'letter'. It could only mean one thing, news of Harry.

As she descended the stairs her smile was brave, but she refused to allow her glance to stray in the direction of the letter Francis Bennett held in his hand, the contents of which held her future in the balance; either happiness or a lifetime's heartache.

Matilda wished him a gracious good-morning then indicating that he should follow, brushed past him into the drawing room. The Squire was still behind her when she heard him say, sounding more pleased that she might have expected, "I've had a letter from my brother Basil. Harry has been slightly wounded in the shoulder, but he's going to be all right."

There was a sound like a sigh then Matilda swung round to face him, her whole face illuminated with joy.

But Francis Bennett found consolation in the knowledge that his next words would wipe that happiness from her face. "There's just one other thing," he went on, "he's also betrothed."

"B . . . be . . . trothed?"

"Yes, isn't it good news? Apparently he met the young lady at a very grand ball in Brussels. She was one of the few people who didn't flee after the war started and she helped nurse him back to health." He opened the letter and began reading it. "'The family live around here, not far from Loughborough. Wealthy too by all acounts. Oh, and her name's Charlotte.'" He studied his brother's poorly formed script more closely. "Charlotte Paget." The Squire finished reading the letter and looked up. He'd imagined it would be a moment to cherish: Harry revealed in his true

197

colours. But even he could find no pleasure in Matilda's white stricken face.

She stood staring at him for a moment trying to control the violent tremors in her body, then with an abrupt, "I fear I have a migraine coming on, I must go to my room," she rushed past him, and he could hear her heartbroken sobs even as she climbed the stairs.

Chapter Fifteen

Joseph Pedley had come back from Nottingham in a towering rage, having lost a considerable amount of money in an extremely volatile and nervous stock market. Rumours of defeat in Belgium, false as it turned out, had resulted in heavy selling, which sent Consols plummeting. Like many other businessmen, Joseph Pedley panicked and sold his when the market was at its most depressed, only to see them go sky high a few days later when hostilities ceased.

"There's a story coming from the Stock Exchange that a certain well-known banker increased his wealth by more than a hundred thousand pounds this week, through his manipulation of the market. But beggared me." He'd been striding up and down the room but suddenly he stopped and glaring at his children said, "You two will have to pull your belts in from now on. No more fripperies for you, Tilda and you, George, will be settling your own gambling debts in future."

Assuming he was exaggerating their financial situation, his children received these facts with their normal air of indifference. Their father threatened them so frequently with poverty these days.

"Don't worry Joseph, we'll manage somehow," answered his wife, maintaining her normal optimistic manner, which was how she dealt with any adversity, no matter how she felt inside. And she felt dreadful. Not out of any personal fear of poverty, but because, on top of everything else, she would shortly have to communicate to her husband information of such gravity, it would cause him to erupt into a rage of volcanic proportions. For she'd finally established that Matilda was pregnant.

It was while Francis Bennett and Matilda had been talking in the drawing room. Under the pretext that she was arranging flowers Mrs Pedley had hovered in the hall, as anxious as her daughter about the contents of the letter. But their voices were little more than a mumble, even when she had her ear pressed hard against the door. And she was quite thrown off guard when the door was unexpectedly flung open. Only just in time did she manage to avoid the embarrassment of being caught eavesdropping. Not that Matilda was aware of anyone. In a state of near hysteria, she'd gone rushing up the stairs to her room. Assuming that Harry must be dead, Mrs Pedley was just on her way to offer what comfort she could when behind her, Francis Bennett said in a nonchalant tone, "The poor girl seems to have taken the news of Harry's betrothal rather badly."

Esther Pedley swung round. "He's not dead then?"

"Good Lord, no. Alive and kicking, apart from a small shoulder wound."

"If you don't mind letting yourself out, Mr Bennett, I'd better go to her," answered Mrs Pedley distractedly and by the time he reached the door, she was was already half way up the stairs.

But with no sense of being snubbed, the Squire walked down the lane whistling happily to himself. There was within him the feeling of a job well done and the certain knowledge that if he approached Joseph Pedley for his daughter's hand, no obstacles would be put in the path to domestic bliss. And due to the unfortunate circumstances in which Matilda found herself, he could also afford to hold out for a hefty dowry. The idea of actually being out of debt for once in his life added so much to his good humour, he began whacking the heads off flowers with a stick.

Up in Matilda's room, Mrs Pedley, who was as angry with her headstrong daughter as she'd ever been in her life, didn't waste time on sympathy. The tears and hysteria would alter nothing, but practical alternatives had to be considered.

"Matilda, stop that noise, do you hear me?" Mrs Pedley said standing over the prone, heaving body of her daughter. "I'm sorry you are so upset about Harry but there is something I must ask you and I want a truthful answer, otherwise I can do nothing to help. Are you with child?"

Matilda gave the merest nod of the head.

"I thought so. You know what this means don't you? You'll have to make yourself extremely agreeable to the Squire and hope that he'll ask for your hand in marriage pretty quickly."

Matilda began pounding the pillow with her fists. "I can't marry him! I can't! He's a disgusting, horrible drunk!"

"Suggest an alternative then," said her mother coldly. "You silly, silly girl, giving yourself to that ne'er-do-well. And you'd better not let Francis Bennett get even a hint of your condition. Men don't like damaged goods you know. Except that now he's at least assured of an heir," she added practically.

"Oh Mama, how could Harry do such a thing to me?" wailed the unhappy Matilda and flung her head against her mother's bosom. And Mrs Pedley, stroking her daughter's curls tried to keep her thoughts calm and wondered if it would look too obvious if she invited the Squire up to supper that evening.

There was a hitch over the dowry but otherwise the courtship went surprisingly well. Francis Bennett was delighted by Matilda's amiability. He could kiss and pet her and she never squirmed away when he pressed his lips against hers. Sometimes, though, he lost control and would try to fondle

201

her breasts. She might object then but only mildly, perhaps with a playful smack of the hand, "Mr Bennett, really!"

"Francis, you must call me Francis," he murmured hotly in her ear. Then, "Matilda, may I speak to your father? Will you marry me?"

They were sitting in the garden, and as he spoke he suddenly went down on his knees, clasping her hand dramatically to his breast. But the sudden exertion made him wince and he looked such an incongruous sight, Matilda felt the sort of mocking laughter that could easily put her future in jeopardy bubbling in her throat. She stifled it with a pretended fit of coughing, cleared her throat then said with a becoming blush, "Isn't this a little sudden . . . Francis?" but at the same time trying to calculate whether with three weeks to wait while the banns were called, she'd still be able to hide her bulge. Still, she thought, a cleverly cut dress from Mrs Dumelow in Leicester ought to hide the worst of it. Although her gowns were expensive. And since she wasn't exactly in her father's good books, he might not feel so inclined to indulge her as he'd done in the past. Her mother had insisted, cruelly Matilda felt, that it was her job to break the news to him of her condition and she could still tremble at the memory of his explosive rage. He'd rarely hit her, even as a child, but Matilda knew she came near to being struck that day. He'd flung words like 'whore' at her, aimed pewter jugs at the wall, threatened her with expulsion from the house. Like all storms it had blown over, although her father was only just beginning to speak to her again. And it had been made clear she was duty bound to accept Francis Bennett's proposal. So if all went to plan, in a short time, she would be Lady of the Manor, which would at least afford her father some comfort amidst all the gloom.

Joseph Pedley's face had turned a violent puce then paled when Francis Bennett made known the dowry price. "Good

God man, where do you expect me to get that sort of money from? I've done very badly on the Stock Exchange recently, business is poor and most of my land is mortgaged up to the hilt."

"Well you'll have to mortgage some more then, or your house. I don't think it's an unreasonable sum for a dowry, just enough to pay off a few outstanding debts and repair the roof. After all you wouldn't want Matilda living in a house with a leaking roof, now would you? Anyway, that's my price, or the marriage is off." To show he wasn't bluffing, the Squire walked to the door.

"But the banns have been called, and the wedding is next week."

"Well let's say it will be as long as you find the money."

With the spectre of a jilted, pregnant, daughter hanging over him, Joseph Pedley slumped down in his chair a defeated man. "All right Bennett, I'll raise it somehow."

"Good."

By no stretch of the imagination could the wedding have been described as a happy occasion. Matilda mumbled her vows and refused to look at her husband, while her mother, standing just behind, wept noisily. Mrs Dumelow hadn't failed her though. At great expense and with careful darting, the wedding gown of cream sarsenet, cunningly disguised Matilda's expanding belly, defying even the most inquisitive eye to detect that anything was amiss.

Deeply unhappy as she was, Matilda still noticed, as they came out of church, that there wasn't one cheer or call of "good luck," from the villagers lining the path, just an uneasy hostile silence.

Afterwards, the parson and his two daughters joined the Pedleys and bride and groom for the wedding breakfast at Thatcher's Mount. But it seemed to Matilda about as joyous as a wake, and even the toasts to their future health and happiness had a hollow ring.

The groom, however, felt rather pleased with life. He'd drunk and eaten well, against all the odds he had the woman he wanted and thanks to her, for the first time in years, he was comfortably in credit. Pleasurably anticipating the consummation of their union, he pulled a watch from his waistcoat pocket. Then as casually as possible he called over to his bride, "I think we'd better go, my dear."

Matilda had been dreading this moment. "All right Francis."

She stood up, thinking to herself that all she'd really done in marrying was change from dutiful daughter to obedient wife. Going over to her father she kissed him goodbye and thanked him, clung briefly to her mother, then like Marie Antoinette on her way to her execution, got in the buggy beside her husband and drove off.

Matilda had always known that Trent Hall was run down, but previously she'd never noticed the weeds sprouting from cracks in the steps. And somehow she'd expected the servants to be lined up to greet their new mistress with a deferential bob. Instead Francis rang the bell and after a long pause, a sullen looking Hodge opened the door, while still thrusting his arms into a threadbare jacket. As she walked over the threshold, Matilda gave him a glance which said, 'you don't know it yet, but there are going to be changes here.'

"Your new home, my love," said the bridegroom with great pride, clasping his new wife tightly and kissing her cheek. "What do you think of it?"

"Very . . . nice," Matilda lied, gazing about her in distaste at the grimy walls, worn furniture and faded hangings. However, she had inherited her mother's natural good taste, and as Francis showed her around she noticed that the proportions of the rooms were handsome and would repay any work done on them. Briefly her unhappiness

204

left her. In her mind's eye she saw herself organizing the redecoration of the house and entertaining the cream of the County. And the fact that the gentry would no longer dare to snub her, was, as far as she could see, the only consolation in being Mrs Francis Bennett.

"Shall we take a turn round the garden my dear?" asked Francis after they'd taken a little light refreshment in the drawing room. He kept glancing furtively at his watch but felt that seven o'clock on a summer's evening was probably a little early for even the most ardent of bridegrooms.

So they fought their way through the overgrown garden. he showed her filthy cowsheds and rusting farm equipment. And on the guided tour of her new home, it struck Matilda, that there was little evidence that the revolutionary farming methods of such men as Turnip Townshend and Robert Bakewell had ever been been heard of, let alone put into practice. The whole estate, the livestock, even the land itself, had a neglected abandoned air.

Matilda was predisposed to discuss the state of the farm with him when they returned to the house, but it wasn't agricultural matters the bridegroom had on his mind, and as soon as the clock chimed nine, he yawned loudly and stood up. "Shall we retire my love?" He held out his hand and together they mounted the stairs, the Squire almost dragging his bride behind him.

Although Matilda had more or less resigned herself to her fate, the sight of the huge four poster bed with its dusty, moth-eaten drapes, and her nightdress, a virginal white against the grimy sheets, brought her situation into sharp focus. "And who's to blame for this," she muttered through clenched teeth. Harry, that's who. But one day she would exact a bitter revenge. How, she wasn't sure. But she swore she would, even if she had to wait all her life.

Francis had disappeared into his dressing room so she quickly undressed and climbed into the conjugal bed. Feeling like a sacrificial lamb, Matilda lay down and closed her eyes. If I don't look at him, perhaps it won't be so bad, she said to herself, as the bed creaked with the weight of her husband's body.

Wasting no time on preliminaries, Francis pulled up her nightdress. "Oh my darling," he whispered hoarsely, then sucked on her lips and rubbed his hand between her legs roughly.

With all her heart, Matilda wanted to push him away, tell him that he she found him totally repellent, but the practical side of her knew the marriage had to be consummated that night. He quickly abandoned his clumsy attempts to kindle desire in his wife and was heaving himself on to her when Matilda suddenly said, "Francis, I've often thought I'd like to go to Bath."

"Then you shall my love, you shall."

"And have my portrait painted?" she shrewdly bargained as her husband poked and prodded, found what he wanted, then began to noisily grunt and sweat on top of her. Trying not to think that she would have to endure this for the rest of her married life Matilda lay there, as unresponsive as a log, wondering how it was that sex could be so pleasurable with one man, while with another it was almost unendurable.

He seemed to labour long at his task but eventually there was a sound like a balloon deflating, after which he thanked her politely then rolled off her. "Was it as good for you as it was me, my love?" he enquired, giving her a peck on the cheek.

"Oh yes, Francis, it was," Matilda murmured huskily, resisting the urge to laugh in his face.

"I thought so," her spouse answered complacently and a moment later loud snores told her he was fast asleep.

Overwhelmed by a crushing desolation, Matilda turned away from him. She was lying beside a man for whom she felt not the slightest affection and who in the morning would again demand his marital rights, this time when his breath was foul and his face dark and rough with stubble. By becoming Mrs Francis Bennett, she was seen to be bettering herself and yet she'd gone from a comfortable, well run household to a pigpen. This must be the worst day of my life, Matilda thought and her mouth trembled. She bit hard on her lips. She would waste no more tears on Harry. She remembered one of her mother's little homilies: 'Grasp the nettle firmly and it will not hurt.' Well she would do that. Concentrate on refurbishing Trent Hall, and when it was finished invite Harry and fiancée over so that she could act the gracious hostess, parade the baby in front of them, show Harry just what he'd lost.

She'd survived today. Now she had the trip to Bath to look forward to, then when they came back from there she'd have her portrait painted. Small crumbs of comfort but better than nothing and there was no telling what she might be able to wheedle out of Francis if she played her cards right . . . Maybe their own carriage with a liveried coachman. Matilda yawned widely and her lids drooped. Yes, she thought, just before she fell asleep, there might, after all, be certain compensations in being Mrs Francis Bennett.

Chapter Sixteen

Rachel was surprised to find herself still working for Jack Brewin several months after his wife died. It had been her intention to leave once the funeral was over and she'd received the wages due to her. Four unhappy and confused little girls with an indifferent father made her waver in this decision initially; later it was the uncertainty of obtaining another position in a town where trade had become increasingly depressed. Looking at it practically, she saw that a roof over her head was something to be thankful for, and even if her employer kept a meagre table, at least she wasn't starving. And Jack Brewin desperate not to lose her, had in a weak moment, offered her a rise in wages and promised to pay her on the dot each month.

But if Rachel was honest with herself she often felt lonely. She missed Susan, Polly and Sam and the familiar routine of country life where the cycle of the year was marked by such events as planting, sheep shearing, haymaking and harvest. Her one link with them might have been Jed, except that she had no contact with him at all. Often on some pretext, she would find herself walking past the shop. Sometimes he would be serving a customer and at others his head would be bent low over a ledger. But even if she slowed to a snail's pace, he never looked up or acknowledged her presence. At first Rachel was put out by his coldness, then thought, just like a man to hold me responsible for what happened and started feeling resentful instead. But their estrangement cut her off from the news and gossip of Halby and often she felt tempted to jump on a carrier's cart and surprise them all. Except that she was uncertain of the reception she might recive if Joseph Pedley got wind of her visit. And a fear of George was still a burden she carried around with her. Looking at it realistically, Rachel realized that as far as he was concerned she was unfinished business; quarry to be stalked until the kill. Sooner or later they must come face to face and her one hope was that she would acquit herself with honour.

The chance to find out came one morning in October. Weighed down with bundles of hosiery she, Primrose and Marigold struggled against a head wind to catch the fly-boat that would leave Leicester Canal at noon. People were optimistic that the recently opened waterway would bring prosperity to the town, and it was the proud boast of Messrs Pickfords that their boats arrived loaded from London in the morning and returned reladen for the Metropolis the same day.

Everything and everyone seemed to move at an accelerated speed. Merchants haggled, piles of timber and slate hampered the girls' progress and Rachel tutted in exasperation. Then they had to dodge round a mountain of coal being heaved by sweating men, naked to the waist and black as Africans. Their shovels threw up great swirling clouds of dust and grit which blew in the girl's eyes, furred the insides of their mouths and left an acrid taste on their tongues. The sisters coughed and spluttered then began to complain. Rachel was telling them to 'shut up,' when they suddenly found themselves faced with an even greater hazard; barrels full of molasses being rolled straight towards them at dangerous speeds by a gang of hefty young men.

"Out of the way!" One of their number shouted and just in time the girls leapt aside, in their fright scattering the parcels of hose in every direction.

"Idiot, do you want to kill someone?" Rachel raged at the cocky youth.

The young man stopped the barrel with his foot, then after regarding Rachel's angry face with more than a passing interest, shouted cheekily, "Well certainly not you, sweetheart, you're far too pretty."

Rachel, who had grown used to the effect her looks had on men, gave a haughty toss of her head, disdaining the compliments of such a callow youth. But the sisters were transfixed in admiration. For he now stood, a proper cock of the walk, flexing his muscles and puffing out his chest for Rachel's benefit. That is until his foreman yelled at him to get a bloody move on, whereupon he turned scarlet and they collapsed in a fit of girlish giggles.

In spite of the these various obstacles they managed to reach the Pickford office in time, had let the heavy parcels fall from their tired arms on to the counter and were awaiting a receipt, when through the window Rachel saw George, making straight towards the office. Although her brain told her there was nothing he could do to her here, not with workmen and bargees milling around, her heart still set up a great hammering against her ribs and her mouth went dry with apprehension. Snatching the receipt from the surprised clerk's hand and with a brief, "Come along girls," she hurried from the office.

However, George already had his foot on the bottom step and when he saw her he extended an arm and tried to delay her. "Why look who it is!" he exclaimed. "And there was me thinking you'd been spirited away by that scoundrel, Jed Fairfax."

"Let me past or I shall make a scene," Rachel muttered.

George let his arm fall. "You are quite at liberty to pass. And your little friends as well." He smiled benignly at Primrose and Marigold, who were now all agog.

Turning to urge the startled girls to, 'Hurry up', she went

to push past him, but his hand fell on her shoulder. "Rachel, couldn't we let bygones be bygones and meet occasionally. I'd treat you well, I really would. Dress you like a lady, take you to the theatre, the races, anywhere you want, just for a few small kindnesses."

"Get your filthy hands off me."

"Please."

"I'm warning you, let go," she repeated very quietly.

"Not until you've said yes."

"Your skin's obviously so thick you don't realize just how much I detest you, George Pedley. Well perhaps this will help you get the message." And throwing back her head Rachel very deliberately spat in his face.

Then coolly, she turned to the astounded younger girls. "Come along, we must be getting back or your papa will wonder where we've got to."

"By God, I will get you one of these days," Rachel heard George spluttering.

Although she maintained a brisk pace Rachel didn't run, not until she rounded the corner of a warehouse and reached the towpath. Then in a tense voice she said to her charges, "Run, like the very devil." Without even bothering to check whether they were following her, she picked up her skirts and fled.

However, rain had made the towpath treacherous and when she heard a plaintive cry of, "Wait for us," Rachel turned just in time to see Primrose go sprawling in the mud. For a second she was tempted to leave the girl there, but she saw that if her life wasn't to be blighted by him she must conquer her fear of George. She gave a swift glance about her, but there was no sign of him. He'd grown hefty and that would check his progress, plus with his gigantic conceit he wouldn't want to spoil the shine on his hessians. Slowly the tension eased and she walked back to where Primrose was lying spreadeagled.

211

"I nearly went head first into the canal," the girl wailed when Rachel reached her.

"Nonsense," answered Rachel and grabbing Primrose's collar, yanked her to her feet.

The child stared at her hands and white apron plastered in mud and tried to assess whether it was worth making a fuss. Deciding it might be, she started to bawl, loudly.

"Shut up, you're not hurt," said Marigold callously. Then her eyes bright with curiosity, she turned her attention to Rachel.

"Who was that man, Abigail? You're frightened of him aren't you? I could tell by your eyes. That's why we ran away, isn't it?"

"Hasn't your papa ever told you it's rude to ask questions?"

"No," the girl replied truthfully, then ignoring the reprimand, went on, "And why did he call you Rachel?"

"I don't know what you're talking about, he didn't call me that."

"Yes he did," said Primrose, forgetting her tears.

"Don't talk daft," Rachel scoffed. "You must be have been hearing things."

"Yes he did! Yes he did! We heard him," they chanted, jumping up and down with excitement.

"I'm not standing here a moment longer listening to your nonsense." And in attempt to ward off further awkward questions, Rachel moved off along the path. But the interrogation continued.

"And fancy spitting in his face like that. You wouldn't have done that without a reason either," persisted Marigold, who was following directly behind.

Finally Rachel, unable to stand the barrage of questions any longer, stopped. "Look are you two going to keep this up all the way home?"

"Yes," they answered, undeterred by her fierce expression.

212

Resigned to the inevitability of some explanation, Rachel thought: Now do I tell them the truth, or do I concoct some story? She was reluctant to go digging about in dark painful memories, but anything else, she knew, would have to be plausible enough to satisfy two inquisitive little minds. And they were standing looking up at her now with the same bright expectancy as they did when they were waiting for one of her bedtime stories. And that is what this will have to be, she decided, a bit of fiction. So thinking quickly, she launched into her tale.

"Right, I'll tell you what happened. But it's to be a secret between us. And mind you don't go telling your papa what you saw today. Because if you did, I would probably have to leave and you wouldn't like that, would you?"

"Don't leave us, Abigail, please," pleaded Primrose, who looked as if she might dissolve into tears again.

"If you keep quiet I won't. But you must give your solemn promise."

"Oh we do, we do," they piped, wriggling impatiently.

"Well it was like this: I was out one day, minding my own business when that unpleasant character started pestering me. He wouldn't leave me alone, followed me round the town, wanted to know my name, where I lived, would I see him again. In the end the only way I could get rid of him, was to tell him my name was Rachel and agree to meet him the following day at the Three Crowns. I didn't go of course and that was why he was so persistent back there. But I sorted him out didn't I?" She laughed, trying to hide her anxiety and glanced from one small face to the other.

"Well I don't know why you didn't meet him. He seemed like a gentleman to me," said Primrose, who obviously felt Rachel could do a lot worse than George and had missed a golden opportunity.

"He might have dressed like one, but don't ever be

213

deceived by fine clothes. It takes more than that to turn someone into a gentleman."

"He had nice blond curls, too," added Marigold enviously, thinking of her own dull locks.

Rachel gave an involuntary shudder. "He's fat and I hate men with blond curls."

"But you haven't got a beau, have you?" said Primrose.

"No I haven't. Anyway when would I have time to go courting? I spend all my time looking after you lot, don't I?"

There was no questioning the truth of this and it silenced the girls briefly. But then they were off again, prattling between themselves and trying to decide what qualities they would be looking for in a suitor when they reached that state of grace, womanhood, beckoning so tantalizingly, and yet still such a long way off.

Grateful that they'd ceased badgering her, Rachel fell to thinking of Harry, wondering if he could have been regarded as a beau. He'd liked her, she knew that and his kiss was something she still recalled with a secret pleasure. She'd remembered him in her prayers at night, right through the fighting and for some time afterwards. But since, as a Christian, she felt she failed miserably, Rachel wasn't sure her feeble petitions had been heard and Harry might well be dead. Except that she found this hard to believe. The charming, opportunistic Harry with his highly developed sense of self-preservation, his lust for life, dead? No, it was impossible. The passing of time had blurred his faults, the way he'd trifled with Matilda's affections. One day, she was certain, she would hear her name called, and turn to find him striding towards her, his blue eyes regarding her in a way that could always make her heart beat pleasurably.

In spite of her warnings to the girls, they were such chatterboxes Rachel still wasn't sure if she could rely on them to keep their mouths shut. So when she'd got them home, wiped the mud from Marigold's hands and tied her into a clean apron, she cautioned them again. "Now remember what I said, not a word to your papa about this morning."

However, their vigorous assurances still couldn't dispel her anxiety, even after their father had come in and they were all sitting around the dinner table. Her edginess made her tetchy and as soon as either girl opened her mouth to speak she would glare at her warningly. This so unnerved them that their chatter petered out and the meal continued in almost total silence.

Jack Brewin spoke only once throughout the meal and that was to complain about his feckless workers before sinking back into a gloomy introspection. If he'd been taciturn and uncommunicative before his wife's death he was doubly so now. He fairly burned with self-pity. What little interest he'd shown in his children had evaporated into indifference and their management was now left to Rachel, who provided the only affection they had. That they were growing increasingly dependent troubled her at times, for she saw she was in danger of becoming a substitute mother. Although she had no immediate plans, Rachel had no wish to spend the rest of her days in Jack Brewin's employment. The risk was that soon she might be bound to the girls by threads too strong to break. Rachel's only hope was that some rather desperate widow would come along and take Jack Brewin and his family, off her hands.

Jack Brewin finished his dinner, belched his appreciation and left the table. Rachel had cleared away, sent the girls to play in the yard and was just measuring flour into a bowl to make bread, when he suddenly appeared again. Looking agitated, he pushed a piece of paper across the table to her.

"This has just come. Someone put it through the door."

"What is it?"

"A letter. Read it but don't let the little un's see it, for gawd's sake." His voice had a tremor in it and he nervously plucked hairs from his bushy eyebrows.

Hiding her surprise, for her employer had never before taken her into his confidence, Rachel wiped her hands down her apron and picked up the letter. But it was so crumpled and ill-written it took a moment or two to smooth out and decipher. "'By Genral Luds orders your childrin will be orfons your masheens broke your busness runed if you dont pay proper wages. Remember you are a marked man Brewin. yrs for Genral Lud.'"

Trying to convince herself it was just a stupid hoax, Rachel read the letter twice, her scalp prickling with apprehension.

She glanced at the letter again then at Jack Brewin who had collapsed into a chair by the fire. His head was cradled in his hands and his whole body shook like someone gripped with the palsy. "What am I to do?" he moaned and began to rock back and forth like a child.

"You must go to the police immediately. And take this with you, it's important evidence." She thrust the letter back in his shaking hand.

"What can the police do? Everyone knows they're useless." He looked up at her and Rachel saw that his eyes were moist with self-pity.

"They'll have a constable of the watch put on guard that's what."

"Fat lot of use one nightwatchman would be against that rabble. There's no protection for honest citizens in this town. What we need is the Redcoats. Anyway I knows who's responsible. It's them workmen of mine." Finding someone on whom to vent his spleen, he recovered a little of his usual blustering manner. "Ungrateful bastards!" He spat contemptuously in the fire. "So I had to reduce their wages, but I've not stood any of 'em off have I?" He looked to Rachel for confirmation of his altruism. "No they're out to get me and there's nothing I can do."

216

Rachel knew that although his business wasn't doing well, there was still a market for his cheap cut-up hose, particularly in London, and he was making a living, which was more than could be said of some hosiers. Thinking she was there to spy on them, the stockingers regarded her with suspicion and their talk was guarded whenever she was around. But she heard their mutters of dissent. And having endured Jack Brewin's meanness, she sympathized with the men and understood their burning resentment when yet again their wages were cut.

Jack Brewin still hadn't budged, and Rachel, exasperated by his ineffectual behaviour, wanted to shake him. Is he going to sit there all day brooding on his misfortunes, she wondered irritably. She'd realized for some time that he lacked backbone and this knowledge had brought about an imperceptible shift in their relationship and Rachel sometimes felt it was five children she had on her hands instead of four. Finally growing impatient of his inertia she said sharply, "Well, what are you going to do? Take that letter down to the police office, or let Ned Ludd's men break your frames?"

"I can't leave them lot. There's no telling what they might get up to on their own."

Them lot, Rachel knew, meant his workmen for whom he had scant regard.

"Yes you can. I'll keep an eye on things in the frameshop. Not that I think it was one of them anyway. With things as they are, they'd have to be pretty stupid to put themselves out of work."

"You're right I must do something," he said and leapt to his feet. "But it's no good depending on the law. No, I'm going out this minute to buy myself a weapon, a pistol or musket. And just let any bugger dare set foot on my premises and I'll blast his bloody brains out." He glared threateningly about him as if he might actually find a Luddite skulking in the shadows. Then before Rachel could warn him against such foolhardy action, he departed, and with the swagger of someone who looked as if he meant business.

"It's the police you should be going to," Rachel shouted after him, following it with, "fool!" when she knew he was safely out of earshot. But she was glad to have him out from under her feet and settle down to the soothing, domestic task of making bread; of mixing flour, yeast and water to a dough, of kneading away her fear of George and anonymous men who came in the night to destroy. When she was done she returned the dough to the bowl, covered it with a cloth and left it to prove. Then sitting down she allowed herself the luxury of ten minutes idleness before facing the stockingers.

She was disturbed by shrill, quarrelling voices from the yard. Rachel opened her eyes, yawned, saw that the dough had ballooned to double its size and jumped from her chair. Scooping up the spongy mixture, she knocked it back, shaped it into loaves, then going to the door, called the girls in. Ignoring their complaints at having their play interrupted, she instructed them to keep an eye on the bread while it baked, warning them that if they were careless and allowed it burn there would be nothing for tea. Hoping it wouldn't be too long before Jack Brewin returned, she left Marigold in charge and made her way to the frameshop.

Although light poured in from three large windows down either wall, these were never opened so as well as being cramped, the frameshop was also stuffy and smelt of flesh too infrequently washed. And the grating, discordant sound of eight stocking frames working in unison always set Rachel's teeth on edge. The men sat back to back, with just enough space between the large, cumbersome wooden frames to give them arm movement. The stockingers, jealously guarding their livelihood, saw to it that she, a woman, who would probably work for even less than they did, never operated one of the frames,

218

and even Jack Brewin knew better than to defy them on this point.

Frame knitting was no mystery to Rachel, though. She'd spent too many hours watching Robert as a small girl. And when she was old enough and her legs could reach the treadles, he'd taught her how to work the frame, shown her how to adjust it to decrease or increase the stitches so that the worsted material followed the shape of the leg. She'd seen the weariness in Robert's body at the end of a long day, knew the sheer physical effort that went into just one row of knitted fabric, the strain on the eyes, the co-ordination required between leg and treadle, arm and heavy iron carriage.

As she squeezed past them to reach the winding-wheel the men made a great show of ignoring her. At first she'd felt intimidated by their hostility. Then she'd felt hurt. It had taken longer to think, 'damn you all'. Now she didn't give a pin for any of them. Occasionally she looked up from winding a bobbin and studied their faces, wondering if perhaps one of them had sent the letter and searching for signs of guilt. But their features were impassive. They might know about the letter but she doubted if any of them would have been so foolhardy as to send it. Anyhow they were probably incapable of penning a letter, even a semi-illiterate one. No, more likely it was someone such as that crony of Jed's, James Towle who was said to go out Ludding not from conviction but purely for monetary gain.

The afternoon progressed into early evening and Rachel waited in vain for Jack Brewin to return. And with the noise and stuffy atmosphere, she could feel an ominous throbbing pain developing over her left eye.

Because they had to supply their own candles, the men tried to work for as long as they could without artificial light. And once lit, the candles were placed behind water-filled glass globes called shiners, which threw light on to their frames, and enabled them to go on working long after it had grown dark.

Tonight Rachel noticed that the shiners disturbed her vision and the stabbing pain in her eye had spread all over her skull and developed into a headache that would split a stone. Pressing her fingers against her temples, she closed her eyes and prayed it would go away. But she knew it wouldn't. She'd suffered this sort of headache before. A migraine was what Mrs Pedley called it, and would pack her off to bed with a vinegar compress on her forehead. To move her head had now become an agony, the light in her eyes a torture. Mumbling to the man nearest her to check that all the candles were snuffed and to lock up, she thrust the key at him and staggered blindly from the frameshop, just making the yard before she was sick. She was still heaving noisily when she reached the house and her knees buckled under her. Without the will to rise again she crawled on all fours up the stairs, and collapsed on to her bed.

The retching tore at her stomach, she sweated and shivered, hammer blows pounded away in her head, so that when she heard Marigold's small frightened voice asking, "You're not going to die, are you Abigail?" Rachel didn't have the strength to do more than groan.

"Don't die . . . please. We didn't burn the bread and I'm sorry we're naughty sometimes, but we won't ever be again," babbled the guilt-ridden child and burst into great hiccuping sobs.

Without opening her eyes, Rachel found the girl's hand and gave it a reassuring squeeze. Finally Marigold's tears subsided to a manageable sniff and after blowing her nose several times, she asked, "Can I get you something, Abigail?"

"I . . . I'm very . . . cold." A short while later Rachel was dimly aware of a huge counterpane being tucked round her then the door being quietly closed.

She lay there for hours, bludgeoned by pain and certain

her skull would crack. But mercifully, sometime in the night, the vice-like grip on her temples eased and the spasms in her stomach subsided. She was dozing fitfully when she half heard a disturbance in the street. At first she thought it was a recollection carried over from a dream. But as she became more fully awake and the din grew louder, Rachel decided that it was a drunken marital dispute, an event common enough for her to close her eyes again. Hardly a second later, she was jolted into a sitting position by the sound of running feet and a voice under her window shouting the command,

"Now see you do your job well, men. Dash them cursed frames into the thousand pieces!"

"The Luddites! They've come!" The words formed on her dry lips and she slid in terror under the bedclothes as the pre-dawn silence was shattered by great hammers splintering wood, buckling metal and smashing glass. Why doesn't somebody do something, she thought frantically, blocking her ears against the destruction. Where's the Constable of the watch? Where's Jack Brewin for God's sake?

Gradually, though, her paralysing fear was replaced by anger and she sat up. How dare they reap havoc and destroy! They would not get away with it. Everybody else might stand by and do nothing but she wouldn't. She would identify them and have them brought to justice. Hobnailed boots striking cobblestones spurred her into action. Thrusting her feet out of bed and on to the cold floor, Rachel wrapped herself in the counterpane and stood up, only to sit down very suddenly again, when her legs buckled under her. She tried again, easing herself up with care and moving to the window.

To avoid capture the Luddites struck then moved quickly on, so she was only just in time to catch sight of about half a dozen shadowy figures in long coats and with blackened faces, erupting from the yard. All she could distinguish was great hammers balanced on shoulders and a musket she knew

221

they wouldn't hesitate to use if confronted. With a wildly beating heart she stepped back into the shadows, heard the curt command from their leader, (was that Jed's voice?) to "Get going," and recklessly moved forward again. As quickly as they'd come, they dispersed, two legging it over the wall of the Great Meeting, the rest disappearing amongst the narrow lanes and back alleys of the neighbourhood.

After this there was nothing but dust and silence and Rachel didn't realize she was shaking violently until, too late a nightwatchman, preceded by his lantern, came puffing round the corner. Then doors opened and neighbours, awakened by the frenzy of the attack but who, she suspected, had decided to stay out of harm's way until it was over, now appeared in the street, everyone talking at once.

"What's going on here then?" the nightwatchman asked importantly.

"By the noise I'd say Jack Brewin's shop's been smashed to smithereens, courtesy of Ned Ludd," a man replied.

"Has it by jove," said the upholder of law and order. "Did you see them?"

"Oh I see'd them arright."

"Why didn't you try and stop them then?"

"What and get me bloody brains blowed out? No thank you."

"So where is this Jack Brewin then?"

"A good question," the neighbour answered. "Because I reckon you'd have to be deaf as a doorpost or dead drunk to sleep through that noise."

The nightwatchman conferred briefly with the man who'd delegated himself spokesman, then he crossed the street and proceeded to pound the door with his stave, calling out at the same time, "Now come on Jack Brewin, be stirring yourself for heaven's sake!"

The banging reverberated through the house and Rachel's head. Why in heaven's name doesn't Jack Brewin open up, she fumed. Her mouth tasted sour, her hair, when she touched it, had the texture of a gorse bush and her clothes, which she hadn't taken off when she fell into bed, were crumpled and stained. She longed to crawl back under the bedclothes, to pretend none of this was happening. Except that it was obvious the noise wouldn't let up until she went down and let the nightwatchman in.

Berating him under her breath, she adjusted her clothes and tried to smooth her hair. Then she lit a candle, opened her door and was nearly sent flying by the four small figures crouched there.

"What on earth . . .!" she exclaimed, and managed to regain her balance, just as four terrified children flung themselves upon her and started to howl.

"It's all right, I'm here," she said, trying to pacify them while at the same time anxiously wondering where their father was.

"Wha . . . what's happening Abigail?" asked Primrose in between sobs.

Since they would soon see for themselves the destruction of their father's business, Rachel saw little point in fobbing them off with half truths. So she kept her voice calm and replied, "I think Ned Ludd's men have paid us a visit."

The sobbing stopped and four pairs of eyes regarded her with interest. "Ned Ludd?"

"Yes, but they've gone now," she reassured them, then realized, as they began to chatter excitedly, that she needn't have bothered. In the way of children, they were elated rather than frightened by this news. The implications were lost to them. This was adventure.

Rachel now noticed that the hammering on the front door had stopped. Going over to the window she threw it open and leaned out. The street was deserted. The neighbours had returned to their beds, and the nightwatchman had given up and moved on to other duties without even bothering to investigate.

But where was her employer? Nobody could have slept through that noise. And just supposing he'd decided to camp out in the frameshop to protect his machines. Remembering the musket and hammer, Rachel shivered. Ordering the girls back to bed, she hurried downstairs. Her migraine had left her hardly able to think straight. Fearful for his safety, in her mind's eyes she saw Jack Brewin, face down in a pool of blood, the back of his head caved in and perhaps already dead.

She was half-way along the passage when her attention was caught by a spluttering candle in the kitchen. Among the shadows it threw up on the wall, was the outline of a man.

Angered that she wasted time worrying about him, Rachel stamped into the kitchen, ready to give Jack Brewin a piece of her mind. But as she gazed down at him, sprawled in drunken oblivion in the chair and unaware that his livelihood had been taken from him, her scorn turned to pity. He was such a weak man and misfortune seemed to dog him relentlessly. He would find out soon enough, let him sleep a while longer, she thought.

But tomorrow morning she would be making a call. On Mr Jed Fairfax. Because she had a strong feeling there was a thing or two that gentleman could tell her about tonight's attack.

Chapter Seventeen

The cacophony of church bells calling their faithful to prayer made it difficult for Rachel to think. But then the noise ceased and a Sunday calm returned to the streets, enabling her to get her thoughts into good order and decide how she would approach Jed.

She'd set off from Jack Brewin's armed with the powerful weapons of self-righteousness and bitter anger. However, as she turned into High Cross Street, she found her steps faltering. With no real evidence, apart from a voice overheard in the dark, and the letter in her pocket, she was about to accuse a man of being involved in a crime for which he could be hanged. Then she remembered again the heart-wrenching scene she'd witnessed earlier that morning. Her employer standing staring at the wanton, savage destruction of his frameshop; smashed windows, splintered wood and twisted metal; unfinished hose and hanks of yarn saturated in oil, bobbins and needles hurled about the room. She heard again his cry of, "Why have they done this to me? Why?" as he sank to his knees among the debris, saw the tears slowly coursing town his cheeks then the slow crumbling of his body into despair. These images of a man pushed beyond reason, haunted her and stoked her anger. Her uncertainty hardened into resolve, at least until she reached the shop, when a nervous dryness in her throat made her cough.

Although it was the Sabbath, Rachel had expected the shop to be open, but the notice in the window said closed.

Was that because of last night? She rattled the handle to gain his attention. It would take a man with no sense of remorse to rest easy after he'd wilfully ruined a man's life. Was Jed that sort of man? From the stack-burning she had evidence that he was. She rattled the handle again, but when he still didn't appear she moved round to the side of the house, rapping insistently upon the door until she heard Jed calling in a sleepy voice, "Who is it?"

"Me, Rachel."

"Rachel?" Was that a wariness she heard in his voice? "Just a minute while I get something on." There was a pause but when he opened the door he was still tucking his shirt into his trousers and trying to smooth down his hair.

"Why, this is an unexpected pleasure."

"Is it?" replied Rachel. Doubting the truth of this she studied his face and shirt collar with unusual interest, searching for the slightest clue, a streak of black, a small abrasion, anything that would confirm his guilt. But apart from an early morning stubble his skin was as clear.

If he felt disconcerted by her scrutiny Jed didn't show it, Instead he flung open the door and with a welcoming smile, invited her to step inside.

It would have been extremely careless of him to leave any evidence lying around, Rachel knew that, but it didn't stop her making a swift inventory of the small room that was so familiar to her, noting the unmade bed, the hand-press, the pamphlets gathering dust on a chair. There were also signs of study: books open on a table, a quill, an inkstand, paper covered in neat cursive writing, the stub of a candle.

"I was working well into the small hours last night, as you can see," Jed said indicating to the writing material. "That was why I was sleeping late."

How plausible he sounds, Rachel thought.

"Sit down, won't you?" said Jed, flicking the dust off a

chair with his handkerchief. "I'll just get the fire going then we can have some tea."

"No thank you, I'm not planning to stay. I just came to ask if you knew anything about this." She handed him the letter Jack Brewin had received the previous day.

He took it from her and read it with a puzzled frown.

"What's this got to do with me?" His eyes narrowed slightly. "And why should you imagine I know anything about it?"

"Because last night my master's frames were destroyed, his livelihood taken away from him."

"You're not suggesting I wrote that illiterate junk and broke his frames?" Jed exploded.

"I . . . not saying you did," Rachel replied, annoyed that her voice faltered.

"Why have you come here, then?" His grey eyes which only a short while ago had welcomed her now looked cold and remote.

"I . . . I . . . just thought you might know who did."

"Did you have anyone in particular in mind?"

Aware that Jed was cleverly manipulating the situation to his own advantage, Rachel rallied. "Yes, James Towle," she said boldly, and watched him carefully for a reaction.

But instead of his face suffusing with guilt, Jed merely gave a derisive snort, "Do you really imagine I'd get myself involved with that scoundrel? I'm not that foolish. And I value my neck."

"I saw you with him, you know I did."

"Oh yes, that day you were with your Dragoon."

Ignoring the reference to Harry, Rachel went on, "You don't deny you know him then?"

"Why should I? It is supposed to be a free country, after all. But if you must know, he's no more than a passing acquaintance. I got talking to Jem in the Three Crowns. At first I didn't know who he was. But he asked me for some legal advice. And since he was a man just out of prison and down on his luck and I'd recently been making a study of the laws of this land, and discovering the truth of the saying that there's one law for the rich and one for the poor, it was something I was glad to give him. Associating with him doesn't make me guilty of his crimes, though."

"You make yourself out to be so innocent Jed Fairfax. But I wouldn't put anything past you," she flung back at him.

"Wouldn't you now?"

A pulse was pounding in her ears but the suspicious she had held so long about Jed now bubbled to the surface and her tongue would not be stilled. "In fact, I know far more about you than you realize," she said recklessly.

"Such as?"

Rachel was gratified to hear that his voice sounded rather more wary, and this gave her the confidence to go on.

"I know, for instance, that sometimes you go in for a bit of rick burning. And if you've fired a stack without it troubling your conscience, you're not going to worry too much about breaking a frame."

The effect of her words was more dramatic then she could have imagined. The colour drained from his face and he moved towards her in such a threatening manner she backed away and searched around for some means of escape. But his bulk was between her and the door and before she had time to do anything he had her wrists in a painful grip.

"Let go, you're hurting me," she protested and tried to squirm from his grasp.

"It was no more than Joseph Pedley deserved, but how do you know about it? Who told you? Was it Susan? Robert?"

"No it wasn't. I saw it all with my own eyes, from my bedroom window. You thought you'd got away with it, didn't you? But one word and I could have a noose around your neck, Jed Fairfax," she taunted.

228

"What about your own pretty neck, eh?" His free hand came up, stroking it with a slow sensuous movement that sent small shock waves through her body. His eyes as he stared into hers were turbulent, his voice menacing. "Do you know, Rachel, I could crush the life out of you in a moment?"

Although her heart was beating uncontrollably, she stared back at him with unwavering scorn. "From what I've seen, you appear quite capable of it."

"Perhaps, but such a waste." Then before she could respond, he pulled her roughly towards him and his mouth came down hard on hers, almost crushing the breath out of her.

Her lips remained clamped shut as she fought him every inch of the way, pushing her hands against his chest, and struggling not to respond. But gradually under the insistent pressure of his mouth her body melted into his, her lips parted, and slowly her arms curled around his neck.

"Oh lovely, lovely Rachel," Jed murmured into her hair, and she felt his fingers fumbling with the buttons on her dress then his hands on her breasts with a shiver of delight. She was allowing him to manoeuvre her in the direction of the bed when unbidden, but into sharp focus, came the gutted frameshop and she pulled sharply away. "Stop it!" she ordered and turning away she adjusted her dress with trembling fingers. "You shouldn't have done that, you know," she accused.

"And you shouldn't have come here. By God Rachel, don't you know how I feel about you?" Jed asked, pacing up and down the small room in a distracted manner.

"No, how do you feel about me?" More or less composed, she tucked in some escaping curls, then turned to face him again.

Jed ceased his pacing and linking her fingers with his and

drawing her close again, said quietly and simply, "I love you Rachel Arden."

"Love . . . me? I don't believe you."

"Damn it, woman, do you really think it's something I'd lie about? It is the last thing I wanted to happen and don't think I haven't fought against it." He sounded angry as if it were her fault. "Would you believe me if I asked you to marry me then?"

Half believing him for a moment, Rachel's head jerked up. "No. You know about politics and the law, you've been to the Grammar school, so you're clever, Jed, cleverer than anyone I know. But what you don't know about is people, or you'd see I'm not the simple country girl of a year ago. And I've already worked out what your game is. You're just trying to save your own skin." Her voice had taken on a high accusing tone and her eyes were bright with indignation. "A wife, you think, would keep her mouth shut about her husband's illegal activities. But you can't buy my silence like that. I don't know for certain whether you're involved with the Luddites and I can't prove that you were involved in last night's attack. But if I could . . ." Leaving the threat unfinished she walked to the door.

She deliberately left it swinging on its hinges and as she strode off down the passage, Rachel heard behind her, Jed hiss, "Why wait? Go to the authorities now. After all there's a good price on the head of any Luddite and you might find yourself the richer by fifty guineas."

Rachel had never heard such contempt in anyone's voice but she tried to shrug it off with an indifferent toss of her head. However, she reached the street to find she was trembling with an impotent rage. To regain some sort of equilibrium, she stood quite still and while families, just out of church or chapel and in their Sunday best, jostled her, she clenched her fists and took in great gulps of air.

Somewhere in the spinning confusion of her mind she knew

230

things had gone horribly wrong. Jed had spoken to her as if she was an informer, someone no better than the notorious spy Oliver, someone prepared to betray for personal gain. But perhaps with her wild talk, she was in a some way to blame. If only she'd kept her mouth shut about the rick-burning. And what had possessed her, allowing him to make love to her like that.

She stood for some time in the warm sunshine, irresolute and unhappy. Her anger had evaporated and she could see she'd achieved nothing that morning except Jed's undying contempt. On top of it all she now had to go back to the tall, gloomy house in Butt Close Lane, which held little attraction at that precise moment. The weather beckoned as well. It was one of those perfect dying days of autumn when nature seemed to be flaunting itself like a defiant, fading beauty. It wasn't a day to be cooped up indoors but a day for taking a stroll up New Walk, or along the banks of the Soar. Except that with everyone else in pairs or family groups, she would look conspicuous on her own.

Trying to put the whole miserable episode with Jed out of her mind, Rachel wandered slowly down the high street. But she was in no hurry so she paused every now and then to gaze in shop windows: at French gloves, fans, gowns and all manner of things she could never afford to buy. She was studying one of Mrs Dumelow's exquisite confections and imagining the delight of real silk against the skin, when she became aware of someone standing close behind her. A quick glance told her that the features reflected in the window were those of a man. Increasingly, Rachel found herself being pestered by the opposite sex and the most effective way of dealing with them, she'd discovered, was to ignore them. So pretending to examine the workmanship on a gown, she waited for the man, bored by her lack of response, to move off. She stuck it for a few minutes then her patience ran out and she was just about to turn and give her tormentor a piece of her mind, when she heard a familiar voice say quietly in her ear, "You'd look an absolute picture in that gown Rachel."

"Captain Bennett!" she exclaimed, and swung round, her face warm with pleasure and surprise.

"Harry, I've told you it's Harry, at least when we're alone. Still as devilish pretty, I see," he went on, stroking her cheek and smiling down at her.

These words, the touch of his hand, the approval in his eyes, were a balm on Rachel's taut nerves. She forgot Jed and she gave him her sunniest smile.

"Now I suppose you, young lady, are in a most frightful hurry and haven't a moment in which to stop a talk to an old friend."

"I've all the time in the world. It's my day off."

Harry took her arm. "What do you say to me hiring a trap then and us taking a jaunt into the country together?"

Rachel tussled only briefly with the possible impropriety of his suggestion, before answering, "I'd love it."

So a trap was hired from The Bell and soon the pony was doing a brisk trot along Granby Street. The steep incline of London Road slowed him down slightly but he perked up again when Harry turned his head into Evington Lane. The fetid smells of the town were behind them now and they were in a lane lined with trees displaying all the rich colours of autumn. Rachel sighed with pleasure. She didn't want to talk, she just wanted to savour the moment of sitting close to Harry, his thigh almost touching hers, to feel the gentle breeze on her face, to hear bird song. They drove for a mile or so and then Harry pulled the pony up outside a country inn.

"I thought you might like something to eat," he said, helping her down from the trap.

While he went to order, Rachel sat outside on a bench. Leaning her back against the warm brick of the inn, she closed her eyes. A couple of elderly men, for whom life obviously

232

offered few diversions, had ceased talking when she and Harry drew up, but their low mutterings indicated that her appearance had been subjected to their close scrutiny. For once it didn't trouble Rachel. Because today she knew there was nothing they could criticise. Her gown, shawl and bonnet had been almost new when she'd bought them in the market, and her shoes, though unadorned were a good quality leather and Rachel felt she could easily pass for a lady.

Until Harry came back with a pitcher of cider, pork pies, pickled red cabbage and home-made chutney, Rachel hadn't realized how hungry she was. She'd eaten little since the day before and even this morning her stomach had rejected food. However, the drive had revived her appetite and Harry didn't have to press her more than once, to tuck in.

"Now tell me what you've been up to while I've been away," said Harry when they'd both finished the simple fare and were on their second tankard of cider.

Rachel didn't know if it was because they were away from the prying eyes of people who might recognize them, but the inhibiting shyness she'd previously felt in Harry's presence vanished. She told him of Catherine Brewin's death and the Luddite attack, although she was careful not to implicate Jed. Then Harry told her what it felt like to be under fire in the battlefield.

"Were you ever frightened?"

"Frequently," said Harry with an honesty that was normally quite foreign to him. "Cavalry casualties were high, but when I was injured I was taken back to Brussels. All the gay blades and their ladies who'd come over to Belgium for the fun, scampered back to England as soon as things got hot but a few brave women stayed behind to nurse the wounded and I owe my life to them." In particular he owed his life to Miss Charlotte Paget, now his fiancée but Harry saw no point in mentioning this to Rachel.

"Have you visited your uncle since you came back?" asked Rachel, who was hungry for news of Halby.

"No," Harry paused then went on, "You haven't heard then?"

"Heard what?"

"My uncle married recently."

Rachel couldn't hide her astonishment. "Who to?"

"Matilda."

"You mean Miss Matilda?"

"That's the girl."

"Whatever possessed her?" asked Rachel, then realizing this might sound rude, stammered, "I . . . I mean he's so much older than her." It was no secret either where Matilda's real affections lay, so her behaviour seemed totally out of character.

"Perhaps the idea of being the Squire's Wife appealed to her," replied Harry, who'd asked himself the same question often enough. He couldn't pretend, it had come as a shock to learn Matilda was married. Eventually he'd arrived at the conclusion she'd done it in a fit of pique and to stop him inheriting, when she'd heard of his engagement. He couldn't see why though. She must have known there was never any real chance of them marrying, but that didn't mean, just because he'd met someone else, that their liaison should end. All in all, he felt, Matilda had behaved rather unreasonably. Although when she forgave him, as she surely would, there was the possibility of some very pleasant diversions on future visits to Trent Hall. It was a pity too, that although Charlotte was an excellent nurse, she was also plain and reserved. And he did have a penchant for pretty, responsive women.

But circumstances had forced Harry to take a pragmatic view of life and he saw little point in wasting time on regrets. One couldn't have everything. He was tired too of being endlessly in debt, of struggling to survive on his army pay and small allowance. And Charlotte did have one

234

qualification which equipped her perfectly to be his wife; she was the only child of a wealthy, doting and elderly father. Meanwhile there was this most tantalizing creature sitting next to him, who had nothing but her beauty and more than a little bit of his heart and who had always proved to be a trifle elusive. By God, he would deflower her today. It was such a golden opportunity and one which might never come his way again. She would cry afterwards, but he would suggest he rent rooms for her in Leicester. After all, he reasoned, if she hated her job she was hardly going to object to giving it up. He could visit her at his leisure then, have access to that lovely ripe body when he pleased. It would beggar him of course, but once he was married there shouldn't be any financial problems.

Draining his tankard, Harry stood up, his loins already stirring in pleasurable anticipation. "Shall we go, my dear?" he said, holding out his hand.

As he pulled her to her feet Rachel said, with a hint of disappointment in her voice, "Are we going back to Leicester already?"

Secretly amused by her innocence, Harry said gravely, "Not unless you want to."

"Oh no. It's so lovely out here. In fact I don't think I ever want to go back to Jack Brewin's."

So they drove on deeper into the countryside, rattling through isolated farms, missing squawking chickens by a feather and stirring wolfish looking dogs into such a fury they would throw themselves at the wheels, snarling viciously and almost choking themselves on their chains. All this seemed to amuse Harry and as he urged the pony into greater effort and the trap bumped and swayed Rachel found herself hanging on to the side with one hand and her bonnet with the other. Finally she was moved to protest. "Harry, slow down, please."

"Only if you give me a kiss," he grinned.

"Certainly not," answered Rachel primly, and as good as his word, Harry kept up the pace, only slowing down when they came to a small wood, glowing in its mantle of autumn leaves.

"Look, a lake." Harry pointed to where the ground sloped away to his left.

Through the trees Rachel could see it, a pool rather than a lake, but warmed by shafts of sunlight it looked serene and inviting.

"Shall we go and explore?" Harry asked then without waiting for Rachel's reply, he jumped down and tethered the horse. Moving round to her side, he stretched out his arms to receive her.

The vigorous ride had caused Rachel's bonnet to slip off and her hair to shake loose, while the fresh country air had given her skin back its peachy bloom. As he caught her, she threw back her head and laughed, seeming to shake off the problems that burdened her young life. Slowly he lowered her to the ground aware of her slightly quickened heartbeat and the soft sweetness of her in his arms. Thrusting aside bothersome and unwanted feelings of tenderness, he patted her cheek and said coolly, "Come on, I'll race you to the lake."

Spiky green shells and conkers lay scattered over the ground, but little sunlight penetrated the arching branches of chestnut and beech, and no birds sang. Apart from the leaves crunching beneath their feet like crisp brown toast it was eerily quiet in the woods.

Anxious not to spoil her one decent pair of shoes, Rachel edged her way cautiously down the steep slope, taking it a step at a time. But Harry, showing off a little, forged on ahead.

He was almost at the bottom of the hill when Rachel saw him slip. She expected him to regain his balance immediately but her hand flew to her mouth when he landed heavily and she heard a sickening crack, as his head hit the extruding root of a tree.

Disregarding her clothes, Rachel scrambled and slipped to where Harry lay, still as death, his thick lashes soot black against the pallor of his skin. Falling to her knees, she took his hand and massaged it frantically, pleading in a distressed voice, "Harry, Harry, are you all right? Say something please."

Harry opened one eye a fraction, saw the concern on her face, gave an exaggerated moan of pain then began to mumble incoherently.

"What was that? What did you say?" Anxiously trying to think where the nearest house was and how she was going to get him back up that hill if he were injured, Rachel leaned closer.

Suddenly Harry's arms shot out and Rachel found herself clamped hard against his chest and with his mouth perilously close to hers. Angry at his deception she struggled to release herself.

"Let me go, Harry, this minute," she ordered.

"A kiss would really make me feel better, Rachel," he said with a wicked grin. Then before she could explode into righteous anger he pulled her head down and very gently kissed her.

He'd expected her to resist, but she remained passive in his arms. His heart pounding like a nervous youth and with some careful manoeuvring, he eased her down into the bed of moss and leaves. Unable to believe his good fortune, he began unbuttoning her dress. Her eyes were closed, but as he began caressing the firm young breasts, she gave a small gasp of pleasure, her eyes opened and there was no mistaking the message in them. But he wasn't going to go at it like a bull at a gate, this would be no hurried affair, Harry decided. He would hold himself in control, his prowess as a lover bringing

237

her to such a peak she would be crying out for it like Matilda did.

The first thing to come off was her shoes. Then easing up her dress his hand found the top of her stocking. With a skill born of years of practice, he rolled first one, then the other down her leg, expecting at any moment a decisive "No." He had successfully negotiated this hurdle and was about to make the final assault, when close behind him he heard a snigger then explosive derisive giggles and froze. Slowly turning his head, he saw two barefooted urchins of about eight or nine, regarding them with bright knowing eyes.

"Ah, we know's what you've bin gettin' up to," jeered the elder of the two.

Harry who daren't look but could imagine Rachel's humiliation, leapt up and grabbed the boy by the ear.

"Let me 'lone or I'll tell me pa an' he's bigger an you," the boy squawked and kicked out at Harry with his feet.

"Bugger off then," ordered Harry, who could have cheerfully submerged the pair of them in the lake.

"Not unless you give us a tanner."

Harry fumbled in his pocket. "Here, now go."

The boy studied the silver coin, tested it between his teeth, spat, then said with true entrepreneurial spirit, "I meant one each."

"Do you want your neck wrung?"

"No mister, just another tanner."

Harry flung the sixpence at his feet and while the two of them scrambled for it in the leaves, then ran off arguing, he turned to Rachel.

She was still sitting on the ground and although she'd adjusted her dress, her stockings and shoes lay where he'd thrown them and her long hair was strewn with twigs and moss.

"I'm sorry Rachel," he said, kneeling down beside her and taking her hand.

She didn't answer, just flushed scarlet and hung her head in shame. Then the urchins, having put a safe distance between them, turned with the final crude suggestion that he could now get on with his 'dive in the dark,' and her eyes filled with tears.

"Little sods," Harry muttered. His hands itched to pursue the pair and wring their scrawny necks, but he knew Rachel was in no state to be left on her own. Instead, feeling strangely ineffectual, he went and picked up the stockings and shoes and handed them to Rachel, who modestly insisted he turn away while she put them on. When she'd finished he helped her to her feet and waited while she brushed herself down. But she still refused to look at him, and they scrambled back up the hill without exchanging one word.

Harry was truly at a loss as to what to do but he knew he must try and make amends before they got back into the trap. "It was terrible for you, what happened, and I can only repeat I'm sorry. I wouldn't have put you through something like that for the world, Rachel, I think too much of you."

For the first time she looked at him directly. "Don't apologize, I'm glad it happened. Those boys saved me and deserved a guinea not sixpence. Because without them I would have done something I'd have spent the rest of my life regretting."

"You don't mean that, Rachel. You can't."

"I do. You brought me out here with every intention of taking advantage of me, didn't you? And what would have happened if I'd got in the family way? Would you have accepted your responsibilities?"

"I couldn't have married you," answered Harry with a rare honesty. "But neither would I have deserted you. I'd have set you up in a little place of your own, Rachel."

"Oh how very convenient. I'd be your mistress, that's what you're saying, isn't it? You're no better than George, I can see that now. You think girls like me are for just for the taking." Rachel climbed into the trap and sat ramrod straight. "Take me home, Harry," she commanded, "this minute. And I never want to set eyes on you again."

Chapter Eighteen

It had taken two days, with bullying and cajoling from her and tears and drunkenness from him, before Rachel could persuade Jack Brewin to set foot in the wreckage of his frameshop.

When she came downstairs on the Wednesday morning and found him, as usual, hunched over the fire with a hangover, her small residue of patience finally ran out. Hardly an appealing man at any time, such an unpleasantly sour smell now emanated from him, Rachel's nose wrinkled in distaste. Her pity for him was also tempered by contempt because more and more she saw he was a man quite lacking in moral fibre and she was landed with responsibilities she felt were his.

He didn't even look up as she pushed past him to rake the fire and put on the kettle. To show her exasperation she banged cups and plates down on the table, made the tea with an excess of energy, but when she handed him a cup of the hot liquid and he took it without so much as a thank you, it was the last straw.

"Mr Brewin, I'm going to say something, which will be my final word on the subject. It's no good you sitting there feeling sorry for yourself, what's done is done. If you want to get your business on its feet again, the frameshop must be cleaned up. Today. Once you've done that you'll probably find that the damage is not as bad as you imagined, and you might even be able to get a frame working."

"Don't ask it of me, I can't face it, not yet," he said in a self-pitying whine that taxed her sympathy to its limits.

"You could if you pulled yourself together," she answered sharply.

He stood up so abruptly the small chair went flying. "For Christ's sake stop nagging, woman!"

Rachel, who had been sawing slices from a loaf, jumped at his sudden bad tempered eruption and the knife slipped, cutting her finger which then began to bleed. "Now look what you've done," she accused, flinging down the knife and binding her finger in her apron. "And don't think you can shout at me, either, I'm not your wife. Or your drudge come to that, because I'm leaving. From now on you can sort your own problems out." She stormed to the door.

Taking her threat with the seriousness it deserved, Jack Brewin moved with more speed than he had in several days, reached the door before Rachel and stood barring her way. "I didn't mean it, I'm sorry. Don't leave, please. Think of the children. What would they do without you?"

"They are your children not mine, though you'd hardly know it at times. Anyway those are my conditions, either you get off your backside now and do something or I'm off."

He put up both hands in a placatory manner. "All right, all right, I'll do as you say," and to Rachel's astonishment, he went and finished his tea, sluiced cold water over his face then looking more purposeful than she could have believed possible, he let himself out through the back door.

Rachel sat down at the table, poured a cup of tea for herself and examined her finger. It had already stopped bleeding and as she sucked the wound absent-mindedly, she wondered for the umpteenth time if there was going to be any other life for her than this.

Wooed with sweet words and an arm around her waist, she'd forgiven Harry before they were half way home on the Sunday. She'd even allowed him to see her to the door

242

and kiss her goodnight. She had no illusions about Harry, knew he was a person of questionable character who used his looks and easy charm to manipulate and exploit women. But what was wrong with enjoying his company, she asked herself. She no more loved him than he did her, but she was still attracted by his devil-may-care attitude, and in his company life took on a rosier aspect.

And Harry had offered her an alternative to the life she now had. If she went to him, he would set her up in rooms and free her from this drudgery and Jack Brewin's doleful countenance. From time to time and when it was convenient, he would visit her and they would make love. Although this would give her an unheard of freedom, she would also carry around with her the stigma of a kept woman. And what would happen when she was older and less attractive, perhaps with a couple of bastard children and Harry's passion had cooled? Would she be able to depend of his financial support then? Possibly not.

But whatever his faults she knew where she stood with Harry. At least he was honest with her, didn't pretend to love her; not like Jed with his passionate declarations and proposal of marriage. And it had been a proposal, whatever his motives. She didn't dislike Jed either and as a married woman she'd be able to hold her head up in society. She said it out loud: "Mrs Jed Fairfax," decided it had a pleasing ring to it and gazed at her left hand, imagining a band of gold on her finger. Except that they hadn't exactly parted on the best of terms, so he was hardly likely to ask her again. Not that she would accept anyway, she quickly told herself. Marriage? To a man with such questionable friends and activities? Why it was out of the question. And he could deny it until he was blue in the face, but she was certain he knew something of the goings-on of the Luddites.

Her musings were interrupted by four pairs of feet clattering down the stairs. Like destructive whirlwinds, the girls burst into the kitchen and as Rachel stood up to meet the full force of their complaints and demands she gave a heartfelt sigh and thought to herself, here I am, performing the role of wife and mother, but without any of the benefits that go with that state. Surely I deserve better?

He'd complained about the expense but she had persuaded Jack Brewin to allow his two youngest girls, Lily and Rose, to attend the Dame school in the morning. But first, hair had to be combed, hands and faces washed. Finally, with a sigh of relief, she pushed them all out of the door. Leaning against it she closed her eyes. Peace, perfect peace. What a luxury it was, particularly when there was so little of it.

She hadn't intended to spy on Jack Brewin. In fact, in the rush to get the girls off to school, Rachel had quite forgotten about him. But she happened to glance out of the window while she was clearing away the breakfast things. Noting the absence of any sign of activity in the frameshop, she thought, blast that man, I bet he's sidled off to the Bunch of Grapes again. Leaving the pots unwashed she stormed across the yard, determined to drag him out of the tavern if that was where he was.

But he was sitting on an upturned box staring at the wall. And as Rachel looked about her, she saw the destruction through his eyes and although it wouldn't have done to let him know it, she caught something of his feelings of hopelessness.

Broken glass crunched like ice under her feet as she approached him but he seemed unaware of her until she was standing over him. "Getting on I see, Mr Brewin," she said in a voice heavy with sarcasm.

Jack Brewin, who had come to recognize that tone in the past few months and the frown of disapproval that went with it, jumped up guiltily. "Oh yes. Just stopped for short rest."

"Well I've come to give you a hand."

244

"Oh good," he said, without enthusiasm and went over to a frame that was less damaged than the rest and started tinkering with it in a half-hearted fashion.

During the night, rain had seeped in through the broken windows and formed large oily puddles and everything was in such chaos it was hard to know where to start. But taking up a broom, Rachel began to sweep, throwing up great billowing clouds of dust. It went in her mouth, up her nose and made her sneeze. It covered her clothes, her hair, even her eyelashes until she felt as if someone had taken a bag of flour and tipped it over her. Out all the debris went through into the yard: bobbins, broken glass, fractured metal, yarn, everything.

Her decisive energy must have shamed Jack Brewin because she'd just about finished and was standing in the yard, leaning on the broom handle when she heard a triumphant shout of, "It works!" from the frameshop.

A moment later he was standing in the doorway bouncing up and down like an excited child, beckoning her in. "Come and look, I've got a frame working!"

"Didn't I say you would. If you got another one going, we could work one each. That way you won't be so far behind with your orders for London."

Somehow he'd also managed to salvage some yarn and was so busy demonstrating his skills on the frame, neither of them heard footsteps crossing the yard.

It wasn't until someone coughed and a voice said, "Can I come in?" that they both looked up and Rachel's eyes grew round with disbelief as Jed sauntered towards them. Quickly she tried to rub some of the grime from her face with her apron.

"I brought this back." He held out a piece of paper.

Rachel stared at him then the piece of paper, but she didn't speak.

"It's the letter. You left it behind." Jed explained. "The police will want it as evidence."

245

It took a minute for Rachel to collect her wits, but then her angered flared. The nerve of him, coming here as if nothing had happened. But she kept these thoughts to herself, took the letter from him and stuffed it in her pocket. Jack Brewin's curiosity wouldn't be satisfied, though, without some explanation. "This is Jed Fairfax. He's a friend of mine who knows something about the law so I took the letter for him to have a look at. I thought he might have been able to help us."

Jack Brewin gave him a curt nod, but this didn't in anyway disturb Jed who was now looking around him. "They've mucked things up a bit here, haven't they?"

They, or you? Rachel felt like saying, but instead satisfied herself with a hostile stare.

Jed was now moving around the shop, examining the mangled frames. "Have you written to the authorities, Mr Brewin?" he finally asked.

Jack Brewin shook his head. "What good would that do?"

"You might be able to make a claim for damages against the county and get some compensation."

At the mention of compensation Jack Brewin's gloomy features cracked into a smile. But then his face fell again. "I'm not much of a scholar or one for putting words into fine sentences. Schooling finished early for me."

"Shall I pen you a letter?" Jed offered.

"I'd be very obliged to you if you would, Mr Fairfax," answered Jack Brewin. Then in a display of great camaraderie, he threw his arm round Jed's shoulder and drew him from the frameshop, across the yard and into the house.

Rachel followed them at a distance. To honour the occasion Jack Brewin installed Jed in the cheerless parlour where no fire was ever lit. Guessing there was little chance of hospitality being offered by her employer, Rachel, stopped outside the door and asked, "Shall I bring Mr Fairfax some ale?"

Jack Brewin, who was searching for a quill, paper and ink, cleared his throat and seemed to think about this.

"Well?"

"Yes, of course, of course," he said, giving a good imitation of a liberal host.

"And some bread and cheese?" she pursued.

"Yes, yes," her employer answered. Alarmed at such profligacy, he waved her away before she suggested something completely outrageous, like sharing the chops he was looking forward to having for his dinner or heaven forbid, his favourite baccy.

When she went back with their refreshment, Jed was preoccupied with composing the letter and Jack Brewin was watching him over his shoulder, forming the words with his lips as Jed wrote. Making as little noise as possible, she put the food down on the table and crept out again.

She was in the kitchen peeling the potatoes for dinner when Jed poked his head round the door. "I'm off now. The letter is written but let me know if you hear anything."

Just behind him Jack Brewin said in a tone very much master to servant, "See Mr Fairfax out please, Abigail?"

Wondering why he couldn't do it himself, Rachel wiped her hands on her apron and indicated that Jed should follow her.

"Abigail?" queried Jed. "Since when were you called Abigail?"

Rachel put a warning finger to her lips. "Hush, don't talk so loudly. If I have to explain, you're not as clever as I thought you were. Anyway, I've some questions to ask you. What do you think you're doing coming here? And the nerve of you, pretending to help." Rachel was facing Jed now, hands on hips and girding herself for combat.

"Look, how many times do I have to tell you, I'm not a Luddite, please get that into your head, Rachel. I'd like to see the stockingers organized, able to strike. But as long we've got men like Sidmouth sitting in Parliament and repressive laws, that will be impossible. So they take matters into their own hands, out of sheer frustration, can't you see?"

"Oh I see all right. I also see you trying to confuse me with your clever tongue again."

"I don't want to confuse you I just want to explain. It's why I came. And because I care about you. Surely you can see that's the truth, Rachel," he said, and the expression in his grey eyes was so sincere, she almost believed him.

"You get my head in such a whirl, Jed Fairfax, I don't know whether I'm coming or going. Now be off with you." Hearing Jack Brewin's steps along the passage, she unceremoniously pushed him out into the street.

But persistent as ever, before she closed the door, Jed blew her a kiss and called, "I love you."

What a man, she thought with a smile and a shake of the head and was so preoccupied, that if he hadn't tapped her on the shoulder, she would have walked right past Jack Brewin standing by the parlour door.

"Could you come in here for a moment, Abigail," he said.

She followed him in, half-expecting a reprimand for taking so long to see Jed off the premises, but he invited her to sit down. He remained standing, cracking his knuckles as he always did when he was agitated and rousing Rachel almost to screaming pitch. Finally he stopped directly in front of her and cleared his throat. At last he spoke. "Abigail I have something of great importance to say to you." He cleared his throat again. "You've been quite a help to me here since Catherine passed on and the children seem to have taken to you too. And because of that and as a measure of my appreciation, I have decided to make you the second Mrs Jack Brewin."

Rachel opened her mouth, closed it again, felt her lips twitch and bit on them hard as she struggled not to burst

248

into hysterical laughter. Surely of all the offers she'd had recently from men, this had to be the most ludicrous. She thought very quickly and finally managed to stammer out, "Well . . . that's . . . that's very kind of you Mr Brewin and I'm really flattered, but you see I'm already spoken for. Shortly I plan to wed Jed Fairfax."

Chapter Nineteen

On the last day of January 1816, Matilda fell hopelessly, irrevocably, unselfishly in love.

She had wanted to return to comfort and warmth of the family home for the baby's birth, but Francis, who indulged her in most ways, had been adamant. "My child will be born here, at Trent Hall," he'd said firmly, and for once Matilda knew better than to pout and sulk because she wasn't getting her own way.

Because from the moment she'd told Francis she was pregnant he'd appeared delighted at the prospect of fatherhood. Whether he'd been entirely taken in she wasn't quite sure, but she had sense enough not to push him too far. Her secret didn't weigh too heavily but when she did experience the occasional twinge of guilt, she would tell herself that even though Francis wasn't the father, at least the child would be of the same lineage, something that could be used to explain away any resemblence it might have to Harry.

So when her pains started, prematurely of course, a message was dispatched to her mother. Taking Susan with her as midwife, Mrs Pedley hurried up to the Hall. Excluding Francis Bennett from this most female of occupations, the pair of them took up residence in the bedroom until the baby was safely delivered.

She'd heard stories about childbirth that had scared her half to death, but Matilda was surprised how easy it all was. She hadn't liked the labour pains, or the mess afterwards, but the actual delivery had been as easy as shelling peas. At half past four in the afternoon she was sitting up in bed, washed, in a fresh cotton nightgown and with her new born son at her breast. The rush of love she felt for the small, red-faced creature was untainted by jealousy and uncertainty. What she gave to him, she gave unreservedly, and if necessary she knew she would die for him. Surrounded by Susan, a proud grandmother and a benevolent husband; cosseted and the centre of attention, Matilda came closer to complete happiness that cold January afternoon than at any other time in her life.

"What are we going to call him, my darling?" asked Francis, gingerly taking one of the tiny hands in his large fist.

"Adam," replied Matilda without hesitation. "Adam Francis," she added diplomatically and her husband beamed.

"I'll have a word with the Reverend Dobbs and we'll have him baptized just as soon as you're up and about," said Mrs Pedley, enjoying the novel experience of seeing her daughter enthralled by someone other than herself. All in all, things had turned out quite satisfactorily. Matilda's marriage had given her the position in life she'd always craved, she had a baby to occupy her and with luck, by now she'd got over her infatuation for Harry.

"Francis will see to that, Mama."

"Oh, all right. But what about help for you with Adam? Have you thought of anyone, Matilda, my dear?"

"No, Mama, I haven't." In fact over the months she'd thought of little except how much she loathed Harry Bennett for forcing her into a loveless marriage.

"Mr Fellowes, the miller, has a daughter coming up to fourteen. She's a sensible girl and bright. Ruth is her name. Do you want me to have a word with the family?" Susan offered.

"Yes, then send her up to me and I'll interview her," said Mrs Pedley.

"Mama, I'm perfectly capable of hiring my own servants." replied her daughter firmly. Tiring of her mother's solicitude, she went on, "Now if you don't mind, I'd like to sleep." She kissed the baby tenderly, then handed him over to Susan, who put him in his cradle by the bed. And the door had hardly closed before she'd slid under the sheets and was fast asleep.

Soon after their marriage Matilda had informed her husband she had no intention of living in a crumbling hovel and had set about initiating various improvements to the house. The first thing to be done was the roof, with fine Swithland slate. Then rotting windows were replaced. After this she had started on the interior and Francis Bennett, protesting feebly, would watch as carpets and samples of curtain material and wallpaper arrived by carrier from Leicester.

But Matilda would brush his protests aside. "Don't be such a meany Francis," she would purr, nibbling on his ear. "You know you've got all that dowry money from Papa."

Francis was so besotted by his beautiful young wife he hadn't the heart to tell her that the dowry money had gone on the trip to Bath, her portrait that now hung in the drawing room and the new roof. And each time he made love to her yet another promise was exacted from him. If he demurred, she would grow cold and he couldn't bear to be denied the pleasures of that soft young body, so now when bills came in he stuffed them away in his desk and tried to forget them.

Although hardly a proper sort of pastime for a woman, her husband felt, Matilda was beginning to take more than passing interest in the management of the estate. She had some new fangled ideas about how it should be run and where previously threshing had been by flail and had kept the men occupied during the slack winter months, now a threshing machine and winnowing machine stood in the barn and he'd had to stand several of his farm labourers off.

"But think of the money you'll save in wages," said Matilda, ignoring the men's sullen, hungry faces. And she'd looked so pleased with herself, Francis hadn't the heart to tell her that what with interest and everything, it would take several years' wages to pay off the infernal machines.

However he did feel that if she was to involve herself in the running of the estate, it behoved him to educate her politically, to see that her interests were broadened beyond Halby. So one morning at breakfast, shortly after Adam was born, he rather laboriously tried to explain about the Corn Laws, how foreign corn couldn't be imported until English corn reached eighty shillings a quarter and the impact this was likely to have on the country.

"Are you listening Matilda?" he asked a trifle tetchily when he saw her smothering a yawn behind her hand.

Matilda, who was only interested in what affected her directly, gave him a winning smile. "Of course dear. But it's really no good talking to me about politics, I do find it so tremendously boring."

"So you might. But you'd do well to remember that Parliament had to be defended with troops against a London mob when the Bill was passed and the discontent could reach Halby."

She'd gone back to thumbing through a fashion journal and he could see she wasn't listening. For Francis Bennett, however, a disaffected population meant only one thing: trouble. And as the year progressed and the price of corn rose, there were reports of rioting in Suffolk, Ely and other parts of the country. Flour was taken from mills and thrown in the river, barns and ricks set on fire, agricultural machinery destroyed. Francis didn't care for it at all, being separated from his wife and denied the pleasure of the marital bed, but because of the unrest and in his role of magistrate, he was frequently forced to spend nights away from home.

Matilda on the other hand, was more than happy with

this situation. Her life was so filled with Adam there was little room in it for anyone else. Her son fascinated her. She loved the soft arrangement of curls on the back on his neck, his plump, dimpled legs, and she would kiss every contour and curve of him, delighting in his baby gurgles of joy. Nothing had prepared her for this fierce love and she wanted to protect him from the ills and afflictions of life, particularly the sort that Harry had caused her. Every night too as Francis heaved himself on top of her, she prayed that he was incapable of siring a child. Because her love was all used up on Adam and she had none left for other children.

When he was still barely six weeks old Matilda wrapped her son in warm clothes and took him for a walk round the estate. It was a still, cold afternoon, the sun a huge marigold-coloured disk low in the sky. Puddles in the lane were frilled with ice, the ploughed fields lay in solid, frozen ridges but already rooks were building their nests high in the leafless elms. Leaning against a gate, she held her son up and spoke quietly to him. "One day this will be all yours, Adam. You'll be Squire here, honoured by the village and a man of substance."

His eyes grew bluer, his lashes darker as each day passed, and when he smiled his toothless smile she saw the resemblence to his father with a sharp indrawing of breath. But to think of Harry was a waste of time. That part of her life was done and finished with. She must make the best of what she had and try to remember that Francis wasn't unkind to her. But she'd vowed that never again would any man get close enough to cause her the heartache that Harry had.

The silence of the afternoon was broken by a 'kark, kark,' and she watched as a skein of geese flew in a V formation across the flaming sky. Now too cold to stand still any longer, Matilda turned and walked back to the house. She stopped briefly to watch some frisking lambs, congratulating herself on how healthy they looked. She knew her interest in the estate wasn't welcomed, but it was obvious to anyone with eyes to see, that through her intervention, things had improved already. She'd insisted the cow sheds were lime-washed every six months and even though Francis had complained of the cost, she felt justly proud of the labour saving threshing and winnowing machines. And it was all being done for Adam. She would see that he inherited fertile grazing land and sheep that produced wool and meat that would make him the envy of the county.

Once indoors she fed her son then took him up to the nursery and handed him over to Ruth Fellowes, the young nursemaid she'd taken on. The eldest child in a family of nine, she had an innate commonsense and was devoted to Adam.

Because Francis was away for the night, she'd invited Jane up for a game of piquet. She arrived at seven and as they embraced, Matilda could sense she was bursting with news.

But Jane intended making Matilda wait. So she sat down and looked around at the freshly papered walls, the new window hangings and the fine Persian carpet covering the floor. "I must say you've made a splendid job of this room, dear."

Silently Matilda agreed with her, but she answered modestly, "Do you think so? I haven't spent a great deal either." She rang for the tea things to be brought in: the caddy, small stove and kettle, and it wasn't until the ritual of tea making had been observed that her friend seemed ready to disclose her news.

"Guess who I saw in Loughborough yesterday?" Jane shifted excitedly on her chair.

Maintaining an air of indifference, Matilda poured the tea, handed a cup to her friend then began dealing the cards. "I've no idea."

"Harry."

Matilda made no comment, although there was an almost

imperceptible tremor in her hand as she dealt the last card.

A trifle disappointed by the cool response she was getting, Jane went on, "He was with his fiancée."

"I'm glad to hear it."

"Don't you want to know what she's like?"

Matilda picked up her cards and studied them intently. "I haven't the slightest wish to know anything about her."

Ignoring this obvious untruth, Jane went on, "She's quite old."

Matilda made no attempt to hide her interest now. She leaned forward. "How old?"

"About thirty. Maybe a bit even more."

Matilda had to ask. "Is she pretty?"

"Distinguished is how I would describe her," answered Jane, who understood too well the misfortune of being plain. "They were getting into a very grand coach with a liveried coachman."

That they didn't keep their own carriage was a bone of contention between Matilda and her husband. She felt not to have one undermined their status, particularly if they went calling. But in spite of her blandishments Francis had remained surprisingly stubborn. "The trap does us very well, Matilda. If and when the need arises I'll hire a chaise." Even a second-hand barouche for sale in the weekly paper had failed to interest him. And now to hear this. It was just too much.

"I suppose the wedding will be soon. Will you go?"

Matilda flung down her cards and stood up, sending tea slopping into the saucer. "What a ridiculous question, of course I'll go. Now will you please change the subject, Jane or I shall go to bed."

"Sorry my dear," said Jane, looking contrite, then further compounded her crimes that evening by winning at piquet and going off the richer by a guinea.

It was gratifying to know Harry's future wife was plain, but talk of him always rekindled the old longing. Lying in bed remembering the excitement of stolen hours together, her body grew moist with desire for him, her need so powerful her skin seemed to burn through the crumpled sheets. Restless, unfulfilled, she heard the clock downstairs chime out eleven, twelve, then one o'clock.

Sometime in the small hours exhaustion overcame Matilda and she slept. Only to be woken again by a roll of distant thunder, then a flash, like lightning. Mumbling bad temperedly she turned over and buried her head under the blankets. But what she couldn't ignore were the dogs, who had started up a great howling. Assuming it must be Francis returned unexpectedly Matilda gave up all attempts at sleep and fumbled around in the dark for her wrap. But even as she tightened the belt round her waist, the distant rumble exploded into a clamour of stamping feet and wooden rattles. When a chant, like a battle cry, went up, she knew what she'd feared for months was happening and her limbs went weak as if they were dissolving into water.

Incapable of placing one foot in front of the other, Matilda sank down on all fours and crawled to the window. With trembling hands she grasped the sill, pulled herself up and peered over it. What she saw made her duck, although almost at once she felt impelled to look again. Cautiously raising her head, she saw through the trees, the shadowy outline of about a dozen or so figures, some dressed in long great coats, others in women's dresses, but all with hats slouched well down and handkerchiefs covering their faces. Anonymous and terrifying, they crashed through the undergrowth shouldering muskets, hammers and axes, their way lit by swinging lanterns and flaming torches.

"Rabble!" She spat it out, all her feelings of contempt and hatred for the mob distilled into that one word. Because Matilda knew without question where the chanting army

257

of destruction was headed: the barn and the threshing and winnowing machines. By now anger had doused her fear and footsteps along the corridor and a fist banging on the door had her scrambling to her feet. Then the voice of the manservant, Hodge called out in a quaking voice, "Madam, Madam, a . . . are you awake, there's something terrible going on!"

"Yes I am," she called back in a composed voice and thinking quickly, went on, "Now I want you to collect all the servants and bring them up here to my room. We'll be safer to—" Matilda stopped in mid-sentence, thought, my God, Adam, flung open the door and pushing Hodge aside, tore along the corridor to the nursery and snatched up her sleeping son with frantic relief. At such rough handling, he started to whimper, but she quietened him with reassuring words of love. "It's all right my precious, your mama's here, she'll see nothing harms you." Hugging him against her breast, she shook Ruth awake. "Don't go near the window, keep your head down and follow me," she said in an urgent whisper to the sleepy, bewildered girl.

The servants were huddled together in the middle of the bedroom when she got back. Hodge, for some reason had lit a candle. She ordered him sharply to put it out, then asked, "Is everybody here?"

"Yes madam," the small, subdued group answered.

Calmly in control now, Matilda spoke in a tone she hoped would reassure. "Right, the house is securely locked and shuttered downstairs, so as long as we all stay here together and keep quiet, we should be safe. It's probably the farm machinery they're after rather than—"

She didn't finish. A terrified scream from Ruth and a pointing finger made Matilda swing round to the window. She caught a glimpse of a blackened, pink tongued, leering gargoyle of a face, saw the raised axe. Glass shattered, wood splintered, there was a rush of cold night air then a flaming torch came hurling through the window and landed by the curtains. Its glow lit up the stunned, terrified features of the servants then mayhem broke loose. But Matilda didn't have time to think of her own safety, because one of the curtains was already smouldering. Thrusting Adam into a servant's arms she rushed to the window. With tremendous presence of mind she picked up the torch and hurled it back into the garden. "Here, you can have it, we don't want it," she yelled as she took aim, and was rewarded with a cry of pain. Tongues of fire were now shooting up the curtain and Matilda tugged at it frantically, trying to pull it from the rail. But the heat scorched her hands and forced her back. "Someone help me for God's sake, or we'll all burn to death," she screamed and grabbed a pillow from the bed.

Coughing from the acrid smoke, eyes streaming, she pounded at the flames oblivious to anything until she heard Ruth say in a voice so terrorstruck it was almost a whisper, "Madam, your bedgown's on fire."

Matilda paused, looked down, saw her wrap curling up like burnt paper, felt the searing heat on her legs, was just thinking she was going to die, when she found herself drenched in cold water.

Gasping and blinking, Matilda stared at her sopping night clothes, then at the nursemaid who was standing with the washstand jug clasped in her hand. "I didn't know what else to do," said Ruth in a small, apologetic voice.

But there wasn't time to explain to the girl that she had probably saved her life, because everyone in the room was now diverted by a glow in the sky.

So they'd done it, set fire to the barn. God damn and blast them all! A great gust of rage surged through Matilda. At that moment her feelings were entirely primitive. She could have killed without the slightest remorse and she cursed her husband for always keeping the gun cupboard locked and the key to it in his pocket.

The sound of running feet intruded upon Matilda's vengeful

thoughts, the atmosphere became taut again, there was the sour smell of fear in the room and one of the younger girls began to whimper in terror. "Shut up," Matilda snapped, listened again and heard the reassuring clank of swords followed by orders being barked out in military fashion.

"Thank heavens, the Militia," Matilda breathed and there was an audible easing of tension.

More shouted orders were followed by a confusion of noise, an enormous crash, volley after volley of musket fire then screams of agony and rage. Adam, now fully awake, began to cry and while Matilda tried to pacify him, the battle raged outside. Whether it was for ten minutes or half an hour she wasn't sure; she was too dazed even to care. But after a while she became aware of the diminishing level of violence. "Listen," she said. Lifting her head, she strained her ears for any sound. "I think they've sent them packing."

There was a collective sigh of relief. Handing Adam over to Ruth, Matilda tiptoed cautiously to the window and peered out. The landscape was obliterated by a pall of smoke and the smell of charred wood, cordite and blood. Matilda had imagination enough, though, to guess the extent of the damage, knew the threshing machine and winnowing machine she was so proud of, would now be no more than a pile of splintered wood. Her hands were clenched and she was muttering vengefully to herself, if ever she got her hands on any of them . . . when an urgent pounding on the door, followed the vigorous pulling of the bell, made her jump back from the window in fright. "G . . . go and see who it is, Hodge."

"Me . . . Madam?" The manservant, who had so far been of little assistance, seemed astonished at such a suggestion.

"Yes you."

"But I'm 'ardly dressed suitable for answering the door, Madam."

Matilda wondered why, in view of his normally unkempt

260

appearance, this suddenly bothered him. "In the circumstances I hardly think it matters. Unless you expect me to
go," she added tartly.

"Supposin' it's one of them Luddites?"

"They've gone, you fool. It will be one of the military
wanting to know if we're all right."

Matilda discerned a reluctance in his step but in the end he
went. Clutching a lighted candelabra, she watched him from
the top of the stairs as he slowly opened the door and eased
his head round it with all the caution of a tortoise emerging
from its shell.

"Hello Hodge. "Is everything all right here?"

The voice, deep, male and oh so familiar, but which Matilda
hadn't heard for almost a year, seemed to suck the strength
from her legs. Her head swam, the blistering hot wax from
the candles dripped on to her fingers, but she was oblivious
to pain – anything but that voice.

"Captain Bennett!" Hodge sounded so joyous, Matilda
thought he might abandon convention altogether and embrace
Harry. Instead he flung the door wide and Harry stepped into
the hall.

Her heart fluttering like a trapped butterfly, her thoughts
in turmoil, she slowly descended the wide staircase. By the
time she'd reached the bottom Matilda had pulled herself
together sufficiently to say in a normal tone, "Hodge, tell
the servants they're quite safe. They can all retire for the
night now. You too."

Harry followed Matilda into the drawing room like a sleep
walker, too exhausted to even notice the sorry state she
was in. Making himself at home he unbuckled his sword,
shrugged off his jacket and threw them over a chair. Then
he poured himself a large brandy, sank into a chair and closed
his eyes.

Although Matilda was as near as she'd ever been to
breaking point, all her concern was for Harry. She studied

261

the beloved features, noticing his pallor, the graze on his forehead, the torn trousers. He didn't appear to have the energy to put the glass to his lips and he was silent for so long, she began to think he'd fallen asleep. She was about to remove the glass from his fingers when he said, "My God, what a night. Halby's in turmoil. Those buggers went right through it, smashing every frame they could find."

"All . . . all of them?"

"Every bloody one. The villagers didn't do much to stop them, either."

"And the barn?"

"Not too bad. You can say goodbye to the threshing machine and the roof is badly damaged. But it can probably be repaired and you're lucky that none of the livestock was maimed."

"Lucky? When we were all nearly burnt to a cinder by that mob. Were any killed or caught?"

"One killed, two caught, and they'll hang for it, the fools."

"Good. I curse them all for their destruction."

"Men in want of employment tend to make mischief, Matilda, particularly if they see their families starving."

"You're not expecting me to feel sorry for them, I hope."

"No. But there are some who call the Luddites the poor man's friend."

"What rot."

"Perhaps." Harry stood up, rubbing his eyes wearily. "Anyway, how is marriage, my dear?" He was standing in front of her now and studying her features with interest.

"Fine, just fine." She smiled up at him, brightly, defiantly. "We have a son, you know."

"Yes, I had heard. Premature, I believe."

"That's right."

"No doubt Francis is pleased to be a father." Harry nearly added, "at his age," thought better of it and said instead, "but where is my uncle?"

"He's away for the night." The unslaked longing for him had come back and her meaning was implicit.

"May I see him, your son?"

"Oh no," Matilda said hastily. "It's been a very disturbed night for him, he'll be asleep."

Harry had always felt that a fit of pique alone wouldn't have driven Matilda to marry and he'd suspected for some time that the child was his; now he was certain of it. Matilda was quite at liberty to maintain the charade and he certainly had no desire to upset the apple cart by putting a claim upon the child. But the boy was of his seed and he was curious to see what he'd sired. Perhaps he could even impregnate her again tonight, make Francis a happy father for the second time. The thought amused him. Earlier he'd imagined himself too weary for sex and had prepared the excuse that he was holding back out of respect for Matilda's married state. But it was such a golden opportunity: an absent husband, a frustrated wife, possibly even a warm bed. Offering her the gift of his smile, he moved closer and started to untie the belt on her wrap. "Never mind, it's you I want to talk to." He murmured as he eased up her night gown.

"Not here, Harry. Let's go upstairs," Matilda whispered as he'd hoped she would.

By the time he'd reached the bed, Harry had divested himself of the rest of his clothes and desire for Matilda had been rekindled. They fell across the bed together, Matilda pulling him on top of her hungrily and he took her without tenderness or preamble, pushing hard into her. She didn't care though. After her flaccid husband with his bulging stomach and bad breath, she ached for Harry's youthful virility.

And throughout the night, every time he got up to leave

263

she would plead with him to stay a little longer, then draw him back in her arms. Just before dawn she allowed him to leave and then only after she'd secured a promise that he would return in two weeks' time, when Francis would again be away for the night. "Promise you'll come Harry," she pleaded, her arms round his neck.

He kissed her. "Nothing could keep me away, my darling."

Reassured, Matilda allowed him to disengage her hands.

Harry kissed her once more then crept down the stairs and let himself out of the back door. He stood there, savouring the crisp morning air, flexing his tired muscles and thinking to himself; well, with one thing and another, it had certainly been quite a night. Moving with stealth, he circuited the house and was soon walking down the drive.

While there was still hardly a streak of light in the sky, a solitary bird sang its first note of the day. Almost immediately another took up the chord, then another, until it seemed to Harry that the whole of England must be filled with the sound of birdsong. He felt spent and his limbs ached, but he was filled with a tremendous sense of wellbeing. Everything seemed to be working out to his advantage. He'd never been sure if Matilda would welcome him back into her bed, but she had and now he had a more than willing mistress and shortly there would be a rich wife. What more could a man possibly want? A child perhaps. Well he had that too, even if he couldn't acknowledge the fact. Rachel continued to evade him, but a man couldn't have everything and that left him something to pursue. A self-satisfied smile played around Harry's lips as he turned into Blackthorn Lane. There was no question of it, his future looked very rosy indeed.

Matilda slept deeply and woke late with the smell of Harry on the sheets. Every aching muscle was a proclamation of their lovemaking and she gave a small secret smile of contentment.

Now, with the promise of nights in Harry's arms, she could even endure Francis's incompetent fumblings. And if they showed discretion, there was no reason why their affair couldn't continue for years. Pleased with herself, Matilda stretched her arms above her head in a languorous feeling of fulfilment, saw the streaks of dirt smearing her skin, felt the pain of the blisters, turned her head slowly to the broken window and leapt out of bed.

Jolted into remembering the true reason for Harry's arrival at her door in the middle of the night, Matilda scrambled into her clothes, ran down the stairs and met her husband walking in through the front door.

"What the devil has been going on here?" He thundered. His colour was brick-red, his forehead beaded in sweat.

For one horrifying moment Matilda thought he was referring to her and Harry and her heart gave a sickening lurch.

Without waiting for an answer he began striding up and down the hall. "The village is in chaos. What else did those bloody Luddites do?" He swung round to face Matilda. "Go on, tell me the worst."

"They nearly set the house on fire. If it hadn't been for . . ."

"Yes. What else?" He interrupted.

She hardly dare say it. "I . . . I think they got the threshing and winnowing machines."

"Do you know how much I'm in debt for those bloody machines you insisted on buying, Matilda?" Francis Bennett raged, banging his fist on a small hall table.

"I should do, you've told me often enough. At least your family is safe, or don't you care about us?" she shot back at him. "It was terrifying. Just me, Adam and the servants. I thought we'd all be burnt alive. You don't know the hell I went through. Look at the blisters on my hands." She held them towards him resentful and tearful.

"I'm sorry, my dear," said Francis, all contrite. "I promise

I won't ever leave you alone at night again." He came towards her, taking her in his arms and patting her like a faithful hound.

Oh Lord, thought Matilda, I've cooked my goose now. She daren't even say, "But you must go Francis, if it's necessary, you're a magistrate," because it would come out that Harry had been there the night before and his suspicions would be aroused. So drawing away from him, she mumbled, "Well, we'll see about that," while her mind continued to grapple with the problem.

"If they hanged a few more, we wouldn't have this trouble. Too many of them are caught then acquitted by lenient judges on the evidence of lying witnesses. In the meantime I suppose I'd better go and see if those black-hearted villains have completely bankrupted me."

"Wait, I want to come with you, I haven't seen the damage yet either," Matilda said, and hurried to get a cloak.

The Luddites had left their evidence behind them in abandoned staves and bludgeons, in flattened undergrowth and branches ripped from trees, but most of all in an oppressive silence, bloodstains and the smell of charred wood. After Harry's description of the damage, Matilda had thought herself prepared. But as they approached the barn, and she saw that the timbered roof was no more than a blackened skeleton, while inside, the two machines had been splintered into a thousand pieces and used for firewood, tears of frustration and despair started in her eyes. So far her husband had remained silent but she was so gripped by her own misery she hardly heard him declare, "I am done for. This will be the end of me."

What she did hear though was the sound, like a hiss, that escaped his lips. She turned to see him hunch his shoulders and grip his chest with both hands. Saw his face crease with pain and the colour drain from it.

"Francis, for God's sake what's the matter?"

He didn't answer. Instead, his legs began to buckle and he reached out and grabbed her. Although she tried, Matilda couldn't support his weight and he went down, pulling her with him then slumping on top of her. Pinned to the ground she heard him exhale once, felt his heart stop like a clock, and knew that her husband had put all earthly troubles behind him.

Chapter Twenty

Rachel had suspected all along that Jack Brewin had asked her to marry him merely as an economy measure and to save on her wages. And her suspicions were confirmed when almost immediately after her rejection of his offer he set about wooing Mrs Spence the midwife, a lady of mature years but who, it was rumoured, wasn't short of the odd bob or two.

It was a few days after his proposal that Rachel came downstairs and found a note, addressed to her, pushed under the door. She stared at it for a moment, wondering who could have written to her, then broke open the seal. It was from Jed, telling her she wasn't to think there was anything sinister in his sudden disappearance but that he was going to a large house in Derbyshire to catalogue their library and wouldn't be back until the job was finished. In the meantime she was to remember he loved her and would be thinking about her all the time.

The fact that Jack Brewin had seen fit to announce to the world that she and Jed were to be married, troubled Rachel's conscience, particularly since Jed was unaware that he'd been partnered off. So she waited to hear from him again and immediately she had his address, she wrote back a carefully worded letter explaining the whole awkward situation. She finished by saying that of course he needn't worry about any of this, because they certainly weren't plighted, even if the whole town now seemed to think they were.

Jed's reply stunned her. In it he said it was fine by him that they were betrothed. And since it had been made public, he had no choice but to hold her to her promise and they would marry as soon as he returned.

Rachel's answer was brief. "You told me when we first met you were no gentleman and you've proved that time and again. Please don't write any more. I can't afford to pay the letter carrier."

Jed's shop was closed for over four months but his return was as sudden and unexpected as his departure, and on the very day Jack Brewin had four new frames installed in the shop. He sauntered into the yard just as the last one was being humped in through the gate and behaving for all the world as if he'd left only the day before. Immediately he was surrounded by four curious but admiring girls and Jack Brewin was giving him matey slaps on the back. Only Rachel kept her distance.

A proud Jack Brewin drew him across to the frameshop. "You must come and see them. Spanking new frames they are. And after all, if it warn't for you I might not have 'em. It's you, lad, who've helped put me back on my feet. And don't think I'm not grateful. Young Abigail here can count herself fortunate she's going to marry a fine upstanding man like you."

Jed glanced over to a glowering Rachel. "She doesn't look very pleased to see me, does she? Do you think she's had second thoughts?"

"Second thoughts, certainly not. Being away 'as made you fanciful, just go and give her a kiss. Go on," he ordered and gave Jed a shove in Rachel's direction.

"Am I permitted to?" Jed asked, smiling down at her. Then without waiting for a reply, he slipped an arm round Rachel's waist and in full full view of her employer and four intensely interested children, he bent and kissed her.

Smothered childish giggles made Rachel blush scarlet and pull away. "Don't do that."

But Jed was still holding on to her as he turned back to Jack Brewin. "We need some time on our own after our long separation. What to you say to giving Abigail the day off tomorrow so that I can take her to meet my kin?"

"Certainly, you take her out for the day, my boy," replied Jack Brewin in an unaccustomed rush of generosity.

With an expression that told her he felt he was winning, Jed turned back to Rachel. "I've got to get back to the shop now. But see you're outside The Bell at eight o'clock. We'll go by Gibbs to Halby."

And so it was that a little after eight o'clock the following morning Rachel, in her best dress and bonnet, a warm woollen cape not quite protecting her against the raw March air, found herself sitting beside Jed in Mr Gibbs' cart, bouncing along the Belgrave Road towards Halby. They battled for space with carpets, rolls of material, blocks of salt and sugar as well as a large box of crockery, all of which Mr Gibbs would deliver round various villages during the day. Mr Gibbs drove with a fine disregard for either passenger or goods and every time they hit a pothole, Rachel would be thrown against Jed while the sound of yet another plate or cup shattering would come from the box,

Jed soon found it necessary to give her the continued support of an arm round her waist, but still not having forgiven him for the day before, Rachel quickly drew away from him along the seat. "Don't try and get familiar with me Jed Fairfax, we're not really plighted you know."

"Oh yes we are. You said so yourself. You can't deny it. One way or another, I shall marry you, Rachel Arden."

"But you know I only said it to get out of marrying Jack Brewin."

"The nerve of him, even asking you," retorted Jed.

Rachel giggled. "He thinks he's a good catch for a woman. But then men are inclined to be like that: vain."

"Does that include me?"

"If the cap fits, as they say," answered Rachel with a toss of her head.

Jed inched himself cautiously along the hard wooden seat and his arm slipped round Rachel's waist once more. "Listen," he said softly in her ear, "I'm doing better now and there are three rooms above the shop I could just afford to rent. Think of it Rachel, if you married me you'd have a place of your own to furnish as you please. You'd like that, wouldn't you? And there's not much future for you at Jack Brewin's, not if he marries again."

There was truth in what Jed said, of course. And recently she'd been giving this subject careful thought and knew that if Jack Brewin did marry Mrs Spence there was no way she was prepared to go back to being a mere household servant.

"Think of a good reason why we shouldn't be wed."

Rachel thought hard.

"Well . . . have you thought of anything?"

She shook her head.

"Good, that's settled then. We're getting married."

Jed was just bending to kiss her when Mr Gibbs' voice came gruff and disapproving from the driver's seat, "Oi, that'll be enough of that carry-on in my cart."

"Now look what you've done," said Rachel as they sprang apart and for the rest of the journey she sat with her hands resting demurely on her lap and refused to allow Jed to touch her.

It wasn't until they'd turned off the turnpike into Halby Lane and Jed pointed his finger and said, "Look, you can just see the church steeple," that Rachel began to wonder what she was doing returning to the village.

"Jed, tell Mr Gibbs to stop the cart, I'm not going to Halby."

"Nonsense, of course you are. We've got to tell Susan and Robert we're to be wed."

"But supposing I bump into Mr Pedley . . . or . . . George?"

"Just let one of them touch you . . ." Jed didn't finish but his face took on the taut, grim expression it always did whenever the hated name of Pedley was mentioned.

Rachel put a hand on his arm. "Please Jed, no fighting or I will go back to Leicester."

He covered her hand with his. "There won't be any, I promise."

All her life Rachel had had to fend for herself but now she had put herself into Jed's care, and he would protect her, fight for her if needs be. Knowing she no longer need fear anyone, not even George, Rachel relaxed and soon they were passing the first scattering of cottages. Perhaps they'd always been tumbledown, perhaps she was just seeing with fresh eyes, gates swinging on broken hinges, panes missing from windows, thatch hanging over eaves like stuffing from a torn mattress, but she doubted it. Then as they drove into the village and up Main Street, she was aware of an unaccustomed silence.

Mr Gibbs dropped them down outside the Weavers' Arms. With a parting warning that they were to be there at four of the clock and not a minute later, if they wanted to get back to Leicester that night, he drove off, muttering grumpily to himself.

"Why is it so quiet?" Rachel asked, looking about her with a puzzled expression.

"I don't know. It's eerie isn't it? Let's go and find out." Slipping his arm through hers, Jed drew her up to the short footpath to Woodbine Cottage.

A whole year had passed since she'd seen Robert, Susan and Polly, and Rachel wondered if they'd notice her town manners, her less countrified way of speaking. She did hope so. Wanting to look her best, she adjusted her bonnet and smoothed her dress. But as soon as he turned the handle, she felt suddenly shy and hung back.

But Jed was having none of it. "Look who I've brought to see you," he said, and pushed her forward into the room.

"Rachel! Good heavens!" Susan stood staring at her for a moment then said, "Come here," and Rachel ran to her, finding herself enveloped in an extravagant hug. "My, it's lovely to see you!" Standing back, Susan surveyed her with interest. "Quite the young lady, aren't you?"

"And shortly to be my wife as well," added Jed proudly.

"Didn't I always say this pair were made for each other, Susan?" Beaming with pride, Robert took Jed's hand and shook it vigorously. "You don't know what a tonic that news is, after all the terrible happenings round here of late."

"Why, what's been going on?"

"Didn't you know about them Luddites coming here and smashing everything in sight?"

Jed shook his head. "No I've been away up in Derbyshire."

But Rachel found herself looking at him out of the corner of her eye. Luddite. It filled her with terror, that word, because it could so easily take away her new-found happiness.

"It were a real bad do. They went right through the village. Even Trent Hall weren't spared. I'd have thought you'd have heard. News of that sort usually spreads round here like dandelion seed on the wind."

"We wondered why it was so quiet."

"Oh, that'll be on account of the funeral. They're burying Squire Bennett this morning."

"Are you telling me he's dead?" asked Jed.

"Dead as a herring. It was the shock they do say. The sight of all that machinery smashed and still not paid for was just too much for his heart and he dropped down dead at Miss Matilda's feet."

273

Rachel shook her head. "Fancy, Miss Matilda a widow, and her not wed a year."

Susan pursed her lips. "Don't go wasting your pity on that young madam. I can't see her shedding too many tears over her late husband. She just used the silly old goat, who couldn't even count up to nine."

Seeing Rachel's puzzled expression, she went on, "But other people can. And that son of hers, Adam, why it's obvious whose child he is."

"Are you saying he's not the Squire's?"

"I think I've said enough to be going on with. You draw your own conclusions. Anyway, I can't stand here gossiping, I've got to go and pay my last respects." Susan drew on a pair of crocheted mittens then began searching for her shawl. She found it, draped it around her shoulders, then turned to her husband. "Are you coming, Robert?"

"The way I felt about that man it would be hypocritical," Robert answered and stretched his legs comfortably towards the fire.

"I'll come," said Rachel. "Jed can stay here with Robert. I won't come to the service; just stand outside. Me and Polly together." Rachel held out her hand to the girl, who she realized had said nothing since they'd arrived.

Polly thrust her hands behind her back and shook her head. "Don't want to," she answered sullenly.

"Nonsense of course you do," said her mother firmly.

"Perhaps she's forgotten me," suggested Rachel, who in the past had always been greeted by Polly with great affection.

"No, she's like it with everybody at the moment. I can't make out what's wrong with her."

"She does look a bit off-colour," said Rachel, peering at the girl closely.

"Well she says she feels all right. And she eats well."

Rachel held out her hand again. "You and me'll be cousins

soon, you've got to come," she coaxed, but still the girl held back.

Susan looked exasperated. "Polly Levitt, I don't know what's come over you. Take Rachel's hand and let's go, otherwise I'll never get to church."

Polly finally surrendered her hand to Rachel. By now, Susan's patience had run out, and she'd already gone, leaving them to catch up if they could, Rachel didn't even try. With a reluctant Polly tugging against her, it would have been impossible anyway.

As soon as they stepped outside the door Rachel noticed a change in the atmosphere of the village. For one thing it was no longer deserted and with a line of spectators arranged along the road that led to the church, it had acquired an almost festive air. Rachel suspected it was curiosity rather than a sense of loss that had brought folk out, for the Squire had done little in his life to earn their affection. But death was the great equalizer, and it would reassure them to know that in the end, the grim reaper recognized neither money nor class.

Searching up and down the line Rachel eventually saw a suitable spot to stand without being conspicuous. It was behind two stout women, close to the lych gate and she pulled Polly towards it, just as a ripple of anticipation ran through the crowd. "Here it comes," whispered one woman to the other and a respectful silence fell as the hearse, pulled by two black horses, followed by a line of carriages, slowly wound its way through the village. The cortège drew to a halt outside the lych gate and the pall bearers, four young men from the estate, shouldered the Squire to his final resting place, while a single church bell commenced its sonorous tolling, one for every year of his life.

Following directly behind the coffin was Matilda, shrouded in a long black veil and leaning in an attitude of great distress against a gentleman who bore a striking resemblance to the

275

late Francis Bennett. Then came Harry, and with him was a rather prim looking woman, her small gloved hand resting on his arm in a manner that told the world he was hers. And as they passed in a waft of lavender water she suddenly knew what Susan had been hinting at: Harry was the father of Matilda's child. The knowledge winded her like a punch in the stomach and she gave a gasp of pain.

Hearing it, Polly looked up with a worried frown. "What's the matter, Rachel?"

"Nothing," Rachel answered and knew it to be true. For in that second she saw that Jed was ten times the man Harry was and never again would he have the power to shackle her with his blue eyes and charm.

She watched him and his lady friend disappear through the lych gate, bid him a silent farewell then turned back to see the the Pedleys approaching, weeping wife, grim husband and fat porker of a son.

At the sight of them Polly's placid features became animated. She gripped herself between the legs and began dancing excitedly up and down. Then pointing in the direction of the group, she said, "Look, Mr Georgie!"

"Hush, Polly," Rachel admonished, ducking down behind the two ladies. "The last thing I want is for them to see me."

"Mr Georgie's nice. He gives me . . ."

"He gives you what?"

Polly looked sly. "I'm not to tell you."

Rachel began to feel uneasy. "What can't you tell?"

Polly swung to and fro on her toes and refused to answer. The grey sky then fulfilled its promise with a few spots that seemed likely to turn into a steady downpour. The few remaining mourners increased their pace and the crowd started to break up. With a worried frown and deepening suspicion, Rachel grabbed Polly's hand. "Come on young lady, we're going home."

Chapter Twenty-One

Matilda watched from the window as the last mourner departed, thanked God it was over, then slumped down in a chair and tried to massage away the tension that radiated from the base of her neck to her shoulder blades.

It was as if over the past week she'd been battered incessantly by tumultuous seas then left floundering on a hostile shore. First there'd been the unparalleled horror of finding herself pinned to the ground by the weight of her husband, his dead fish eyes staring at her, while her hysterical screams for help went unanswered. Close on this had followed a visit from the lawyer, Mr Penny. Dark clothes mildewed with age, he'd smelt as fusty as the documents he fiddled with, before informing her she'd been left the entire estate and with it a large mortgage. Matilda hardly had time to absorb this devastating news, when going through Francis's personal effects, she'd found great handfuls of unpaid bills stuffed away in his desk, mostly, she noticed with a jolt of guilt, for all the new furnishings she'd demanded. And if this wasn't enough to cope with, before her husband was hardly cold, the creditors had come howling round the door like a pack of scavenging wolves.

Today convention had demanded she play the grieving widow. But even while Francis was being interred, resentment and anger had bubbled away inside her. And when her lips should have been moving in pious prayer, they'd instead been cursing her husband for his total lack of consideration in dying, leaving her and Adam penniless in a world that didn't look kindly on poverty.

But pain, anger and self-pity required energy to feed on and for the time being all her emotions were spent. Tomorrow she would have to start thinking about her future, maybe pay a visit to her father. Dependable Papa, who never refused his little girl anything. He wouldn't want to see her without a penny to her name. He'd help her out financially, get her back on her feet, he was bound to.

At the thought of possibly being able to shed at least one burden, Matilda relaxed and rang for tea. Sipping it she fell to thinking of Harry and Miss Charlotte Paget and her mood lightened even more.

It had been as well that her veil had concealed her fury when Harry, going well beyond the bounds of good taste, had introduced her as his Aunt Matilda. The veil had also provided her with opportunity to study his fiancée and confirm there was no exaggeration in Jane's report that she was a real 'miss prunes and prisms'. Although behind those unprepossessing features Matilda suspected there lurked a will of iron. Not that it would help her to hold on to Harry, no matter how tightly she grasped his arm. A small smile played round Matilda's lips. No, Miss Paget didn't offer much of a threat and it was her bet that after a barely decent interval Harry would be around expecting to share her bed.

But Harry had played fast and loose with her for the last time. From now on there would be conditions. She was respectably widowed and after a decent interval there was no reason they shouldn't marry. And he must see he'd find no sexual pleasure in that flat-chested, dessicated fiancée of his. Then there was the estate. Wasn't it something he'd always wanted, land of his own, even if it was mortgaged up to the hilt? But her trump card, she knew, was Adam. Because surely once she admitted to Harry that he was his son, conscience and a sense of duty would demand he do the right thing by them.

That Harry was rarely troubled by conscience she chose to ignore and soothed by rain pattering against the window, Matilda closed her eyes. Her body had relaxed to a wonderful inertia when she heard the click of the drawing room door. Drowsily imagining it was Hodge come to take the tea things away and light the candles, she didn't trouble to open her eyes. A prolonged silence and an uneasy sense that someone was watching her finally forced them open and she was startled to find her brother standing over her.

"George, what on earth are you doing here?" Matilda exclaimed.

Because of the rain, daylight was fading rapidly and much of the room was in shadow, so it wasn't until he moved over to the fire and spread his hands towards the flames that she noticed he had no overcoat. His trousers too were torn and smeared with mud. Even more startling was the expression on his face. He had the terror-struck look of a cornered animal and his teeth were chattering violently.

"You . . . you've go . . . got to . . . to help me, Matilda," he finally managed to stammer out.

At this demand she stood up and moved over to the fireplace, drawing a quick breath of alarm when she saw that as well as one of his eyes being badly bruised, his lip was also split and a trickle of blood ran down the corner of his mouth. "Whatever's happened to you?"

"Robert and that bloody Fairfax came into the Weavers' Arms and beat me up. I managed to get away but Robert's out there somewhere with an axe and he's threatened to kill me. I didn't dare go home, so I've been hiding in the woods waiting until it got dark so that I co . . . I could come here." George's voice shook with a sob of self-pity.

"But why on earth should they want to kill you?"

279

"They've found out about me and Polly. Stupid bitch! She's been and got herself pregnant."

"Oh my God!" Clasping her forehead, Matilda sank back down in the chair. Then angrily. "As if I hadn't had enough for one day, you come and tell me this. Didn't I warn you? It was disgusting, taking advantage of the poor imbecile. I don't know how you could."

"Never mind the lecture. If the needs be the devil must. Are you going to help me or not? They could be here at any minute."

Matilda leapt up again and began pacing the room. "No, you deserve everything you get. And if you stay here they might hack me and Adam to pieces as well."

"Don't turn me away, Matilda," George whined. "I'm your brother, your own flesh and blood. I promise I'll be away at first light."

"Before first light," she amended. "Where will you go?"

"As far away as possible. To one of the colonies. But I've got to get to London first, if you could just lend me the fare."

"Sorry, you'll have to walk. I'm in dire financial straits myself. A change of clothes is about all I can spare. I think what you've done is despicable, but I'll put you up for the night only because you're my brother. And I hope you appreciate the risk I'm taking."

"Oh I do." His tone was now ingratiating.

Matilda stopped her pacing and chewed thoughtfully on her thumb. "Which way did you come in?"

"The back."

"Did anyone see you?"

"No."

"Right. Get behind that chair over there. Don't move. I'm going to ring for Hodge."

"Christ, don't do that!?"

"You've asked for my help, haven't you?"

"Yes."

"Well shut up and do as you're told," she answered. She waited until George had ducked out of sight, then went and tugged on the bell.

When the servant entered, she was sitting with her head resting against a wing-backed chair. "Just take the tea things, Hodge, don't light the candles, my eyes couldn't stand it," Matilda said faintly. "My head is throbbing fit to kill . . . it . . . it's the strain of the day. And Hodge . . ."

"Mam?"

"I shall shortly retire for the night."

"Would you like a tray sent up?"

"I have no appetite for food. I'm just totally exhausted . . ." Here her voice faded to a mere whisper and Hodge had to move nearer to hear what she said. "What I need is uninterrupted sleep, so I shall take some of my drops. And I won't wish to be disturbed. Is that clear?"

"Yes mam."

"Good. You may go now."

Matilda waited until she heard his footsteps cross the hall and fade away down the corridor to the kitchen, then got up and eased open the door. She checked that the way was clear then hissed to George, "Quickly, up to my room. Get under the bed and stay there until I come."

Matilda watched nervously as he took the stairs two at a time, checked once again no one had seen him, then sedately ascended the stairs herself. After making sure Adam was all right, she hurried back to her room, locking the door behind her. Resisting the urge to peer out she drew the heavy curtains across the window then lit the candles. "You can come out now, we won't be disturbed."

George's head hardly had time to emerge when there was a slow, threatening banging of fists on the front door. "It's . . . them," George stuttered and shot back under the bed again.

Matilda tiptoed to the door, held her ear against it and heard a loud male voice she recognized demand, "Where's that bastard, George Pedley? I'm going to kill him after what he's done to my . . . my Polly." The sentence ended on a heart breaking sob and hearing it, Matilda wondered why she was putting herself and her child at risk for a brother she so despised.

"He's not here, Robert, I swear it. Nobody comes to this house without me knowing it," Hodge answered firmly.

"Let me speak to your mistress, then."

"Please, show a little respect for her grief. Don't you think today's been enough of an ordeal without you barging in? There's nothing she can tell you. Anyway she's taken a sleeping draught. A few drops of that stuff and she's really out for the count. Come back in the morning, she might be able to help you then."

Some further mumbling followed, but finally persuaded by Hodge, Robert offered his parting shot: "Right, I'm going, but I'll be back first thing, unless in the meantime I've found that bugger and split his skull in two like a log."

There was the crunch of feet on gravel then Hodge called after him, "What about Thatcher's Mount, have you tried there, Robert?"

"It was the first place we went to. And I don't think he'll be welcome back there. We left his mother in hysterics and the old man threatening to do his son in as well."

"I never liked him," Hodge offered. "Sly, spiteful little sod. And to do that to your Polly . . . well, he deserves all he gets. If I get wind of anything I promise I'll let you know."

They exchanged a few more words then the manservant came back into the house, bolting the door behind him. Matilda imagined him hesitating in the hall, and wondering whether to come up or not. To her relief he decided against it. But it wasn't until the house had returned to its funereal silence that she dared to turn back to George, now half-emerged from his hiding place.

"Well, did you hear any of that?" Matilda asked.

George stood up and dusted himself down. "Not really."

"Just as well. But you're right about one thing, Robert intends to kill you. And the way things have been round here lately, I wouldn't be surprised if the whole village wasn't out hunting for you in the morning." She made the statement matter of factly but watched, with satisfaction, as George's face grew white with terror. Serve him right, she thought spitefully, it was a change to see a man suffering, they got away with far too much.

"For God's sake don't say things like that, Matilda," George pleaded.

"Rachel, Polly, who else will there be? I warned you ages ago what might happen. Perhaps if you'd listened, thought about the consequences . . ." Her voice trailed off in disgust. "Anyway its too late to go over that. You can stay here for a few hours. It'll give you time to clean yourself up and get some sleep. I've no money but you can take some of Francis's clothes, you might be able to sell them. But I want you out of the house by four o'clock. As long as you're here, we're all in danger."

"Thanks, sis. Don't think I'm not grateful."

"I'm not doing it for you, George. It's for mama. Heaven knows why, but she always makes excuses for you, in spite of all the pain you've caused her. If anything happened to her darling boy it would break her heart. I only ask one thing, if you do get away, see that you write to her, let her know where you are. Will you promise me that?"

He made a sign over his left breast. "I will. Cross my heart."

"Have you got one?" she couldn't resist asking, then turned away from his reproachful look and started sorting through Francis's shirts. She came back with a pile and dumped them in his arms. "Here, take these and while you're at it, try and mend your ways, George. Women weren't put on this earth merely for your pleasure. Now get yourself washed and tidied up. Then put your head down and try and get some sleep. You're going to need all your energy in the next few days."

With a sigh, Matilda lay down fully dressed on the bed and wearily reflected that for her family, problems seemed to be piling one upon the other. Knowing if she wasn't careful she would fall into a great yawning pit of depression she watched George pour water into a bowl, douse his face and head, dry himself, change into one of Francis's shirts, then lie down on the the chaise longue. It's all right for him, she thought resentfully, by tomorrow he will have shaken off his past, but me, Mama and Papa, will still be here, having to face Susan and Robert's hatred, the hostility of the village, plus a bastard child with our blood but probably simple like its mother. Her lids grew heavy but she forced them open. She must stay awake, make sure George got away before daybreak . . . she wouldn't give much for his chances . . . otherwise and . . . there'd been enough tragedies of late . . .

. . . A slight movement woke her. It was pitch dark and she called out cautiously, "George, are you there?" When there was no reply, Matilda scrambled off the bed and lit a candle. The chaise longue was empty. Downstairs a clock chimed four. So he'd gone. Thank God! She undressed, letting her clothes fall in an untidy heap, then climbed back into bed. She'd done what she could for her brother. The rest was up to him.

Not until she and Jed were back on Mr Gibbs' cart did Rachel breathe easily again. The hood was up and the rain drummed steadily on the tarpaulin. Conversation was made difficult by a rumbustious family with whom they were making the return journey, although Jed seemed disinclined to speak anyway.

So instead she sat thinking about the day which had started out so full of optimism and degenerated into one of hatred and violence.

Should she voice her suspicions or keep quiet? Was she allowing her dislike of George to cloud her judgement? Trying to hammer out these questions, her mind had worked feverishly as she'd hurried with Polly to the cottage. Polly was a young woman with a child's mind and she often babbled like one. Rachel knew herself that George went for the weak and unprotected, but would even he take advantage of a girl not quite right in the head? It was an extremely serious accusation to make and supposing it was unfounded? And she had little to go on, just some incidents in the past which had bothered her and, of course, Polly's rather physical response to his presence today.

By the time she lifted the latch on the gate, how she was even to bring herself to mention such a distasteful subject to Susan and Robert, was something that troubled Rachel even more. So to see Sam with the same red mop but several inches taller, opening the door to them, filled her with guilty relief. Caught up in the joy of their reunion, she pushed the problem to the back of her mind.

And later sitting round the dinner table listening to Robert's banter about their forthcoming marriage and exchanging shy glances with Jed, Rachel was glad she'd said nothing to spoil the atmosphere of happiness and good will.

They were half way through the meal when Polly suddenly got up and rushed out into the back kitchen. Susan followed her and Rachel heard her commiserating with her daughter as she was violently sick.

After a short while Susan came back into the parlour. "Get on with your dinner, I'm putting Polly to bed."

But Rachel had lost her appetite and when Susan called for Robert from the top of the stairs, she knew from the harshness of her tone something was amiss. After a short while Robert came back down, spoke quietly to Jed, then he too disappeared upstairs.

"I wonder what's wrong?" said Sam. Then seeing, Rachel's half-finished plate of jam roly-poly, asked, "Don't you want that, our Rachel?"

Rachel pushed her plate towards him. "No, I'm full up. You have it."

"Coo, ta," Sam said and dug his spoon into his third helping of the suet pudding, managing to eat and talk at the same time.

But Rachel was listening with only half an ear and when heavy boots clattered on the stairs, she jumped up gripping the table nervously. She had a glimpse of Robert's face, distorted into a mask of grief and hatred, before he rushed into the back garden. And when he crashed back through the house, wielding an axe above his head and roaring, "I'll get that black hearted son of Satan," she knew he intended to kill George.

Jed was close behind him and gripping his arm, she shook it urgently. "You've got to stop him. George Pedley's not worth hanging for."

Jed's grey eyes flashed with an icy hatred. Pushing her away, he strode to the door. "Stop him? I'm going to help him."

"No, Jed, no," she screamed, then sobbing loudly she ran to the bottom of the stairs. "Susan, you must come otherwise something terrible will happen. They intend to kill George, I know it."

The face that stared down at her was one from which all human responses had flown. "I hope they do."

Hot tears ran down Rachel's face. "How can you say that?"

"Because he's used my Polly for his own evil ends and now she's with child. He deserves to die."

"Do you want them to hang? Because I'm sure I don't.

You do what you like but I'm going to try and stop them."

Forgetting her shawl, Rachel raced after the two men, closely followed by Sam. Outside she stood peering helplessly around her. "Where have they gone?" she wailed, clenching her fists and stamping her feet in frantic despair.

"Why don't we try the Weavers' Arms," said Sam. "Mr George spends a lot of time in there. Although I hope you know what you're doing, Rachel, it could get nasty."

"It'll be nastier if I don't do anything."

A roar loud enough to take the roof off the ale house suggested Sam might be right. So did the circle of men, the bets taking place, the money changing hands and the encouraging shouts of, "Give it to 'im, Jed," Rachel heard as she burst through the door.

"Hey, where do you think you're going?" grumbled several of the men as she elbowed her way through the crowd.

"You'll see," she answered tartly and reached the ringside to see that Jed had George by the scruff of the neck and was pulverising his face into the colour of raw liver.

"Stop it!" she screamed and hurled herself upon Jed, grasping him around the waist and trying to drag him off.

A roar of laughter went up and an astounded Jed momentarily loosened his grip on the enemy. George staggered back in a dazed fashion, shook his head to clear it, wiped the blood from his nose then wisely made a swift exit.

"Don't let the bastard get away," Jed yelled to Robert because although he tried to shake her off, Rachel still clung to his coat tail. Swearing savagely, he finally wrested it from her. "Damn you girl, what did you have to do that for?"

"To stop you killing him," she panted.

"Don't tell me you've been nursing a secret passion for Master George all this time," he jeered.

Rachel's felt her cheeks burn and her hand itched to slap

287

Jed's face. "How dare you say that, knowing what you do." She swung round on her heels and marched to the door. When she reached it she paused and said imperiously, "I'm catching the carrier's cart at four. Either you're on it with me, Jed, or our marriage is off."

Rachel had plenty of time in which to regret her ultimatum and as the cart lurched down Main Street, now a river of mud, she sat staring dejectedly out at the desolate, rainswept landscape. A figure stumbling and splashing through potholes made her straighten.

Yelling "Stop, Mr Gibbs," She scrambled to the rear of the cart, held out her hand and pulled a panting Jed aboard.

His clothes were splashed with mud, his hair lay flat against his skull, and he shivered with the cold. Forgiving each other, they exchanged hesitant smiles. But she sensed that Jed was in no mood to talk. A carrier's cart was no place to iron out their differences. Whatever needed saying between them would have to wait.

The jolting cart smelt of damp clothes, the chill air seeped into her bones, and Rachel found it impossible to respond to the family's unremitting cheerfulness.

When Mr Gibbs stopped to pay at the tollgate, she said quietly to Jed, "What happened?"

"The rabbit's run."

Rachel gave a deep sigh of relief. "Thank heaven for that." The strains of the day left her then, Jed's arm went round her waist, her head fell on his shoulder and she slept soundly until they reached Leicester.

Chapter Twenty-Two

In the early part of May, while the country seethed with unrest, Princess Charlotte of Wales, married Leopold George Frederick, Prince of Saxe Coburg. The Royal nuptials were reported in the newspapers, but the Regent, with his wanton extravagances, was held in such contempt by his half-starved subjects, the country was no mood to celebrate his daughter's marriage. Instead hunger fanned their republicanism. In spite of hangings and deportations, rioting continued unchecked in most counties and in Leicester the odd brick heaved through a window had nervous magistrates sending the town crier round warning innkeepers against staying open later than nine at night.

Rachel knew her own marriage would take place with rather less pomp than the Princess's, But she felt no envy. She and Jed loved each other. Poor Princess Charlotte, who could say if she loved the husband that had been chosen for her?

Although he had taken possession on Lady Day, Jed's pride wouldn't allow any wife of his to live in rooms that weren't decently furnished. So the slow process began of saving for every piece of furniture then scanning the newspaper advertisements for bargains.

Rachel also hunted through the market and would bear home her treasures for Jed to admire; a glazed jug bid for at the crockman's stall, small ornaments with hardly a chip on them, lengths of material, pictures for the wall. As each piece of furniture arrived she would wax it with loving care. And while Jed whitewashed the walls, she swept mouse droppings from corners, knocked cobwebs off windows and ceilings and watched with a sense of pride as the once empty, dusty rooms began to bear the stamp of their personalities.

Rachel trod through those early days of summer with an inner glow of joy. But sometimes her happiness would be disturbed by a nameless dread that everything could suddenly be snatched from her. It would often hit her when she was watching Jed as he went about some task, his face intent, serious and she would be moved by an unbearable sadness. Just as there was a beginning to our love, she would think, so there will be an end to it. One day I will kiss him for the last time. She never mentioned her fears to Jed in case he thought her foolish. Instead, in an effort to dispel them, she would go over and bury her face in his shoulder, and inhale the reassuring, comforting, masculine smell of him that could banish any terrors, for a little while at least.

Because there were other fears to disturb her serenity, the ones that still fell, like a shadow, between them and caught her unawares . . .

As they did one evening just after she and Jed had struggled upstairs with a cumbersome washstand: They shuffled with it into the bedroom then collapsed laughing and panting against the wall, as the last rays of the setting sun pierced the room, illuminating Jed's face and reminding her of the first time she'd seen him, his strong features lit by the lanthorn. It wasn't something she cared to think of, that wild, impetuous streak, the ability to leap in where other, more cautious people might fear to tread; the anger that could flare suddenly against a perceived injustice and threaten her security. Moving over to him, she slipped both arms under his coat and gazed up at him with a serious expression. "Jed, you would never let yourself get involved in . . . in anything, would you? Do anything to spoil all this?"

Jed looked momentarily surprised then a a line etched itself between his brows. "If you mean the Luddites, I swear Rachel, I have never been one of them, ever." He shook her gently. "Do you believe me?"

She nodded her head, wishing at the same time that she could shake off the wretched nagging doubts.

"Good. It's this waiting, it's making you fanciful. I think we've got enough in the way of furniture. Tomorrow I want you to go out and buy yourself a new gown, bonnet and silk shawl, while I pay call on the the parson. Four weeks from today I intend to make you my wife." Keeping a tight rein on his passion, Jed bent to kiss her. It was difficult, though, with her soft mouth and lovely body pressed against his. But he curbed the explosion of feeling out of respect for Rachel and her wish that their love be consummated with the blessing of the church and in the marriage bed. And what was a month, he thought, when they had a lifetime in front of them?

As their wedding day drew near Rachel spent more time in the bookshop, learning how it was run. Jed showed her on which shelf to find a book, explained the way in which they were arranged under subject and in alphabetical order. "And when you make a sale you write it down in that ledger." He pointed to a large brown book on a high desk. "And no credit, Rachel. They pay on the nail, or don't get the book. If people really can't afford it, then I'll put a book by for them and they can pay a bit off each week, but you and me have got to eat and no book goes out of this shop unless it's paid for first."

It was on the Monday afternoon, just four days before her marriage and Rachel was on her way to put the finishing touches on her new home, when Jack Brewin called from the kitchen, "Have you heard?"

Rachel paused, "Heard what?"

"There were a real bad do up at Loughborough late Friday night. Firm of Heathcoat and Boden had a visit from Ned

Ludd and his men. Did about eight thousand pound's worth of damage. Smashed fifty-three lace frames, burnt the lace and nearly done one of the nightwatchmen in."

"Was anyone caught?" Rachel could ask the the question calmly. On Friday night Jed had been with her until ten o'clock.

"Yeah, that Jem Towle, he's under lock and key, and about time too. I hope the bugger swings for it this time, although if I had my way he'd be hung drawn and quartered, along with the rest, when they catch 'em. Sixteen or seventeen there were said to be and I shall be at the hanging of every one." Swinging his feet up on the table, Jack Brewin closed his eyes and Rachel left him happily contemplating the miscreants' possible fate.

Rachel understood his feelings, but when people spoke of being poor as a stockinger, it was no exaggeration. Yet another petition on the distressed state of the trade and signed by over six thousand men, had been presented to the Commons in April. But it had been to little effect and families were being thrown on the parish daily. Soup and cheap coal had been distributed to those in most need but still the streets were littered with ragged, hollow eyed beggars. And along with the beggars there were the more enterprising; the prostitutes, the confidence men, the young nimble-fingered, fleet-footed pickpockets, people who could still rustle up enough money to briefly drown their misery on a Saturday night.

Jed had talked to her a lot of late about their plight too. "If they live like animals, it's because that's the way they're regarded by our masters in Parliament. What chance have they, to get out of those hell-holes most of them live in? It's the same with framebreaking. Strikes are made illegal, wages are lowered, the price of corn and potatoes goes sky-high, so they take the only action open to them. It's the government that's addle-brained, not the men. The laws of this country are wrong and they need changing."

As always when he spoke of these injustices, Jed's grey eyes would darken with anger and he would push into her hands, yet another of the many pamphlets he had on parliamentary reform. This was a subject so dear to his heart that he'd recently joined a radical organization called the Hampden Club. And this bothered Rachel. In such unsettled times, clubs like these, whose aims were the extension of the franchise, were regarded with the deepest suspicion by the Home Secretary, Sidmouth, who considered them iniquitous dens of revolution.

But Rachel refused to allow herself to be burdened by such nagging worries so near her wedding day. Instead, her countenance remained determinedly cheerful as she stopped to buy to buy cheese, bread, bacon and a small quantity of tea for her and Jed's meal that evening, thinking to herself as she paid for her purchases, that this time next week she would be doing her shopping as Mrs Jed Fairfax.

She swung into High Cross Street and waved to several shopkeepers standing on the footways. They didn't respond which was unusual, but as she went to push open the shop door, Rachel had the uneasy sensation of several pairs of eyes on her back. When the door didn't budge, she put her shoulder against it and almost fell in to a scene of total devastation.

"Oh my God, what's happened?" she cried, gazing about her with a stupefied expression. Pamphlets, leaflets and papers were flung around the shop. Books had been pulled from shelves, the pages wantonly torn from their bindings, splattered with ink, then trampled underfoot. For several dazed minutes her brain refused to register this act of vandalism, but then like an automaton she bent and began to shuffle the papers together, in an attempt to bring order to the room. But as she saw the extent of the damage, the money it would cost to replace the books, Rachel began to

293

shake with rage. But who could have done it? Who could hate them that much? And where was Jed? She spun round on her heels then frantically calling his name, rushed into the small back room. Here she found the hand-press gone and a similar scene of chaos. Somewhere in the region of her bowels, Rachel felt an unpleasant, churning sensation. Beset now by a nameless terror, and clinging to the banister for support, she made her way up the stairs. At the top she paused and called out cautiously, "Jed, are you there?"

There was no reply but her jagged nerves heard danger in the faint creak of a floorboard and she froze. Eventually she gained enough courage to push open the door, preparing herself for what she knew she would find. But there was no smashed furniture, no Jed lying in a pool of blood, just everything as she'd left it: flowers in a vase, the fire laid, the room neat and untouched This domestic calm in comparison to the scene downstairs only increased her bewilderment and she raced downstairs again and into the street, gazing up and down it as if Jed might suddenly appear. But there was only one person to be seen, a shopkeeper still standing in his doorway. "Have you seen Jed? I need to get hold of him right away. By the look of things we've had a burglar." For his benefit she tried to maintain a calm manner.

The man shifted from one leg to the other. "It's the law what's bin rummaging around in there, A couple of constables came and took Jed and a load of books and leaflets away 'bout midday."

Rachel felt a cold trickle of fear down her spine. "What are you talking about?"

"Like I said," the man repeated patiently, "the law came and took him. If you want 'im he's down there." He pointed in the direction of the Borough Gaol. "I should cancel your wedding. As things are, I don't see 'im getting out in a long while, or maybe even ever."

*   *   *

294

It had been a wretched few months for Matilda. Creditors had continued to hound her and when she'd gone to ask her father for a loan, he'd rounded on her angrily.

"Don't you know how things are? Do you walk around with your eyes shut, Tilda? My frames smashed by those thugs; consuls sold for a pittance. And you're not the only one with a mortgage. If you remember, I had to take out one to pay off Francis for your indiscretions. Then there's that bastard child of George's, which your mother is insisting we help support when it's born. Why it was my misfortune to produce two children like you, I don't know." Working himself up into a fine old lather, he strode up and down the room, contemplating his children's excesses. "I'm bloody well fed up with the pair of you, from now on you'll stand on your own two feet."

Matilda's eyes filled with tears. "But Papa, we'll starve."

"I doubt it. You'll maybe have to live a bit more frugally. Sack some of the servants; buy a few less dresses."

"If I sacked the servants I'd have to pay them first. They haven't had wages since Francis died."

"Well sell off some of the estate, although land isn't fetching a good price at the moment."

Matilda's head went up. "That's Adam's land. I shall never sell an acre of it, if I have to go out and till the fields myself."

Her father's eyes bulged with aggression. "Yes, why don't you do that? Get some good honest muck under those perfectly manicured fingernails, rise summer and winter at four o'clock in the morning, slosh around up to your ankles in cowshit, find out how money has to be grafted for, learn that it doesn't grow on trees."

"Well I will," she screamed back at him. "You don't think I can, do you? Well just you wait and see." Father and daughter, each unwilling to give an inch, stood glowering at each other in open hostility, until Matilda finally turned on her heels and strode out. Her fury hadn't abated by the time she reached home and as well as being directed at her father it now also encompassed Harry and her dead husband, in fact the whole world. Well I'll show them all, she muttered defiantly. This place is going to pay for itself if it kills me. With a little knowhow, she could run it as well as any man, learn how to get the best price for her wool and corn, attend farm sales, plant turnip for animal feed, do all the things she suggested to Francis but which he'd failed to put into practice. Driven by what she considered to be her father's unreasonable attitude, she strode into the library and pulled several books on farming and animal husbandry down from the shelf. But it needed only a brief glimpse to realize they were about a century out of date. Flinging them aside in disgust she thought, right, tomorrow I shall go to Leicester and buy some.

Matilda was footsore and hot, it was getting late and she still hadn't purchased one book on her list. If she had she might have paid a little more attention to the sign swinging above the bookshop, might have looked up and seen the name Fairfax, and might have had second thoughts about entering.

Rachel saw her first through the window, although by the time Matilda entered, she had her dark head bent over a ledger, industriously adding up a column of figures. Matilda didn't give her a second glance but instead went over and ran her eyes over the shelves of books.

Laying down the quill, Rachel said politely, "Good-afternoon, madam, may I help you?"

Her voice brought Matilda's head up with a jerk of recognition. Moving to the counter she looked Rachel up and down in a patronizing manner then exclaimed, "Good heavens, it's you. Papa will be interested."

Rachel's reply came back in a flash. "So will Halby, when

I tell them why I left. How is Mr George by the way? And Polly? Now she must be near her time, and her hardly more than a child."

It was unusual to see Matilda lost for words and Rachel watched with malicious enjoyment as her mouth fell open in consternation. But just as quickly it snapped shut like a mantrap. "Well . . . yes . . . then, never mind about that." She fumbled in her reticule and drew out a piece of paper. "Now have you any of these books?"

Rachel's ran her eye down the list. "Yes, all but one."

"Be so good as to wrap them for me. And if you'd just send me the account, I'll settle with you at the end of the month."

Rachel gave her a sweet smile. "I'm sorry, Mrs Bennett, my instructions are that no books leave this shop without they have been paid for first."

"Well I never . . ." With an expression of haughty indignation, Matilda searched for some money. "Here you are." She flung the coins on to the counter.

"Thank you," said Rachel, thoroughly at ease with herself. "Now if madam would just care to take a seat, I'll get the books from the shelf."

Matilda said no more, but while Rachel searched for the books then parcelled them up, she sat drumming her fingers impatiently on the counter.

Rachel refused to allow this to bother her. Instead she wrapped them unhurriedly, handed the package to Matilda then walked to the door and held it open for her. With an imperious swish of her skirts, Matilda stepped into the street. But Rachel couldn't resist a final stab, to make up for the years of spitefulness. "By the way, how is Captain Bennett? I hear he is soon to be wed, to a lady of some means. If you happen to bump into him, do give him my regards. You see he was very kind to me when I was forced to leave Halby so suddenly."

Matilda turned and glared at her. "I'll do nothing of the sort . . . you . . . you . . . chit!"

Rachel, whose mood had been sombre all day, watched with a brief sense of achievement as Matilda, her back stiff with displeasure, marched off down the street. Early that morning she'd watched James Towle, John Slater and Benjamin Badder make the same journey, but they'd been accompanied by gaolers taking them to the Castle to stand trial at the summer Assizes. A dismal sight it had been too, the three scarecrow figures, their ankles and wrists manacled, clanking past surrounded by jeering rabble.

Jack Brewin, not a man to miss out on anything of a grisly nature, was attending the trial and he'd promised he would call in as soon as it was over and let her know whether the men were to be hanged or transported.

Distracted by the knowledge that the jury would shortly be delivering their verdict, Rachel found it difficult settle to book-keeping. It was a warm August day and as afternoon passed into early evening, her body began to sweat uncomfortably. Her tension increased and the columns of figures in the ledger danced before her eyes. Slamming the book shut, she went to the door and peered down the silent, waiting street. She continued to do this every ten minutes, growing more and more agitated as seven, eight, nine o'clock came and went and there was still no sign of Jack Brewin. She knew intuitively that her own and Jed's future hinged on today, on whether the judge delivered a harsh or lenient sentence on the defendants.

Although always half expecting it, Jed's arrest had devasted her. And following so closely on the Loughborough job, in spite of his frequent denials in the past, in her own mind her fears were confirmed, his guilt established, his death warrant signed.

Rachel's early, frantic attempts to see him in prison were unsuccessful and it wasn't until she got wise to the system and scraped together enough money to bribe the gaolers that she was able to visit him. It was then she discovered that Jed's only crime was to own a hand-press and to stock Tom Paine's *Rights of Man*, and William Cobbett's *Weekly Political Register*, works considered by the authorities to be both seditious and blasphemous. Jed, a free man, it seemed, was a danger both to government and society. He'd been incarcerated now for nearly two months but when he would go on trial remained as uncertain as the day he was arrested. But he had made her promise that she was to keep the shop open. So on the whim of an edgy magistrate her life had once again had taken a drastic, unforseen turn, her marriage to Jed no longer a certainty. But any tears were spilled at night away from curious eyes. Determined to put a brave face on it and keep her promise to Jed, she moved into what was to have been their home and took her first blundering steps into the world of commerce.

When it reached nearly ten and Jack Brewin still hadn't put in an appearance, Rachel decided she was too tired to wait any longer and was about to shut up shop when his unprepossessing features appeared at the window. He looked pleased with himself and as she opened the door to him he was rubbing his hands with glee. "They nailed that Towle at last. He's for the long drop. Too bad about Slater and Badder, though, they were acquitted."

"Poor Jem," Rachel murmured.

"Don't you go feeling sorry for 'im now, not after what 'e's done."

"But he's so young and he's got a wife and child."

"He's old enough to know right from wrong. It was diabolical what he did and a bit of killing wouldn't have troubled him neither. He threatened to blow the brains out of one of the nightwatchmen. No he's just a common criminal who was in it for the money. And Slater and Badder were just as bad. They only got off because the witnesses perjured themselves left right and centre, said they was 'ome at the time of the attack. Towle would have got off too on their evidence if his big mouth hadn't got the better of him and he let slip a few things when he was arrested."

"How is it all going to end for Jed and me, that's what I want to know?" Rachel said with an unhappy sigh. Because although the acquittal of the two men might have given her some hope, James Towle's death sentence had crushed it.

"You know Jed should curb those radical notions of his. It don't do to bring attention to yourself in these troubled times." Jack Brewin advised.

Rachel rounded on him angrily. "This is supposed to be a free country, or so we're told. He's done nothing wrong and he shouldn't be in prison."

"Perhaps, but think yourself lucky they didn't arrest him on suspicion of treason like they did John Pares, because that's a hanging affair. As it is, he might get away with twelve months, it depends on the judge. There again if things go really bad against him, he could be transported for life."

Chapter Twenty-Three

It was her mother who told her Polly had died, standing in the hall, her body wracked by noisy sobs and indifferent in her grief to the inquisitive eyes of Hodge.

Waving him away, Matilda drew her mother into the drawing room, sat her down, then slumped in a chair herself. "I can't believe it, Polly dead." She shook her head as if to deny such a tragedy could occur. "What happened, Mama?"

Several minutes passed before Mrs Pedley spoke. "The baby, it came suddenly. Perhaps early and something went wrong." Mrs Pedley looked at her daughter with brimming eyes. "They'll never forgive us, Susan and Robert, not after this, and I don't blame them."

Matilda lay back in the chair and rubbed her forehead in a weary, defeated gesture. She felt ground down, crushed by life, a failure. "Why does misfortune seem to dog us so, Mama?"

"As you sew . . ." Esther Pedley's voice trailed off in a fresh bout of weeping.

Forcing herself out of the chair, Matilda went to her mother and took her in her arms. "Don't distress yourself so. You always treated Polly kindly and none of this is your fault.

George is the only one to blame. He killed Polly just as surely as if he'd run a knife through her heart. But he gets off scot-free. Men never have to account for their sins," she said bitterly, thinking of Harry.

Mrs Pedley checked her tears with a small lace hand-kerchief, her head jerked up and in a voice that rang with conviction intoned, "All of us are accountable to the Almighty in the end."

"Do you imagine such thoughts will keep George awake at night?"

Mrs Pedley considered this point for a moment. "Probably not. But he must realize that it's unlikely he'll ever be able to set foot in the village again."

"Well since he hated everything about the places that's hardly going to bother him. No, it's us who are left with the consequences of his actions. Us who'll have to deal with the vindictive remarks, the wagging tongues."

"Perhaps when I tell him he's got a daughter he'll mend his ways," said Mrs Pedley without much conviction.

Matilda gave her mother a startled look. "I assumed the baby was dead. Are you telling me it's still alive?"

"Only just and no bigger than a skinned rabbit."

"Well it would probably be a merciful release if the poor mite did die then, particularly if it's going to grow up simple like Polly."

Mrs Pedley gazed at her daughter reprovingly. "In the good Lord's eyes, whatever their disabilities, every human being is special. And she's my grandchild, just as much as Adam is. So as long as she's got breath in her little body, she will remain this family's responsibility. That's the least I can do for Susan and Robert . . . and Polly, God rest her soul."

Matilda refused point blank to go to the funeral. Grieving parents, the silent recrimination as the coffin was carried into the church, was more than the could endure. And because the baby was such a tiny scrap of humanity, it was accepted that mother and child would lie in the same grave. So the name Clare was chosen and she'd been hastily baptised. Whether it was the Holy water or not no one could say but the infant immediately rallied, then further confounded her grandparents by proceeding to flourish.

Matilda was glad she had the estate to occupy her in those days following Polly's death. She who had never read anything more demanding than a romantic novel, now pored over the farming books she'd purchased from Rachel. She also had her father's shrewdness and accounts and columns of figure held no mysteries. Knowing too how servants could cheat and steal, she demanded to know from the cook, the price of everything that was bought, down to the last candle. She might not get up at four, but Matilda was in the dairy soon after, supervising the making of cheese and the churning of butter, which she then arranged to have dispatched to Leicester.

Matilda was enough of a country girl to know, without consulting a book, that gathering in the harvest was a fight against time and weather, so she was out in the fields early with the reapers, helping to tie the corn into sheaves then prop them into stooks. In spite of a wide straw hat, her pale skin turned the colour of a gipsy's, the palms of her hands developed callouses and her fingernails broke. She sweated in the heat of the sun, immodestly hitched up her skirts like the other women, shared their casks of beer and saw respect growing in their eyes. She also discovered there was a therapy in hard work and though her body ached like it had never done before, she slept so soundly she hardly had time to think of Harry. And if she could have found time to look in the mirror, she would have seen that the fretful expression had gone from her eyes, the petulance from her mouth, to be replaced by energy, confidence, determination.

Matilda was also slowly learning that contented workers laboured more willingly than discontented ones. So although she could ill afford it, when the last load was in, she had the large barn swept out and decorated for a harvest home supper and dance.

The food was done with, the tables cleared and the fiddler had struck up a tune. Immediately couples were on their feet. Matilda, her own feet tapping in time to the music, was watching them enviously, when suddenly she felt her waist gripped and a moment later she was whirled into the middle of the floor.

"Harry!" Matilda's face lit up with the joy she reserved exclusively for him. "What are you doing here? I thought you were away on manoeuvres."

"That's a fine greeting. Aren't you pleased to see me?"

She let her head fall briefly on his shoulder and felt again that old longing, "Of course I am."

"Good, let's get out of here then." He grabbed her hand, led her out of the barn and into the brightness of a full harvest moon, so low in the sky it looked as if it was impaled on the treetops. Pulling her into the undergrowth, Harry began kissing her hungrily, trying to undress her and press her down on the ground at the same time. "I want to make love to you here, under the stars, like we used to," he murmured into her hair.

Keeping control of her feelings, Matilda pushed him away. "Just a moment Harry. Who says we're going to make love?"

Harry's handsome features looked momentarily perplexed. Matilda had never once denied him access to the delights of her body. Then remembering the problems women often had to cope with, his face cleared. "Oh, I understand, it's that time of month, isn't it my darling?"

"No it's not actually." Holding him at bay as he tried to kiss her again, Matilda went on, "But there are some matters I want settled first."

"What matters are those, my dear?" said Harry, who was now concentrating on the buttons of her dress.

"Where, exactly, do we stand, you and me?"

"In regards to what?" Harry's voice sounded instantly wary.

"To our future. There's nothing to stop us marrying now. Money's not everything. And think, with me you would have all this estate."

"And the debts," Harry reminded her.

"I've already paid off some of those," she said with pride. "And if we worked together, we could soon make a go of it. I've got all sorts of plans worked out. And we're young, we've got energy. Francis had lost his that's why the estate went to rack and ruin."

"I wish I could marry you, I really do, Tilda," Harry said gently and stroked her face with the back of his hand.

Matilda felt her temper rising and pushing his hand away, she stamped her foot. "Don't tell me you're going to go through with it and marry that frozen-faced fiancée. You'll never be happy, I warn you. Why you've only got to look at her to see she'll never enjoy sex. I bet you've never got near her so far. Come on, tell me the truth. That's why you keep coming here, isn't it?"

Although Harry wasn't going admit it, unfortunately what Matilda said was true. With all his charms, a chaste kiss on cold, rather thin lips was all Charlotte ever permitted and if she did have feelings she had no trouble in keeping them firmly under control. Harry was beginning to suspect she might be frigid, which didn't augur well for their marriage, which she was insisting take place soon. However, he always comforted himself with the thought that there would always be Matilda, sexual, compliant, and who gave her love unstintingly.

"I come because I love you."

"Don't lie. You come for sex. If you loved me you would marry me."

Harry raised his shoulders in an apologetic shrug. "I can't,

305

my darling. It has nothing to do with Charlotte, the estate or money. There is an impediment to our marriage. The law forbids it."

Matilda stood very still. "What are you talking about?"

"Look in your prayer book. I may not marry my father's brother's wife, you may not marry your husband's brother's son."

A shaft of moonlight shone on Matilda's stricken face and although her mouth trembled and her breasts heaved with emotion, she didn't cry. "Blast and bugger your eyes, Harry, you've done this deliberately, you unprincipled pig."

"Don't be unreasonable, Matilda, I didn't make the laws. And if we just let things rumble along as they are I don't see what the problem is."

In the background the fiddle sawed away and the barn reverberated with the sound of thumping feet.

Matilda pointed to the driveway. "Go," she ordered, "Now! You've made a fool of me once too often. Set foot in my grounds again and I'm warning you, I'll turn the dogs on you."

Harry shrugged. "If that's the way you want it . . ."

"I do."

But Harry had one last card up his sleeve . . . "What about Adam?"

"What about him?"

"He's my son, isn't he?"

"Adam is Francis's son."

"I don't believe it."

"You'll have to. I was no more faithful to you than you were me," she lied. "Now if you won't go, I will."

In a passion of grief she turned from him. Her thoughts and emotions a swirling confusion of hate, regret and betrayal, Matilda stumbled away through the undergrowth. She reached the footpath, stopped, smoothed her hair, took several deep breaths, then with amazing composure, walked towards the barn. Looking diminutive and vulnerable against its cathedral-like proportions, she seemed to hesitate at the door and half turn. But then she changed her mind and in a gallant, heartbreaking gesture of farewell, Harry saw her square her shoulders and walk in to join the dancers.

And at that moment of losing her, Harry had to face his own pain. Because too late, he'd been awakened to the terrible truth that beyond a doubt, the woman walking out of his life was the only one he would ever truly love.

Chapter Twenty-Four

"Jem died game, wanting no prsons about him," was the defiant boast of James Towle's family and friends after he'd swung from the gallows a few yards from the Infirmary on a dull November day.

On the morning of the execution the town had a carnival air and Rachel had watched with a feeling of revulsion, the huge crowds, behaving more as if they were on their way to a fair than a hanging, swarm through the streets. Vulgar and raucous and coming from as far afield as Nottingham, there was a great deal of undignified elbowing in the vying for positions; scuffles broke out and punches were exchanged. And amidst all this mayhem, fathers still managed to stoop and hoist excited children on to their shoulders to enable them to better enjoy the spectacle of a man having his neck snapped in two. Ballads recounting Jem Towle's exploits and the manner of his end were selling like hot cakes, clowns and jugglers performed spectacular tricks, a sad, muzzled bear danced to the flick of its master's whip, and pickpockets had a field day.

Jack Brewin, who had no intention of missing a moment of Towle's last few minutes on earth, had tried to persuade Rachel to join him. "You might as well shut up shop and come. Everyone's treating it like a holiday so there won't be no business. They've had a new drop specially made so it should be a good day out."

Rachel had shuddered and shaken her head. "No thank

308

you. I've no taste for seeing a man launched into eternity in such a barbaric manner, whatever his crime."

"Go on, it'll do you the world of good, take your mind off things," he urged.

"I said I didn't want to go."

Hearing a tone in her voice he had learned not to argue with, Jack Brewin lifted his shoulders in a placatory gesture. "All right. But if you don't mind, I'll be off otherwise won't get a decent view of the proceedings."

Rachel suspected that Jack Brewin despised her faint-heartedness but she didn't care, even when she saw that she was the only shop open in a deserted street. She tried to occupy herself by taking books down from shelves and dusting them but soon gave up. Because try as she might all she could see was young James Towle, once so broad set and jaunty, the life choked out of him and swinging on the end of a rope. In her distress all her fears for Jed multiplied and she sank down in a chair, twisting her hands and biting her lip until she could taste blood. What was to become of him? What chance was there of happiness or a life together now?

By twelve an uneasy quiet had fallen on the town. Then in the distance she heard a great swell of voices, a thousand or more, singing so firmly and clearly Rachel could hear every word. "Oh, for an overcoming faith, to cheer my dying hours; to triumph o'er the monster death, with all his frightful powers."

Several more verses followed but she couldn't bear to listen. "No more," she sobbed and pressed her fingers tight against her ears to block out the soaring voices. Only when she was certain the singing had died away did she allow her hands to fall to her side. Then closing her eyes, she bowed her head and murmured the only part of the burial service she knew. "The Lord gave and the Lord hath taken away . . ."

By one o'clock, people started to filter back through the

town. She splashed her face with cold water and felt more composed, although snatches of conversation did threaten that composure. Some people were discussing in detail the execution but others were more subdued and there were several hysterical children who no parent could pacify. A little later she had her first customer. He came into the shop, picking over the details of the hanging like carrion over a carcass and telling Rachel that immediately after the body had hung for the regulation time, it would be cut down, handed over to a relative then conveyed back to Basford for burial there.

She listened without comment, banged the book he wanted down on the counter, said, "That will be one shilling please," escorted him to the door and bid him a curt good-afternoon. Another figure was fast approaching the shop, but Rachel quickly put the closed sign in the window, turned the key and pulled down the blind on the face at the door.

The man was demanding to be let in. Ignoring him she tiptoed away but was stopped dead in her tracks by the voice itself, so familiar and dear to her. She stood in disbelief while the handle was rattled once again, but more imperatively this time. "Rachel, open up, it's me."

"Jed!" With a surge of joy, she raced to the door, wrenched it open and flung herself into the arms of the gaunt, ragged stranger who stood there. Then she started back and glanced fearfully over his shoulder. "But what are you doing here?" Without giving him a chance to reply, she grabbed his hand, yanked him into the shop and bolted the door.

"It's all right, you've nothing to worry about I'm free, free as a bird!" In an explosion of happiness he took her up in his arms and executed a dizzying dance round the room.

But the months without proper food or exercise had weakened Jed and he was soon out of breath. But he couldn't bear to let her go and as he held her tight against him, his thinness frightened her. But then Rachel felt his heartbeat, it was strong and regular and although she suspected it would be sometime before he regained his old vigour, she was reassured. A bath, fresh clothes and several hearty meals would work wonders.

"I can't believe it, you're here and not two hours ago I thought I'd never see you again," she murmured against his chest.

"They reckon hanging poor Jem will be a lesson to all us radicals and so put the fear of God in us, we'll swear off any further activities." He gave a bitter laugh. "But we're not that easily cowed."

Rachel pulled away from Jed's embrace then and studied him with a grave expression. Finally in a steady voice but choosing her words carefully, she said, "Jed these past months have been terrible, the loneliness, not knowing what was going to happen to you, wondering if you would be transported, in my darkest moments thinking you might even be hanged. I don't know if I could go through that again. I want us to live a normal life, to get married in the knowledge that our children will have a father who isn't continually in and out of prison. You've been lucky this time, you might not be in future. Please no more politicking."

"But I've done nothing wrong," Jed protested.

"I know, but I still want you to stop."

"They will have won then. No, I'm sorry Rachel, you shouldn't ask it of me. In prison, time is the one thing you have plenty of. I did a lot of thinking while I was locked away, I know what I'm doing is not criminal and I refuse to be silenced."

In spite of the months in gaol his voice had lost none of its resonance and his grey eyes blazed with the same fire. Jed wouldn't change, she knew that. Putting him behind bars had only hardened him in his opinions. She had to accept too that in spite of his love for her, politics would always come first. Without question she loved Jed but was

311

it strong enough to face an uncertain future, or did she walk away from him, out of the door and out of his life? It was a decision she had to make now.

Unaware of her fears, he began eagerly formulating plans. "And I shall get a new hand-press, publish pamphlets, fight for the stockingers . . . for the extension of the franchise . . ."

Rachel watched his face while he spoke, mobile and lit with an inner conviction and knew that she couldn't change him, indeed didn't want to, because without these qualities Jed wouldn't be the man she loved. Suppressing her doubts, she gave a small sigh, almost of regret, then making her choice, her arms slid round his neck. Pressing herself against him she silenced him with a kiss. "Hush Jed," she said softly, "no more of that talk, not for a while anyway. Too much time has been taken from us already. The world and its problems can go to the devil. For today at least I refuse to share you. Today I want there to be just you and me." She kissed him again, more lingeringly this time, felt his response and taking his hand she drew him through the shop. "Come my love, let's go upstairs – to bed."